Tempted and Taken

ITALIAN STALLIONS
BOOK SIX

MARI CARR

To the Golden Girls.

We may have started as work colleagues, but that quickly gave way to a true sisterhood. I love knowing you're always up for skinny dipping, wine time, traveling the world, and that you're never more than a text away when I really need you.

This one is for you - Deb (Dorothy), Lisa (Rose), and Nan (Blanche) from Mari (Sophia).

Naughty and Nice

<h1 style="text-align:center">Naughty and Nice</h1>

One unforgettable night...with the wrong man.

If there's one thing Liza excels at it's making bad decisions. Which is why she knew it was stupid to invite the guy she'd just started dating to the gala she was hosting. When he gets overly familiar, she asks him to leave. He refuses...

Until sinfully sexy billionaire, Matt Russo, intervenes, leading to Liza's worst decision ever. Because a holiday hook-up with Matt, her family's enemy, would definitely land her on the naughty list for life.

If Matt's past has taught him anything, it's that true love doesn't exist. Then he spies Liza—the only threat to his simple existence—across the hotel ballroom. A slow dance leads to a heated embrace that ends in his hotel room. And for the first time ever, he imagines a very different future for himself.

Unfortunately, it's one he can never have.

Chapter One

Liza Moretti looked across the crowded hotel ballroom and smiled. Months of planning and preparation had come together much better than she could have hoped. As Executive Director of the Philadelphia Initiative—a foundation that worked to increase philanthropic donations in the community—she was no stranger to fundraising, part of which included organizing shindigs like this one.

Tonight, the Initiative was hosting a Snowflake Gala, the proceeds going to support a local shelter, Promise House, that offered a place to live for young people facing homelessness and survivors of sex trafficking. The home was very near and dear to Liza's heart, and she'd begun volunteering there every weekend since first touring it shortly after her promotion to the executive director position.

She'd put countless hours into planning tonight's festivities, making sure it was considered a not-to-miss event amongst Philadelphia's wealthiest. Sometimes she felt like she had dissociative identity disorder as she lived in two very distinct worlds, working with the city's most troubled and destitute youth at Promise House, while rubbing elbows and hobnobbing with the elite, all in an attempt to get them to open their wallets to help.

The Ritz-Carlton's Grand Ballroom was dripping in twinkle lights and white tulle, looking so elegant, it took her breath away. Her team had been working since yesterday to fashion the romantic atmosphere, creating a true winter wonderland. The soft lighting from the massive chandelier in the center of the room added to the effect, and she had been pleased by the number of astonished—impressed—gasps she'd heard when the guests first arrived.

They'd just completed the three-course dinner, so guests had begun to mill around, some opting to socialize, while others were dancing to the five-piece orchestra that had played throughout the meal. The orchestra's time was winding down. In a little while, she would take the stage to give a presentation about the Promise House. After that, she'd hired an extremely popular local band to liven things up and take the party to the next level.

"Here you go," Davis Taylor said, handing her a glass of champagne.

"Thank you," she said, smiling at her date for the evening.

Ordinarily, she attended work events stag so that she could handle any last-minute problems that might surface. However, when she turned Davis down for a date tonight, due to this work obligation, he'd asked if he could accompany her, reassuring her it wouldn't bother him if she was called away to deal with any emergencies.

This was her sixth official date with Davis, which made him this year's record holder.

No. Liza reconsidered that. That wasn't true. He had the distinct honor of being the record for this year *and* last, the first man in at least the last twenty to make it past her three-strikes-you're-out dating regimen.

Liza, single and thirty, was a professional when it came to weeding out the unsavory candidates in her ever-dwindling dating pool. As such, she had a system. Her dates—found either online, through setups, or even the occasional met-in-line-somewhere—started with the coffee break. If that went well, they moved on to the lunch date, which ensured that if things went south, her pain was limited due to the need to return to the office. After that, they graduated to a proper dinner date.

Davis had soared through the first three dates, and even made a decent showing for the fourth and fifth—both dinners, with the added drinks and dancing at a nightclub afterward.

So tonight, after a two-year dry spell, she was on an honest-to-God sixth date and hopeful that perhaps Davis would clear the next and most important hurdle.

Sex.

Her girl parts were hungry. Starving, in fact.

Liza was anticipating a full-on pussy rebellion if she tried to get herself off with her vibrator one more time. She'd worn out every fantasy in her vast repertoire, struggling to find anything new on porn sites or in erotic romance novels that could get her motor revving. She'd hit the limit on ways to turn herself on.

She needed a man.

Stat.

So, she'd gone ahead and offered Davis the invitation to tonight's gala and, unbeknownst to him, if all went well, she had a room reserved upstairs.

"This is quite an event," Davis said, surveying the room much as she'd just been doing. "You should be very proud, Liza. Not everyone could pull off something of this magnitude. And with this many big names. Your guest list is a who's who of Philadelphia society."

"Well, it's for a very good cause. Plus, I've discovered the secret to increasing the number of yes RSVPs is to up the price. At ten thousand dollars a plate, this suddenly became the social event of the season."

Davis laughed. "You're as brilliant as you are beautiful."

Liza hoped that wasn't a line. Then she decided she didn't care if it was.

She reached up on tiptoe to give her charming date a kiss on the cheek. They'd shared four good-night kisses so far. The first two were too sweet and short to give her any real insight on his abilities in that area. However, the third and fourth kisses had opened her eyes. They were what had convinced her to reserve the room here. Because Davis had some skill. For which she was very grateful. She'd kissed way too many frogs in her life.

"Would you like to dance?" Davis gestured to the floor. The orchestra was playing a waltz, the tune familiar though she didn't have a clue what the name of the song was. Classical music was not her forte. Instead, her music tastes—much to her rockin' and rollin' family's dismay—began and ended with country. She'd been introduced to it by her college roommate, and she'd been hooked ever since.

She took Davis's proffered hand, then stepped into his embrace once they found an empty space on the dance floor.

She rested her head against Davis's shoulder. He wasn't a tall man, but he was taller than her by a couple inches. They fit physically in a way that wasn't always true of her and other men. She wasn't particularly tall, rather she considered herself medium height. However, she'd had a couple of dates fall apart when the men—shorter than her—decided they couldn't handle looking up at a woman. Which, in truth, suited her fine because she looked banging in a pair of heels, always willing to suffer for fashion. Flats weren't something she'd ever switch over to, just to soothe some insecure man's pride.

When she looked back on her track record, she figured she could check just about every dating failure box there was, which was why tonight felt steeped in promise. And while Liza was too much of a realist to let herself get carried away, there was no denying that she was genuinely hopeful and happy.

God, please let him be good in bed.

Davis's hand remained firmly on the small of her back. She'd splurged on the deep-red ball gown, knowing the moment she saw it in the shop window she had to have it. It had hurt her bank account a little but given the fact she was a single woman with a good-paying job, and precious little debt, she'd decided to call the dress a Christmas gift to herself.

The A-line style suited her frame and made her feel elegant and sexy. The top was lace with cap sleeves, the full skirt chiffon with a long slit that reached the middle of her right thigh. The back of the dress had an open keyhole that revealed quite a lot of skin and meant she couldn't wear a bra. Not that that was a problem, as it had a bra built into it, and it wasn't like she was overly endowed.

The devil in her wished Davis would lift his hand a little higher to touch her bare back. While he'd proven himself to be a very nice guy, she sure as shit wouldn't complain if he revealed a tiny bit of a bad boy side.

Ugh. She dismissed that thought.

Beggars can't be choosers. He had ticked off every box that mattered, so who cared if he toed the "gentleman" line when it came to politeness and public appropriateness and didn't sneak a touch.

That was her hormones talking.

They swayed together and she let herself sink into his embrace, enjoying the peacefulness of the moment after so many long, stressful hours spent making sure everything about tonight went off without a hitch.

"I can't believe the mayor is here," Davis murmured. "I've been trying to get an appointment with him for the past two weeks, but I can't get past his secretary."

Davis worked in the district attorney's office, though he'd confessed at dinner the other night, he was considering pursuing a career in politics somewhere down the line. Then he'd regaled her for the better part of an hour, discussing some of his more fascinating cases. He was intelligent and witty, two things she was certain would help his political career.

Truthfully, so far, that was the only tick mark in the *meh* column. She wasn't a fan of politics or politicians, but she wasn't ready to call it a deal-breaker. Especially since he was only thinking about it.

Liza gave him a playfully narrowed gaze. "No distracting my guests, Mr. Taylor," she teased him. "Tonight is all about raising money for homeless teens."

He gave her a quick nod and smile. "Of course, of course."

The sound of a woman's loud laugh captured Liza's attention, and she looked toward the source. It took all the strength she had not to roll her eyes.

Patricia Eddington was Philadelphia society's It Girl, though Liza had a hard time understanding why. Obviously, she was beautiful in the typical style of all rich-bitch blonde Barbie dolls. She and Liza were the same age, though their paths had never crossed when they were younger. Liza was public school, Patricia private. Liza was nightclubs; Patricia was country clubs. And while Liza had known who Patricia was, thanks to the local paparazzi and their fascination with the socialite, they hadn't met in person until Liza began working for the Initiative, hosting events like tonight's.

Heiress to a fortune, Patricia had cut a wide swath through the most eligible bachelors on the East Coast over the past decade. She'd also been engaged something like twenty times—Liza was exaggerating, but not by much—though she'd never once made it down the aisle.

Liza figured Patricia might have completed one of those trips if Philadelphia had ever managed to land a *Real Housewives* reality TV show. That kind of shit was right up Patricia's alley as she insisted on being the queen bee no matter where she was, her need to be the center of attention in every single room she occupied borderline obnoxious.

Actually, scratch the borderline.

Patricia's latest billionaire bachelor boyfriend—say that real fast three times—was none other than Liza's arch-nemesis, Matt Russo. Matt served as chairman of the Initiative's board, and he'd managed to be a constant thorn in Liza's side, ruining what was otherwise her dream job.

In addition to their work issues, she and Matt also had a long family history that ensured they would always be on opposites sides of whatever lines formed between them. Matt was a Russo, Liza a Moretti. Two names as infamous in Philadelphia as the Hatfields and McCoys, the Montagues and the Capulets.

The animosity between the two families had started way back with Liza and Matt's great-grandfathers, and it continued still today, four generations later.

She couldn't begin to guess what Matt—or any man, for that matter—saw in Patricia. Perhaps it was the sizable inheritance she had coming her way, although Matt was already richer than Midas. Or maybe she was just shit-hot in bed; all those men couldn't be wrong. Either reason wouldn't be enough for Liza to spend more than three minutes in her presence.

Of course, it didn't help Patricia's case that she had an annoying habit of treating Liza like she was the hired help.

Matt caught her staring at him and his date, but he offered her nothing—no smile, smirk, or even middle finger. Instead, his eyes held hers for three beats too long before looking away as if he hadn't even seen her at all. It was always that way with him. He'd capture her gaze and...time slowed down. Just the tiniest bit, and it always took her too long to recover.

Liza turned her attention back to Davis as the song came to an end, the musicians rising and carrying their instruments backstage.

"I need to get ready for my speech," she said, as the two of them stepped apart. She'd prepared a special video about the Promise House, featuring interviews with some of the teens living there, for whom they were trying to raise money. She'd also prepared a few words—her pitch, for lack of a better term. "Will you be okay without me for a few minutes?"

She'd put the finishing touches on the video yesterday morning with help from the Initiative's media department, and even though she'd seen the footage a hundred times, she'd still blown through half a dozen tissues as she watched the completed show.

"I'm perfectly capable of entertaining myself. I might go over and say hello to the mayor," he joked, winking at her.

"Talk only about the Promise House." She swatted him playfully on the shoulder as he walked away, giving her the crossed-heart motion.

She walked over to her table to grab her notecards from her clutch.

"Davis Taylor?" a deep voice rumbled from behind her.

She sighed as she turned around.

"You have a problem with that?" she asked, staring Matt Russo down, despite her surprise that he was commenting on her date.

"Do you think that's two last names or two first?" Only Matt Russo could make a joke in such a deadpan voice—and without cracking a smile—that she wasn't even sure if he was trying to be funny.

"Careful, Matt. Someone might mistake that for humor and your reputation as a grumpy bastard would be shattered forever."

Matt's only response was the slightest narrowing of his eyes before his expression flattened out to his typical look—stoic, solemn.

Typically, their conversations were restricted to work. And, for better or worse, most of those discussions became contentiousness, given the fact Matt viewed her as overly ambitious when it came to her goals for the Initiative, while, in her opinion, he was far too conservative, too slow to act.

During their last meeting, he'd told her she needed to scale back on her planned fundraisers for the upcoming year, claiming that too many philanthropic projects would "wear out" her contributors.

Wear them out.

Those were the words he'd actually used. As if the wealthy had a limited amount of endurance when it came to writing checks and spending money they wouldn't even miss. She'd told him that when the needs of the less fortunate were smaller than the overflowing coffers of the wealthy, she'd slow down. But until then, her project goals would remain the same.

Tonight, he was breaking the pattern by touching on something more personal.

"You never bring dates to work functions, Ms. Moretti."

Ah. And there it was. The connection. The son of a bitch stressed the word *work* like she was breaking some sort of rule or something...which she wasn't. She also didn't appreciate him talking to her like she was his subordinate. She didn't work for him; she worked *with* him, a concept he struggled to grasp.

Plus, it bugged the hell out of her that he always called her Ms. Moretti rather than Liza. What the hell was that about? It made her feel like a naughty schoolgirl, and not in a sexy way.

"Not that it's any of your concern, but I am perfectly capable of handling my duties." She held up her notecards to prove her point. "Now if you'll excuse me, I have to—"

"I'm surprised to see you with him," Matt interjected.

Liza hesitated to reply for a moment, thrown for a loop.

Wait.

Was he pissed that she brought a date to a work function? Or was he pissed she'd brought a date, period?

"What does that mean?" she finally managed to ask.

"He's not your type."

And what the fuck did *that* mean?

As always, Mr. Aloof was impossible to read, so she had no idea if he was insulting her or Davis.

"Thank you so much for that unsolicited opinion," she replied sarcastically.

And there it was.

The Matt Russo smirk.

The only reaction she ever managed to provoke from the man was that infuriating smirk.

"Ladies and gentlemen," Charles Dunning, president of the Initiative, announced from the stage. "If you will please take your seats, Liza Moretti, Executive Director of the Philadelphia Initiative and our wonderful hostess for this evening, has a special presentation for you."

"Shit," she murmured. That was her cue.

She shot Matt a dirty look, then skirted by him.

The orchestra had packed up and cleared the stage and a screen was being lowered. Once the presentation was over, the band would quickly set up and her responsibilities for the evening would wind down to schmoozing the bigwigs and answering questions, most of the heavy lifting done. In a couple more hours, the guests would be well on their way to intoxicated and shaking their asses on the dance floor, at which point she could finally begin to relax.

She hurried to the stage, cursing her heels—her feet really did hurt, but she also knew they looked fucking awesome—and pissed as shit at Matt. Of course, the asshole *would* fluster her right before she had to speak.

What the hell was his problem?

Stepping behind the podium, she took a deep breath and looked out across the room as the lights began to dim for the video.

Davis was sitting next to the mayor, grinning from ear to ear as he lifted his glass to her, though she wasn't sure if his silent toast was meant as thanks or encouragement. She caught sight of Matt, reclaiming his spot next to Patricia. He whispered something to his date, then his attention returned to Liza, holding her gaze captive for too many seconds before she managed to escape and turn her eyes back to the crowd.

After delivering her brief address, she stepped off the stage as the video began to play. She remained in the wings, though she didn't watch the show. Instead, keeping her attention on the reactions of everyone in the room. She prayed they'd be as moved by what they were seeing and hearing as she had been. The Promise

House was in bad need of repairs, but more than that, Liza hoped to raise enough money for expansion as well. They never had enough beds to meet the need, which meant too many kids were still sleeping on the street.

She watched several women wiping their eyes and saw quite a few people filling out the contribution forms. Thank God.

"Well done, Ms. Moretti."

Liza turned to see Matt standing next to her.

"My part will be easy. Looks like you've already won the crowd over to your cause." As chairman of the board, he was the next speaker, the one who would ask for the contributions and explain how to donate.

"Our cause," she corrected, before saying, "thank you," a little more shortly than she should have. She was still annoyed about his dig at her date.

"You look lovely tonight. Red suits you."

She stared at him, trying to figure him out. The man had a knack for keeping her on her toes, she had to give him that. Most of the time he looked straight through her. Or, when it came to Initiative business, he managed to push every button she had. But sometimes, on the rare occasion, he would pay her a genuine compliment, looking at her like...

Like she was beautiful.

She didn't have a chance to respond as the video ended, the lights rose, and Matt took the stage. His deep voice carried as he insisted they had a duty to help these young people, the future of their city, of their community. His speech was short, succinct, and powerful, and Liza was moved, despite the fact it was Matt Russo doing the talking.

With the presentation over, the guests rose, milling around and socializing as the band set up. She was delighted when they began their first set with a wildly popular, upbeat number that had everyone rushing to the floor. Happy people having fun tended to be more generous.

Countless guests came up to Liza, asking questions about the

Promise House or about some of the teens interviewed and praising her work for such a worthy cause. She answered questions and thanked those who promised to help. Once the crowd around her thinned, Davis rejoined her. He had remained true to his word, stepping aside so she could do her job. It was another tick mark in her "Yay, with jazz hands" column.

"You are incredible," he said, giving her a kiss on the cheek.

"Thank you."

"Tonight has been a huge success, Liza. You must be very proud."

"The true proof of my success is yet to be seen. I hope the contributions are enough that the Promise House can add that second wing. It would double the number of beds available, which still wouldn't be enough. I swear, I don't think I can rest knowing there are still sixteen- and seventeen-year-olds sleeping on the streets, falling victim to traffickers or gangs or..." She stopped mid-sentence, then joked, "Aaaand thanks so much for coming to my Ted Talk."

"You are a passionate woman. Never apologize for that. The mayor was quite impressed by your presentation, called you a force to be reckoned with, I believe."

Liza laughed. "Did he mean that as a compliment?"

Davis nodded. "He did. He said any man would be lucky to call you his wife."

"Correct me if I'm wrong, but I'm pretty sure the old guy has been married for nearly fifty years."

"I think he was dropping that hint for me."

Liza smiled, though she was surprised by his comment, as well as the way he was looking at her. His gaze was suddenly too intent and way too serious for a sixth date.

"Did you tell him we'd only just started dating?" she asked, hoping to slow his roll.

"Liza," he continued, grasping her hands in his. "Since the first time we met for coffee, I've had this feeling about you."

"Feeling?"

"Like you and I are two sides of the same coin."

She had noticed—and tried to discount—Davis's downright giddiness tonight as they'd rubbed elbows with Philadelphia's elite, his excitement growing with each introduction she offered. While she considered that part of the job a chore, Davis had looked at her as if she was his golden goose, opening doors to places he wanted to be.

So, despite her better judgment, Liza asked, "How so?"

"We're both ambitious, driven, and we know how to get what we want from people."

That didn't sound horrible on the surface, but Liza's Spidey-senses were screaming. "Tonight isn't about *me* getting what *I* want. It's about encouraging people to support a very worthy cause. The Promise House needs help, and I want to open people's eyes to that."

"Of course, you do," Davis said, though his tone felt a bit too nudge-nudge, wink-wink to be sincere. "All I'm saying is the two of us could go far together. My political ambitions partnered with your connections and fundraising talents...we'd be unstoppable."

Liza was starting to draw lines between dots she didn't want to connect. "Unstoppable how?"

"The sky's the limit," he responded, wrapping his arm around her shoulders. "The mayor's office, the governor's mansion, maybe even the White House."

"Those sound like your ambitions. What about my career goals?"

"You'd still be using your skills. You're good with people, with getting them on board and in support of a cause. Why does it matter if you're working for the Initiative or...for your husband?"

Her eyes widened. "This is our sixth date, Davis," she reminded him again, wondering how she'd slipped so deeply into the twilight zone.

"I know, and I'm certainly not proposing tonight. I'm simply saying I've played the field for enough years that I know what I'm looking for in a woman, in a wife. And, Liza, when I look at you, I see the potential for an amazing future for both of us."

"It's way too soon to discuss the future." She hoped her tone was stern enough to penetrate the idiot's thick skull. "But you should know, as you're looking ahead, that I will always work for the Initiative, for those less fortunate."

"That's what I'm saying, Liza. You could do that with me. When I'm in office, I'd have the power to affect real change."

It took Liza a few moments to let the dust settle on his comments. Partly because she was amazed that he would make such a tremendous leap—from dating to marriage talk—and that he would assume she would be fine with abandoning her career to support his.

"Davis, if you knew me better, you'd realize that I have no intention of giving up my job. I love it."

"You're not listening to me. I'm not suggesting you quit working completely, at least not until my political career is off the ground."

She looked around for video cameras because she had to be getting punked.

"Your career would have zero bearing on mine," she said, trying to use smaller words in hopes that he'd get it.

Davis frowned. "Liza, you and I...we're the dream team. Surely you see that? Think about how much good you could do for all your pet projects as the wife of the governor."

"Pet projects?" she said through gritted teeth.

He scowled, as if her anger was unjustified. "That's not what I meant, and you know it. You're being overly sensitive. I can see I shouldn't have brought this up after you've had such a busy day."

Why did it suddenly feel like he was patting her on the head like a cranky child?

"Take a few days to consider what I've said and—"

A few days?

"Oh no. I don't need to consider a damn thing. I think you should leave." She was suddenly very sorry she'd invited him to this gala. She'd obviously given him a false impression of herself, somehow made him think that she would be perfectly fine propping up some asshole man and making him the center of her motherfucking universe.

Bringing him here had been a mistake of epic proportions because if this conversation was happening in a restaurant versus this place, where she was technically working, she would toss her drink in his face and storm out. As it was, she was trapped here.

So he was the one who needed to get out. She just wasn't sure he'd do that willingly.

"Leave?"

"Leave," she repeated. "This date is over. It's *all* over."

"Don't you think you're overreacting? I wasn't saying we should run out and get married tomorrow."

"*That's* the part you think—" She stopped talking, aware of the fact her volume was rising. She sucked in a deep breath and counted to ten, even though it went against every grain inside her.

Liza was the youngest of four kids and the only girl. That meant she'd grown up with a bunch of rough-and-tumble brothers. It was the kind of upbringing that ensured she knew how to stand her ground, to never say die. It was that or be run over roughshod by the male contingency. She'd learned to throw a punch about three seconds after taking her first step. Her brother Elio had been a shameless toy hog at four, always wanting whatever she had. And at three years old, she'd managed to correct him of that shortcoming.

"Liza," Davis started again.

"Davis," she said, relieved to discover her voice was quieter. "I promise you; I'm not overreacting. If anything, I'm underreacting. You need to leave. *Now.*"

Her temper was close to the surface, but she refused to do anything that would jeopardize all the work she'd done for the shelter. The last thing she was going to do tonight was make a scene.

So, she did something she never did.

She stepped away from the fight.

"Lose my number." She turned her back, walking in the opposite direction, praying he didn't follow.

She hadn't made it more than a half dozen steps when another voice stopped her in her tracks.

"Davis. How are you?" The sound of her date's name, too close behind her, told her the fucker was giving chase. Or at least, he had been. She glanced over her shoulder, watching as Matt drew the asshole into conversation, deliberately drawing him farther and farther away from her.

Spying an easy escape—thanks to Matt Russo, of all people— she continued her retreat, not stopping until she reached one of the large windows at the back of the ballroom. She considered trying to open the damn thing but dismissed the thought instantly. As it was Philadelphia in December, and cold as fuck outside, people would bitch, even though she was sorely tempted to see if the single digits could cool the furious anger raging red hot inside her.

Placing her forehead against the chilly glass, she blew out a long, slow sigh. She should have known Davis was too good to be true.

God, she hated that she'd let herself hope, even for a second, that he might be the one.

The one.

Yeah, right.

As the years passed, she was genuinely beginning to fear that person didn't exist for her. Especially as she'd stood on the side-lines, watching her friends Jess, Penny, Gianna, and Keeley, all fall madly in love and settle down with their perfect matches. She'd never considered herself a particularly jealous person, not the type to covet what others had. But lately, she was so overwhelmed by bone-deep envy, it felt as if it was eating her alive.

"Ms. Moretti."

Liza closed her eyes wearily. She was too tired for round seven hundred and forty-seven with Matt. Though she supposed she needed to thank him for running interference. His timing with Davis was too perfect to be anything but, which meant...he'd been watching.

She stiffened her spine and turned, glancing over Matt's shoulder to look for Davis.

"He's gone," Matt said.

"Thank you."

Matt nodded, his typical lack of expression replaced by something that looked a bit like concern, which was definitely a new one.

He turned away from her briefly, taking two glasses of champagne from a passing waiter, before offering one to her. "Davis's ego is only surpassed by his ambition."

"I'll drink to that," she said miserably, taking a sip of the champagne. Then she decided to hell with it. She upended the glass, draining it in one long swig.

For a split second, she thought Matt looked almost amused.

"Did we make a scene?" She was concerned Matt wasn't the only one to notice her altercation with Davis.

Matt shook his head. "No. I happened to be passing by when I heard you ask him to leave."

"Not one of my better dates," she muttered. "Of course, it wasn't one of my worst, either."

Before he could reply, Patricia stepped next to him.

"All work and no play, Matt." Patricia pouted. "I'm sure there's nothing you and Liza have to say to each other that can't wait until the next board meeting. Come dance with me. I love this song."

Matt accepted Patricia's hand, barely sparing Liza a parting glance as he let his girlfriend lead him to the dance floor.

Patricia Eddington had claws. She didn't like her date paying attention to any woman who wasn't her.

Not that the socialite had a damn thing to worry about in that regard.

Liza was as likely to date Matt Russo as she was to agree to be Davis Taylor's First Lady.

Handing her empty glass to a waiter, she helped herself to another, though she only sipped this one. Feeling a bit more fortified, she shook off the disastrous date, put on a fake smile, and went back to work.

Sadly, it was the only part of her life where she didn't feel like a complete and utter fuck-up.

Chapter Two

Matt murmured "mm-hmm" for the third time, though he didn't have a clue what Patricia was talking about. The two of them had been on a dozen dates, serving as each other's plus-one-with-benefits because they both lived in a world where high society events like this were as common as a Monday-morning staff meeting.

He'd originally asked her out because Patricia ran in the same social circles, had expressed an attraction to him, and, in truth, though it made him sound shallow as hell, she was very easy on the eyes.

She ticked off all those columns, as well as the mandatory one.

The one that had to be marked before he asked out *any* woman.

He was in absolutely no danger of falling in love with her.

Patricia had been engaged four times in the last ten years or so, but all those relationships had failed. The reason he'd continued to call her was because she didn't pressure him for anything more serious than the occasional date and hook-up.

He'd made his feelings about marriage clear from the onset of their association, and she'd commented that after so many failed engagements, she was in no hurry to accept any future proposals. She insisted the next man she said yes to would be the one. And if that wasn't going to be him, then so be it. She'd promised they could keep it casual and have fun for as long as they wanted.

It had been the perfect response. So, apart from accompanying each other as they attended events like tonight's—all of which ended in sex—he never saw or spoke to her. She didn't even demand a morning-after phone call. It was the best relationship he'd ever had. No muss, no fuss.

Unfortunately, while Patricia didn't want him as a boyfriend, she did want his attention—all of it—whenever they were together, and it was starting to grate against his nerves. Tonight, she'd been uncharacteristically clingy and dropping hints that seemed to indicate perhaps the status quo was changing.

When he added in the fact Patricia was incredibly vain, spoiled, and entitled—all things he noticed before but had managed to ignore—tonight was looking like it was going to be their swan song. Which meant he would be sleeping alone in the penthouse suite he'd reserved in this hotel.

"And that was when I gave the ring back," Patricia said, retelling him the story of why she dumped the latest in her string of ex-fiancés. He didn't bother to point out he'd already heard this particular tale of woe the last two times they were out, mainly because it meant he didn't have to listen.

"I just realized," Patricia continued, placing her hand on his arm, leaning toward him in a way that ensured he got an eyeful of her generous cleavage. "I couldn't spend the rest of my life with a man completely incapable of finding my clit...or G-spot. I'm not the type of woman who should have to take care of her own needs. That's what pool boys are for."

She followed her joke with a laugh that was far too loud, though it had the desired effect. He saw no less than six people nearby lift their heads to look over at them. Patricia covered her mouth with her hand, pretending she hadn't meant to make so much noise, but she was clearly delighted to have so many eyes on her. She preened and he looked away, the act one he'd seen a few too many times lately.

He glanced two tables over at the sound of a much softer laugh. Liza was chatting with Arnold Jackson, the director of Promise House, and his partner, Johnnie, clearly enjoying whatever story the older men were telling her.

Bringing Patricia to this event had been a foolish move on his part because it meant he'd spent too much of the evening comparing his date to Liza Moretti.

Liza.

Moretti.

She was becoming a problem. A big one.

Simply the fact that her last name was Moretti should have ensured his interest in her was limited solely to the disdain he felt for the rest of her enormous blue-collar clan. As a general rule, he gave anyone with the last name Moretti a wide berth.

Or he had.

Until her.

He'd first noticed her a year and a half earlier at his brother Conor's club, Enigma. She'd been out with a couple girlfriends, including his now sister-in-law, Penny. He and his brother, Gage, had been sharing a drink when he'd spied her on the dance floor. He'd known who she was, of course, but he hadn't seen her since she'd been a young girl, still in middle school.

As she was five years younger than him, the two of them hadn't gone through school together, hadn't had a conversation, or even been properly introduced. He'd simply caught glimpses of her when they were younger, her always tagging along with her older brothers or cousins to high school football games and such.

That night...he'd seen her, and he hadn't been able to look away. When she caught him staring, she didn't blush or lower her eyes.

Instead, she met his gaze, held it.

And she'd been holding it ever since.

When he first learned she was being named Executive

Director of the Philadelphia Initiative, he'd briefly considered resigning his position on the board, thinking it best to keep a proper distance between his world and hers. Of course, that plan fell apart when he was asked to run for chairman and instead of saying no, he'd foolishly agreed.

"Are you listening to me?" Patricia's eyes narrowed as she looked over at Liza. She'd caught him staring in the other woman's direction one too many times tonight.

Matt turned his attention back to her. "Of course I am."

God help him if she asked him to repeat what she'd just said because he didn't have a clue.

For the next half hour, he forced himself to tune in to Patricia, while making a concerted effort not to turn and look for Liza. He wished he didn't have to try so hard.

It should be a simple matter. He wasn't the type of man to have his head turned by any woman. He'd sworn off serious relationships and marriage a long, long time ago, and he'd held true to that commitment, never once faltering.

Typically, he was better able to keep his wits about him when in Liza's vicinity, but tonight...

God...tonight, in that red gown, she looked like something ripped from his most wicked fantasies, and he was struggling to rein in his baser instincts, the ones screaming at him to march over to her, toss her over his shoulder, and drag her to his lair.

Matt ran a hand through his hair and pushed that unruly desire down deep. Because he would never—*could* never—give in to that impulse.

And not simply because she was a Moretti, and he was a Russo.

But because she didn't tick the mandatory box on his list, and that was a problem.

"I'm surprised your brother Gage didn't come tonight," Patricia said. "Still in the honeymoon phase?"

"Probably," he replied without inflection.

"Where did they go on their honeymoon again?" Patricia had

become interested in his brother of late, working Gage's married state into conversation the last couple of times they'd been together. Subtlety was not her strong suit.

"New Zealand," he replied. "Conor called it Penny and Gage's nerd honeymoon. Their first choice was Comic-Con, but since they married in February and the convention is in July, they decided to visit the Shire and went on the Hobbiton tour instead."

Matt was about ninety percent certain Patricia didn't give a shit about anything he'd just said. That was the other thing about her that was getting old. She always talked but never listened.

"I'm sure Gage would take on some of these society chores if you wanted to spend more time at home."

"In truth, my brother has never attended parties like this. Gage's interests run more along the lines of dungeons, dragons, and grand theft, the auto variety."

Patricia tittered, a much quieter laugh that told him this conversation wasn't one she wanted others to hear. "He's quite the devoted husband. Do you think that's a common trait shared by you Russo brothers?"

"Hard to say considering Gage is the only one who's succumbed."

Patricia wasn't swayed. "He's the only one...so far."

"Chances are good he'll be the only one, period. Conor and I are both married to our work."

Patricia bent even closer, her breasts brushing against his arm. "You don't have to be."

"Patricia. I've never made any secret about my feelings regarding marriage. You and I have an arrangement—" he started, but, of course, she cut him off.

"And we still do," she reassured him. "I'm fine with things the way they are. It's just we get along so well, and you have to admit we're well-suited in the bedroom. I was thinking..." She paused, studying his face too closely.

"Thinking?" he prodded.

"We should take what we have and expand on it. We're both rich, beautiful," she said without an ounce of humility. "And if your reasons for rejecting marriage stem from a lack of desire to be monogamous, I'd be fine with looking the other way, as long as you're discreet. And, of course, I'd offer the same discretion with my dalliances."

"My reasons for not getting married have nothing to do with monogamy. I simply don't want to tie my life to another person's," he reiterated. "If you're asking to change the details of our arrangement—"

"I'm not," she stressed. "I'm simply pointing out there are things I think you're overlooking."

Matt found his patience wearing thin. "Like what?"

"You and I have so much in common. People look at us and see a true power couple. Together, we would set the standard for the elite in Philadelphia. Can't you feel everyone's eyes on us tonight? Watching us, interested in us, wishing they *were* us."

He'd felt nothing of the sort, but he had come to learn the one thing Patricia prized above everything else in the world—even over her massive wardrobe—was attention. In her mind, money equated power and fame, and she wanted both.

To be honest, she was correct in those beliefs. God knew he'd gotten lots of doors opened for him that remained locked to those without the ability to grease the palms of the greedy bastards with the keys.

"And you're suggesting marriage because...why? You want people looking at us?"

"I know you have no interest in marriage, but perhaps that's because you've been looking at the institution from a romantic perspective. I'll admit that's what I did wrong the first few times I said yes to the ring as well. I've changed my mind. What I'm suggesting would be more of an...alliance."

"I'm not looking for an alliance, either."

Patricia waved his comment away. "We're well-suited to each

other, Matt. Similar lifestyles, common interests. And...we both need heirs."

"My brother Gage, and perhaps Conor, will continue the family line. Their children will inherit the Russo businesses."

"Or our children would inherit both the Russo and Eddington fortunes. They would be wealthy beyond compare."

Matt shook his head, but before he could say no again, she interjected.

"I'm not saying we need decide anything immediately. We have an arrangement that I'm happy with. It works well, and it can stand...for now. However, what I'm proposing is not something you should dismiss out of hand. I'm merely asking you to give it some thought."

"If you're happy with the way things are between us, why pursue marriage?"

Patricia grinned. "Because I want more. And you *have* more."

He wasn't interested in the deal she was offering, that truth driven home even further by the fact she wanted children. He wasn't about to bring life into his fucked-up world.

The more she pushed her agenda, the more he was convinced it was time to end things with her.

"Patricia," he started, trying to decide if he should give her the "this is over" conversation here or wait until they were in private. She was the type of woman who would make a scene, raise her voice, or even use tears to sway him. If she got a sense he was serious in his desire to break things off, she would be certain to make a spectacle of it. The last time she broke off her engagement, several bystanders had recorded it, posting her tirade—complete with her tossing a quarter of a million-dollar diamond ring into the Schuylkill River.

The video had gone viral on YouTube, Patricia obsessed with the number of views it had received. She was determined to live her life in the spotlight, constantly putting on a show for the local paparazzi. He had no interest in drawing that kind of attention.

Unfortunately, something in his tone must have tipped her off that things weren't going her way because she doubled down, going for distraction.

"We don't have to say anything else tonight. Actually, how long do we have to stay here? I want to open my present. Please tell me it's sparkly and obscenely expensive."

He'd mentioned earlier that he had a gift waiting for her upstairs. Though, in his mind, it was now less Christmas present and more parting gift.

Before he could reply, Patricia leaned toward him until her lips touched his cheek. "I have a Christmas gift for you too," she whispered in his ear. "But I can't give it to you here. Because it involves unwrapping...me."

The tip of her tongue dashed against his earlobe, in what he could only guess she considered a seductive move.

Now that he'd decided to break things off with her, his attraction had cooled to the point that her closeness was off-putting.

"It's still early." He shifted away to put some space between them. "As chairman of the board, I have a responsibility to stay, to promote the cause." That wasn't necessarily true, but it gave him a way to start circulating the room rather than continue to sit here with her.

Patricia stuck out her lower lip. "That's what Liza is paid to do. Make her do it. And you know, as chairman, you should probably talk to her about her bad habit of playing dress-up and pretending she's one of the guests," she said, her tone dripping with disdain.

"Dress-up?" Matt repeated, not bothering to mask his anger over her rude comment.

Patricia was either patently oblivious to his tone, or she simply didn't give a shit. This wasn't the first time tonight she'd revealed jealousy toward Liza.

Unfortunately, this was the first time they'd attended a function together with Liza present. He mentally kicked his own ass again for putting the two of them in the same room.

Before tonight, Patricia had never had to compete for his unwavering attention, and she wasn't taking it well.

"She's an *employee*," she said, haughtily. "She should dress like one."

"Let me explain something to you," Matt began, but before he could call her to task about exactly what Liza's role was within the Initiative, they were interrupted.

"Patricia, I've been trying to get over here to talk to you all night," Bethany Rogerson said, as she approached the table.

Patricia squealed as she stood up, the two women giving each other those stupid double-cheek air-kisses.

"Oh my God," Bethany exclaimed. "You look gorgeous. Is that a Thom Browne?"

Apparently, seducing him and insulting Liza took a backseat to fashion as Patricia lit up. "Of course, it is. He designed it just for me. He said he absolutely loves dressing me."

"Is it any wonder?" Bethany gushed. "You have a figure to die for."

Patricia preened, then added, "You look nice too."

"Oh posh," Bethany dismissed Patricia's obviously less-than-sincere compliment. "I've just been pea-green with envy as I've looked around at all the ball gowns. Juliet Marshall's pink Carolina Herrera is to die for. And Liza Moretti looks stunning in that red dress."

Patricia rolled her eyes. "Please. It screams bargain basement. You wouldn't catch me flitting around in that twenty-dollar off-the-rack rag she's wearing tonight."

And that was when Matt hit his official limit of Patricia Eddington. Not just for the evening, but forever.

"If you ladies will excuse me." Matt rose, grateful for the opportunity to escape. He rarely lost his temper, but Patricia was pushing him to the brink. "I need to have a word with the mayor."

Bethany and Patricia didn't spare him a glance, already

comparing notes on their latest shopping adventures in New York and Milan.

Matt walked to the open bar. "Scotch and water."

Once the drink was in hand, he shifted to the opposite side of the room, keeping the crowded dance floor between himself and Patricia, lest she wrap up her conversation too soon and decide to seek him out. He felt strangely out of control tonight, and that feeling didn't sit easy with him.

"Mr. Russo." Arnold Jackson stepped next to him, reaching out to shake his hand.

Matt shook the other man's hand and fought to beat down his scowl. He genuinely liked the director of the Promise House —which wasn't true of most people in this room—so it wasn't hard to do. Arnold was an attractive man with thick gray hair, bushy eyebrows, and deeply grooved laugh lines by his eyes due to his permanent smile. In his early sixties, he had the energy of a much younger man, and Matt could only hope to age as well.

"Please, call me Matt. I'm glad you could make it tonight," Matt said.

"I'm delighted to be here. I wanted to take the opportunity to thank you and the Initiative for all the work you've put into this event," Arnold said. "I can't begin to express how much good we can do with the money raised tonight."

"I think that thanks should go to Liza Moretti. She did all the heavy lifting."

Arnold slapped him on the shoulder. "The best thing the Initiative ever did was hire that girl. She's a godsend for our community. Never seen anyone work harder. She's one of our best volunteers."

Matt tilted his head. "Liza volunteers at the Promise House?"

Arnold nodded. "Every weekend. Never misses. And there's no job too hard or dirty that she won't roll up her sleeves to do."

"I didn't realize," Matt mused.

"She's been a true champion for our cause. And the kids love her."

Matt wasn't sure what to say to that. It wasn't that he didn't know Liza was an extremely compassionate person. She'd proven that to him time and again when they went toe to toe on the Initiative's goals, always pushing hard to bring real change for the poor, working overtime to help those who needed it the most.

He'd spent most of his life turning a blind eye to those less fortunate. Until he'd met Jess Monroe and heard her story, learning that she and her young son, Jasper, had been forced to stay in homeless shelters and even sleep in their car. She'd been living paycheck to paycheck, barely hanging on, until medical bills delivered the knockout punch, causing her to lose her apartment.

He'd hired her briefly to work at Russo Enterprises, but that ended when she fell in love with Tony Moretti and his roommate, Rhys Beaumont.

It was Jess's situation that led him to volunteer to serve on the Initiative's board. He'd viewed going to the meetings and making financial contributions as him doing his part to improve things in the community...but Liza was giving so much more. Not just talking the talk but walking the walk.

The song changed, and Arnold's eyes lit up. "Better go find my partner. He requested this song."

Matt chuckled when Arnold's partner, Johnnie, danced over to them, inviting Arnold out onto the dance floor with a crook of his finger and a swish of his hips.

Taking a sip of his scotch, Matt surveyed the room once more, not even attempting to lie to himself about whom he was looking for.

Liza was standing near the back of the room, alone, seemingly lost in thought. He'd hated seeing her look so sad earlier, after she'd given her date the heave-ho. She was a million times too good for the likes of Davis Taylor—and he'd been more than happy to let the man know that fact as he'd escorted him out, right after issuing Davis a warning not to contact her again.

Before he could think better of it, he was walking toward her.

She didn't seem surprised or even bothered by the fact he'd sought her out again.

"How much money do you think is out there, swirling on that dance floor?" she asked when he stepped next to her.

"I couldn't begin to estimate how much the attendees spent on their attire."

"Bet it's enough to keep a small Third World country full of starving children in rice and medicine for six months."

Matt refused to take his eyes off her to glance around and play the game. Besides, he'd spent the last hour watching the couples dance as the band played, the women in their richly colored designer gowns and ornate, expensive jewelry.

Liza's estimate was too low.

"Two years," he corrected, and she shook her head.

"Ironic, isn't it?" she asked. "I mean, the whole purpose of this holiday gala is to raise money to expand a homeless shelter for teens. Why can't we just skip the formality of this overdone, expensive party and simply ask them to donate the money they spent on their ticket and their clothing to the cause?"

"The wealthy are only compelled to open their wallets and purses if they can do so while dripping in diamonds and designer suits. It's no fun giving money if no one sees you doing it."

"Such a waste," she murmured. "Speaking of dripping in diamonds, where's your girlfriend?"

Matt wanted to correct her on the term, but instead he merely gestured toward their table. "Like you, discussing fashion. Comparing price tags."

Liza surprised him by laughing. "She's appalled as well?" Her tone made it clear she knew that wasn't the case.

"Appalled isn't the word I'd use."

"Neither of your brothers came tonight," she pointed out.

Matt casually lifted one shoulder. "They decided a long time ago that I would be the face of Russo Enterprises."

"They decided for you?" she asked.

"Gage prefers to spend his time with the nerd circle and Conor has no patience for this kind of thing. So...that left me."

"Oh." She looked away, and he could see she was trying to extricate herself from their conversation...and him.

"Do you have plans for the holiday?" He was resorting to making small talk simply to keep her next to him.

Mercifully, he'd chosen his subject well because the holidays didn't appear to be a topic she minded discussing. She grinned widely. "I have *allll* the plans for the holidays. Tonight is my last official work function before the New Year. Which means I can shift toward the craziness surrounding Christmas Eve with the Morettis."

"Sounds like a bad rom-com," he said sarcastically.

"It's my favorite time of the year."

"Let me guess," he said. "You attempt to squeeze all seven hundred of you into someone's too-tiny house, gorge yourselves on homemade pasta and cases of wine, and," he paused, "draw names? Or shop for everyone?"

Liza narrowed her eyes, trying to decide if he was making fun of her or not. "We draw names," she replied at last.

Then, because it was the nature of their relationship, she turned the tables on him. "I suspect you Russos do it much differently." She tapped her chin with a finger. "A late-night Christmas Eve dinner at some bougie restaurant, the kind that charges a couple hundred dollars a plate for three bites of food. I'm thinking expensive champagne, not wine. And...no gift exchange at all."

She nailed it in one, and he knew why. "Penny filled you in, I see."

Liza nodded, her smile fading a bit. "Doesn't feel very festive, does it?"

Matt didn't reply. The truth was, he dreaded the holidays every bit as much as she looked forward to it. She probably wouldn't be surprised if he confessed that more often than not, he spent Christmas Day in his office at work. There were too many sad memories attached to the holiday, so he found it easier to pretend it didn't exist, treating it like any other day.

Liza must have taken his silence as a signal that their conversation was over, as they both turned their attention back to the room, standing next to each other in silence. The band struck up a slow number, the large groups of dancers dispersing, breaking up into couples.

"Dance with me," he said, before he could think better of the request.

Liza looked at his hand like it was a snake...but then, she slowly lifted hers, placing her palm in his, allowing him to lead her to the floor.

She stepped into his arms, glancing over her shoulder toward his table.

He followed her gaze and saw Patricia still deep in conversation with Bethany.

"Patricia won't like you dancing with me," Liza said. "She strikes me as the jealous type."

"That doesn't concern me."

"Trouble in paradise?"

"No paradise," he replied. "No girlfriend," he added, strangely bothered by the fact she thought that's what Patricia was to him.

"Does *she* know that?" she asked with a cheeky grin. "Because you're dating a serial fiancée."

Matt didn't respond. Primarily because she wasn't wrong, but also because he couldn't. Her goddamned red dress was going to be his downfall tonight. He'd failed to take into account the fact it was cut low in the back.

As they spun, his hand shifted, and he found skin.

A gentleman would lower his hand, put some of the silky material of her dress between his palm and her back.

He couldn't do it. And because he was apparently a masochist, he began to caress her soft skin, his thumb slowly stroking her, up and down, up and down.

Liza lifted her face. He expected her to call him out for his too-familiar touch, but instead, he heard her soft intake of air. And what he saw in her beautiful brown eyes left him struggling to catch his own breath.

Desire.

Now, as she had on that night at Enigma, Liza held his gaze as they moved in time to the music.

The moment felt surreal. It was as if they were the only two people in the room.

Their closeness allowed him to see things he'd never noticed before, like the specks of gold in her eyes, the small beauty mark on her left cheek, the fact she had two piercings in her ears instead of one.

He and his brothers were tall men, all of them well over six feet, but he'd never noticed the difference in his and Liza's heights until this moment, as he held her. The top of her head came to his chin, and she felt small in his arms.

Which seemed wrong. Someone who'd captured and held his attention with such strength and tenacity should have been so much taller.

She'd opted for an elegant updo tonight, and his fingers itched to pull out the pins to watch the thick, chestnut-brown mass of waves fall over her shoulders.

"Why did you ask Davis to leave?" he asked, curious about her failed date.

"A misogynist and a feminist are always going to be a bad combination. Turns out his attraction to me had less to do with who I am and more to do with what I could do for him."

"So he's still holding on to those grandiose political aspirations."

She nodded. "Six dates in and he'd planned our whole future. One where I would give up my career to support his, putting my stellar fundraising skills to better use, garnering campaign contributions for him as he shook enough hands and kissed enough babies to land the big gig in the White House."

Matt had been surprised when Liza walked in with Davis for

the very reasons she just espoused. The man was far too full of himself. However, it was the first thing she said that captured his attention and held it. "Six dates?"

She grimaced, clearly annoyed with herself. "Typically, my bullshit meter works better than that."

"I suspect you figured him out quicker than most women."

"Careful, Mr. Russo," she said in a teasing tone. "That's dangerously close to a compliment."

He bowed his head. "I'll tread lightly."

Unable to resist, Matt ran the tips of his fingers down the center of her back, feeling her response as she shivered, as she lost the ability to focus for just a moment, obsessed with the touch. She was giving herself over to him, letting him lead the dance, control their movements, their direction, and it was heady, intoxicating to have this woman under his command.

It brought needs he'd buried for so long to the surface.

She was so responsive, so sensitive, so in tune with him, that his cock began to thicken. He needed to get a grip or risk embarrassing himself.

Liza swayed closer, but it didn't feel intentional or premeditated, like the moves Patricia had been putting on him earlier.

Liza's actions seemed almost instinctual. Like the pull was too strong to resist.

He recognized it because he felt the same. Placing his palm flat on her back, he let his fingers slide lower, until he found the edge of the material that began only a couple inches above her ass. What would he give to slip his fingers beneath the skirt, to stroke all the way down?

Suddenly, he was curious to know what kind of panties she wore. Liza carried the air of a practical, nice girl, but he'd bet every dollar he had, the naughty woman was wearing a thong right now.

He drew a single fingertip along the edge, watched Liza's cheeks flush, her lips part, her gaze holding his with just the hint of dare in them.

They remained there, speaking volumes without saying a

word. However, before he could answer her unspoken taunt, the song came to an end, and Matt was forced to let her go.

She released an unsteady breath. And then, he watched as she stiffened her spine, gathered her wits, and took back the control she'd entrusted to him during the dance.

Matt wanted to reject the changes in her, to pull her back into his arms, demand that she submit to him, but that way would only lead to disaster. For both of them.

So they left the dance floor, neither of them touching or speaking until they'd reached the bar. If Matt hadn't been so distracted by her, he would have steered them in a safer direction.

As it was, he guided them both to where Patricia stood.

"You stole my dance partner," Patricia said to Liza, her tone a bit too loud and laced with accusation.

"Patricia," Matt said quietly, infusing as much warning as he dared.

"I'll have to keep a closer eye on you." She pointedly ignored Liza as she ran her hands over the front of his suit, straightening his bow tie, before stretching up on tiptoe to give him a hard, possessive kiss. "I wouldn't want you to forget who you're with tonight."

Her words chafed, and if he'd harbored an ounce of doubt about ending his association with her, it was gone now.

"Dance with me," Patricia demanded, grasping his hand in hers and tugging. He wasn't the type of man to be led around by any woman, but in this instance, he allowed her to do it, simply to get her away from Liza before she made a scene.

He glanced back at Liza...but for the first time, she looked away from him, refusing to hold his gaze.

And he hated it.

Chapter Three

L iza sat watching as the crowd on the dance floor began to thin. Many of the guests had already gone home, calling it a night.

She wished she could do the same.

Glancing over, she saw Matt and Patricia rise, leaving for the night as well. She tried to beat down the ridiculous spark of jealousy she felt when he put his hand on the other woman's lower back, guiding her out of the ballroom.

That jealousy morphed into an even more unwanted annoyance over the fact he hadn't bothered to look back at her. She'd gotten too used to his eyes on her tonight and, fool that she was, she was starting to like it.

"You're an idiot," she murmured under her breath, chastising herself for her behavior. She'd gotten far too carried away during that dance with Matt, fantasizing about things she had no business longing for.

Karma was having a lot of fun at her expense. She'd wished for Davis to be less of a nice guy, hoping for him to reveal some level of bad boy during their dance.

Well, she'd gotten a bad boy.

Only it was the wrong one.

The Russo and Moretti animosity had started decades earlier, generations of Russo men all finding ways to hurt her family, either through affairs or financial ruin. And Matt had added his own sins to those of his father and grandfather.

He and her cousin Tony had been rivals their senior year, competing in sports and clubs. When Tony won the class president election, as well as the position of quarterback on the football team, Matt had retaliated, in true Russo fashion, by having sex with Tony's girlfriend, his first love. Then, he'd taken it one step further by ensuring Tony caught them in the act.

That story had been retold so many times it was practically family legend. Yet, Liza couldn't reconcile that younger Matt with the man she knew today, no matter how many times she tried.

The face Matt projected to the world was cold, impassive, aloof, yet her instincts told her that was nothing more than a mask. She couldn't shake the sense there was a much different man buried deep beneath the layers of...God...she wasn't sure what. Anger? Arrogance? Sadness?

Her feelings, her suspicions, about him were driving her as insane as the man himself. She should be able to resist him, but she couldn't. Maybe it was because every time she looked at him, she saw something no one else seemed able to recognize.

Matt seemed broken.

Wounded.

And every instinct she possessed told her to step closer, to look deeper. But doing so felt too much like baring her throat to the beast.

Liza sighed. It was nearly one a.m. Time to put all thoughts of Matt to bed. Preferably forever.

"Liza," Charles said, dropping down into the chair next to hers. "There's no need for you to remain any longer. Go home. I'll hang around and lock up the store," he added with a wink.

"Oh, but I feel like I should—"

"There's nothing else you need to do. The party is as good as over. You did a wonderful job. I can see you're exhausted, and I'm perfectly capable of entertaining these last few stragglers. There will always be a handful who never want to say die."

She felt like she should argue, but she didn't have it in her. "Thanks, Charles. I appreciate it."

He rose and she followed suit, resisting the urge to wince as she did so. Her shoes were killing her, so much so she was considering ripping them off the second she hit the elevator.

Charles gave her a fatherly hug. "I'm so proud of what you accomplished here tonight, Liza."

"What *we* accomplished," she corrected.

"I'll stop by your office Monday morning, and we can see where we landed on contributions."

She crossed her fingers, then reached for her clutch. "Good night."

She slowly dragged her weary body out of the ballroom, and she had just reached the end of the long hallway that led to the hotel's front foyer when she heard a familiar voice raised in anger, and then a loud slap.

"How dare you end things this way!" Patricia yelled.

Liza caught only a brief glimpse of Matt and Patricia facing off in the foyer of the hotel before she quickly took one huge step to the right, hiding behind a large pillar so she was out of sight of the couple.

She glanced back down the hall and considered returning to the ballroom, but dammit...her feet hurt too much.

Unfortunately, there was no way to pass Matt and Patricia without them seeing her.

She had enough energy to get to the elevator and up to her room and that was it. She had zero desire to have yet another confrontation with Patricia or another...whatever the fuck had been going on between her and Matt.

"Keep your voice down, Patricia. I have no interest in drawing a crowd," Matt said, so low Liza barely heard him.

"I will *not* keep my voice down. I don't think it's unreasonable for me to expect my date to treat me with courtesy. To pay atten-tion to me. I didn't enjoy watching you staring at her all night."

Staring at...her?

"She has nothing to do with this," Matt replied.

Me?

"Bullshit," Patricia scoffed.

"You're looking for excuses that don't exist," Matt replied wearily.

"Is this because I suggested we get married?" Patricia asked.

Liza sucked in a quiet gasp. *Married?*

"You see a much different future than I do, Patricia."

Patricia laughed, though there was no humor in the sound. "You're wrong, Matt. Everything I offered you is exactly what you want, what you need. You're making the wrong decision. And one day you're going to realize it. I suggest you figure it out soon because I wait for no one."

"I'm not asking you to wait," Matt said softly, though Liza wasn't sure Patricia heard, considering she'd already started walking away. Liza tracked the angry stomping of the other woman's heels across the marble floor.

She remained hidden, out of sight, listening for Matt's retreating steps as well.

Luck was not on her side tonight.

"You can come out now," he said.

Great. Busted.

She stepped around the pillar. "I didn't want to interrupt." As far as excuses went, that was probably the lamest.

And Matt called her on it. "So you opted for eavesdropping instead." He didn't sound angry. In truth, he sounded like she felt.

Exhausted.

Numb.

Done.

Just fucking done. With everything.

Liza moved closer, looking at the bright red mark on his cheek, shining out even through his beard.

"She slapped you?" She fought not to roll her eyes at herself. *Of course she did, Captain Obvious.*

"Yes." Matt didn't bother to touch his cheek. "I will admit she's not the first woman to slap me."

Liza couldn't resist. "I suspect she won't be the last, either."

The edges of Matt's lips twitched and for a second, she thought she might get a real smile out of him.

It wasn't that he was a humorless bastard all the time. She'd seen him smile on a few occasions, but it was never directed at her.

"You broke things off?"

Wow. She was batting a thousand on the stupid questions.

Matt nodded.

"Because you were staring at...someone?" If she wasn't running on fumes, she never would have asked that question. But he'd thrown her for one too many loops tonight. She was off-balance, and she hated it.

"You know I was," he said, holding her gaze. "Because you were staring back."

Fuck.

There was no response to that.

"Right," she said. "Well, I'm going to..."

She started walking, and Matt fell into step next to her. Soon, it became apparent neither of them was headed for the exit, both walking in the direction of the elevator.

"You got a room here for tonight?" she asked.

"I did."

"Hoping for a romantic interlude?"

Matt shook his head. "Hoping for sex."

"Oh." She'd walked into that one.

"You have a room?" he asked.

She nodded.

"Romantic interlude?" he threw back at her.

"Nope," she replied with a cheeky grin, feeling far too punchy.

She was in a reckless mood, which wasn't a good thing, given the company she was keeping. "I was hoping to get fucked."

She wasn't sure why she'd thrown those words at him. Perhaps it was because part of her wondered if she could spark a reaction.

Sadly, she got nothing, and she felt the need to recover the upper hand. "So, I'm resorting to plan B."

"What's plan B?" he asked as the elevator doors slid open.

"A long soak in a hot bath." And then, because she wasn't finished playing yet, she added, "And self-care."

She'd really thought that would at least earn her the smirk, but nope. Again. Nothing.

They stepped into the elevator. Matt pulled his key card out, tapping it over a screen she hadn't noticed earlier today when she was dropping off her overnight bag in the room. Then he pressed the button to the top floor, and she realized he'd sprung for the penthouse suite.

She rolled her eyes at him, then reached out to press the button to the fourth floor, one with a much less impressive view of the city, no doubt.

Before she reached the button, however, Matt's large hand flew out, grasping her wrist to stop her.

She tried to pull it back, but he didn't release her.

Liza twisted toward him to call him out, but Matt was faster. Using his grip on her wrist, he dragged her to him, his lips descending on hers in a kiss that was urgent and hard and rough and...God...*desperate*.

And because all those words matched her needs, Liza didn't waste a second thinking about the wisdom of this. She shook off his grasp on her wrist and lifted her arms to his neck, pulling him closer, deepening the kiss, pressing her breasts to his chest.

Matt's hands slid along her back, those deadly-to-her-libido fingers tracing lines up and down her bare skin, the same way he had on the dance floor. She'd never been so affected by such a simple touch, but her panties had been damp ever since that dance.

Matt shifted the two of them as they continued to kiss, pressing her against the back wall of the elevator. She was vaguely aware it was rising, but everything vanished when Matt pushed her lips open, his tongue invading her mouth.

She stroked hers against his, tasting the Scotch on his breath. She wanted to get drunk on it. His fingers moved even lower, and he captured her gasp with his mouth as his hands gripped her ass, pulling her body tight to his, letting her feel exactly how much this kiss was impacting him.

Her legs parted as he thrust his large, strong thigh between hers, and she grated her pussy against it, wantonly, shamelessly.

They broke apart at the sound of a bell chiming, the elevator doors sliding open. Both of them were breathing so heavily, one might believe they'd just run a marathon.

Liza's gaze drifted to the hallway, relieved to discover it empty. Otherwise, someone would have gotten an eyeful of her dry-humping Matt Russo's leg.

Looking up, she realized they'd taken the elevator all the way to the top.

"I missed my floor," she said, suddenly struggling to face him.

Matt didn't reply. Instead, he stepped off the elevator, stopping just outside the door. When it started to close, he slammed his hand against it, holding it open.

"Have a drink with me."

Liza was shaking her head before he even finished issuing the invitation. "No," she said, forcing herself to look him in the eye. "We both know if I walk into that room with you, it won't end with a drink."

He didn't bother to consider that, replying instantly. "You're right. It won't."

"That would be insane."

"Why?"

She narrowed her eyes. "You know why."

"It's the holidays, Ms. Moretti. A time when people loosen the reins."

She had to get a grip, had to find solid ground again. As it was, she was teetering precariously on shifting sands and one wrong move was going to have her tumbling to her ass. "Now isn't the time to lower my guard. Santa is watching," she said, hoping humor might cut through the sexual fog threatening to suffocate her.

"I have no interest in those on the nice list."

"But you're interested in me?"

"I am," he replied.

"Are you insinuating I'm naughty?"

Matt shifted closer, pushing a piece of hair that had fallen into her eyes away from her face, tucking it behind her ear. "There was very little insinuation in that statement."

"This is a mistake," she whispered.

"Do it anyway." Matt hit her with that dark, demanding voice that ensured her pussy would win the battle over her brain.

She stood there, her feet rooted to the floor, searching for a way to do the right thing.

In the end, she realized she didn't want to do the right thing, so she made the monumental mistake of stepping off the elevator and following Matt down the hall to the door of his room.

He lifted the key card, but she took a page from his book, gripping his wrist to stop him.

"Just a drink," she said, in one last weakhearted attempt to put the brakes on this runaway train.

Matt didn't even bother to respond to what they both knew was a lie. Not with a nod or a shake of his head. Instead, he tugged his wrist free and unlocked the door.

Stepping aside, he allowed her to walk in first.

Liza's eyes widened as she took in the sheer opulence of the room, catching sight of the Philadelphia nighttime cityscape through the window. "So this is how the other half lives?"

"I'm not sure half is accurate, considering I'm in the one-percent."

She shot him a dirty look over her shoulder. "That's probably not something to brag about."

Matt's lips tipped up in something that could almost be considered a smile. She was making progress.

She walked to the window, anxious to put some distance between them by pretending to look down on the city below, even though she was hyperaware of his presence.

Liza fought to steady her breathing, not quite finished fighting with herself. Maybe there was still a chance she would come to her senses.

Part of her expected Matt to join her at the window, so when she heard him walking around the room, she turned to look.

He took off his tuxedo jacket, hanging it over the back of a chair, and it occurred to her that she'd never seen him without a jacket. Matt was the epitome of corporate America fashion. As such, he was always in a suit. Always. Part of her wouldn't be surprised to discover he slept in his bespoke three-piece suits.

Without the jacket, she had a much better view of his build. She'd clearly given his suits too much credit for his extra bulk, his arms large and muscular. She licked her lips, wishing he'd go one step further and roll up his sleeves.

Shit.

She really had gone too long without a man if she was this ridiculously turned on by the sight of Matt without his jacket.

He caught her staring—she hoped she wasn't drooling—but he didn't call her out, didn't smirk, but his expression was too knowing, too amused for her pride.

So she narrowed her eyes and turned away...briefly. Until Matt headed to the kitchen.

Because, of course, the penthouse suite had a full kitchen that, sadly, rivaled the one in her small apartment. Matt grabbed a corkscrew from the counter, then he held up a bottle of red, looking for her approval.

She nodded and he uncorked it, pouring two glasses. The whole scene felt too familiar and almost domestic.

She accepted when he handed her a glass, tapping his against it. "To a job well done."

"Thank you." Liza took a sip, making a mental note not to consume too much. She'd indulged in at least three glasses of champagne over the course of the night, and while she was far from intoxicated, she needed her wits about her if she was going to maneuver her way safely through this.

Matt gestured toward the couch, and she accepted the invitation to sit, placing her glass on the end table so she could reach down to pull off her shoes with a relieved groan.

He watched her curiously, then, to her surprise, he toed off his own shoes.

"Too long in heels," she explained. "Part of why plan B was the hot bath. My feet are killing me." She wore thigh-high stockings, and she wished she could strip them off as well.

Matt put his glass on the coffee table before sitting down next to her on the couch. Then to her surprise, he lifted her feet onto his lap, his thumbs pressing against the soles.

"Relax," he urged her, twisting his body so that his back was against the arm of the couch. She assumed the same position, reclining against the opposite cushioned arm. They were mirror images, facing each other. He leaned one leg against the back of the couch, bent at the knee, while the other remained on the floor. He held her feet in his hands between his outstretched thighs. It felt strangely decadent, sitting here while Matt gave her a foot massage.

He dug his thumbs in deeper, hitting a particularly sore spot, and Liza moaned. It felt like bliss, like heaven. Too much more of this and she thought she might actually have an orgasm.

"That feels...amazing."

"You need more sensible shoes." He cupped her feet with his large hands, working absolute magic.

She laughed. "But those shoes were so perfect with my new red dress."

She hadn't meant to draw his attention to her outfit, but now that she had, she realized the slit in the skirt had fallen open, revealing the long expanse of her thigh.

Liza started to pull the material together.

"Leave it," Matt demanded, and damn if she didn't find herself obeying, dropping the skirt. It fell open once more, revealing most of her right leg, riding high enough to show him the top of one of her thigh-high stockings.

He stared at her leg, but she didn't call him on it, though she *did* make sure to flash him that same knowing look he'd given her when she checked him out without his jacket.

They remained there on the couch, in quiet solitude for several minutes. His massage was so soothing, and she was so exhausted, she might have expected to fall asleep. Instead, his touch had the opposite effect, waking up all the party places in her body.

At one point, he lowered his grip and one of her heels brushed against the crotch of his pants. She felt the bulge of his erection. Her eyes flew up to his, and she realized his actions had been intentional. He wanted her to feel what she was doing to him.

Slowly, she slipped her feet from his lap, shifting closer, wanting to offer him some measure of comfort as well. Reaching out, she untied his bow tie, slipping it from the collar before unbuttoning the top two buttons on his shirt. Matt watched as she worked, making no move to stop her.

She was tempted to close the distance between them and resume the kiss they'd started in the elevator, but there was still a part of her trying to fight this, to resist him and this unexplainable pull.

It was that determination that had her pushing away, reclaiming her side of the couch, tucking her bare feet beneath her.

"You really don't exchange gifts with your brothers?" she asked, seeking to end the silence.

"We're wealthy men. If we want something, we buy it. A gift exchange just for the sake of observing some holiday tradition is pointless." He picked up his wineglass from the coffee table and took another sip.

She followed his lead, reaching for her wine as well, hoping it would provide some level of defense. "Gifts aren't just about buying something the person wants. They're meant to be meaningful, thoughtful."

"For example?"

"This fall, I managed to get my brothers and I together in the same place at the same time for a portrait. My mom has wanted it for years, but it's been impossible to synch our schedules because Bruno always had something with the kids or Aldo was on duty or Elio was on the road with the team."

While Aldo was still a paid firefighter for the city, Elio had hung up his skates at the end of the last hockey season, returning home to be with Gianna.

"Elio and his wife just had a baby, right?"

Liza smiled. "A little girl. In September. She's absolutely adorable."

"You like being an aunt."

"I loooove being an aunt," she corrected. "You know, Penny said she and Gage are trying to get pregnant. Are you ready to become Uncle Matt?"

Matt sighed, lifting one shoulder. "I don't have a lot of experience around small children. Conor can assume the role of fun uncle."

Liza waited to see if he added a "just kidding" to that comment, but she could see he meant what he said. "So no kids in your future?"

Matt shook his head. "I have no plans to get married or have a family."

"Oh." She started to ask why, but Matt seemed to anticipate the question and he shut her down.

"So you're giving your mom the portrait for Christmas?"

Liza nodded. "Actually, I got two of the pictures framed, and I can't wait to see her face when she opens them. I bought all of us flannel shirts in coordinating colors. We paired them with blue jeans, and in one we're doing the usual cheesy smiles, but the second one wasn't posed.

"Bruno's a big guy, with a big appetite, and the most obnoxiously long, thick, unruly lumberjack beard. Mom and I have been begging him to shave, but he says his wife Vivian is crazy about it. Anyway, we're sitting there, waiting for the photographer, when Bruno runs his hand down his beard...and a French fry falls out and lands on Aldo's shoulder. All of us fell apart laughing, and the photographer snapped a picture of it. It was our favorite of the bunch. We're pretty sure that's the one Mom's going to hang up in the living room for guests to see."

"You're close to your parents, to your brothers."

"Yeah. Very. Mom and I talk on the phone at least three times a week. And my brothers...well, they're more than brothers. They're my best friends too. You know how it is. You have Gage and Conor."

Liza wished she could take back her comment, even though she wasn't sure what she'd said wrong. The shadows that never completely left his eyes grew darker, and she knew she wasn't imagining the outright pain that flashed on his face.

Of course, Matt was the master of control, so she only got a glimpse before he schooled his features and turned to put his glass on the coffee table once more.

She'd become very good friends with Gage over the past year, but the subject of Matt wasn't something they discussed much. At least not from Gage's perspective. When she looked back, she realized the only times she and Gage talked about Matt, it was her doing the talking, and by talking, she meant bitching.

She didn't know much about the Russo brothers' relationship other than the fact the three of them ran the family business together. Now...she was curious.

Matt, however, was good at dodging subjects he didn't want to discuss. He shifted closer, taking her glass from her and setting it next to his.

Then he began pulling the pins from her hair.

The familiarity should have felt strange, but like her unbuttoning his shirt, it seemed natural, right.

Once he'd removed the last pin, he ran his fingers through her hair, his fingertips rubbing against her scalp in such a sensual, gentle, hot-as hell way, she closed her eyes and sighed.

"That feels good."

"You have beautiful hair. So thick."

Her eyelids lifted and she watched as he continued to run his fingers through her long tresses. Before she could think better of it, she reached out to draw her hand along his cheek, rough from his beard.

The redness from Patricia's slap had faded, only the slightest tinge of pink remaining.

"Contemplating slapping me?" he joked, always with that deadpan voice.

"Not yet," she murmured. "But I suspect it's just a matter of time."

He chuckled, and she was completely taken aback by it, even though she couldn't help but notice it wasn't a wholly happy sound.

There was a tiredness in his eyes that she didn't think was driven by the late hour. She recognized it because it was the same thing she saw whenever she looked in the mirror.

She was lonely...and there didn't seem to be an end in sight. So along with the loneliness, she carried around a boatload of resignation.

She wanted off this particular treadmill. And it looked like Matt did too. She was beginning to feel like he might be a kindred spirit, that he was as lonely as she was. But there was something else there as well, something lurking deep beneath the surface.

He was...haunted. It was the only word she could think to describe it.

It called to her in ways she couldn't explain, couldn't understand. The only thing she *did* know was...this thing between them...

It was dangerous.

Chapter Four

Liza pushed away again. And he let her go. She was wrestling with a decision.

Sleep with him or walk away.

In truth, he should be facing the same dilemma because she wasn't wrong when she called this a mistake.

Unfortunately, any internal debate ended the moment his lips touched hers in that elevator. Hell, it had probably ended during that dance, when his fingers stroked her smooth, soft back.

He wanted her. More than he'd ever wanted another woman, and he was arrogant enough, cocky enough about his skills as a lover, to know he could seduce her into his bed.

But he didn't want to resort to seduction. He wanted her to come to him willingly, without reservation, so he'd made more small talk, showed her as much of himself as he was able, in hopes that it would be enough to convince her to spend the night with him.

Liza resumed her previous spot, leaning back against the arm of the couch, turned sideways to face him.

"It's late," she mused.

"It is."

"I should be face down in a pillow by now, especially after the week I've had, but instead I..."

"Second wind?" he asked.

She nodded. "Yeah."

He felt the same. His mind kept telling him he should be sleepy, but his body hadn't gotten the word yet, too focused on the gorgeous brunette sitting next to him.

She was absentmindedly toying with the ribbon on a present he'd stashed on the table behind the couch earlier today. It was meant to be Patricia's Christmas present, but she hadn't taken well to his assertion that they should stop seeing each other.

Part of him had been surprised by her response because he didn't doubt for a moment that she had no feelings for him apart from sexual desire and a strong attraction to his bottom line. If she was a gold digger, perhaps he could understand her losing her shit and slapping him. But Patricia was wealthy in her own right. She didn't need his money. She just wanted it.

His surprise faded when she mentioned Liza, pointed out the way he'd been staring at her all night. He hadn't hurt Patricia's heart; he'd wounded her pride. She demanded the attention and admiration of every man in her vicinity, and because she was beautiful, she was accustomed to receiving it. She'd been livid that Matt had made the cardinal mistake of finding another woman more beautiful.

Once he understood the reason for her fury, the slap made sense, and he'd taken it as his due. Because he *had* been staring at Liza.

Liza suddenly realized what she was doing. She stopped fiddling with the package, picking it up. "Was this for Patricia?"

"It was."

"Thought you didn't do Christmas gifts?" she teased.

"Patricia, like you, is a firm believer in presents. Though her pleasure seems to be derived more from receiving than giving, which is *unlike* you."

She picked up the small square box, as if testing out the weight. "Well, I hope you can get a refund on whatever it is."

"Open it," he said.

Liza shook her head. "No." She put it back down quickly.

"You're curious. You want to know what it is. So open the gift."

For a moment, he thought she might continue to refuse, but Liza's inquisitive nature was strong. "Fine." She untied the ribbon, then lifted the lid, gasping. "Holy shit. That must have cost a fortune."

He shrugged. He didn't have a clue what it cost because he hadn't picked it out. He'd sent his personal assistant, Henri, to shop for Patricia.

She placed the box in his hand. "You're definitely going to want to get your money back on that."

Matt lifted the diamond tennis bracelet out of the satin-lined box and unfastened the clip, laying the thing over his palm to look at it. Henri had wrapped it as well, so it wasn't just Liza who'd been curious about the box's contents. He recalled Henri saying he'd bought a bracelet, but Matt hadn't cared enough to ask for details about the gift. Instead, he had viewed it as one less thing on his to-do list.

His personal assistant had a great deal of experience when it came to shopping for Matt's lovers, always finding the perfect token, be it something for the holidays, birthdays, the morning after one-night stands, or parting gifts. Knowing his very capable assistant, Henri probably had a chart for every category, complete with price range, what certain flowers or jewels represented, as well as the female's preferences.

Matt reached for and grasped Liza's hand, pulling it toward him, his intent clear.

"Don't put that on me," she said immediately, trying to tug her hand from his grip.

Matt was amused. God knew she was the only woman who had ever rejected diamonds from him. "Humor me." He tightened his grip so that she couldn't pull away. He fastened the bracelet around her wrist, maintaining his hold so he could look at it.

"Whoa," she breathed. "It's beautiful." She admired it for a moment or two longer. "Take it off."

He shook his head, drawing his fingers over the diamonds, noticing the way she shivered lightly when he brushed the pulse point of her wrist.

"It's very pretty," he acknowledged, not bothering to remove it. "But this isn't what I would have bought if I'd been shopping for you."

He didn't bother to point out he hadn't shopped for this. Something told him that if he ever decided to give Liza a gift, he wouldn't send Henri to buy it.

He'd do it himself.

"No diamonds for me?" she asked, attempting a playful tone but falling a bit short.

"No. Diamonds pale next to your skin."

"Nice line," she murmured, trying to play off his comment by cheapening it. It annoyed him, even though he knew where her opinions of him came from. She'd formed them based on his past actions, things he'd done to hurt her family, which he couldn't defend. So he didn't try to.

"It's not a line," he insisted as he shifted closer to her, running the backs of his fingers over her soft cheek. Liza's skin was tan, despite the fact it was the middle of winter. It betrayed her Italian ancestry, as did the deep brown eyes a man could get lost in, framed by long black lashes.

She wasn't a classic beauty, unlike Patricia, who fit the more traditional standard for female attractiveness. As such, Patricia was a cookie cutter of every other woman he'd ever dated—blonde hair, blue eyes, a shapely figure, courtesy of time spent with her personal trainer.

Liza's beauty was unique, exotic. Breathtaking.

His gaze fell to her lips when her tongue darted out to wet

them. It was an invitation to kiss her, but he held back, still wanting the next move to be hers.

"If I'd been shopping for you, I would have bought you rubies. I can imagine how the rich, vibrant red hue would shimmer against your skin." Leaning closer, he placed his lips against her ear. "I'd cover you in rubies. They'd dangle from your ears." He pulled away. "From your throat." He placed his open hand at her neck, the touch possessive, perhaps even slightly threatening, though it didn't provoke that response from her.

Liza's breathing stuttered, her eyes drifting closed.

"From your wrists," he continued, listing all the places he'd wrap up in rubies. He took both of her wrists in his hands, lifting them over her head, giving the illusion of holding her captive.

Liza responded with a quiet whimper, though he could tell she was embarrassed by the sound. He hadn't meant to draw them down this path, but now that he had...he couldn't stop. Her lowered eyelids, her flushed cheeks, her panting breaths were telling him things about Liza he was going to wish he didn't know.

He released her wrists, stroking his hands down the inside of her arms, loving the way it took her a few extra seconds before she remembered to lower them.

He wasn't finished. There were still so many places he'd yet to adorn.

"And I wouldn't stop with the traditional pieces." He was aware that he was about to reveal a part of himself he typically guarded closely.

"What do you mean?"

"My rubies would dangle from your nipples," he whispered, using the backs of his fingers once more, running them over the lace bodice of her dress, over her breasts. He could feel the tautness of her nipples, knew the effect his words were having on her.

"Where else?" she asked, her voice husky with need.

"From the clamp I'd put on your clit."

He heard her slight intake of breath, desire naked in her big brown eyes.

"But the largest ruby would peek out from the plug I'd put in your ass."

"God," she breathed.

After that heated kiss in the elevator, he'd purposely slowed things down, giving Liza time to decide if this was what she wanted.

Now, time was up.

Matt leaned toward her, placing his rough cheek against her smooth one. "You would be my naughty red queen."

Liza's response was instant. She grasped his shoulders, placing her lips against his in a kiss that was hard and hungry.

He cupped the back of her head, holding her there, pushing her lips open with his. Kissing wasn't part of his sexual repertoire. It wasn't that he didn't kiss his lovers. He did. But they were glancing touches, a small part of the experience he utilized to increase the woman's arousal.

Kissing had never done anything for him, never left him gasping for air, desperate for another taste.

He pulled away, fighting to regain control. Tonight was about sex. Nothing more.

It had to be, or he'd lose what was left of his sanity.

"Bedroom," he said, rising from the couch.

She took the hand he proffered, letting him lead her to the master bedroom. Once they were there, he lifted his finger, gesturing for her to turn around.

Liza presented him with her back, pulling her hair over one shoulder as he unbuttoned the two buttons holding her dress together at the base of her neck, before lowering the zipper at her lower back.

Liza looked back at him, not a hint of timidness in her gaze. It was one of the first things that had drawn him to her. He had no interest in innocence. He liked her boldness, her confidence. It called to him.

Once the dress was loose, she let the material fall away, stepping out of it as it hit the floor. She kept her back to him, giving him a bird's-eye view of her ass.

Fuck *him*.

He was right. She wore a thong.

Pushing his fingers into the thin elastic, he shoved it down, stroking her ass as he did so. It was round and pert and full and so goddamned perfect.

Liza kicked off the thong, then turned to face him.

She didn't seek to hide her body. Instead, her hands hung loose by her sides, and she let him look his fill.

He took his time, painfully aware that this would be his only night with her. To pursue more would be madness.

Liza was patient with his perusal, up to a point, then she reached for him and finished unbuttoning his shirt. Like him, she touched every place she bared, her fingers sliding along his pecs, down to his stomach. She shoved her hands beneath the material, her hands stroking his arms as she peeled the shirt off completely.

Unsatisfied with just touching, she moved closer, drawing her lips over his chest, her tongue darting out to steal a taste of his skin, and then another, and another.

Gripping the back of her head, he held her lips to his chest, wincing when she sank her teeth into his right pec.

"Do that again," he demanded, loving her lips on him, her teeth, wanting to wear her mark and to mark her as well.

She bit the left pec, then lifted her face to him. Holding his gaze captive with those dark, expressive eyes, Liza went to work unfastening his belt and pulling it from the loops. The buckle clattered as it hit the floor.

She started to unhook his pants, but Matt stopped her. The second his cock came out this shifted into overdrive. He refused to go too fast.

He was already taking more than he deserved, but he wasn't a good enough man to stop. So he was going to steal every minute, every second, and then pay penance for this night's folly for the rest of his life.

Gripping her wrists in his hands, he lowered his head, kissing her as he slowly pushed her away from the bed. The wall at her back stopped them, so he lifted her hands above her head as he'd done in the living room. Holding her hands against the wall, he gave her the sensation of being held, trapped, bound.

"You're mine," he murmured, then because it was imperative that he regain some grip on reality, he added, "all night."

It was a line he needed to draw, a limit he had to place.

Liza's eyes narrowed slightly, but then she nodded. Just one bob of the head.

He tightened his grip on her wrists, and she moaned, losing herself to the sensation, falling headfirst into his possession.

What would he give to tie her to his bed? To keep her beneath him, helpless to do anything more than take what he gave her. He'd withhold her orgasm for hours, demanding her submission, her body, her soul, every fucking thing. He'd touch every inch of her skin, all while making her beg and plead and even cry. He wanted to taste her tears, wanted her to know that he would own those as well.

Matt wasn't a possessive man, but Liza made him want to lock her up in a cage and throw away the keys—forever.

Releasing her arms, he lowered his lips to her neck, cupping her breasts, squeezing them, nipping at the taut buds, giving her the same bite of pain she'd given him. Liza hissed, then groaned, her hands finding their way to his hair. She closed her fists in the strands, pulling it in an attempt to keep him where she wanted.

He wasn't a man who would be commanded. Not outside the bedroom, and sure as fuck not inside it.

He'd lived under another's authority once...just once...and it had destroyed him. He would never give anyone that kind of power over him again.

He drew her hands away from his head, pulling them behind

her back, holding them there as he studied her face, saw something he was certain Liza didn't even know she was revealing.

She was a powerhouse, a go-getter, a take-charge, take-no-prisoners woman...but not here. Not with him.

He released her hands before he took this to a place neither of them had any business going. Instead, he forced the tide to turn, to shift to something less dangerous.

He kissed his way down her body, moving lower and lower, not stopping until he was on his knees in front of her.

Liza's eyes widened in surprise, especially when he lifted her right leg and placed it over his shoulder. The wall at her back gave her the support she needed to remain upright on one leg. She still wore her stockings, but as they didn't hinder him from his goal, he left them on.

"Oh my God," she cried out when he gave her a much more intimate kiss. Matt sucked her clit into his mouth roughly, then stroked her slit with his tongue, leaving no part of her untasted. She was so hot and wet, he almost expected to see steam rising.

He teased her clit with the tip of his tongue, holding her open to his assault with his thumbs, until her hips began to gyrate, thrusting toward him in an obvious attempt to steal more.

She was going to get what she wanted, but only on his terms, only when he was ready. He wasn't familiar with Liza's past lovers, but there was something about the way she was holding herself that told him she hadn't chosen wisely.

"Hold still," he demanded.

Liza froze, but only for a second. She wasn't finished trying to take control. Her hands snaked out, gripping his hair once more.

He pulled his head away even as she reached out, trying to bring him back.

"Hold still," he repeated darkly. "Do that again and all of this ends."

"But I..."

He lifted one eyebrow, daring her to finish that statement. She wisely fell silent, and he saw it again, clear as day.

Submissiveness.

If someone had told him this morning that Liza Moretti was a submissive, he would have scoffed.

And he could tell by Liza's face that he wasn't the only one shocked by the discovery. She frowned, and he could almost read the struggle in her eyes, the part of her that couldn't figure out why she was responding to him.

He didn't give her time to think about that too hard. Instead, he lowered his head once more. He sucked and nipped at her clit, adding his fingers to the mix, pushing two inside her wet pussy.

It clenched strongly, greedily grasping his fingers as he thrust them in and out. She was tight, almost too tight.

"How long?" he asked.

She didn't need clarification. "Two years," she confessed. "Maybe a little more."

Matt struggled to make sense of that admission. Liza was sexual, vibrant, beautiful. How could it have been so long? What the hell was wrong with every single man in this city?

He increased the suction on her clit as well as his pace, pushing her hard, taking her to the brink fast. His girl needed an orgasm.

His.

His.

Fuck...no.

"Matt," she said, her hands digging into his muscular shoulders, her nails scraping the skin there.

God, he loved the sound of his name on her lips.

"I, I..."

He lifted his face, gazed up at her, waiting for her to return it. She looked down.

"You're going to come for me and you're not going to hold a goddamned thing back. You try to give me less than everything, I'll punish you for it." He placed his mouth back on her, his fingers thrusting harder, and within seconds, she was there.

Liza's knee began to buckle in the midst of her orgasm, so he lowered her other leg, quickly reaching up to press on her stomach with one hand, holding her steady against the wall as she rode out the storm. With his other hand, he continued stroking her, milking every ounce of pleasure from her clenching pussy.

He'd never seen anything more beautiful than Liza Moretti in the throes of an orgasm.

Her grip on his shoulders tightened as she bent forward, trembling with the force. She called out his name. Just his name. Over and over.

It wasn't a scream. It was quieter, almost reverent.

Matt rose slowly, retaining his grip on her, his eyes locked on her flushed face so that he saw the moment her wits returned.

Liza's eyes blinked open, her lashes fluttering. Then she looked him dead in the eye and...smiled.

Matt tried to recall the last time anyone had ever smiled at him like that. Years, he decided. It wasn't the smile that was unusual; women flashed him flirty grins all the time.

No, Liza's smile was something else altogether.

It was genuine happiness and affection and, God help him, even trust.

His chest tightened, and he suddenly found it difficult to draw a deep breath.

Her comment earlier drifted through his brain as the magnitude of what he'd just done struck.

This is a mistake.

He'd known that going in, yet he'd tossed all sense of self-preservation aside, thinking with the wrong head. Now he could see this wasn't just a mistake.

It was a catastrophe, a tsunami, cataclysmic destruction.

Before he could find a way to extract himself from the situation, Liza took the decision away, all hope of escaping before they hit the point of no return vanishing the second she lowered herself to her knees in front of him.

"Fuck," he muttered under his breath, watching as she unfastened his pants, drawing them and his briefs down. He stepped out of them, groaning when Liza reached between his thighs and cupped his balls. He reached out, placing his hands flat against the wall behind her for support.

She glanced up at him briefly, the fucking smile that would be his downfall still on her face, before she turned her attention to his cock.

It was hard as concrete, the head an angry red. This erection had first appeared during their dance, and it had ridden at half-mast since. He was an unpinned grenade, ready to blow, and Liza was on her knees in front of him.

She wrapped one of her hands around his cock, the fingertips not touching. While his dick was an average length, it was thicker than most, something past lovers had either complained or raved about. Liza didn't appear intimidated as her lips parted and her tongue darted out to steal her first taste.

She tightened her grip around his cock, running her hand up and down his hard flesh as she took the head into her mouth completely.

Matt closed his eyes, gray dots clouding his vision as he sought control. There was nothing like Liza's lips, or the confident way she sucked him in. Her tongue teased the sensitive spot just beneath his head, and he groaned again.

She was pushing him too far, too fast, but nothing was going to stop him from coming inside her sweet, sexy mouth.

He wrapped his fingers in her hair, closing his fists around it, using that grip to tilt her head back, careful to keep his cock lodged inside her mouth.

"I'm going to come," he explained. "And you're going to swallow. All of it."

She nodded just once, the most she could accomplish. She was struggling to keep him in her mouth while also dislodging his grip. Liza, foolishly, still believed she could take the upper hand, thought the power would be hers.

She was wrong.

He pulled her hair, her slight whimper a sign that her scalp stung. He didn't relent.

"This isn't going to be the end of the night."

He saw from Liza's scowl that was exactly her intention. He'd realized it the moment she dropped to her knees.

She still wasn't finished fighting this thing between them. And while he appreciated her efforts, wishing he had her strength, they'd already gone way too far.

"This doesn't end here," he repeated. "You think you don't want me, but you do. So I'm going to bury myself in that wet, tight cunt of yours, and we're going to come again...together."

She stilled for just a moment, and he wondered if she'd pull back, drop his cock, rise, and walk away. He wasn't a hundred percent certain he'd be able to let her go.

"But first..." He prodded, pushing his cock the tiniest bit deeper into her mouth.

Mercifully, she didn't fight him, taking him even deeper, her tongue stroking in a way that had him seeing stars.

He released her hair but kept his hands on her head, cupping the back of it, using that touch to drive his cock deep. She gave herself up to him, whatever internal struggle she'd waged done now.

She relinquished the reins, allowing him to direct her movements as he fucked her mouth, stealing as much as he could from her, all the while knowing...it would never be enough.

He shoved his hips forward, forcing more of his cock inside. She was at her limit, maybe even a touch beyond, but she didn't cower or try to pull away. Instead, it felt as if she was fighting to give him even more.

She flexed her hand around his balls, squeezing gently, the action pushing Matt over the edge.

"Fuck!" he grunted as come spurted from the end of his cock, but Liza didn't relent. She drew the pleasure out as she kept fucking him with her mouth, her lips, even the tiniest touch of her teeth.

Once his climax passed, he slowly withdrew, watching as Liza swallowed. Her lips were puffy, red, well-used. She ran her fingertips over them, touching the juices that remained there.

He gripped her upper arms, tugging her up from the floor, drawing her into another kiss, needing to taste—her, him, what they'd created together.

Liza's kisses were going to be his new obsession. He would spend the rest of his life craving them, dreaming of them, addicted to the memory of them.

After minutes, maybe hours, he broke the kiss, cupping her cheek, trying to memorize the way she looked right now, storing it away for all the long, lonely nights to come.

Then he turned them toward the bed, reaching out to pull down the covers.

"Get in."

Rather than obey, she perched on the edge, slowly stripping away her stockings. He lifted one foot, then the other, stripping off his own socks. They'd been too impatient to remove those earlier. Completely naked, Liza twisted around and crawled across the mattress, his hand itching to reach out and spank that perfect ass.

Then she shifted, sitting in the middle, waiting for him patiently, expectantly.

"You're mine," he said, lacing as much warning as he could muster into his tone. "Tonight, you're all mine."

Chapter Five

Liza shuddered at Matt's words.

Jesus Christ.

She sat there watching him, waiting for him, fighting like the devil to convince herself that Matt wasn't the greatest lover she'd ever had—and they hadn't even fucked yet.

She tried to tell herself she'd just gone too long without.

She'd had too much champagne.

She was succumbing to that old "want what you can't have" adage. He was forbidden fruit, so she was building this all up much bigger than it was.

Yeah.

Right.

Those were all bold-faced lies. Weak attempts to lessen this, to make it something more manageable, controllable.

Because, God help her, she wanted to be his.

He'd made the comment twice, each time making sure to let her know that possession only lasted until morning. Part of her wanted to test that timeline, to push him on it.

But something told her if she did that, if she pushed for more, he'd walk away from her right now—and she couldn't let him do that.

Fuck. Hadn't she already taken enough shit from karma tonight?

First the super-sexy dance and now...this.

Clearly, she'd been a serial killer in a past life. It was the only way to explain why the greatest lover she'd ever had would be Matt Russo, a man her family hated, a man who made her professional life difficult, a man she could barely tolerate and who could barely tolerate her.

Matt climbed into bed with her as she mentally patted herself on the back for not drooling. She had never—NEVER—seen such muscular arms on a man. The guy had to be bench-pressing two hundred pounds, his shoulders something she would have attributed to Photoshop if she'd seen him pictured in a magazine. Plus, he was sporting an honest-to-God eight-pack, which she had to admit she assumed was super rare when it came to normal men.

Movie stars, bodybuilders, her brother Elio, the former hockey star, sure...an eight-pack.

Matt Russo, a man who spent his days pushing papers behind his oversized desk?

Wow.

Actually, every second since they'd walked into this bedroom had been one huge wow. She was still trying to figure out if she'd imagined Matt Russo dropping to his knees and going down on her.

Liza couldn't recall the last time a man had done that. It had been a very, very long time ago. Maybe even as far back as college, now that she thought about it.

Matt wasn't the type of man she'd ever thought to see on his knees, not that the position made him less intimidating, less powerful. He was dominance personified, and she was here for it.

She'd never been a passive lover, never let a man take charge in the bedroom. She was a sexual woman with needs and desires, and her past lovers had sadly needed a little—a lot—of instruction on how to get her where she wanted to be.

It felt as if Matt had gotten his hands on her owner manual, and he hadn't just glanced at the thing; he'd read it cover to cover, memorized it, studied it like she was his final exam.

After giving her an orgasm that literally shook her so hard it hurt, he took care to hold her steady, keep her safe, which was a good thing because her bones had melted at some point in the midst of it all.

Of course, the second the last pulses of her orgasm faded away, Liza knew she was in way over her head.

Originally, a blow job seemed like the quickest, easiest way out of the situation. He'd gotten her off, she'd get him off, and then she'd run like the hounds of hell were chasing her all the way back down to her hotel room.

Shared orgasms with Matt were one thing. But more of those incredible kisses...sex...lying in bed with him.

God, she wasn't strong enough to come back from that, and she knew it.

So she'd gone to her knees.

But she'd given herself away. Somehow, he'd known her plan. And he'd called her on it.

In truth, Matt had looked shocked when she'd knelt before him, and that same...awareness...crept in. The feeling that Matt wasn't just lonely.

He was wounded—and she wanted to ease his pain.

That was when she'd been forced to admit she wanted to give Matt a blow job, wanted to be there on her knees in front of him because his pleasure felt tied to hers. She'd gotten seriously turned on when she'd taken his—holy fuck—thick cock in her mouth. She had just had the mother of all orgasms, but as she sucked him, it felt as if she hadn't come in years.

Now...here she was, watching as he crawled across the bed toward her.

"Matt," she started, though she didn't have a clue what she was going to say after that.

He gripped her ankles, pulling roughly until her back hit the mattress, so that he could cage her beneath him.

Before she was forced to think of something else to say, he lowered his head and kissed her. This kiss, unlike the previous ones, was slower, gentler, but just as dangerous to her sense of self-preservation.

Who the hell taught him to kiss like this?

He held himself above her, his weight resting on his elbows, his body covering hers. His hard-on brushed against her stomach.

He smirked when her eyes widened.

"That's some world-class recovery time." She was striving for humor, something to minimalize what they were doing, to break it down into something she could handle.

"If you want to leave, now is the time. I'm not sure...I..."

He was offering her an out, a chance to escape with her heart still intact.

Because that was what was on the line.

She could offer up a million excuses, a million lies, and none of that would change the fact she could very easily fall in love with Matt Russo.

"Do you want to go?" he asked, his voice gruff when she didn't reply.

Liza shook her head. A smart woman would walk away, but she'd lived on her own for too many years, watched love strike this friend, then a cousin, her brothers, while missing her time and time again.

If this was it for her, if this was all she got, she was going to take it.

"I don't want to leave," she whispered.

Matt's brow creased, and she got the impression she'd given him the wrong response.

"Do you want me to go?" she asked.

He shook his head. "No. Though..."

"I should," she finished for him.

"I don't want you to leave," he said, though she could tell those words cost him something.

"Kiss me," she murmured.

It looked like they were both resigned to paying the piper tomorrow.

He lowered his head and gone was the soft lover. Matt's kisses took on a life of their own, and he laid claim to her lips, her mouth, her tongue. He took and she gave.

And the need for words vanished.

Her back arched when Matt's lips drifted along the side of her throat, sucking and biting in such a way that she was grateful it was winter because she was going to be wearing turtlenecks for a week.

She groaned when his lips found her nipple, drawing it into his mouth roughly. She recalled his comment about dangling rubies from her nipples. She wondered if he'd envisioned clamps or piercings, then she realized she'd wear either for him.

Liza wasn't sure where these desires were coming from, but there was no denying they were genuine. It felt as if she'd finally discovered the woman she was meant to be. No wonder her previous sexual encounters were so lackluster. She'd been a shadow of herself, hiding the truth of who she was and what she needed. Not only from her lovers but from herself.

Matt had reached through all the protective layers, torn down the walls, and dragged out the real her.

How was she going to survive this?

Survive *him*?

A sharp pain pierced her heart.

Liza cried out again when Matt pinched one nipple while biting the other.

"Don't go away," he growled. "Not even in your head."

"I didn't."

"Don't lie," he barked.

"I...won't," she promised, her words soothing him.

"You're with me," he said, before adding that hated last word, "tonight. Only me. Put the bullshit away."

Her only reply was to nod. She ran her fingers through his

hair. He was the most intense, serious, even scary man she'd ever known.

He was also the most handsome, and she found it impossible to look away.

Matt held her gaze for only a second longer, his eyes troubled, and that was when she realized he was asking for something from her he wasn't giving in return.

"You're with me," she repeated, adding as much strength to her tone as she could. "Stay with me."

Matt blinked once, twice, his frown too pronounced. Then, something lifted in his eyes, his face clearing.

"I'm with you," he promised.

She lifted her face, kissing his cheek, loving the roughness of his beard, then Matt resumed his travels around her body, kissing, licking, nipping at every bare inch of skin. She'd never had a lover take so long simply exploring.

She loved it as much as she hated it.

"I need you," she gasped, not for the first time. Hell, not for the thousandth time.

"Keep begging," he said, darkly, not lifting his head. He was currently nipping at a sensitive spot on the inside of her upper thigh.

"Dammit," she bitched. "Please!"

"More." His tongue brushed her clit, but it was too light, not enough.

"Sex, *now*," she demanded, reaching for his arms, trying in vain to drag him where she wanted him. She was convinced the man was made of steel.

"Be more specific."

"Your dick. My vagina. Like peanut butter and jelly, all smooshed together. Make it happen."

She was pleasantly surprised when this time—finally—it appeared he was going to give her what she wanted. He lifted his head, amused, his lips slightly lifted at the corners.

"Peanut butter and jelly," he murmured.

"Please," she whispered, pride be damned. "Matt...please."

He reached toward the nightstand, pulling a condom out of the drawer.

"I have an IUD too," she offered, wanting him to know that they would be doubly protected, as she recalled his vow to never have children.

The package crinkled. Then he put the condom on and pushed her thighs apart before settling between them, lining his cock up with her opening. His cock was way thicker than that of any man she'd ever been with, wide enough that it belatedly occurred to her this could hurt.

Not that she'd needed to worry. Matt seemed cognizant of the need to go slow, so he see-sawed in, then out, in, then out, giving her time to adjust to his girth rather than forcing his dick in with one hard thrust.

Both of them were looking down, watching the process, as his cock slowly disappeared inside her body. She'd never seen anything hotter.

Once he was fully seated, he lifted his face to hers. He cupped her cheek with his hand, offered her a kiss so soft and tender, it almost made her want to cry.

Then, he gave her the world's most wicked grin. "Now," he said in that dark chocolate tone that made her entire body clench with need, "we're getting serious."

"Serious?" she asked breathlessly. She was barely hanging on. And all he'd done was slide in.

"Serious," he repeated. "Hold on."

As far as warnings went, that one fell short—because Matt fucked her like a man possessed, pounding into her body, giving her no quarter, no reprieve, no time to catch her breath.

Within seconds, she was in a freefall, and there wasn't a damn thing tethering her to the mountain.

"God. Fuck!" she yelled.

She was coming again.

How in the hell was she coming again? Her body wasn't wired this way.

Or so she'd thought.

Matt grunted, giving her a somewhat astonished look. "So fast."

She might have taken offense, but the truth was, he was looking at her with...wonder? Awe? He couldn't be that oblivious to the fact he was an amazing lover, could he?

"I..." It was on the tip of her tongue to apologize, which was stupid. Because she wasn't the tiniest bit sorry.

"So tight," he said through gritted teeth, and that was when she realized he was struggling to hold back, just as close as she was. Matt slowed his thrusts, but he didn't stop moving.

Electricity shimmered along her skin, her spine, lighting up every hot zone she had. At this rate, she could provide enough power to light up New York City.

When the last remnants of the orgasm stilled, Liza went for broke. She wrapped her legs around his waist, tilted her hips, and they groaned in unison as he slid in even deeper. Her fears about pain seemed ridiculous now. Matt filled her to the brink, but it didn't hurt.

God, nothing that felt this incredible could ever hurt.

She lifted her hips in time with his downward thrusts, their actions so rough, so animalistic, they both grunted, clawing, scratching.

"You're going to give me another one," he demanded.

If she'd had the breath, she might have fought him on that, but she was too close to deny the truth. Especially when Matt's fingers found her clit.

The clever man was too talented with her self-destruct button, and she came again, loudly. Liza had never screamed in bed. Not once in her whole damn life, but this orgasm was too big for silence.

Her body thrashed, the pleasure so intense it hurt. White lights flashed relentlessly behind her closed eyelids.

And Matt, damn him, never missed a beat, fucking her through this orgasm too, drawing it out so long, she feared she'd pass out. Once the tremors subsided, her legs—now jelly—fell to the mattress.

Matt still didn't stop.

Until he did.

He pulled out, too quickly, and she shouted, ready to complain, her masochistic pussy clenching in an attempt to keep him inside. But the sound was cut short when he grasped her hips, twisting her.

"Roll over. I want to spank your ass while I fuck you from behind. And you're going to come for me again. Another one just like those last two."

"I'll die," she said, even as she struggled to push her knees beneath her, to shove her hips upward.

"You'll do as I say," he said, punctuating that comment with a hard slap to her ass. She gasped at the burn. Matt wasn't holding anything back, wasn't working her up to his rough touches.

He fucked like he lived—taking what he wanted without apology.

Part of her wanted to hate that, but she couldn't. Not now when he spanked her ass again, then again, six hard slaps that set her on fire—inside and out.

While she was on her knees, her head was lowered to the mattress, held there by Matt's palm cupping the back of her neck. She was beginning to feel like his rag doll. He put her where he wanted her, and for reasons she couldn't explain to herself, she stayed there. Thrilled by his possession, his dominance, his control.

This time, when Matt pushed back inside her, there was no easing in. Just one hard shove, and—oh my God, HOW?—she was there. *Again.*

Her third orgasm took her unaware, and Matt cursed.

"You're killing me. So fucking good!" His fingers clenched,

gripping her hips so tightly, there was no way she wasn't going to have bruises tomorrow.

Liza cried out, this climax striking fast and fading quicker than the last. Not that it mattered. It still packed one hell of a punch.

Again, Matt continued taking her as if nothing had happened. She'd never been fucked through an orgasm before, never thought she'd want such a thing.

Finally, his motions slowed, though she couldn't understand why. He hadn't come yet.

He reached down, taking a huge handful of her hair in his grip, using it to pull her upper body away from the mattress. Her scalp stung from the tight pull, but it also ramped her arousal even higher.

Liza's sexual fantasies had always leaned toward rough sex, hard fucking, hair pulling, spanking. She'd dreamed of it all and even tried bits and pieces with past lovers, but Matt was the first to act without her asking, to tap into those darker desires without her having to draw him a road map.

He continued to pull her upward until her back was flush with his chest. He retained the grip of her hair with one hand, the other snaking around her to pinch her nipple.

She tried to back away from the pain. Her body was on sensory overload, and every single thing he did to her was amplified a thousand percent.

She loved it.

She hated it.

Matt growled, biting her neck. "Take what I give you."

Liza was too far gone to pretend offense. There was nothing she wouldn't give him, wouldn't offer up freely.

He'd proven himself worthy...capable.

The only man to ever do so.

He pinched her other nipple and this time, she moaned but held steady.

"Good girl," he whispered.

Why did those two words elicit two very opposite reactions in her?

For one, she liked being good, but the second he said it, she felt the need to be very, very naughty.

Reaching around, she gripped his ass with one of her hands, tightening her hold on his firm, muscular ass cheek, squeezing it in a way that had to hurt.

"Bad boy," she said, her voice huskier, sexier than she'd ever heard it.

Matt's eyes narrowed, and he frowned. She wondered if she'd gone too far poking Mr. Dom Bear.

Until he murmured, "You're going to be trouble," so low that she wouldn't have heard him at all if his lips weren't right by her ear.

She liked the idea of being trouble. She wouldn't say she'd been the perfect child like her sister-in-law, Gianna, but she'd been far from the wild child her best friend Keeley had been when she was younger.

It was her sarcastic nature that pushed her closer to the naughty line rather than her actions.

However, before she could consider all the ways she wanted to be bad—with Matt—he wiped those thoughts away, shoving her back down on the mattress. The push was so sudden, so quick, she just barely got her hands up to catch herself.

Then he was there...fucking her like it was his last night on earth. It was too brutal, too rough, too much after so many orgasms, but at least, mercifully, it was brief.

Matt came loudly, his body slamming into hers once, twice, three times more before he held steady, erupting.

They remained there for several minutes, locked together, neither moving. Liza's head spun as the consequences of what she'd just done began to crash down on her head.

When she was lost in the throes of pleasure, overwhelmed by a bliss so big it was all-encompassing, she could forget all the reasons why being here was a huge fucking mistake.

Matt didn't say anything as he slowly withdrew. Her body betraying her, her pussy gripping him, one last rebellion.

He didn't touch her, didn't ask if she was okay, didn't do anything other than rise from the bed and walk to the bathroom.

She closed her eyelids quickly when he turned the light on, the bright beam shining in her eyes after so long in the dark almost painful.

She listened to his progress. To him throwing the condom away, washing up.

She couldn't continue to lie here. Time to make her escape, regroup, figure out next steps. Throwing her legs over the edge of the mattress, she tried to summon enough energy to get dressed and leave.

Because she had to leave.

Matt's shadow lay across the floor at her feet. She could tell he was leaning on the doorframe between the bedroom and bathroom, but she wasn't ready to face him yet.

His shadow remained where it was, and she wondered if he was struggling to find the right way to end this as well.

Enough, Liza, she chastised herself.

She wasn't a coward, and she wasn't going to start acting like one now. Taking a steadying breath, she forced herself to look at him.

He was a gorgeous, naked silhouette, backlit from the bathroom lights above the mirror. She could just barely make out the features of his face, but she saw enough to see his scowl.

While she was in freak-out mode, Matt looked...angry.

"Lay down," he said in *that* tone. When he'd used it earlier, she'd found herself responding before she could think about her actions.

This time, she managed to hold her ground.

"I need to leave," she said, refusing to look away from him. "Now."

Matt crossed his arms, his frown deepening. "Lay down, Liza."

She hadn't thought there was anything he could say that would make her stay.

But that...

He'd called her by her first name. For the first time ever.

She sighed dramatically, unable to give in with good grace, though she *was* giving in. She dropped down onto the bed on her back, staring at the ceiling.

Matt turned off the bathroom light and padded to the opposite side of the bed, pulling the duvet down. The mattress dipped as he climbed in. She glanced over and saw he was lying on his back as well.

Liza would have expected this to feel awkward, but it didn't. Then she realized nothing about tonight had felt strange.

Which made this all so much harder.

She twisted to face him, drawing his attention as he turned his head to look at her.

"A mistake," she said softly, wondering if he would agree or try to argue the point.

He didn't respond to that. Instead, he simply reached out to cup her cheek affectionately as he said, "Go to sleep, Liza."

Liza wanted to push, but she'd used up her second wind and there was no third coming. Plus, he'd used *that* voice.

So...she closed her eyes and made one last mistake. A whopper.

She fell asleep next to Matt Russo.

Chapter Six

Matt stirred, fighting his way back to consciousness, roused by...movement, a sound. Given the darkness of the room, it was still night, and considering his current level of exhaustion, he'd guess he hadn't been asleep long. Probably not more than an hour or two.

Then he heard another rustle, like the one that had woken him up. He didn't bother to open his eyes. He already knew what —or he should say, who—was making the noise.

He didn't have to reach across the mattress to confirm he was alone in the bed.

Feigning sleep, he listened as Liza made her way around the bedroom. He could chart her progress even without the benefit of sight. He heard her slip her dress back on, the gentle rasp of the zipper, before her footsteps grew softer.

He tracked her progress to the living room, but he remained where he was, not bothering to give chase, even though that desire, that instinct was stronger than he was comfortable with. He didn't want her to leave, hated that she'd escaped the bed they should be sharing until morning.

He'd laid claim to her several times, making it clear that, for tonight, she was his. It was still the goddamn night.

Matt took in a long, slow breath, stilling the voices in his head that told him to stop her, to drag her back to the bed and take her again. His dick began to thicken at the thought. Fucker was destined for disappointment because Matt had no intention of following her.

He simply...couldn't.

After a few minutes more, he heard the hotel door open, then close again.

She was gone.

Opening his eyes, he rubbed them, blinking to clear his vision. They were scratchy from too little sleep, but getting more rest wasn't in the cards for him tonight.

Pushing himself upright, he sat on the edge of the mattress, much like Liza had done when he'd gone to the bathroom earlier.

Jesus, sex with her had been life-altering, amazing. It was as if her body had been made just for him. And her unexpected submissiveness...

Fucking hell.

He'd taken countless lovers to his bed, but none of them— not one—had made him feel so...well, the only word that came to mind was *complete*.

In her arms, he felt whole.

Like he wasn't missing the big chunks of himself he'd learned to function without.

When he'd returned to the bedroom after cleaning up, he had been unsurprised to see that she was ready to run. Her reaction was logical, given who they were to each other and what they'd done.

What hadn't been expected was his visceral reaction to seeing her there, about to leave.

He'd gotten so pissed off that she was trying to cut the night short, he'd demanded she lay back down. And he'd used the tone that—up until then—had gotten him everything he'd wanted from her.

When she failed to move, he took it one step further, calling her Liza.

It was the first time he'd spoken her name—just Liza—aloud to her, though it was what he called her when thinking about her.

Liza.

Liza.

He was tempted to add the word *his* in front of it, but it was time for him to put that foolishness aside.

He'd indulged in one night—a mistake she'd called it, and she was right, though Liza had no idea just how big a mistake it had been, how big the can of worms they'd just opened.

Matt sighed, trying to shake off the heavy thoughts beating inside his head. He'd expected the regret over his actions, been waiting for it.

But he'd underestimated how large, how brutal it would be.

He stood, pacing across the bedroom floor. He pulled on his boxer briefs but nothing else before padding to the living room.

Crossing the room to the bar, he poured himself a glass of Scotch, taking a long sip, the heat of the liquor burning down his throat, a lame attempt at warming him—inside or out.

It didn't work.

He walked to the window, looking down on the cityscape. The streets—decorated with twinkly lights for the holidays—were quiet in the wee hours of morning, as they were still a couple of hours away from sunrise. There was a light dusting of snow on the sidewalks, winter making its first—late—appearance. Typically, Philadelphia's first snow came long before now, but this year, it had held off until mid-December. Looked like they'd get that white Christmas everyone always longed for.

He swallowed hard, fighting to dislodge the lump in his throat that always appeared whenever he thought about the holidays, likening himself to a soldier with PTSD. Only his trauma had nothing to do with war and everything to do with fucking Christmas.

Shoving those unwanted thoughts deep down inside, he imagined Liza returning to her hotel room, stripping off that gorgeous red dress, toeing off the torturous heels. Was she standing in this same spot, too many floors below him, studying the same view?

The urge to get dressed and go after her was powerful.

Too powerful.

So he took another drink of Scotch. And another. Willing it away.

This was why he'd stayed away from her, always watching from afar, keeping his distance. She'd been a threat to him since the first moment he'd laid eyes on her at Enigma. And she was still a threat.

Because while Liza may have run tonight, she wouldn't go far.

She'd begin to play tonight over in her mind, recalling all the things he shouldn't have revealed, and she would come to believe that there could be something between them.

At some point, she'd convince herself that this wasn't a mistake, and she'd come back to him. She was a fighter, and she never said die. He admired that about her as much as he hated it because it was what made her so dangerous to him.

Liza thought he was holding her at bay because of their families' feud, because of long-ago slights and hurts.

But that wasn't the truth, wasn't the reason at all.

His need to stay away from her stemmed from something more, something that—should he ever try to explain to her—would do what he was trying to do now. It would push her away forever.

Those flashes of fondness, of trust that he'd seen tonight would turn dim and sputter out completely if she knew the truth.

Which was why he would never tell her.

Turning away from the window, a flicker caught his eye and he walked over to the coffee table. The diamond bracelet lay on the surface, shining in the moonlight.

Liza had taken it off, left it behind.

God, he was so tempted to race after her, to drag her back to his bed...*where she belonged.*

Picking it up, Matt closed his fist around it, looking at the hotel door, taking two steps toward it before forcing himself to stop.

Chasing her down now would be the action of a fool. And he wasn't a fool.

No. That wasn't quite true because he was most definitely a fool for *her*. God, every second of the evening, from the moment they stepped onto that elevator until they fell asleep next to each other, had felt like a dream.

For the first time in his life, Matt closed his eyes and allowed himself to imagine a different future for himself. One where he didn't live alone, eat alone, sleep alone.

One where he was able to offer love and receive it in return.

One that included Liza.

Matt stopped fighting it, letting the amazing visions play out in his mind.

Liza in a white dress, walking down an aisle as he waited for her.

Liza's stomach round with his baby.

Liza, with streaks of gray in her hair, as they sat side by side, watching their child graduate from high school, then college.

He even let himself picture the proverbial front porch swing, the two of them old and gray in the later years of their lives, slowly rocking back and forth as they reminisced about a life well lived.

Before tonight, he'd never wanted those things, certain they were meant for others—like his brother, Gage—who had revealed himself to be a romantic at heart after falling in love with his now-wife Penny.

Matt had never fallen in love. Not once in his entire life. So here he was at thirty-seven, confident—no, fucking *cocky*—in the belief that love wasn't an emotion he was capable of feeling. Until...

Liza.

Liza.

He stared at the hotel door, a war raging inside him.

Follow her or let her go?

He knew which was the smart, practical, safe answer.

"Fuck," he muttered to himself, as he returned to the bedroom, quietly dressing. Sleep *definitely* wasn't happening tonight.

Returning to the living room, he poured a larger glass of Scotch, slowly sipping it as he hardened his heart. He controlled the narrative, controlled the outcome.

Controlled it all.

He couldn't—wouldn't be swayed from his path.

Dropping down to the couch, he did something he never did. Took himself back in time, forced himself to remember exactly why he couldn't have Liza.

Now, as always, the dark memories swallowed him whole.

The constant drip-drip-drip of water.

Dark red blood congealed on the snowy-white tiles.

Before he knew it, two-thirds of the bottle of Scotch was gone, and the sun was well up in the sky.

It was just after eleven o'clock. He should get up, check out, put last night out of his mind, and move on with his life.

He didn't move.

His phone rang, crashing through the silence, and he glanced down at the caller ID, closing his eyes wearily when he saw her name. That didn't take long. He should have known she wouldn't be the type of woman to simply walk away.

Let it go to voicemail.

Let it go to voicemail.

His eyes drifted to the diamond bracelet, and in the end, a sleepless night and liquor made his next poor decision for him.

Picking up his phone, he said, "Hello."

When she spoke, her voice was strong, confident. "I don't like the way last night ended. I shouldn't have left like that. We need to talk. Will you have dinner with me tonight?"

He paused, considering her request, for a long time. Too long. Matt sensed she was ready to begin pleading her case, so he cut her off with just one word.

"Yes."

Tempted and Taken

Tempted and Taken

Some mistakes are worth repeating.

Liza knows that cocky billionaire Matt Russo is the wrong man for her. She could make a long list of reasons why she'd be smart to stay away, including his tenacious ex-girlfriend, the fact he's trying to destroy her family, and, oh yeah, did she mention he's a cold, distant bastard? However, after their tempestuous one-night stand, she's finding it hard to hang on to their well-established nemesis routine.

Matt is the master of control—of his life, his emotions, his future. Except, of course, for that night he slipped up...with Liza Moretti. Reassuming his grip on the reins, he's determined it won't happen again. Unfortunately, doing the right thing in regards to the tempting woman fails because doing the wrong things with her—to her—are too alluring to resist.

An impromptu invitation to share his private plane leads to an unexpected break from reality and some very steamy nights in Hawaii. Until real life comes knocking and Matt is forced to face the mistakes of his past. Mistakes that could destroy the one thing he can't control, and the one thing he can no longer live without —Liza.

Chapter One

Matt Russo rubbed his forehead wearily, then swung a right at the next light, kicking his own ass for agreeing to this dinner. He was too hungover—an uncommon state for him—to deal with this shit tonight. He never drank to excess, but he had last evening. Or more accurately, this morning.

The bottle of Scotch he'd consumed in the wee hours before dawn had been the final fuck-up in a long list of mistakes he'd made last night.

Matt sighed, concerned the three ibuprofen he'd just taken weren't going to kick in before he got to the restaurant. This dinner date was going to be tricky enough with all his faculties functioning. Doing it with this nonstop, throbbing pain behind his eyes...shit.

He applied the brakes at a red light, his mind drifting back to why he was in this predicament to begin with.

Last night had started just like any other night. He'd donned his tuxedo, picked up his current plus-one-with-benefits, Patricia Eddington, and headed to the Ritz-Carlton for the Snowflake Gala, a fundraiser held by the Philadelphia Initiative to raise money for the Promise House. The charity was a good one, one he was more than happy to support, seeing as the money went toward helping teenagers in the city who were facing homelessness or who had been victims of sex trafficking.

The problem wasn't the fundraiser; it was the organizer.

Liza Moretti.

Simply the name Moretti should have been enough to ensure Matt kept his damn distance from her, but Liza had captured his attention a year and a half ago, and since then, she'd been the cause of too many sleepless nights.

As chairman of the board overseeing the Philadelphia Initiative, Matt crossed paths with Liza more than was comfortable—for either of them—as they tended to butt heads regarding the Initiative's goals. Of course, their professional disagreements notwithstanding, they were also dealing with the fact their families had participated in a four-generations-long feud fueled by marital infidelity, broken hearts, destroyed businesses, and outright petty revenge.

Matt wasn't stupid enough to pretend the Russos hadn't been the perpetrators of most of the bullshit, and that he hadn't contributed more than his fair share to the continued ill will.

The moment he'd walked into the gala last night and seen Liza in that deep red ball gown, he'd known he was in trouble. He hadn't been able to keep his eyes off her, and in a moment of weakness, he'd asked her to dance. That dance had been his first mistake because holding her in his arms, recalling the softness of that tiny bit of skin exposed by the keyhole slot in the back of her gown, had sent his thoughts down paths best left untrodden.

Unfortunately, his date hadn't appreciated him paying so much attention to another woman. Asking Patricia out had originally seemed like a smart move because they traveled in the same circles, both had more money than God, and neither of them was looking for a relationship. In hindsight, he could see he'd been short-sighted, given the fact he had quite a few business ties with her father—her doting, spoiled-Patricia-rotten father.

Matt hoped Richard wouldn't be petty after the way things

had ended between him and his daughter, but he couldn't bet the bank on that, either. Patricia had given off "woman scorned" vibes when she'd stormed out the hotel last night.

Matt pushed the gas when the light turned green, recalling his argument with Patricia. After the gala, he had broken things off between them in the lobby of the Ritz, proclaiming their relationship—the word he'd really wanted to use was "association"—had run its course. Patricia, whose jealousy had reared its ugly head throughout the evening, took his rejection badly.

Very badly.

"How dare you end things this way!" Patricia yelled.

"Keep your voice down, Patricia. I have no interest in drawing a crowd."

"I will not keep my voice down. I don't think it's unreasonable for me to expect my date to treat me with courtesy. To pay attention to me. I didn't enjoy watching you staring at her all night."

"She has nothing to do with this," Matt replied.

"Bullshit," Patricia scoffed.

Absentmindedly, Matt raised his hand to his cheek, the one Patricia had slapped before stomping off. The argument had been unfortunate, but he hadn't viewed it as something he couldn't recover from. He suspected everything might have been okay...if his night had ended there.

But there had been a witness to his and Patricia's confrontation.

Liza Moretti.

She'd seen—and heard—everything.

"She slapped you?" Liza asked.

"Yes." Matt didn't bother to touch his cheek. "I will admit she's not the first woman to slap me."

"I suspect she won't be the last, either. You broke things off?"

Matt nodded.

"Because you were staring at...someone?"

"You know I was," he said, holding her gaze. "Because you were staring back."

After that, they had walked to the hotel elevator together. They'd both gotten rooms at the Ritz, anticipating very different endings to their nights. Matt had planned to spend the night with Patricia in his bed, Liza with her date for the gala, Davis Taylor.

Liza had given her date the heave-ho before the party had even ended, and it had bothered Matt to see her looking so...depressed didn't seem like the right word. No. Liza had looked resigned. Like she was so used to getting the short end of the stick in her relationships, she didn't even feel disappointment or sadness anymore.

He had to give it to her. Liza rallied quickly, bantering with him as they walked to the elevator.

"You got a room here for tonight?" she asked.

"I did."

"Hoping for a romantic interlude?"

Matt shook his head. "Hoping for sex."

"Oh."

"You have a room?" he asked.

She nodded.

"Romantic interlude?" he threw back at her.

"Nope. I was hoping to get fucked. So, I'm resorting to plan B."

"What's plan B?" he asked as the elevator doors slid open.

"A long soak in a hot bath. And self-care."

• • •

Matt wasn't sure what had driven him to kiss her the second the elevator doors closed. All he knew was one second, she was reaching out to push the button for her floor, the next, he had her back against the elevator wall as he drove his thigh between her shapely legs, working them both into a frenzy.

That had been his second mistake.

And because he was on a roll, he'd made the third—and deadliest—mistake just moments later when he asked her to join him for a drink in his room. She'd accepted the invitation, the two of them making small talk on the couch in his penthouse suite. Liza had spotted the gift he'd bought for Patricia, and he had insisted she open it. Her curiosity won out as she unwrapped the diamond tennis bracelet. He'd put it on her, despite her demands that he not. He'd loved the way the gems sparkled against her skin, even as he pictured her in something much different.

"This isn't what I would have bought if I'd been shopping for you."

"No diamonds for me?" Liza asked.

"No. Diamonds pale next to your skin."

"Nice line."

"It's not a line," he insisted. "If I'd been shopping for you, I would have bought you rubies. I can imagine how the rich, vibrant red hue would shimmer against your skin. I'd cover you in rubies. They'd dangle from your ears. From your throat. From your wrists. And I wouldn't stop with the traditional pieces."

"What do you mean?"

"My rubies would dangle from your nipples," he whispered.

"Where else?" she asked, her voice husky with need.

"From the clamp I'd put on your clit. But the largest ruby would peek out from the plug I'd put in your ass."

After that, any reticence that lingered between them vanished and they'd moved to the bedroom, all restraint gone.

Matt had slept with countless women in his life—beautiful, sophisticated, experienced women—yet none of them, not a single one, had made him feel the way Liza had. Sex with her had been life-altering, amazing. He'd always suspected the chemistry between them would be explosive, which was why he'd kept his distance from her for as long as he had.

Now having it confirmed was going to be hell on his self-control because he hadn't expected to discover *exactly* how compatible they were.

Liza Moretti wasn't just beautiful, intelligent, his kryptonite.

She was submissive.

When she'd snuck out of his hotel room before dawn, it had taken everything he had not to go after her, to capture and drag her back to his bed where she belonged.

Matt closed his eyes, wincing at the pain in his head.

Not where she belonged.

He'd resisted the temptation to follow her, opting instead for the Scotch. He wanted to call the alcohol mistake number four, but there was an annoying voice inside his head insisting that the fourth mistake was not chasing her down and going for round two.

Matt pulled up to the restaurant, sighing heavily, girding his loins. He was perfectly aware that if he hadn't been three sheets to the wind this morning, he wouldn't have answered the phone, and he sure as hell wouldn't have agreed to this dinner date.

Not that he didn't need to talk to her. Because he did. But he would have liked to have had this conversation without the hangover and after a good night's sleep. Right now, he was running on fumes, which put him at a definite disadvantage.

He patted his inside suit pocket, feeling the gift box tucked there, the diamond bracelet Liza had left behind when she'd snuck out of his hotel room.

The valet walked to the driver's side as he opened the door, and he handed the young man his car keys, even though every fiber of his being wanted to snatch them back, jump in his car, and get the hell away from here.

Instead, he took a steadying breath and walked toward the entrance of Vetri Cucina. The hostess smiled when he gave his name, pointing toward the intimate table for two by the front window. If he hadn't been so distracted, he might have seen her sitting there when he'd entered.

Walking toward her, he worked overtime to turn his grimace into a smile.

"There you are, darling," Patricia cooed as he bent down to give her a quick kiss on the cheek. She tried to turn her head at the last minute, hoping to take the platonic out of his kiss, but he moved too quickly, avoiding her lips.

He claimed his chair, aware she'd reserved them a table that ensured everyone who walked by outside would see the two of them dining together. Patricia Eddington loved nothing more than being in the limelight, the center of attention, while Matt preferred to lurk in the shadows.

"I'm so glad you agreed to join me tonight. I wanted—" She paused mid-sentence, frowning when the sommelier arrived to pour him a glass of wine. She didn't like that whatever speech she'd prepared had been interrupted.

"Sir?" The man held the bottle so that he could read the label.

Patricia reached over, grasping Matt's hand, giving it a squeeze. "I hope you don't mind. I took the liberty of ordering a bottle for us."

"Not at all," Matt said, though wine—hair of the dog or not —was the last thing he wanted. Nothing short of water...a gallon of it...was going to help his head.

The sommelier poured him the obligatory taste, which gave him an excuse to pull his hand out of Patricia's, using it to lift the glass. He took a sip, then nodded that the wine was fine. He planned to nurse a single glass, so he didn't give a shit what they drank. Pleased, the man filled their glasses, then left.

Patricia took a sip of the wine. "Oh, that's delicious."

And knowing her, extremely expensive.

Looking across the table, he was somewhat surprised to realize this was their first time dining together alone in a restaurant, as he'd only dated her in that plus-one-with-benefits capacity, inviting her to galas and fundraisers and charity events—all of which came complete with meals at tables for eight to ten people. That had saved him from having to converse with her too much, so now—on top of the hangover—he was stuck having to make small talk with the obnoxious woman. Previously, there had been no expectations between them for dates such as this, no morning-after calls, and no contact between swanky events.

It had been perfect.

Until last night.

It belatedly occurred to him that Patricia was viewing this as a date. Yet another reason why he'd been stupid to accept the invitation. He should have suggested they meet for lunch in the middle of a workday somewhere a hell of a lot less romantic.

"I've heard wonderful things about this restaurant," Patricia continued.

"I'm sure it's very nice." Matt glanced around the small dining room. There were no more than a dozen patrons, all couples, all looking as in love as his brother, Gage, who spent ninety-nine percent of his time these days walking around with damn hearts in his eyes.

Gage, much to Matt's surprise, had fallen head over heels in love with Penny Beaumont, the quirky woman who had worked in the IT department of Russo Enterprises for seven years. Married not quite a year, it appeared the honeymoon was nowhere near over for Gage and Penny.

It was Gage's marital state that had opened his eyes to Patricia's changing view of their—fuck it—association. What they'd shared had not been a relationship, and he didn't give a shit if Patricia took offense to that word. Last night, she'd wondered aloud if all Russo men made good husbands before suggesting the two of them get married. He'd dismissed the idea out of hand, but she'd doubled down, and that was when he had known it was time to cut his losses.

Patricia put her wineglass down, then leaned closer in a blatant attempt to draw his attention to the cleavage revealed by her low-cut dress. She had seduction in mind.

The small table ensured they were too close for Matt's comfort, especially when she reached out and cupped his cheek in a way that, from any other woman, might feel like affection, but from her felt more like a calculated move.

He reached up and grasped her hand, pulling it away from his face. "Patricia," he started, ready to set her straight.

"I was unhappy with the way things ended last night." She'd said as much on the phone this morning when she called to invite him out to dinner.

If he'd been clear-headed, he would have pushed her off, suggested the lunch date, but Scotch, a lack of sleep, and fucked-up feelings about Liza had worked against him, and his brain had failed to engage.

"I handled things poorly," he said.

Patricia lit up, her smile wide, and Matt realized he'd given her the wrong impression. Score one for the hangover.

She laid her hand on his forearm. "I'm afraid neither of us was at our best. Such a silly misunderstanding."

He hadn't misunderstood a damn thing.

Patricia had proposed the marriage idea not because she'd caught feelings but because she coveted power and fame, and she viewed merging her family's billions with his as a way to catapult herself into the same category as the Bezoses, Mark Zuckerberg and Priscilla Chan, the Gateses—pre-divorce—the Beckhams, and God only knew who else.

As she'd said last night, she wanted more.

And he had more.

"It *was* an unfortunate misunderstanding," he said, though he meant it differently than she did. Time for damage control. "I hope the two of us can remain friends."

He had to hand it to Patricia. Her poker face was rock solid, her smile firmly in place.

"Of course." She lifted her glass to take a sip of wine. "But I don't see any reason why we shouldn't continue our previous arrangement."

Matt wasn't about to consider that offer, though he was curious about Patricia's motivation. She was, by society's standards, a very beautiful woman and heiress to a fortune. Men would line up around the block to marry her, as evidenced by the fact she'd already been engaged four times to men she claimed to feel a romantic attachment to. Matt suspected the reasons Patricia hadn't made it down the aisle yet had everything to do with the fact those previous fiancés hadn't had that "more" factor and the only person she would ever truly love was herself.

He shook his head. "No, and I'm sorry if by coming here tonight I gave you the impression I was interested in pursuing that. I'm here because I wanted to make sure there are no hard feelings between us. We're bound to run into each other from time to time and, as I said, I hope we can do so as friends."

Friends was a stretch, as that was something they'd never been and never would be. Too many nights out with Patricia had opened his eyes to who she really was. Her stuck-up nature was only surpassed by her narcissism, and neither was attractive.

The waiter returned with their first course. Clearly, Patricia had taken the liberty of ordering more than just the wine. He mentally cursed, annoyed by the prospect of having to sit through a five-course meal with her.

He took a drink of water, relieved to realize the ibuprofen was kicking in, the throbbing in his head reduced to a dull ache.

He braced himself, expecting her to pick up the argument where they'd left it last night—Patricia wasn't the type to go down without a fight—so he was pleasantly surprised, and somewhat suspicious, when she dropped the subject.

"I understand," she said genially. "And to show there are no hard feelings..." She reached into her purse and pulled out a small square box. Holding it on the palm of her hand, she presented it to him in what felt like a "voila" manner, which was strange. "Your Christmas present. I intended to give it to you last night."

Last night, it sounded as if her "gift" was sex with her, so he couldn't help but wonder if this was purchased today. Matt reached for the box, grateful he'd had the foresight to grab the bracelet at the last minute. He'd intended to use it to "buy" her forgiveness if she persisted in making things difficult.

He'd only just touched the box when Patricia flipped open the lid, her smile odd. In some ways, it looked as if she was the one receiving the gift rather than him.

He thanked her for the diamond-studded cuff links, then he reached into his suit pocket, retrieving her gift. "For you."

She oohed and ahhed over the bracelet, asking him to put it on her. It had looked much better on Liza.

After that, the conversation turned to superficial things, as Patricia talked about her plans for the holidays. Apparently, the Eddingtons celebrated Christmas and the New Year in Aspen, skiing 'til they dropped, according to her. He was content to let her do the lion's share of the talking, nodding and responding appropriately as she gossiped about people in their social circles, bemoaned the lack of good restaurants in the city, and discussed her plans to start her own fashion show on YouTube.

It wasn't the most stimulating dinner he'd ever had, but considering he had expected Patricia to be difficult about him breaking things off, he couldn't complain. His coming here had achieved what he had hoped, put him back on steady ground with the Eddingtons. Last night's mistake-apalooza hadn't been completely detrimental.

Even if his emotional state was on shaky foundation, professionally, he was fine.

Once the bill was paid, they walked out together, her driver waiting at the curb.

She turned to him as he opened the back door to the limo. "I will miss our nights together." She lifted her face to his. He bent slightly, giving her a quick kiss on the lips, but Patricia was better prepared for him this time, her hand capturing the knot of his tie. Using a strong grip, she managed to lengthen the kiss a few seconds longer than he wanted. He was about to break the connection when she let him go.

"Goodbye, Patricia."

"Goodbye, Matt."

He walked back to his car, accepting the keys from the valet. As he slid behind the wheel, he frowned.

The dinner had gone better than he dared to hope for, yet some niggling, suspicious voice in the back of his brain told him it had been *too* easy.

And now there was only one thing he knew for certain. He hadn't heard the last of Patricia Eddington.

Chapter Two

Liza and her cousin Luca dropped down on the couch dramatically and at the exact same time.

"Why?" Luca moaned. "Why do I always eat too much?"

Liza wanted to answer, but she was too full to speak. The food coma was setting in hard. She leaned back and debated unbuttoning the top button of her jeans. She'd watched her dad, Nonno, and two uncles do it while still at the dinner table.

"I should have worn sweatpants," she finally managed to force out.

It looked like Luca would have laughed if he weren't in such pain. Instead, he grimaced and nodded. "Next year, let's suggest a pajamas-only dress code."

That wasn't a bad idea, Liza thought, making a mental note to do just that. Her extended family was close enough and crazy enough that they'd probably make a contest out of the best pj's. Plus, it was Christmas Eve, and they did tend to party until the wee hours, so the relaxed dress code would just make things easier when they all returned home three sheets to the wind.

Or at least, they used to party until dawn. Now the next generation of kids had come along, and her brother Bruno and his wife, Viv, had to leave early so their children were asleep before Santa came. The same held true for her brother Elio, and cousins David, Holly, and Tony, who also had milk and cookies to leave out for Santa Claus and kids to put to bed.

While she adored her nieces and nephews, sometimes she missed the times when they'd been a family of adults and the wine had flowed until daybreak as they sang, laughed, told stories, and ate themselves into oblivion.

She'd been blessed with a huge, close-knit family, most of whom still lived in Philadelphia, so the holidays were always a big-ass affair. Liza looked around the room and counted no less than twenty-five people crammed into Nonna and Nonno's living room with her, all of whom appeared to be talking at the same time—at full volume, with those truly Italian hands gesturing wildly.

Of course, there weren't just twenty-five people in the house. That was just the people in the living room. There were at least that many more in various other rooms, including both kitchens and the dining room.

Keeley stepped over to her and Luca, perching on the arm of the couch and holding up her phone. "Penny just texted. She and Gage finished dinner and they're on their way now."

"Cool," Liza said, sharing a glance with Luca, who smirked. Liza had been shocked when Nonna had invited Penny and her husband, Gage, to join them for Christmas Eve dessert.

Penny, at Liza's request, had stopped by a couple of weeks earlier to help her grandparents set up their new computer. Nonna had finally downloaded enough sketchy spam to cook the old one entirely. Penny, the family's go-to IT guru, had suggested what computer they should buy, then offered to set it up and teach her grandparents how to use it. She'd also done a tutorial on what emails and links not to open, though Liza was certain Nonna hadn't understood half of what Penny had said.

When Nonna had issued the dessert invitation, Liza and

Penny laughed it off, certain her grandmother hadn't thought it through, forgetting that Penny Beaumont was now Penny Russo.

While the younger generation of Morettis had—for the most part—gotten over the long-standing feud between their family and Gage's, the older generation—Liza's nonno, dad, and uncles —most certainly had not.

Penny had politely demurred, not mentioning why, but Nonna hadn't taken no for an answer, insisting it was time they put the past behind them, and that Penny brought her husband to meet the family.

Nonno, who had been standing there, hadn't rejected the idea, but he hadn't exactly embraced it either, remaining uncharacteristically quiet, which made Liza suspect her grandparents had discussed the invitation prior to Penny's arrival.

Penny had given a very noncommittal "we'll see" because neither she nor Liza expected Gage to voluntarily step into the lion's den. They should have known better because Gage, the charming idiot, had been thrilled by the invitation, asking Penny to call Nonna immediately to accept.

When Liza had told her brothers and cousins about the possibility of a Russo coming to Christmas Eve dinner, they'd started a betting pool on how long it would take before one of the older men broke their promise to Nonna to be on their best behavior, then they debated who it would be.

Of course, none of the older men had taken that vow to mind their manners until Nonna had started threatening to cut certain favorite dishes from the Christmas dinner menu. Then, suddenly, they were all singing a different tune, begrudgingly promising to be civil.

Luca leaned toward Liza. "I've got Uncle Cesare losing his shit after twenty minutes."

Liza laughed, sure Luca was going to lose that bet. Cesare, Liza's dad, had gotten an earful from her mom before they'd arrived tonight, Mom swearing up and down that she would make his life a living hell if he embarrassed her by being rude to "the Russo boy."

Gage would probably love that he was being referred to as a boy, even though he was in his mid-thirties.

"That's hilarious," Liza said. "Because I picked *your* dad. Uncle Frank will be the first to crack, but he'll make it a whole forty minutes."

"What are we talking about?" her cousin Joey asked, perching on the edge of the coffee table in front of them.

"Gage is on his way," Luca replied. "We're comparing our bets."

Joey's eyes lit up, the damn pool his idea in the first place. "I've got Nonno blowing a gasket within the first ten minutes."

They all laughed, Keeley shaking her head. "You guys are terrible. You should be ashamed of yourselves. This is a historic occasion, and I think it's wonderful of your nonna to try to build a bridge between the families."

Joey snorted. "You know, your little speech might make me feel guilty if I didn't know you've also put money down on Nonno."

"Yes, but I have more faith in the dear man than you. He'll make it an hour, for sure," Keeley replied, giggling.

"I think you're all going to be disappointed," Rhys, Penny's brother, said, as he and Tony joined the conversation. "My money is on Gage winning them all over."

Tony chuckled. "I'm with Rhys. This is Gage we're talking about. Now, if it was Matt Russo, it would be a different story."

Joey stood up, punching his older brother on the shoulder playfully. "Nobody would have bothered with a betting pool if that had been the case. Everyone would have picked you, kicking Matt out within the first sixty seconds."

"See, that's where you're wrong." Luca gestured toward Liza. "My money would have been on her, and Matt wouldn't have even cleared the front door."

Everyone, with the exception of Liza, laughed at Luca's joke, though she understood why they would believe that to be true. She'd made no bones about her disdain for Matt.

Unfortunately, the mere mention of Matt's name had her insides fluttering.

If the same conversation had happened a month earlier, Liza would have been leading the charge, but then...a week ago, the Snowflake Gala had happened.

Well, not the gala, per se, but what came after.

She'd slept with Matt Russo. She'd been saying those words to herself constantly since that night, trying to make them sink in. Even now, every second of that night still felt like...God, like a fever dream, though it sure as shit hadn't been unpleasant.

Anything but.

Because it had been the best sex of her life.

Liza had replayed it over and over until she'd gone nearly mad. She didn't even bother putting her vibrator away anymore. Every night, she crawled between the sheets, reran the memory of Matt Russo going down to his knees before her, giving her that orgasm that rattled every bone in her body, and within seconds, she was going off like a bottle rocket. Then she'd replay the second and third and—God help her—fourth orgasms, and before she knew it, she would be there again and again, her heart racing, her sheets soaked in sweat.

He'd awakened something inside her that she couldn't silence.

No. The truth was she didn't want to silence it, which was dangerous and terrifying and even a little bit exhilarating.

Matt had been a demanding lover, more so than any man in the past, and she'd responded to it in ways she didn't fully understand or expect.

Liza didn't have a submissive bone in her body. She forged her own path, knew her own mind, and did as she pleased. She didn't let others dictate to her. Ever.

Yet, that night with Matt, she'd found herself wanting to— Jesus—obey him. Even the mere thought of that word left a bad taste in her mouth, but there was no denying that when it came to sex with him, she'd felt herself softening, responding to his demands, even longing for them. She'd wanted to put herself completely in his hands, and for some insane reason, she genuinely trusted him to take care of her.

After Matt insisted she spend the *entire* night with him, she'd lain next to him, only managing an hour or two of restless sleep before she woke up and freaked out. She'd gotten out of his bed in the middle of the night, anxious to escape his overwhelming presence in hopes of coming to her senses.

That hadn't happened yet, and she was beginning to lose hope it would.

The worst part was they had to work together, so it wasn't like she could lay low until she *did* get her shit together. Something told her she could avoid Matt Russo for ten years and still not get him out of her system.

"You okay?" Keeley said softly, nudging Liza's thigh with her foot. "You've been quiet tonight."

Liza nodded, the response a lie. She hadn't told a single soul about her faux pas following the gala. Not because she was embarrassed by it. Hell, she couldn't truly convince herself it was a mistake. For the last couple of days, she'd actually begun to wonder if she should call him. They were both single adults and they'd shared a strong sexual chemistry. What would be the harm in expanding on that? Exploring it?

No, it wasn't shame or even that silly feud keeping her quiet with her friends and family. It was simply that she couldn't find the words to accurately describe that night and what it had meant to her.

Best night ever just didn't feel strong enough.

Keeley didn't look convinced, but fortunately, before she could press for more, the doorbell rang.

Luca rubbed his hands together gleefully. "Nothing I like more than dinner and a show."

Liza rolled her eyes, grinning, then she rose and walked over to answer the front door. Nonna and Nonno got there first.

Nonna pulled Penny and Gage into the living room, out of the cold, giving Penny a big hug.

"Merry Christmas, Nonna," Penny said cheerfully. While Nonna had countless grandkids, that didn't stop her from acquiring "adopted ones," including Kayden and Keeley, whose parents were killed in a plane crash, as well as Rhys and his sister, Penny, Aldo's girlfriend, Hazel, and one of Liza's best friends—who was now her sister-in-law—Gianna.

Nonna was the greatest hugger on the planet, her squeezes tight and warm and wonderful. When she released her, Penny smiled, then introduced her to Gage.

"This is my husband, Gage."

Gage held out his hand. "Mrs. Moretti, it's a pleasure to meet you. It was very nice of you to invite us for dessert. Penny has told me so many great things about you."

Nonna frowned as she looked at his outstretched hand and, for a moment, Liza and Luca shared a surprised glance, especially when she put her hands on her hips. Because nobody had put money on Nonna.

"If she told you about me, then you'd know to call me Nonna, like everyone does. And we don't shake hands in this family, young man. We hug."

The Russos, unlike the Morettis, were low on family. Like, way low. She and Gage had discussed it once, and Gage admitted the only family still living that he knew of were his two brothers, Matt and Conor. Apparently, they'd never met their mother's family at all, and their paternal grandparents had both passed away.

So Liza didn't miss the outright shock on Gage's face as Nonna pulled him into her arms. Nor did she miss the way it quickly morphed to absolute delight. Gage was a jovial guy, rarely without a smile, but she'd never seen him so moved.

When the embrace ended, he said, "Thank you, Nonna," in a thick voice that had Liza blinking a few times to beat back tears.

Nonno must have noticed it too because something softened

in his stiff posture. He gave Gage a genuine smile. "I'm Nonno Moretti."

Those introductions set the tone for the rest of the family, and it became apparent immediately that no one was going to win the betting kitty. Not that anyone cared because it was Christmas Eve, and the party was just getting started.

Her father and Nonno brought out their accordions, the wine glasses were either refilled or—for some—exchanged for coffee cups. Dessert was served and even though Liza was so full she thought she would pop, she managed to put down enough tiramisu to choke a cat. Her annual diet always started the day after New Year's Day, as she was forced to drop the five pounds she gained in this single night.

Liza walked over to join Penny and Gage on the couch, laughing at Gage, who looked shell-shocked as he took in everything—the table overflowing with food, the noise level driven by the music and the nonstop talking, as well as the laughter, hand gestures, and hugs.

"You hanging in there, Gage?" Liza asked.

He nodded, grinning from ear to ear. "Penny tried to warn me, but until you experience it for yourself..." He paused, shaking his head. "Your family is awesome." He'd spoken loud enough for Liza to hear over the din, which meant Uncle Frank and Uncle Tommy, who were standing nearby, had also heard, both giving Gage approving nods.

"How was dinner?" Liza was aware that the couple had arrived here following their annual Christmas Eve dinner with Gage's brothers. Liza told herself she was asking because she was interested in her friends' holiday, but the truth was, she was fishing for any tidbit she could get about Matt.

Not that she was worried Matt would kiss and tell about their evening together. She suspected he'd been as blindsided by it as she had.

"It was good," Gage said. "Though I was glad for the invitation to have dessert here. I swear to God, Matt's goal every year is to find a restaurant that charges more money for less food. I was hungrier when we left than I was when we got there."

Penny rolled her eyes, but Liza noticed she didn't disagree. "At least he didn't bring Patricia."

Liza frowned. "Was he going to? I mean...I thought they broke up."

She didn't think. She knew. She'd witnessed Patricia slapping Matt after the gala before storming off. It was that confrontation that had led to Matt and Liza sharing the elevator to their hotel rooms. Not that she'd slept in hers. After sneaking out of Matt's room an hour or so before dawn, she'd gone to retrieve her overnight bag, then left the hotel completely, partly because she was desperate for the comfort of her own bed in her apartment and partly because she was worried he would follow her, and she wouldn't be able to resist falling right back into his arms and his bed.

"Broke up?" Penny asked, perking up. "What makes you think that?"

Liza wasn't sure how Matt would feel about her telling tales, so she kept it vague. "They appeared to have a fight just after the Snowflake Gala last Saturday."

Penny groaned as she pulled out her cell phone. "Damn. I was hoping you knew something we didn't." She clicked a few buttons, then turned it around so that Liza could see the screen. "Unfortunately, these were taken last Sunday, the day after the gala, so it looks like they patched things up."

Liza took Penny's phone, recognizing the website as a tabloid-style one that spread gossip about the East Coast elite. She never looked at it because she couldn't give two shits about the Patricias of the world.

"Toby has an annoying habit of reading this crap out loud at work. He's addicted to *Real Housewives*, *Married at First Sight*, and anything with the Kardashians. The guy's got issues and way too much time on his hands," Penny explained. "He really needs to find a girlfriend."

Liza wanted to laugh because she'd spent quite a bit of time with Penny's IT colleagues, Toby and Rich—the nerd circle, as the three of them called themselves. There was no denying Toby would have been right at home on the set of *The Big Bang Theory*.

However, she was too hung up on what she was seeing. The photos were of Patricia and Matt, sitting in the window of a ritzy restaurant. In the first picture, it appeared that Matt was giving Patricia a ring-shaped box, her hand outstretched as she smiled. In the second, they were talking and drinking wine, a harmless enough pose...until Liza spotted the diamond tennis bracelet dangling from Patricia's wrist.

Liza felt her face flush as she recalled Matt encouraging her to open Patricia's gift, putting the bracelet on her, then declaring if he'd been shopping for her, he wouldn't have given her diamonds. Instead, he'd told her he would give her rubies, listing all the scandalous places he would put the jewels. It was that racy list that had been her downfall, that had propelled them from the couch to the bedroom, her resistance in tatters.

She'd worn the bracelet right up until she'd made her middle-of-the-night escape. Dressing quietly, she had slipped back to the living room, sitting down to put her shoes back on, catching sight of the bracelet as it glittered in the moonlight. She'd taken it off and left it behind. Apparently, Matt had decided to go ahead and give it to its intended recipient.

The final photo was taken outside the restaurant, beside a limo, the couple locked together in a kiss.

While the pictures were damning enough, it was the headline that had Liza's stomach clenching, her foolish heart pounding painfully.

It said, "Is That Wedding Bells We Hear?" There was an article attached, but Liza didn't read it, handing the phone back to Penny. She told herself she wouldn't look up the story when she got home tonight to read it word for word, but that lie wouldn't stick.

"So what did Matt say about it?" Liza forced herself to ask.

Penny scowled, shooting Gage an annoyed look. "I'm not exactly comfortable enough with Matt yet to bring it up, and Gage won't ask. Just swears Matt isn't marrying her."

"How can you be so sure?" Liza asked him.

"Because my brother is never getting married. Period. End of sentence. He's married to his work."

Gage spoke with such assurance that Liza almost felt better. Almost.

Then she thought about the pictures again and hated herself for feeling disappointed and angry, both misplaced emotions.

She and Matt hadn't made any promises to each other. Christ, the last thing they said before falling asleep was that it had been a mistake, so she was an idiot for feeling hurt and pissed off.

It was just...she hadn't been able to think about anything but him for seven days and nights, the man consuming her thoughts and her dreams.

To discover that she'd been entirely forgettable, that she'd been just another woman taking a spin in the revolving door that led to Matt's bedroom, cut like a knife and made her feel like a fool.

Even as she struggled to quash those feelings, she *still* couldn't bring herself to regret that night.

"I hope you're right about Matt's determination to stay single," Penny said to Gage. "Because Patricia gives off serious 'we wear pink on Wednesday' vibes. I had to deal with too many of her type in school when I was growing up."

Gage's eyes softened and he kissed his wife on the forehead. "Assholes like that are always the worst to people who are the biggest threat. You're gorgeous, brilliant, funny, and perfect, so obviously, women like Patricia Eddington are intimidated."

"Oh, well, of course," Penny said sardonically. "I'm sure that was their problem with me back in school." She laughed, dismissing his words even though she was clearly delighted by Gage's compliment. "Thank you for saying that."

"Saying the truth? No problem." Gage wrapped his arm

around his wife's shoulders. "You're worrying about nothing," he reassured her. "Matt's never getting married, Penny. Not to Patricia or any other pink-wearing mean girl. I promise."

The more Gage reiterated his point with such undeniable confidence, the more Liza wondered how he could be so damn sure.

It was true that Matt had never given any indication he was interested in giving up his bachelor status—no long-term relationships, no broken engagements—so Liza wasn't sure why she would question Gage's conviction.

Then she considered that maybe she wasn't questioning the words so much as she was bothered by them.

Why didn't Matt want to get married? What the hell had happened to make him so opposed to the institution?

She didn't know much about Matt and Gage's parents' relationship. Actually, she didn't know a damn thing about it, other than they had both died when their sons were young, in their early twenties. Conor, the youngest brother, might have still been in his teens.

The easy thing would be to blame Matt's aversion to marriage on his mom and dad, assuming they had a fucked-up relationship.

But then she looked at Gage and Penny and saw the way he'd embraced his marriage to her. If that had been the case, obviously Gage hadn't taken away the same lesson.

So perhaps he didn't want to get married for some other reason.

And that was when Liza recalled something at the gala.

She'd caught a glimpse of emotion in Matt's eyes, something resigned, something lonely. Originally, she had seen it and thought she'd met her kindred spirit because she was no stranger to those emotions.

But when she thought about it now, the only word she could come up with was...

Broken.

Chapter Three

"It sounds like a great deal, Conor. One that will make you a lot of money." Matt sat with his arm resting along the back of the couch in his brother's office in Enigma.

His youngest brother, Conor, was sitting in his desk chair, his feet propped up on the surface, crossed at the ankle. He nodded, the edges of his lips curving up in what Matt assumed was supposed to pass for a smile.

Ordinarily, Matt didn't notice his brother's expressions, but he'd spent the last hour with Conor, the two of them discussing what was going to be a very lucrative project for his brother, one that Matt could see he was looking forward to, and yet, Conor hadn't smiled. Not once.

It wasn't that his brother was miserable. Like Gage, Conor had a good sense of humor and a cutting wit. Matt had been a witness to it over Christmas Eve dinner, his two brothers joking around with each other, teasing in that way only brothers could get away with.

Matt had watched from the sidelines because he hadn't been included in that bubble of fun. He didn't think he'd been purposely excluded, rather they probably assumed he wouldn't join in. After all, he never did. With him, his brothers were all work and no play, those relationship parameters set when Matt had still been in his teens.

He'd been fascinated by their behavior because the playfulness between Conor and Gage was relatively new. Or perhaps it was more accurate to say it was something old that had vanished for nearly a decade only to reappear recently.

For ten years, following the deaths of their parents, Matt and his brothers had retreated to separate bunkers like enemy generals in a standoff. The close relationship they'd shared as young boys was so far in the past, Matt struggled sometimes to convince himself it ever existed. Because when he looked back at those years when they'd been kids, waging epic Nerf gun battles, building countless models out of Legos, and racing up and down the driveway in front of their house on their bikes, he felt as if he was watching his own memories like a TV show, from an outsider's perspective rather than someone who'd experienced them.

That closeness went away when their parents died.

No. Matt reconsidered that.

It had gone away much earlier than that, the distance between them growing when Matt's father decided that his oldest son—at thirteen—needed to stop acting like a "fucking kid" and start learning the family business. Being yanked away from his brothers —who'd been his best friends up until then—was hard for Matt, and he'd been resistant initially. But much like the Borg, resistance was futile when it came to Dante Russo. He was determined to bring Matt to heel and, much as it chafed to think about nowadays, Dad had been successful in molding him into the man he wanted Matt to be, a mirror image of himself.

The emotional distance between him and his brothers had remained in place for way too long, despite the fact they'd taken over Russo Enterprises after Dad's death. All they'd managed to maintain was a professional relationship, sprinkled with what his brothers probably considered "family obligations," like the holidays, occasional happy hours, and birthday dinners.

However, things between them began to change after Gage

fell in love with Penny. His brother had tried hard to deny his feelings for her, Gage's fear of losing her so strong that he pretended what he felt wasn't love.

It had killed Matt to see his brother so lost, so sad, so he'd staged an intervention, dragging Conor along.

Matt wondered now if he'd realized where the conversation would lead them that day if he would have initiated it at all. Because it became clear Gage's resistance to Penny had everything to do with their mother's suicide.

For the first time ever, they'd opened that door, talked about her, about their grief, and it had helped Gage, helped his brother face his fears and admit he was in love with Penny.

In the past year, Matt had watched as the brother he hadn't even realized he'd lost re-emerged.

The same couldn't be said for Matt.

He swallowed, fighting to dislodge the lump that clogged his throat. The memories of his mother that he'd managed to hold at bay for so long had returned full force after that intervention. Because he'd learned that Gage had blamed himself for Mom's suicide, and that realization had gutted Matt.

Fucking *gutted* him.

There was someone to blame for her death...but it sure as hell wasn't Gage.

It was him.

And now, the memories—and the nightmares—were back, battering him relentlessly as he recalled the days, weeks, and months after his mother's death, when his anger at the world, at his father, at himself, burned so brightly he should have been rendered to ash.

The constant drip-drip-drip of water.

Look deeper.

Matt closed his eyes, pushed the memories from his mind before they could fully form.

"Harper plans to move to Philly by March. In the meantime, I'm in charge of looking for a potential property to purchase."

Conor had signed on to become an investor in supermodel Harper Branson's new restaurant. Harper had semi-retired from modeling and gone to culinary school, and now she was looking to open a restaurant in Philadelphia. The plan had been in the works for over a year, but Harper had extended her studies to include earning a degree not just in culinary arts, but in restaurant management as well.

"You sure you're going to be able to work with a partner?" Matt asked. "All your past endeavors into club and restaurant management have been solo ventures. I'm not sure I can picture you working with a partner."

Conor was an incredible businessman with the Midas touch. However, he was also—like Matt—a bit of a control freak, so he'd been surprised his brother agreed to an equal partnership.

Conor shrugged. "Harper has very definite ideas about the type of restaurant she wants to run. We've discussed the business model we plan to follow and it's sound. She's got a winner on her hands, and I want to be involved. Ideally, she would probably prefer to do it on her own, but she knew she needed someone with restaurant experience. After chatting a few times on video calls, it became obvious that we had similar visions. Besides, the only way I would agree to invest was if we were partners, fifty-fifty, and she agreed to it."

Matt smirked. "Well, I look forward to watching you try that."

Conor snorted, not bothering to deny the truth. His brother wouldn't hold his peace if Harper veered in a direction Conor didn't agree with, so this might not be all smooth sailing. Regardless, Matt agreed that if it all went well, Conor stood to make a lot of money from the venture.

"I tried to call you a couple of times earlier to reconfirm tonight, but it went straight to voicemail. Don't tell me you scheduled another meeting on New Year's Eve."

Matt shook his head. "No. Actually, I was at the Promise House."

"The homeless shelter for teens?" Conor asked, clearly surprised.

Matt had stopped by the shelter the week following the Snowflake Gala because he'd been moved by Liza's presentation. With the holiday just days away, he'd wanted to do something for the kids.

Arnold Jackson, the director, had been all too happy to latch on to his offer of assistance. The man had given him a tour of the place, discussing his desire to buy the empty lot behind the large building so they could expand, pointing out that could only happen if enough funds had been raised at the Snowflake Gala. Seeing the need for more beds firsthand had convinced Matt to up his initial contribution.

Matt's original intention had been to simply give money so that the teens staying there might be able to receive Christmas gifts. However, Arnold was a persuasive bastard and before he knew it, Matt had been dragged into a basketball game with several of the kids living at the house, Arnold insisting that what the teens *really* needed were adults willing to spend time with them and act as positive role models.

Matt had noticed the state of the kids' shoes during the basketball game. Devonte, one of the teens he'd been playing with, had used duct tape to keep the soles of his tennis shoes from flapping. The duct-taped shoes had bugged Matt all week, so he'd returned to the Promise House today, requesting every kids' size so he could get them all a new pair. Arnold had been delighted by his request, and then, somehow, he'd convinced Matt to engage in a rematch with the kids, where—once again—he'd had his ass handed to him.

Matt was no stranger to the gym, but damn if he wasn't feeling aches and pains in more than a few of his muscles right now.

"What the hell were you doing there?" Conor asked.

"I attended the Snowflake Gala before the holidays, and I was very impressed by the director and the work they're doing there. I wanted to see more." Matt went on to tell Conor about the basketball games, his brother's eyes so wide with surprise, Matt wasn't sure whether or not to be pissed off. Why was it so out of the realm of believability that he'd play basketball with homeless teens?

Of course, as soon as that thought crossed his mind, he understood Conor's shock. Because it was a completely implausible scenario. Or, at least, it had been. Until Liza encouraged him to pull his head out of his ass and look around at all the genuine need in the community. She'd opened his eyes to things he'd been far too content to remain blind to.

Liza.

The second her name crossed his mind, he felt that same ache in his gut that only went away when he managed to forget about her.

Which was next to never.

Though he *had* managed to put her out of his mind for two whole hours today as he played basketball. Maybe he'd go back for another game, once his glutes stopped screaming at him.

"Well..." Matt rose from the couch, glancing at his watch. "It's getting late. I think I'll head home."

Conor stood as well. "What's your rush? It's New Year's Eve and we're only an hour away from midnight. I was hoping you'd join me for a drink in the VIP area."

Matt shook his head, ready to give his regrets, but Conor cut him off.

"I need help increasing the Russo headcount because Gage has dragged too many Morettis along with him tonight."

Matt wondered if Liza was included in that crowd. The self-destructive part of himself hoped she was. Then his brain engaged, and he prayed to God she wasn't.

He'd had two weeks to get his head screwed on straight over Liza Moretti, and he'd made zero headway. If he was smart, he'd get the hell out of there until he felt ready to do what needed to be done.

For most of his adult life, Matt restricted himself to dating women he stood no danger of falling in love with. It was his only requirement when asking a woman out. It was why Patricia had fit the bill as a plus-one. Until the night of the Snowflake Gala, she'd been tolerable, and while they didn't set the sheets on fire, she was a decent lover. Matt didn't take women to bed for any reason other than to sate his physical needs.

Liza, however, fell into a completely different category. She was intelligent, compassionate, and beautiful, and sex with her had been a goddamn religious experience. He'd never considered what his "type" was because he wasn't looking for it. Now, he could see that Liza was it, which made her dangerous.

So he should go home now...instead of saying, "I can stay for one drink."

Shit.

"Great!" Once again, Conor looked a little too surprised, but there was no denying his kid brother was pleased, and that thought warmed Matt. He made a mental note to try to spend more time with his brothers outside of work. He'd liked the way they were with each other on Christmas Eve, and while he didn't hold out hope that the three of them could return to the same close relationship they'd had as kids, he wouldn't mind having conversations with them that didn't revolve around business deals.

Conor slapped Matt on the shoulder as they left the office, walking downstairs to the roped-off section reserved for special guests.

"Only Gage could convince me to host a bunch of Morettis in my VIP section," Conor murmured as they walked over to the bar and ordered drinks. "I'd hoped to celebrate with a lot less fanfare and people. Original invitation was meant to include just you, me, Gage, and Penny. So much for that," he grumbled.

While Gage was an open book, Conor was the quiet loner, always in his room with his books when they were kids, or now—

as an adult—choosing to work in his office here rather than keeping one in the Russo Enterprises building.

Matt thanked the bartender for the Scotch then drifted over to the balcony. The second-floor VIP section overlooked a large part of the club, including the dance floor.

Matt let his gaze travel over the mass of bodies bumping and grinding. He pretended he was watching the dancers, even though he knew he was looking for her.

And then, he found her.

She was in the middle of a circle of her friends, laughing and dancing. Matt studied the group, spotting Penny and Gage, Toby and Rich—two of Russo Enterprises' IT guys. Liza's cousins, Luca and Joey, were also there, as well as another man he didn't recognize.

When the current song ended, another fast-paced one taking its place, most of the group peeled off, leaving the floor. The only ones who remained were Joey, who'd found a woman to dance with, and Liza, who'd partnered up with the stranger.

The attractive man wrapped his arms around Liza's waist, pulling her closer, and while Matt could admit the dance was more friendly than sexy, he still found himself clenching his teeth, his jaw locked tight.

Voices behind him forced him to look away as Gage approached.

"Hey, Matt. Didn't expect to see you here tonight."

Penny followed Gage, giving Matt an unexpected hug. While he was very fond of his brother's wife, their relationship as in-laws was still in that "getting to know each other better" phase.

She wrapped a supportive arm around Gage's waist when he stumbled a bit. "Next drink is water, Gage, or you're gonna have the mother of hangovers tomorrow."

Gage bopped Penny's nose playfully. "I think the hangover is a foregone conclusion."

"Yeah. Probably. But better try to save yourself. I'll go get some water. You want anything from the bar?" Penny asked Matt.

Matt shook his head, holding up his still-full glass of Scotch. Gage pointed to Matt's drink, silently asking for the same, but Penny shook her head. "Water."

She walked away as Gage stepped next to him at the railing.

"I'm glad you're here." Gage bumped shoulders with him. It was a friendly, casual gesture, and it made Matt smile.

"You're clearly wasted," Matt teased.

Gage laughed. "I'm sober as a stone...ish. Penny and I are celebrating."

"Celebrating what?"

Gage paused for a second, then said, "The new year, of course."

Matt wasn't a fan of the holiday season, so it hardly felt like a reason for celebration. Then he glanced back down at the dance floor. "Who is that man dancing with Liza Moretti?"

Gage followed the direction of Matt's finger. "Oh. That's Miles Williams. Joey's cohost on *ManPower*."

Joey Moretti had landed his own TV show and had been traveling the country for the past two years filming episodes.

"I met him last year at Keeley, Rafe, and Gio's Christmas party. Great guy. Lot of fun," Gage went on to explain, unaware of how much Matt hated his description of Miles. Especially when he looked back toward the floor, watching as the man's hands drifted lower, not quite on Liza's ass but not quite on her back either.

Matt saw red and, for a split second, he imagined himself marching down to the floor and dragging Liza out of the other man's arms.

Fortunately, the song ended, Liza and Miles stepping apart and leaving the floor. Matt relaxed, only until he realized the two of them were climbing the stairs, headed for the VIP section. Liza made a beeline for the bar, she and Penny laughing as they talked to the bartender.

She hadn't noticed him yet, and he couldn't help but wonder if she'd be as carefree when she realized he was there.

They hadn't seen each other since the night of the gala.

Liza thanked the bartender for her drink, then turned around. Her gaze met his in an instant, and he watched a myriad of expressions cross her face—surprise, desire, wariness, sadness, and then—the one she stuck with—anger.

That one surprised him because he couldn't think of anything he'd done that night that would make her angry with him. She was the one who'd walked out, not the other way around.

Their gazes remained locked across the room, and he wished he could tell what she was thinking.

Given the fact none of her male relatives had done much more than give him a cursory glance when they walked into the VIP section, he assumed she hadn't told anyone about their night together. Because he was certain Luca and Joey wouldn't be happy to discover he'd taken their cousin to bed.

Then, he felt his own temper kick up when Miles joined her at the bar, stealing her attention away from him. Her annoyance over seeing Matt vanished when she talked to Miles. Toward him, she was all smiles and flirty looks.

Matt fought to unlock his jaw.

"Hey, Mr. Russo."

Matt recognized the voice and forced his gaze away from her, turning to acknowledge Toby and Rich.

"Matt," he corrected. Matt had told both men to call him by his first name countless times over the past year. Because, while they were still employees, they'd also become two of Gage's closest friends, so the three of them were running into each other more frequently at social occasions, like tonight.

"Matt," Rich said, grinning as he did so. Matt didn't hold his breath that the name change would stick. Next time they ran into each other, either at work or socially, he would be Mr. Russo again.

"Happy New Year!" Toby's volume was a shade too loud. Clearly, he was as sober-ish as Gage. Both men attempted to make small talk about Enigma, about their excitement at being in the

VIP section. Gage joined the conversation, the three men determined to draw Matt into a discussion about the new Dr. Who. Matt listened with half an ear, nodding when appropriate even though he didn't give a damn about Dr. Who, Dr. What, Dr. When, or Dr. Fucking Why.

Eventually, the three men finally excused themselves, seeking out Penny to settle some debate about their last Dungeons and Dragons game night. Now, as always—when it came to Gage's friends—Matt felt as if he'd just engaged in a conversation where he didn't have a clue what any of the words meant, even though they'd been spoken in English.

Glancing back toward the bar, he was surprised to discover Liza wasn't there. Surveying the area, he could see she'd left the VIP section. Foolishly, he was relieved when he spotted Miles, sitting at a round table with Joey and Luca. Turning back to the floor, he wondered if she'd gone back down to dance, but she wasn't there either.

He waited a few minutes more, then gave himself a mental kick in the ass for hanging around in hopes that she would return. He had no business talking to Liza. Time to cut his losses and get the hell out.

Matt crossed the room to say goodbye to his brother, who had claimed a quiet table in the corner, opting to sit alone versus socializing.

"You're going to miss the ball dropping," Conor said.

Matt snorted. "That's not something I'll miss. Happy New Year."

"Happy New Year, Matt," Conor said.

Matt walked downstairs, fighting his way through the crowd to the front door. Handing his ticket to the valet, he stepped away from the entrance, tugging his jacket closed at the front. The temperature had dropped significantly since he'd arrived at the club, and flurries were starting to fall.

Shoving his hands in his pocket, he was surprised when he noticed Liza, leaning against a light pole about halfway down the block. She appeared to be lost to the world, deep in thought.

Before he could think better of it, he walked toward her. "You picked a cold night to hang around outside."

She glanced up at him, her surprise over his presence proving just how lost in thought she'd been. "Hi, Matt," she said somewhat coldly before looking behind him as if expecting to see someone else. "Where's Patricia?"

Ah. And now he understood the anger. Henri, his personal assistant, had sent him the link to that ridiculous article about him and Patricia getting married. He'd been annoyed when he'd seen it because—when he replayed the dinner date—it became obvious that Patricia had instigated not only the photographs but the article as well.

She'd made certain they were seated by that front window, the perfect location for some member of the paparazzi to snap countless pics. The photos that accompanied the article were clearly staged, as he recalled the odd way Patricia had handed him the cuff links. He could see now it had been premeditated, her actions making it look as if he'd placed that ring-shaped box in her hand, not the other way around.

He'd been half tempted to call Patricia to force her to confess, but in the end, he decided it didn't matter. He had no intention of seeing her again, so no harm, no foul.

Now that he suspected Liza had seen the same article, he could use it to his benefit as there was no love lost between the women. Allowing Liza to think he and Patricia were back together might be enough to break this pull he felt toward her. Because regardless of his wayward, unwanted feelings, he and Liza Moretti could never be.

And the sooner he—and she—accepted that, the better.

He had worried that as time passed and Liza replayed their evening together, she might develop feelings for him, that she would begin to see him in a different light.

The wrong light.

So he fanned the flames.

"Patricia's in Aspen," he replied, recalling the woman's holiday plans.

"Why aren't you with her?"

Matt lifted one shoulder casually. "I always spend the holidays with my brothers."

She narrowed her eyes. "Penny said you spent Christmas Day at the office."

Navigating through this endless minefield with Liza was going to be even trickier if his sister-in-law kept feeding her information. Rather than reply, he changed the subject. "Why are you outside?"

Liza turned her face away from him, and for a moment, he didn't think she would answer. When she looked at him again, he saw that damn resignation he'd seen in her eyes one too many times.

When she replied, it was with that same forthright, blunt honesty he'd come to expect from her. "I don't have another still-single, stroke-of-midnight New Year's Eve kiss in me."

Goddammit.

Her words felt like a punch to the gut. Was it because he now cared about her happiness?

Or because her words struck a vein deep inside him? Reminded him just how lonely he was.

Liza held his gaze, let him see. Her pain, her loneliness, everything was right there, reflected in those gorgeous brown eyes. He was seeing the real her.

It was as beautiful as it was heartbreaking.

She'd captured his attention a year and a half earlier, her eyes meeting his, full of fire and challenge and even desire. She never looked away, never hid who she was.

Before he could begin to formulate a response to her confession, the countdown began, loud voices yelling from inside the club.

"Ten! Nine! Eight!"

They'd just hit "Seven!" when Matt moved. He gripped her upper arms and pulled her toward him, her chest hitting his at the same time their lips touched.

If he'd taken her by surprise, she gave no indication. Liza's hands gripped his waist, her fingers burrowing beneath his jacket, finding his shirt. She tightened her hold, tugging him even closer as their mouths opened.

His tongue brushed hers, stealing her taste, her breath, her sensuous moan. He released her arms so that he could touch her face, cup those rosy cheeks, twist her head to deepen the kiss even more.

Sliding his fingers around her neck, he grasped her silky hair. Closing a fist around it, he pulled her head back, fighting like the devil not to slam her against the lamppost and fuck out all this excruciating need.

Liza groaned again and he captured the sound, her hands slipping down to his hips as she pushed herself against him. He recalled the night of the gala, the way he'd thrust his thigh between her legs in the elevator, the way she'd humped against it, seeking stimulation, completion. What would he give to hear her cries as she came again?

Every instinct in his body was screaming out for him to take this woman, claim her, own her, make her his in every single way he could.

She nipped at his lower lip, attempting to claim control of the kiss, a purely bratty move that had his cock growing even harder. She was playing with him, trying to force his hand.

Fuck if she didn't know how to push all his buttons. Matt gave her a taste of her own medicine, as he pulled her hair harder, held her tighter, made certain she knew exactly who held the power.

Another full minute passed before Matt's wit returned and he became cognizant of the sounds around them, the honking of car horns, the blaring of noisemakers, people belting out "Auld Lang Syne."

Liza appeared to have come to her senses as well, and she pulled away. The conqueror inside him almost dragged her back. He wasn't finished with her. Not by a longshot.

But...

They were both panting, fighting to find their breath as they stared into each other's eyes.

And that was when he realized he'd fucked up *again*. Because the resignation he'd seen in her beautiful brown eyes was gone and, in its place, he saw something much worse.

Hope.

He released her quickly, taking a step away. And then another.

"Happy New Year, Liza."

Liza frowned, confused by his retreat, but before she could call him back, he found the strength to do what had to be done.

He left.

Chapter Four

"**S**o does that make sense?" Liza asked, putting her pencil down.

Ashley nodded. "Yeah. I think so."

"Good. Then I think we're done for today."

"Algebra is still stupid. It's not like I'm ever going to use this crap."

Liza had heard the same argument from Ashley every single Saturday for the last three months. She'd gotten roped into tutoring the girl, one of the teens living at the Promise House, back in October after Ashley had failed four algebra quizzes in a row.

Arnold had been talking to Ashley about the importance of good grades when Liza had shown up that chilly Saturday in fall. He'd dragged Liza into the office, asked her if she understood algebra, and before she knew it, she and Ashley had a standing Saturday morning date to go over variables, coefficients, quadratic equations, and a bunch of other crap Liza hadn't used since high school. Not that she'd ever confess that to Ashley. When Liza asked Arnold why he wasn't tutoring the girl, he'd laughed hysterically, claiming he still used a calculator for simple multiplication because the nine times table had eluded him since elementary school.

"It doesn't matter if you use it later in life or not. What you need to do is concentrate on passing this week's test. You're doing so well. We just have to stay on top of it." The first thing Ashley had done when Liza arrived this morning was pull out her report card and show her the C she'd received in the class. That second-quarter grade, combined with the first quarter's F, pulled her semester up to a D, aka passing. Halle-fucking-lujah.

Liza was determined to see the girl finish the year with at least a C in the course, though given Ashley's progress lately, she didn't think a B was entirely out of the realm of possibility. She'd said that aloud after hugging Ashley for the good report card and promising to bring her a surprise next week as a reward.

"You really think I could end up with a B in this class?" Ashley was clearly warming up to that idea.

"I do. You're kicking algebra's ass," Liza assured her.

Ashley laughed, and together they cleaned up the table, putting the study guides, textbook, and notebook away.

"All finished?" Arnold walked into the rec room. Four kids were hunkered down on the couch and chairs surrounding the television, trash talking loudly as they played Mario Kart on the new gaming system someone had donated to the house over the holidays. There were eight other kids sitting around the same large table where she and Ashley had been, working on homework, doing crafts, or playing cards.

"Yep," Liza replied. "I was about to stop by your office to see if you needed me to do anything else. Because if not, I think I might take off early this week."

Arnold studied Liza's face, frowning. "You look tired."

Liza considered denying it, but why would she? Tired had been her permanent state since the Snowflake Gala. Sleep appeared a luxury she could no longer afford because it had been shut off due to lack of payment.

Night after night, she found herself tossing and turning, torn between frustration, self-recrimination, and overwhelming horniness.

She wanted Matt Russo, but she didn't want to.

It was as simple and as difficult as that.

She gave Arnold a weary smile. "I didn't sleep well last night."

Or the night before. Or the night before that one. Or…

Liza had been volunteering at the Promise House for just over a year and during that time, she'd become very close to the home's director, Arnold Jackson, as well as his life partner, Johnnie. The three of them had begun their own little dinner club, meeting up at a different restaurant or each other's home two or three times a month. Liza looked forward to those nights more than she could say, which was a testament to how lacking her social life was. Now that most of her girlfriends were in relationships, she found herself eating dinner alone at least ninety percent of the time.

She hated eating alone.

She, Arnold, and Johnnie hadn't had dinner together since before the Snowflake Gala because of all the hustle and bustle associated with the holidays. Their next date was Tuesday night, and they had invited her to join them at their house because Johnnie had some new recipe for curry chicken he'd found online that he was dying to try.

"You sure you're not coming down with something?" Arnold asked. "The flu has been making the rounds ever since New Year's."

"I'm not sick," she reassured him.

"Hey, Liza," Devonte said as he entered the room, spinning a basketball on the tip of his finger. She'd never seen the boy when he wasn't wearing his beloved Celtics jersey or without a basketball in his hand.

"Hey, Devonte." The two of them fist-bumped, their standard greeting.

"You up for a game of hoops?"

She shook her head, grinning. Most Saturdays, she took him up on the offer, but she couldn't summon enough energy for a lousy game of Horse right now, let alone the one-on-one she and Devonte usually got into. She'd played on the girls' basketball team in high school, but that experience did not help her when it came to playing against Devonte. "Not today."

"Yeah, you probably don't wanna take me on now that I've got these sweet KD16s."

Liza glanced down at Devonte's new tennis shoes and whistled. "Damn. Nice shoes. Santa bring you those?" she teased.

Devonte shook his head. "Nope. Matt gave them to me. Got us all new shoes. Let us pick out whatever we wanted."

"All of you? You mean every kid here?"

Devonte nodded, grinning widely.

"Wow. That's super nice." Liza glanced over at Arnold. She knew everyone on staff, as well as the counselors and volunteers, and she'd never met anyone named Matt. "Is Matt new?"

Arnold nodded. "You could say that. He's been by the place a few times since the gala. Apparently, your presentation really impressed him."

It took a second before Liza could process what Arnold was saying. Because there was no way...

"Matt Russo?" she forced herself to ask.

It was Devonte who answered him. "Yeah. Dude is rich as shit, but he's aww-right." He drawled the word *alright*, making it clear he thought Matt was totally cool. "Not too bad on the court either, but he can't keep up with me and my mad skills, y'know."

"He's played basketball with you?" Liza didn't mean to sound so shocked, but dammit...she was.

"Coming back again next week." Devonte was obviously excited to see his new friend. "Gonna help me break in my new kicks."

"Come on, Liza. I've got something in my office I want to discuss with you," Arnold said before Liza could question Devonte further.

The two of them walked together, stopped several times along the way by teens who wanted to say hello to Liza or ask Arnold a question.

Once they reached his office, Arnold gestured toward the "seen better days" couch before shutting the door. She sank down on the faded but comfy cushion, as Arnold took the overstuffed armchair across from her.

"I'm worried about those dark circles under your eyes. It feels like we haven't talked in ages," Arnold started.

"It's only been a few weeks and I'm coming to your house on Tuesday. We can chat then."

Arnold's eyes crinkled with an amusement that confused her until he explained. "Oh, my dear Liza. You and I won't have the opportunity to say anything Tuesday night. Johnnie is full speed ahead on the wedding plans, so please, for the love of all that's holy, come armed with strong opinions on everything from flowers to color schemes to menus. Because apparently, my feelings regarding all those things are either wrong or too lukewarm. I'm counting on you to pick up my slack."

After twenty-five years as partners, Arnold and Johnnie were finally tying the knot at a destination wedding in Hawaii, and Liza couldn't be happier for them. Johnnie had grown up on the islands and most of his family—apparently as big as hers—still lived there.

"Yes, sir." Liza gave him a salute. "Operation Groomzilla is underway. I'll do my best to soothe the beast."

"Got your plane ticket?" Arnold asked.

"Fully booked." She was living for the trip, which was only about a month away. She'd been delighted six months earlier when they'd asked if she'd like to attend. Arnold had mentioned it one night over dinner, telling her they would understand if she couldn't afford it, either financially or timewise. It hadn't taken her five minutes—she'd needed to check her vacation leave at work—to accept.

The idea of a week soaking up the rays and drinking fruity

cocktails in Hawaii rather than being stuck here, freezing her ass off—mid-February in Philly was relentless—sounded like bliss.

Now the trip had an added bonus because she was hoping the break from reality would be just what she needed to stop obsessing over Matt.

"So about these dark circles..." Arnold was like a dog with a bone.

"I'm just tired," she lied. "Truly."

Arnold didn't look like he bought it, but he let her off the hook. At least, until he unwittingly changed the subject...to the same damn subject.

"I know that you and Matt Russo have a somewhat contentious relationship," Arnold said.

Liza didn't hold back whenever she and Matt butted heads, which meant she'd found herself bitching about him often to Johnnie and Arnold over drinks and dinner.

"We did. Do," she quickly amended, not because she thought the past tense was wrong, but rather Arnold would be expecting the present tense.

"I hope his presence here at the Promise House won't be an issue for you."

"He really is coming back?"

Arnold smiled. "I will admit, I didn't expect to see him after that initial visit. He'd emailed to request a tour, which I'd been perfectly happy to give. Then he asked what immediate needs we had, and I knew he meant financially."

Liza gave him a crooked grin, perfectly aware of where this story was going. Arnold had roped her into volunteering in a similar fashion. After being promoted to director of the Initiative, she'd visited the Promise House intent on raising funds to help the teens living here. She'd asked almost the exact same question. *What do you need?*

And Arnold had answered, *"You and as much time as you can spare for these kids."*

"And because you're you, you roped him into volunteering."

Arnold chuckled. "He wasn't that hard to rope in, if you want the truth. I gave him his tour, told him what the kids needed more than anything was a positive male role model, someone willing to spend time with them. Then I threw him out there on the basketball court with Devonte and a few other kids. You should have seen him in his six-hundred-dollar Brunello Cucinelli dress shirt, sleeves rolled up, sweating his ass off."

Liza laughed. "Oh my God. I would have paid good money to see that."

"He thanked me for the tour and game when he left, and I figured I wouldn't see him again. Didn't expect him to show back up on New Year's Eve, asking for every kid's shoe size and their 'sneaker wish list.' He's been going the extra mile since then, challenging Devonte to a rematch after every game."

"Bet Devonte is loving that," she added.

"I swear to God, that boy would sleep on that ratty old court using the ball as his pillow if I'd let him."

Truer words were never spoken. Liza wished there weren't always a million more pressing needs at the Promise House because she'd love to raise enough funds to renovate the "makeshift" gym. It was an old storage room with concrete floors and a dozen or so dented, folding metal chairs serving as bleachers. There wasn't a damn thing regulation about the basketball court, the hoops hanging up on opposite ends of the space, the size of the room dictating the distance between. The hoops didn't even have nets.

"As Devonte said, Matt's promised to come back, and I have no reason to believe he won't follow through on his commitment." Arnold stood up and picked up an Amazon box from the edge of his desk. "This showed up this morning. No name, but I can figure out who sent it." Reaching in, he pulled out two crisp white basketball nets.

Liza leaned back, trying to find something to say. When she did open her mouth, what fell out wasn't what she'd intended at all.

"I slept with Matt Russo the night of the Snowflake Gala." Liza held Arnold's gaze, waiting for his stunned reaction.

She was sure he'd be shocked and probably even amused. Arnold had a wicked sense of humor, so finding out she'd had a one-night stand with her so-called arch nemesis felt like the kind of thing that would tickle his funny bone.

What she didn't anticipate was his calm nod. "Good for you."

There was no censure, no astonishment, nothing except...approval?

"I don't think you heard what I said."

"You slept with Matt Russo." Arnold repeated what she'd considered a big bombshell as casually as if he was telling her they were having grilled cheese and tomato soup for lunch.

"Seriously? That's all you have to say? Good for me?" Liza hadn't told a soul about her and Matt. It wasn't like she was going to bring it up to any of her Moretti relatives, and while she had plenty of girlfriends to talk to, they all had a bad habit of falling for her cousins and brothers, which meant telling them would basically be the same thing as confessing it to her family. It was a vicious circle.

In the back of her mind, she'd been considering bringing up the subject to Arnold and Johnnie on Tuesday night at dinner because she really—REALLY—needed an objective opinion. But until she just blurted it out, she'd still been on the fence about telling anyone at all, thinking perhaps it was a secret best kept just that...a secret.

"What were you expecting me to say?" Arnold put the nets away, walked back to his chair, and sat down again. "I was there the night of the gala, Liza. I saw you and Matt together, saw the dance you shared. Johnnie commented on it when we got home, said there were so many sparks flying between the two of you, he was shocked the ballroom hadn't gone up in flames."

Liza had been so swept up in that dance, she hadn't even considered the fact there'd been witnesses.

"Regardless of that," she started. "Don't you think I made a mistake?"

"Do *you* think it was a mistake?" Arnold was a licensed therapist, so she wasn't new to his infuriating habit of answering questions with questions. Questions meant to make her think about her feelings and do a bunch of introspection and other shit she sucked at.

"Of course, I do," she said hotly.

"Why?"

Liza scoffed and threw her head back against the couch, her gaze focused on the ceiling. "Because our families hate each other," she spat, giving him the cop-out response.

And because Arnold knew the Moretti/Russo stories—she tended to overshare after a few glasses of wine—he called her on it. "Try again, because that feuding family bullshit is getting old. A lot of what you're pretending to be pissed off about is ancient history, sins perpetuated by people who aren't even still alive."

"Matt pulled some of the shit," she countered, though she knew her argument was weak.

Arnold smirked. "When he was eighteen. Everyone is an asshole at eighteen. So try again. Why was it a mistake?"

Liza fell silent because this was what she'd been struggling with ever since Christmas. Immediately following the gala, she'd tried to tell herself it was a mistake, and she'd failed. How could something so earthshaking and incredible be wrong?

For a few days, she'd toyed with the idea of calling Matt and suggesting a second-night stand. And maybe a third, a fourth, etc., just to see where things took them.

Then Penny had shown her the pictures of Matt with Patricia the day after what she couldn't stop thinking of as the best night of her life, and, well, dammit, her pride had been tweaked. Because while she'd been reliving every freaking second of their night together, Matt had been making plans to go out with Queen Bitch.

Less than fifteen hours after Liza left his hotel room, he'd moved on. Or actually, back. Which told her it hadn't been as amazing for him...and that had hurt her as much as it had pissed her off.

Under the guise of making herself feel better, she'd recalled all those "old stories" about Matt stealing Tony's girlfriend, Adriana, seducing her and making sure Tony found them, to prove to herself that he was still the same old dog employing the same tricks.

Unfortunately, that ploy didn't work because in the end, all it did was make her feel stupid. Like she should have known better, like she'd let herself get played by the playboy.

God. She hated feeling stupid. She'd spent the week between Christmas and New Year's Eve determined to forget him completely.

Until that kiss at midnight.

She realized Arnold was still waiting for an answer, but she didn't have one to give him. "I don't know why it was a mistake."

"Does Matt agree that it shouldn't have happened?"

Liza sighed because she wasn't looking very intelligent in this conversation. "I don't know. He and I haven't talked about it."

"What did he say in the morning?"

Liza bit her lower lip, hating her response to that question. "I snuck out in the middle of the night."

Arnold's eyes softened. "Oh, Liza. You haven't seen him since?"

"Actually, he kissed me on New Year's Eve," she confessed.

"So it wasn't a one-night stand?" Arnold asked, clearly confused.

Liza waved her hand. "No. It was. The kiss came at midnight and that was all it was. Just a kiss." A kiss that had left her nipples so hard and her panties so damp that she'd left the bar immediately, headed home, and gone three rounds with her vibrator.

"And you didn't talk to him then either?"

She shook her head.

"Do you want this thing with Matt to be more than a one-night stand, Liza?"

That was the million-dollar question, wasn't it? And the one that might be moot because...

"The thing is, Matt may have a girlfriend-slash-fiancée."

"*May?*" Arnold asked.

"The night after the gala, after we were together, he was photographed at a restaurant with Patricia Eddington."

The way Arnold crinkled his nose pleased her, grateful to know she and her dear friend were on the exact same page regarding the obnoxious socialite.

"This date happened before the New Year's Eve kiss?"

Liza nodded.

"I can't see Matt with Patricia," Arnold said. "He's not stupid and he's not shallow, and a man would have to be both of those to deal with her for any amount of time."

Liza couldn't argue with that. "The pictures were on one of those online gossip sites and pretty damning. They looked really chummy."

Arnold snorted. "You should know better than to believe everything you read in the tabloids. How do you know they were taken when they say they were? They could have been old, rehashed material, used to jazz up a slow news day."

Liza shook her head. "Patricia was wearing a bracelet that Matt had intended to give her the night of the gala. They had a fight, and she left the Ritz without it. She was wearing it in the pictures."

Arnold nodded slowly, processing that information. "Did you ask Matt about it? Ask him if he's in a relationship with her?"

Liza had questioned why Matt and Patricia weren't together on New Year's Eve. His response had been vague at best. The problem was that between seven days of restless, horny sleep and consuming three strong-as-shit margaritas over dinner, she hadn't exactly been firing on all cylinders that night.

Then he'd planted that blow-your-brains-out kiss on her, and her cylinders had shut down completely, total meltdown.

"We're not exactly…I mean…just because we had sex doesn't mean…"

Jesus Christ.

Wake up, brain. Formulate a complete thought.

"You don't think you have a right to question him about who he's seeing because the two of you aren't dating," Arnold said, filling in the blanks succinctly.

"It was just one night. We made no future plans for more dates."

"But you would like to date him?" Arnold pressed.

Liza shook her head, even though her response to that question wasn't no. "It would be impossible. He's a Russo. I'm a Moretti. And while the feud may seem ancient to me, I can assure you my dad, uncles, Tony, and Nonno have very long memories."

Or at least…they did. Liza considered Gage's presence at Christmas Eve dessert and realized that wasn't completely true anymore.

Arnold laced his fingers in front of him, his elbows resting on the arms of the chair. "Take the last names out of the equation. Pretend you're Liza Smith and he's Matt Jones. Do you want to date him?"

"I…"

Did she?

She closed her mouth and shrugged.

Arnold didn't let her off the hook. "You're not a coward, Liza. It's a straightforward question, one you already know the answer to."

If all that was holding her back was their last names, Liza's response would be as simple as Arnold believed. It would be yes.

The reason it wasn't easy had nothing to do with family rivalries or even Patricia. It had to do with the way Matt had made her feel that night. Because the sex had been eye-opening and slightly terrifying. He had revealed something… Well, something she'd probably known was there but hadn't ever allowed herself to consider. She'd spent too many years sleeping with idiots who didn't realize there was this little thing on a woman's body called the clit...

Matt not only knew it existed. He knew exactly what to do with it.

She raised her gaze to Arnold's, aware she was doing something she *never* did. She was blushing. Serious flames licked her cheeks, and Arnold, the observant asshole, not only noticed but interpreted exactly where her thoughts had gone.

"You and I have talked about everything under the sun this past year, haven't we?" he asked casually.

"We have." Somewhere along the line, Johnnie and Arnold had become two of her best friends. Probably because her girlfriends were dropping like flies, Cupid flinging arrows in every direction except hers, which meant Penny, Jess, Gianna, and Keeley now spent their nights in committed bliss with their soul mates rather than cruising the nightclubs with her.

"Everything except sex." Arnold claimed he liked her because she didn't mince words, but she couldn't hold a candle to him when it came to being forthright.

"That's true," she replied.

"And we don't have to start now if it makes you uncomfortable, but, well, the door is open."

Liza appreciated the offer, even though she wouldn't have a clue how to begin. If she couldn't manage to say the easy stuff, how the hell could she tell Arnold, a sixty-two-year-old gay man who'd become an extra brother/best friend, that she was...

Fuck. She couldn't even think the word inside her own mind. How could she say it out loud?

"I...I... He...um..."

Arnold frowned. "Did he hurt you?"

"Oh my God, no. At least, not in any way that I didn't want. He was strong and demanding and..." Liza resisted the urge to fan herself, certain she was probably past the red stage and now turning purple.

"I see," Arnold mused.

She was afraid he did. "He awakened something in me that I'm not sure I can turn back off, now that I've... God. Why is this so hard to admit?"

"Say the words, Liza. Tell me what he showed you. Tell me what you discovered. Not speaking them doesn't mean they aren't true."

"I think I might be sexually submissive."

"You think?"

"I've never been with a man who made me feel the way Matt did."

Arnold nodded his head slowly, considering that, the silence drifting too long for her comfort.

She broke first. "Say something."

"It's clear that night with him made quite an impression on you, shook your foundation, rattled the windows."

"You can say that again," she mumbled.

"So don't you think something that impactful is worth taking a closer look at, worth exploring?"

"Are you talking about Matt or the sex?"

"Are they separate in your mind?" he countered.

"Not at all," she whispered. Liza's shoulders drooped. Because while his words were right, they were also hard.

"Well then, in that case, I think you know what you have to do," Arnold said, driving his point home.

"I need to talk to Matt."

Dammit.

Chapter Five

Matt leaned back in his desk chair, his gaze drifting to his weekly schedule on the computer.

To her name.

It wasn't like he needed to consult the damn schedule to know what his afternoon looked like. He'd been anticipating this one o'clock meeting ever since Liza had called his PA, Henri, a week ago to request it.

It had been almost a month since he'd seen her on New Year's Eve. Three and a half weeks since he'd piled onto the mistakes he'd made after the gala by kissing her at midnight.

He'd been a fucking idiot because Liza had given him the perfect out that night when she'd questioned him about Patricia. Clearly, she'd seen that stupid article and believed he was back with the annoying socialite.

It would have been the ideal solution to his "How Do I Solve a Problem like Liza?" dilemma.

If it really *was* a problem.

That was why he'd been anticipating this meeting. It was time for the two of them to clear the air. If Liza was happy to hang on to that "it was a mistake" viewpoint and give him a wide berth, he'd be golden.

But if she wanted more…

He recalled the hope in her eyes after that ill-advised kiss.

He really should have taken the opening she'd provided, lied and told her—in no uncertain terms—that he and Patricia were an item once more.

What he should *not* have done was kiss her again.

He thought the kiss they'd shared in the elevator had been explosive, but it didn't hold a candle to the one outside Enigma as snow flurries fell around them.

He glanced at his phone. T-minus twenty minutes until her arrival.

Matt had considered canceling the meeting, telling Liza she could share the foundation's annual report with him via email. It would have been a perfectly valid request because that was how they always handled reports. The fact she wanted to meet in person told him she was ready for the face-to-face he'd been avoiding.

The sooner he discovered what kind of fallout he could expect from their one-night stand, the better. He hated not having all the information. Going into situations blind was bad in business and in personal affairs. He'd never been the type to pull his punches, so the fact he was doing so with Liza was a problem. One he needed to address.

Of course, regardless of her intentions, Matt's would remain the same. He wasn't interested in pursuing anything more.

No. That wasn't entirely true.

It was more accurate to say he *couldn't* pursue anything more.

Because their night together had blown the door he'd kept locked for well over a decade right off the hinges, his nightmares growing more frequent, regret eating away at him like cancer.

The constant drip-drip-drip of water.

Dark red blood congealed on the snowy-white tiles.

Look deeper.

Stop. He shut the images down, then rubbed his eyes wearily. This was why it would be better to let her down easy now rather than let things go too far between them. Because he had no intention of ever letting her see who he really was, nor could he tell her about the things he'd done.

Those were his secrets and he would take them to the grave.

His eyes drifted to his phone again. T-minus nineteen minutes.

"Enough," he muttered, minimizing his calendar and opening his email, allowing work to distract him.

As soon as he clicked on the first message, the door to his office swung open and he looked up, scowling. No one entered without knocking. Not even his personal assistant.

He mentally groaned when Patricia Eddington sauntered in, his PA hot on her heels.

Henri shot Matt an apologetic grimace. "I asked her to wait so that I could see if you were available."

Matt waved his hand at Henri, aware Patricia wasn't the type of woman to follow any protocol that required her to wait. She'd mentioned countless times in the past that she expected others to accommodate her busy schedule. Her self-importance was off the charts. Every time she made the comment, Matt had to practically bite his tongue off to stop himself from retorting that getting manicures, going for coffee, and "doing lunch" at the country club with girlfriends hardly classified as "busy."

"It's alright, Henri."

Henri frowned behind Patricia's back. His PA was a stickler for perfection and Patricia had just broken a cardinal rule by making him look incompetent. "You have a meeting in fifteen minutes," Henri reminded him, not because Matt didn't know but because he wanted to let Patricia know she was on the clock.

Like that would work.

Patricia glanced at Henri over her shoulder. "Leave. Now."

"That's enough," Matt said, his tone low and threatening enough that Patricia actually looked chastened...for a moment. He hated the way Patricia spoke down to anyone she considered her lesser, which seemed to include anyone with less than ten million dollars in the bank. She was rude and insulting to everyone from waiters, doormen, chauffeurs, and now, his personal assistant, something he'd made clear to her he wouldn't stand for.

Henri sniffed, then left, closing the door behind him.

It would be polite of Matt to rise and greet her, but Patricia was the one who'd shown up here without an appointment, so screw that. He'd wanted a distraction, but she wasn't it.

"Patricia," he said coolly.

Her well-plucked eyebrows lifted when he remained seated, but only for a moment. Then she skirted around his desk, bending down to press a kiss to his cheek. "Matt, darling. You couldn't believe how much has happened this past month."

Matt forced himself to be civil. "How was Aspen?"

Patricia perched herself on the edge of his desk, taking care to make sure the slit in her pencil skirt parted just enough to give him an eyeful of her thigh. "Wonderful! The powder was fresh and soft as a pillow. You simply have to come with us next year. Daddy and I insist."

Hell would have to freeze over before he'd make that trip or any others with the Eddingtons.

Matt offered no reply, not that Patricia needed one as she prattled on about the ski conditions in Colorado. "And then, we decided we were having so much fun that Daddy surprised me and Mommy by whisking us off to Switzerland to ski at our chateau for a couple of weeks. We only just got back to Philadelphia yesterday. I'm sure you must've been wondering if I was ever coming home," she said with a giggle.

Matt hadn't realized she wasn't in Philadelphia. He hadn't cared either. After all, he'd broken off their relationship the last time he'd seen her.

"I'm sorry to rush this along, Patricia, but I do have a meeting." If he didn't get her out of there very soon, there would be little chance of Liza and Patricia not running into each other.

And while that was something he could use to his advantage,

he refused. He despised the way Patricia talked down to Liza, so there was no way he'd subject her to that if he could help it. "Was there something you needed?"

Patricia pushed away from his desk, walking around it to sit in one of the chairs opposite him. He didn't like the way she settled in like they had all the time in the world. "I suppose you saw that article about us on the internet. It's terrible how the two of us are never out of the public eye. I mean, we couldn't even enjoy a quiet dinner together without the paparazzi bombarding us."

Bombard wasn't the word he'd use, considering neither of them even saw the cameraman.

Matt sighed, infusing as much boredom into it as he could. "That site is infamous for gossip. I doubt anyone takes the lies written there seriously."

"Oh, I know. It's just...Daddy saw it and he thought it was true. He got very excited about the possibility."

And with that, Matt's suspicions that he hadn't seen the last of Patricia were confirmed. As were his feelings that she'd set up the pictures and the article. Because there was no way in hell Richard Eddington would have just happened upon that article if Patricia hadn't shown it to him.

"I hope you explained to your father that it's not a possibility and that we're no longer seeing each other." He refused to feed her the "just friends" bullshit again. It was time to be a lot less subtle with Patricia.

"I did, but you know Daddy. Once he gets something in his head, he's relentless. It's why he's such a successful businessman. He never says die."

"This isn't a business deal."

"It could be." She'd said the same at the gala, assuring him that theirs wouldn't be a love match and that they could both have affairs as long as they were discreet about it.

"Patricia," he started.

"He thinks, like I do, that a marriage between our two families would be incredibly lucrative."

Matt was trying to figure out if Richard Eddington truly believed that or if he was simply telling Patricia what she wanted to hear. Richard didn't need Russo money any more than Matt needed the Eddingtons.

However, as far as Matt could tell, there was nothing Patricia had ever wanted that she hadn't received. The word *no* hadn't played a role in her upbringing. So if Daddy Eddington thought she wanted Matt, he'd move heaven and earth to get it—him—for her.

"As I told you when you brought up the subject of marriage, I have more than enough money. I don't need to increase the family coffers."

Patricia's pout was pronounced, making her look like the poster child for spoiled brats everywhere. This was the kickback he'd expected the night of their dinner date, and while he was grateful he was able to address it without a hangover, he still wasn't functioning at his best because he was anxious about Liza's imminent arrival.

"I know you said that." She brushed that reason away as inconsequential. "But Daddy was hoping now that some time has passed, you might have reconsidered."

Daddy or Patricia?

"I haven't."

"He plans to call your PA, to set up a meeting so that the two of you can discuss—"

Matt's patience was at an end. "I am always happy to meet with your father about business opportunities, but as far as I'm concerned, this marriage discussion is over. I am not getting married to you for money, love, sex, or fame. I am not getting married. Period."

Patricia looked ready to continue the battle, so he stood up, circling his desk, gesturing toward the door and giving her no choice but to follow suit, though she stood up reluctantly. "If you could just talk to Daddy, I think—"

"No, Patricia."

Her eyes narrowed, her cheeks flushed with anger, and her nostrils flared. She really didn't like hearing that word.

However, he had to hand it to her. She was good at keeping her flashes of tempers just that. A flash, then gone again.

"Matt," she said sweetly, reaching out to place her hand on his forearm, leaning toward him so that her breasts would brush against him. "You're making a mistake."

"No. I'm not." Subtlety would never work with this woman. Matt had hoped to be able to maintain a comfortable working relationship with Richard, but he was over that now. He'd make up the loss of income somewhere else if Richard tried to sever ties. At this point, Matt would embrace the pauper's life if it meant he didn't have to deal with Patricia again. "In the future, please contact Henri if you'd like to schedule an appointment."

Patricia's lips thinned, and he could see her struggling for a way to continue pressing her case.

"Goodbye," he said, dismissing her once and for all.

She walked to the door, flinging it open. He didn't bother to see her out, so he was surprised when she twisted back to him, the fury he'd just seen in her eyes gone. She gave him a seductive smile as she blew him a kiss. "See you later, lover," she purred, before turning and walking out.

It was then that he saw Liza standing next to Henri's desk, her expression unreadable.

"Oh, hello, Liza," Patricia said, her tone pure venom. "I didn't know they let you out of your cubicle during the day."

Liza's eyes narrowed, but before she could offer a retort, Patricia tittered at her own joke, then sauntered down the hall to the elevators like she owned the place.

"Ms. Moretti is here for your one o'clock," Henri said, stating the obvious when neither Matt nor Liza spoke.

"I can see that." Matt gestured for Liza to enter the office. She walked in as he closed the door behind her.

Liza, damn her, looked gorgeous in her silky white blouse, fitted black slacks, and tailored maroon blazer. Her jewelry was understated, a thick gold chain around her neck, a pair of drop earrings, and her Apple watch with a chunky, knotted gold band.

"Why don't you have a seat, Ms. Moretti?" he offered.

She snorted. "Back to that, are we?"

Matt sighed. Sixty seconds in and he was already fucking up. "No, Liza, we're not."

"Actually, I've changed my mind. Let's do a full reboot, *Mr. Russo*." She drew out the mister in his name. "I prefer it when you call me Ms. Moretti." The anger in her voice didn't quite reach her eyes. He wished it did because he hated thinking he'd been the one to put that disappointment there.

She stared him down, one hand on her hip, and damn if his fingers didn't itch to pull her over his lap to spank the sass and sadness right out of her. Matt hadn't opened the door on his sexual proclivities in a long, long time. Leaving them behind hadn't been hard to do because, before Liza, he hadn't felt the desire to dominate a woman in the bedroom since...

Since his world crashed around his head and all he'd managed to drag from the wreckage was this shell of a man.

"I know you've come to discuss the annual report," he said, resuming his composure. "But perhaps—"

"The budget was an excuse," Liza interrupted him. "You and I both know it could have been shared in an email. I thought perhaps we should talk, but..." Her gaze drifted back to the closed door, clearly recalling that nasty insult of Patricia's as well as the kiss she'd blown to him.

She thrust the folder with the annual budget into his hands, gearing up to leave. "But that's not necessary now. I have all the information I need." She took a couple of steps toward the door. Patricia's presence had shaken her up.

He'd always admired Liza's spunkiness, her fire, so it rubbed against the grain to see her backing down.

"Running away again, Ms. Moretti?" he drawled, giving her exactly what she'd just asked for. Whether she realized it or not, Liza was issuing an unspoken challenge to his dominance, and he found himself replying to it. She wanted him to stop her. He could see it in her eyes.

The second his taunt landed, she paused, spinning to face him.

Liza crossed her arms, drawing his attention to her breasts. He could still recall how they'd filled his palms, how tight and utterly suckable her nipples had been. Her body was a goddamn masterpiece. She should be on display at the Louvre.

"You're right. Let's do this. It would be better if we cleared the air. You and I fucked."

She was purposely using the stronger, cruder description to minimize what they'd shared. In Matt's mind, what they did was a million miles away from fucking. It had felt too steeped in importance, in meaning...in danger.

But he couldn't say that to her. "We did."

"And we agreed it was a mistake."

That wasn't entirely true. "*You* said it was a mistake," he reminded her, his response taking her by surprise.

She fell silent, and Matt got the sense she was waiting for him to agree with her. Or maybe she was hoping he'd disagree.

Liza was poised, her gaze unwavering, patient. She intended to wait him out.

Matt wasn't sure why he didn't just give her the words, didn't agree that it had been a mistake. Because she was correct. It had been a mistake of epic proportions.

But the words wouldn't come, so the silence lingered too long.

In the end, she broke first.

"We're adults and we've been playing the game for a long time," she continued, "so it's not like we're new to one-night stands. We'd both had a bad evening, and we reached out to each other. It was just sex, so no harm done."

"No harm," he repeated, perfectly aware those words didn't fit the situation.

"But for the sake of our working relationship," Liza forged

on, her eyes slowly drifting downward until she was staring resolutely at his tie, "it would be best if we put that night behind us. Forget it ever happened. Actually, it looks like you already have."

She was saying exactly what he'd been practicing, and he should be grateful for that, for her willingness to put that night in the rearview mirror and return to the status quo. He should take her words at face value and move on.

But he couldn't. Because for the first time since his and Liza's worlds collided, she wasn't holding his gaze.

"*Can* you forget it?" he asked.

She nodded instantly, not bothering to look at him.

Matt stepped closer and pushed her chin up with a knuckle, until she had no choice but to look him in the eye. The position left them standing too close to each other, her upturned face with those full lips right there.

"Don't lie," he warned, his voice stern. Fuck him if Liza didn't respond to it.

Their proximity allowed him to see the way her mouth parted; the rapid blinks meant to shield her aroused reaction until she could school her features again.

She took a deep breath and then—because Liza was fearless—she gave him what he couldn't give her.

Honesty.

"I don't regret that night, Matt, and I don't want to forget it. You opened my eyes to things I've never allowed myself to acknowledge, and while it was somewhat terrifying, it was also exciting."

Matt hadn't recognized her submissiveness until that night. However, he found himself too hung up on the idea that she found it exciting. Did that mean she intended to expand on it? To seek out lovers who would give her what she wanted sexually?

Matt felt like burning the whole world down as the image of Liza exploring her newfound sexual desires with any man who wasn't him flashed behind his eyes. The possessiveness that coursed through him was uncomfortable. He'd never felt a drop of jealousy in his life, but he was desperate to close the distance between them, to lay claim to her lips, her body...to her. All of her.

"I don't regret what we shared either." She'd opened up to him, given him a glimpse of her feelings, so he owed her that much. "But—"

She laughed, though it wasn't a joyful sound. "There's always a but, isn't there?"

"I'm afraid so." His next words would be some of the hardest he'd ever spoken. "But—"

She cut him off again. "But you're back with Patricia, so it can't happen again." Leave it to Liza to rip off the Band-Aid.

He wasn't sure he heard or imagined the slight inflection at the end of her sentence that made it sound like she was asking rather than telling him.

"It won't happen again." Matt steeled himself to hold steady, refusing to let her see just how much those four words killed him to say. He closed his hands into fists, resisting the urge to pull her into his arms, to kiss her again.

Because damn if he didn't want those soulful, expressive, beautiful brown eyes in his life...for the *rest* of his life.

Liza licked her lower lip, but he couldn't tell if it was an invitation or a show of nerves.

It didn't matter because now that he was looking at her lips, the devil on his shoulder prodded at him, telling him to claim another kiss.

Just one more.

He'd almost convinced himself he could do it. Could kiss her one last time and then let her go. He unclenched his hands, ready to reach for her, but in the end, Liza proved herself to be the stronger person.

She gave him a sad smile, stepped back, and then walked to the door. Opening it, she glanced back at him over her shoulder.

"Goodbye, Matt."

The door was closed behind her before he could manage to whisper the words, "Goodbye, Liza."

Matt wasn't sure how long he stood there, staring at the closed door, but when his cellphone rang, he jerked, startled by the sudden noise in his too-quiet office.

He walked to his desk, intent on sending the call to voicemail. Then he read the screen and before he could think better of it, he answered.

"Devonte wants to know when you're coming back."

"Hello to you too," Matt joked, chuckling at Arnold's greeting. He turned to look out the window of his sixteenth-floor office, grateful for this distraction.

Arnold Jackson was a tenacious son of a bitch, something Matt typically found annoying as hell. However, for some unknown reason, Arnold's phone calls didn't fall into that category. In fact, Matt enjoyed speaking to the older man.

Matt didn't have a lot of friends. Unless he counted his brothers. And his old college roommate, John Kelly, who refused to say die on the friendship. Of course, all John managed was to drag Matt out for lunch once every two or three months. None of those relationships were close enough that he felt comfortable sharing confidences.

That was something he hadn't done in a very long time. One of the first lessons Dad ever taught Matt was to trust no one. *"Everyone's looking for a weakness, Matt. Don't reveal any and they'll never be able to hurt you."* Dante Russo had been a regular Dr. Spock.

However, his gut told him that should he ever want to confide in someone, Arnold was the type of friend he *could* trust, one who might even understand him.

Arnold didn't back down. "So?"

"Dammit, Arnold. I was just there two days ago. I'm not in any hurry to have those kids wipe the floor with me again."

Since his initial visit to the Promise House just before the holidays, Matt had returned almost a dozen times more, dropping by two or three days a week. He told himself he was going back because playing basketball with the teens added variety to his fitness routine and was a great cardio workout, but the truth was, he liked going there.

His life for the last fourteen years had consisted of work and home with the occasional social event sprinkled in, and he'd always told himself that was the way he liked things. Uncomplicated. Predictable. Organized.

Lately, it just felt mind-numbingly boring.

The Promise House was anything but dull. The place was raucous noise, nonstop activity, interesting people...things that were missing from his quiet-as-a-tomb penthouse. The Promise House was full of energy and life and laughter, all painfully absent in his day-to-day routine.

And while he couldn't win a basketball game to save his soul, he gave himself a W in another category because he'd managed to restrict his visits to weekdays when he knew Liza wouldn't be there.

He hated just how hard that battle had been. Once, he'd gone so far as to get into his car and drive halfway to the Promise House on a Saturday morning before his brain kicked his libido to the curb and he turned around.

The damn woman consumed his thoughts, and the lack of sleep was leaving him distracted and irritable. Something both his brothers had noticed and pointed out. Conor had suggested he see his doctor for sleeping pills; Gage had told him to loosen up and get laid.

"You almost beat Devonte's team last time," Arnold said, both of them aware that there was a double-digit difference between the teams' final scores. It had been an old-fashioned butt-whooping—there was no other way to describe it. "Devonte said he'll let you have first pick for teams next time."

Matt chuckled, aware that wouldn't help. He and Devonte had somehow been granted eternal dibs on the captain roles whenever he was there, each of them handpicking different teams every time they played. Matt always selected those most likely to be picked last early in his lineup so no one's feelings were hurt. Devonte, competitive from the word go, hadn't quite managed to let empathy overcome his desire to win.

"That's very generous of him," Matt replied sardonically.

Arnold laughed. "Well, if I can't entice you back for another game, how would you feel about going out Friday after work to grab drinks—maybe dinner—with me and Johnnie?"

This was the fourth time Arnold had extended such an offer. Matt had turned him down the first time because he was rusty as hell when it came to making new friends and that was clearly what Arnold was offering. The last two times, he'd gone and had a great time.

"Let me check my calendar." Matt returned to his desk, dropping down to glance at his computer monitor. Friday evening was clear. "Sure. That sounds great. Did you have a place in mind?"

"There's a new little pub that opened just down the street from the Promise House that looks pretty inviting. Feel like checking it out with us?" Arnold asked.

"Absolutely." Matt was warming up to the idea of kicking back in a bar with a couple of guys and a cold beer, something he'd never really done before.

When he was younger, his idea of a good time was sitting in a leather chair at the club, sipping Scotch with his dad and his cronies, all of them plotting world domination like the arrogant assholes they were.

Since then, he'd eschewed a social life, opting for a more solitary existence, and he'd gotten away with it because—thanks to his less than warm and fuzzy personality—there'd been no one offering true friendship. Arnold refused to give up on him and it felt...nice. On top of that, Johnnie and Arnold were an interesting couple and a lot of fun to hang out with.

"Text me the name of the place and I'll meet you there. Five thirty work?" Matt asked.

"Perfect. Johnnie will be thrilled you're joining us. He was quite amused by Devonte's play-by-play recounts of your last game."

"Terrific," Matt grumbled. "So he already knows of my shame."

"You're spending your evenings playing basketball with a bunch of homeless teens. Loser or not, Johnnie's probably your biggest fan these days."

It was a nice compliment, but the words still hit Matt hard. Because he didn't have fans...didn't deserve any.

"We also wanted to talk to you about something," Arnold continued.

"Oh?"

"As you know, we're getting married in Hawaii in a few weeks."

He was aware of the upcoming nuptials. He, Arnold, and Johnnie had chatted at length one night about past trips they'd taken to the islands.

"Johnnie may have talked about nothing else the last time we went out for drinks," Matt joked.

"He's obsessed. I honestly don't know what we'll talk about once this is all over."

"I suspect Johnnie will keep the conversation from lagging for too long."

Arnold chuckled. "You've gotten to know him well. Listen, I know it's late notice, but I'll plant the seed now and then Friday, I'll let Johnnie convince you."

"Convince me of what?"

"We'd like for you to attend our wedding."

Matt didn't have a clue how to respond to that. The invitation was coming out of left field. While he'd been introduced to Arnold years ago, the two of them running into each other occasionally at various social functions, they'd only started hanging out regularly about a month ago.

"Arnold—" he began.

"Don't answer me now. Take some time and think about it.

You and I both know you're a workaholic, so a week away would do you a world of good. We enjoy your company, and we'd love to have you there with us. Besides, Johnnie's family has reserved a hotel ballroom that is ten times bigger than we need, so you'd be helping us fill the space."

Matt's knee-jerk reaction was to refuse because he knew who else was attending. Then he wondered if Liza was the reason he was getting this invite. Had she told Arnold about their night together? He'd gotten the sense the night of the gala that she'd grown quite close to him and his partner...but close enough to share those kinds of confidences?

It didn't matter either way because he and Liza together in Hawaii would be a huge fucking problem.

Matt had spent weeks trying to figure out how to get his life back on track, his head in the game, and whatever other stupid cliches might work in terms of forgetting about Liza.

But after seeing her just now...he knew that was going to be nearly possible.

And that was when it occurred to him...he'd been approaching the entire situation from the wrong angle.

Ever since the night of the gala, he'd been reacting to the situation each time he'd seen her rather than driving the outcome. Matt never played defense, and yet that was the role he'd been taking.

He'd allowed his emotions to blind him to what should have been obvious.

Control had never been a problem for him, and he wasn't sure why that should change now. If he set the parameters and stuck to them, there might just be a way he could have his cake and eat it too.

Now it was time to regain the upper hand, tighten his grip on the reins, turn the tide in his favor, and start employing some new, better cliches.

Matt rubbed his chin, a smile emerging as the answer to his Liza problem became crystal clear.

So instead of refusing Arnold's offer, he said, "I'll think about it."

"Wonderful. We'll see you Friday," Arnold said.

They said their goodbyes and Matt hung up the phone, feeling—for the first time in weeks—like he was in control again.

Chapter Six

L iza limped off the elevator and trudged to her office, cursing everything from the weather to her damp clothing to her messed-up hair. Today had been an utter clusterfuck. One of those days where she would have been smarter to turn off the alarm, burrow under the covers, and sleep the day away.

Unlocking her office door, she walked to her desk and grabbed the laptop she'd forgotten to take with her yesterday. Charles had told her not to pack it because she was going on vacation, but this was the longest she'd been away from work since taking the job as director and she wasn't quite comfortable going cold turkey. She figured she'd just check email every morning and put out any fires that might flare up.

But thanks to her excitement about flying to Hawaii—she'd been looking forward to this trip for months, complete with a countdown since September—she'd said her goodbyes to everyone in the office yesterday and bebopped home without it. She'd considered stopping by on the way to the airport to get it but decided Charles was right about her needing a break, so she figured it was fate telling her to take the whole week off without worrying about work. Besides, she had her phone and could deal with email on that just as easily as the laptop.

This afternoon, fate had given her the middle finger, ensuring she had more than enough time to grab the stupid laptop.

She sniffled, wiping her nose with the back of her hand, determined she wasn't going to cry or throw something or both. God, she really wanted to do both, wanted to pitch the mother of all fucking temper tantrums.

Sliding the strap of the laptop case over her shoulder, she left her office, locking it behind her, trying to ignore the way her knee was screaming at her. Every time she bent it a little bit too much, it started to bleed again. She needed to sit down and clean it up, but she'd decided to stop here before heading back to her apartment. Because once she got there, there was no way the tears weren't going to start flowing, and once they started, she feared they wouldn't stop until tomorrow.

"Liza?"

She turned at the sound of Charles's voice.

"Shouldn't you be on a plane to Hawaii?"

Liza started to reply—but then Matt stepped out of Charles's office.

She hadn't seen him since the day they'd decided the one-night stand and New Year's kiss had been one-offs. Matt had made his choice—though she couldn't for the life of her understand why he would choose Patricia. She'd spent too much time the past three weeks trying to figure it out, and all she could come up with was perhaps he preferred to date rich women so that he wasn't in danger of falling for a gold digger—not that she was one. It was twisted logic, but somehow it was easier to swallow that bitter pill than accept that she'd come in second place after Patricia Eddington.

"Hello, Liza." Matt's gaze slid down, taking in her torn, muddy jeans.

"Hey." She waved somewhat awkwardly, as the laptop case slid off her arm and she almost dropped it.

"Are you okay, Liza?" Charles asked. "Why aren't you on the plane?"

"Because Murphy's Law decided today was my day."

Charles frowned. "Oh dear. What does that mean?"

Maybe someday, many, many years from now, she could find the humor in this situation and get a few laughs out of the story, but today was not that day. "I got a later start than I wanted to, leaving for the airport. My suitcase broke."

The pull bar on her suitcase had broken just as she was on her way out of the apartment, the whole thing sliding out completely, making it utterly useless. She'd considered saying fuck it and dealing with the broken bag, but it had been heavy—she'd over-packed—and too awkward to drag without the handle, so she'd decided to repack everything in a different case, which had taken some time.

"Then I got a flat on the highway."

"Were you able to call someone for help?" Matt asked.

Liza scowled. "Why would I call someone? I'm perfectly capable of changing a tire."

"That could have been dangerous," Matt said, frowning.

She blew off his concerns. "My oldest brother, Bruno, is a mechanic. He's also the one who taught me how to drive. He flat-out refused to put the key to the ignition in my hand until I learned how to change a tire, check the water and oil, and a few other things he insisted I had to know in order to be safe on the road."

Charles smiled, clearly amused. "That's a fine big brother you've got. Every teen should have such a good driving instructor. I must confess, I don't have a clue how to change a tire. It's why I belong to AAA."

"Blasphemy," Liza joked.

Matt wasn't as amused. "Did you get the tire changed?"

She nodded. "Eventually. But one of the nuts was tight as shit and the ground was slick, thanks to the couple inches of snow we got last night." She gestured to her ripped jeans. "I fell trying to loosen it and tore my jeans, skinned my knee."

"Your knee is still dirty, Liza. You need to clean that up." Matt was looking down at her injury.

"Yeah. I will when I get home."

"I'm guessing all of this is leading up to you missing your flight," Charles said.

She tapped her nose. "You got it in one. I got to the airport, checked my bags, but because the universe hates me, the security line was a hundred and fifty miles long. By the time I got through and ran to my gate, I could see the plane backing away from the terminal."

"There wasn't another flight?" Charles asked.

"The next available flight is the same time tomorrow, so I've lost a day in Hawaii *and* my luggage, torn my favorite jeans, I'm flying standby—which means I won't get a wink of sleep all night worrying—and... Screw it." She shrugged. "I'm going home and falling into a bottle of wine. Maybe two. Then I get to try all of this again tomorrow."

Apparently, her tale of woe was boring Matt, who'd pulled his cellphone from his pocket to text.

She shot a dirty look at the top of his head, then turned her attention back to her boss. "I forgot my laptop yesterday, so, since I have plenty of time, I thought I'd swing by and grab it."

Charles shook his head. "I told you not to work. It's a vacation."

She nodded, not bothering to argue. She was too depressed.

Charles placed a comforting hand on her shoulder. "I'm so sorry, Liza. I know how much you were looking forward to this trip. And while I know it sucks now, losing one day isn't so bad. You'll be on that beach drinking cocktails before you know it."

If there was one thing she loved about her boss, it was his optimism. But right now, and for the first time ever, it was grating on her nerves. She wanted to treat herself to the pity party of the century, so the last thing she needed was someone trying to make her feel better.

"Thanks," she muttered. "I'll see you when I get back."

If I ever get there, she silently added.

She was surprised when Matt followed her to the elevator, the doors sliding closed behind them. "Is your meeting over?" she asked.

"Yes. I'm finished for the day. Just needed to confer with Charles on one thing, and now, I'm on my way to the airport."

She gave him a sidelong glance, trying to decide if he was joking. "The airport?"

He nodded. "My driver is downstairs waiting for me. I was wondering if you would like to come with me?"

"To the airport? I told you, the next flight isn't until tomorrow."

"But my private jet is leaving for Hawaii within the next two hours."

"You're going to Hawaii?" If this was a joke, Liza didn't get it.

"I've been invited to the same wedding as you."

"Arnold and Johnnie's?"

There's no way in hell Arnold wouldn't have told her that he'd included Matt on the guest list. Unless...

Oh God. Unless he was playing matchmaker.

"I didn't realize you and Arnold were so close," she mused.

"To be honest, I didn't realize it either. I was surprised when he called to invite me. I'd intended to give my regrets, but Arnold Jackson is the most persuasive man I've ever met. Only surpassed by—"

"Johnnie," she interjected.

"They've invited me out to dinner a few times since New Year's. They're really good company."

Liza was going to have a long heart-to-heart with Arnold when she got to Hawaii because her friend had clearly been holding out on her. Then she pictured Johnnie and Matt having dinner together. "Johnnie must love you," she said with a grin.

Matt narrowed his eyes, catching her drift. "He's a shameless flirt."

"Let me guess, he's trying to convince you to bat for the other team."

Matt sighed. "It would be annoying if it wasn't so damn funny."

Liza had to admit he'd summed up Johnnie perfectly, which meant he really had spent some quality time with the two men.

"Anyway, Arnold wouldn't take no for answer, so here I am. On my way to Hawaii," Matt said.

"Beats the hell out of Philly in mid-February."

"It really does. I'm afraid I'm on a tight timeline because my flight schedule is locked in, so there's no time for you to take your car home." The two of them stepped off the elevator and crossed the foyer to the exit.

Liza blinked a couple of times. "You were serious about me coming with you?"

"Of course I was. Why would you wait an extra day when I can get you there today?"

Part of her thought she should say no. They had agreed to maintain a professional relationship and nothing more. And by they, she meant him. Because she had wanted to expand on the one-night stand.

But Matt had chosen Patricia.

Shit.

Patricia.

There was no way in hell Liza was hopping on a plane for fifteen hours with that woman.

"I don't think it's such a good idea."

Matt tilted his head, clearly surprised she was turning him down. "Why not?"

"To be perfectly honest, I can't spend fifteen minutes with Patricia, let alone fifteen hours."

"Patricia isn't coming."

"Oh." She wasn't sure what to make of that. Patricia didn't seem like the type of woman to turn down a trip to Hawaii.

"Will your car be okay if you leave it here?" It felt like Matt was taking the decision away from her.

"Bruno can come get it," she said. "He was going to replace the spare with a new tire anyway." She'd called her brother right after missing her flight to see if he could do it tonight, as she thought she was going to be making another trip to the airport tomorrow.

"Very good. Is there anything else you need from your car?"

She shook her head. "No, my luggage is already en route, so this is all I have." She lifted her shoulders, gesturing that she was good to go with just her purse and laptop.

"Great." Matt pointed to a large black SUV waiting by the curb. The driver had gotten out and opened the back door.

Liza thanked him, climbing in, as Matt crossed behind the vehicle and took the bucket seat next to her rather than riding shotgun.

The first thing she noticed when the two of them were closed in together in the backseat was the way he smelled. God, she loved the cologne he wore. She'd noticed it the night of the gala when they'd been dancing. There had to be some sort of aphrodisiac mixed in with the scent, pheromones or something, because damn if it didn't get her motor revving.

She was glad she'd tossed her vibrator into her luggage at the last minute. She had considered leaving it at home, but her sex drive had kicked in big-time these days, and now that she knew Matt was going to be walking around the same Hawaiian resort, she was going to need a way to burn off the excess hormones.

Matt pulled out his phone, texting. "Let me confirm with the flight crew, tell them there will be another passenger."

Oh my God.

What the hell was she doing? The reason she'd excelled at maintaining a professional relationship with the man was because she hadn't seen him since that day in his office. To be honest, their paths rarely crossed, so she figured she'd have at least a couple months to get her act together before having to face him again.

Three weeks hadn't been enough time. Nowhere near enough.

She still spent practically every waking hour thinking about him, lusting over him. This flight—hell, this whole week—was going to test her, tempt her.

Matt tucked his phone away. "All good. I assume you got a room in the hotel Arnold suggested."

"Yes. You?"

"I was fortunate to be able to reserve an oceanfront suite, considering it was such short notice."

She snorted. "Of course you got a suite."

Matt's smile was smug. "When I travel, I like to do it right."

"Well, I don't do it wrong," she countered. "I just do it on a budget. Since private planes and fancy suites are out of my price range, I'm forced to fly economy and make do with a plain old hotel room."

Matt pretended to shudder. "Economy?"

She smacked his shoulder. "Snob," she teased. "Oh shit, let me text Bruno really quick about the car." She grabbed her phone from her purse, firing off a text to her big brother, asking if he could tow her car back to his garage.

Her brother's response was immediate.

Get an earlier flight?

Yes

She skipped over the finer details, like she was going on a private plane with Matt Russo. Because that information would go over like a lead balloon.

I'll take care of the car. Safe flight.

She loved her big brother. He always had her back. She sent back a heart emoji and put her phone away.

"All taken care of?" Matt asked.

Liza nodded.

The rest of the trip to the airport was made in silence as Liza gave herself the mother of all pep talks, reminding herself that Matt was dating a woman she found abhorrent, that he was uninterested in pursuing anything with her, and that—goddammit—she was a professional. Or, at least, she was playing one on TV.

Because her thoughts of Matt were anything *but* professional as she snuck a glance at him. It was hard to keep her attraction to him under control now that she knew what he looked like underneath his bespoke Tom Ford suit. That knowledge was hell on her libido.

Forcing herself to stop looking at the pretty man, she realized they weren't headed to Philadelphia International.

"Where are we going?"

"Northeast Philadelphia. That's where my jet is."

Jesus. She couldn't imagine how much it must cost to own and park a private jet.

When they arrived at the airport, the SUV drove right onto the tarmac, coming to a stop next to a jet. It was larger than she'd imagined. Liza had done a bit of traveling when she was in her early twenties, though she hadn't lied to Matt about being on a budget. Her destinations were typically a lot less exotic than Hawaii and much closer to home. As such, she was no stranger to puddle jumpers, the small planes airlines used for their shorter flights.

Matt's jet was bigger than those planes.

"Overcompensating much?" She decided the only way to get through this trip was to keep her sense of humor firmly intact.

Matt reached over, his hand cupping the back of her neck, tugging her toward him. She forgot how to breathe when his lips brushed against her ear.

"We both know I'm not."

He released her, and Liza felt herself weaving a bit, suddenly light-headed. This was not going to end well.

The driver opened the door for her, and it took her a moment to steady herself enough to climb out. She wondered what the chauffeur must think of her, with her lack of luggage and ripped, dirty jeans. A big chunk of hair had escaped her ponytail holder, a chilly breeze blowing it into her face. She'd broken a sweat hauling ass across the airport earlier, trying to catch her plane, so she knew she looked like a hot mess right now. Probably nothing like Matt's typical parade of wealthy, elegant arm candy.

"Thank you," Matt said, when the driver retrieved his luggage from the back of the SUV. Matt took the suitcase from him, then tilted his head toward the plane. "Your carriage awaits."

"Do carriages usually fly?"

"This one does."

She snickered then walked to the plane, climbing the stairs that had been wheeled to the open door.

Liza had only taken a few steps inside when she stopped in her tracks. "Holy fuck."

Forced to pull up short, Matt stopped right behind her. His hand touched her lower back. "Liza. Are you okay?"

"*This* is your plane?"

He followed her gaze, and she could tell he didn't seem to understand her question. "It's just a plane."

"Jesus, Matt. I don't know when you last flew commercial, but this is not just a plane. This looks like something from a James Bond movie. It's gorgeous, luxurious. Bigger than my apartment."

Matt chuckled, then gave her a gentle push down the aisle. The flight attendant stepped out of an alcove at the front of the plane, taking Matt's suitcase from him.

"Shall I put this in the bedroom?" the woman asked.

"That would be fine," Matt replied.

The attendant glanced to see if Liza had anything that needed to be stowed as well. "Do you have anything you'd like me to put in the room for you?"

Liza shook her head. "No, thank you."

The flight attendant walked away.

"There's a bedroom?" Liza murmured, glancing at Matt, who was amused by her reaction to his bougie-as-fuck private jet.

Matt led her to an oversized seat, and she slipped her laptop case off her shoulder, placing it on a side table. Then she pulled her cross-body bag off, putting it on the floor before sitting down. Matt took off his suit jacket, draping it over the back of a nearby chair, then claimed the seat across from her.

"Dinner will be served about an hour after takeoff." He loosened his tie. "Where do you stand on red meat? Because I'd arranged for filet mignon before I realized I'd have a guest."

"I love steak." Liza recalled the snacks she'd packed for her "dinner" on the flight she'd missed. She wasn't going to have a problem pitching the ham and cheese sandwich she'd made before leaving home. "It sounds wonderful."

"The jet can't fly directly to Honolulu, so we're stopping in Denver to refuel before continuing on. That'll take about an hour."

"Okay."

"Then we'll be on our way to the islands. We should, if all goes according to plan, land in Hawaii at three a.m. their time. I realize that is less than ideal, but I had several meetings scheduled for today and I couldn't leave any sooner."

"Lucky for me. My original flight had me getting in around eleven p.m., so being four hours late versus twenty-four hours is a gift. Matt, I really appreciate you letting me hop on board."

"You're helping me reduce my carbon footprint," he said, winking shamelessly.

"Damn, I wish you hadn't pointed that out because I'm not reducing it enough," she chastised.

Matt acted as if she hadn't spoken. "I've arranged for a car to pick us up when we land and drive us to the hotel."

The flight attendant returned from the bedroom. "Can I offer you anything to drink while we wait?"

Liza started to take her up on the offer, dying for a glass of wine, but Matt shook his head. "Not at the moment."

The woman walked back to the front of the plane, disappearing from view.

"I could have gone for a glass of wine." She was sort of annoyed that he'd spoken for both of them.

"And you can have some. Later." Matt rose, offering her a hand to help her up as well. "First, I need you to come with me."

"Where are we going?"

Matt kept hold of her hand, leading her down the wide aisle until they stood at what she assumed was the bedroom door. It was where the flight attendant had taken Matt's luggage.

He was acting different today, more at ease, almost playful, if that was something he was capable of, and she wondered what had changed.

Maybe he felt more comfortable with her now that they'd established sex was off the table. Or maybe—God, she hated to think this—he was genuinely happy with Patricia, and she was hanging out with a man in love.

Ugh. That thought made her want to vomit.

Before she could come up with another, less puke-inducing idea, Matt opened the door and pulled her inside the bedroom.

Liza's curiosity overrode the part of her brain screaming at her to turn around and go back to the main cabin of the plane. Because the last place she should be with Matt was a bedroom.

Instead, she surveyed the room, amazed by the sheer luxurious elegance. She didn't know who Matt's interior decorator was, but they had great taste.

"Wow," Liza whispered, taking in the king-size bed with an ornate mahogany headboard, the matching nightstands and dresser, the soft lighting, and the large-screen TV hanging opposite the bed that was one of the kinds that looked like artwork when turned off. The bed was adorned with a fluffy white duvet and at least a half dozen deep blue throw pillows. "This room is incredible."

"Glad you approve." With a hand on her lower back, Matt moved her farther into the room, before stepping in front of her and pointing to her ripped jeans.

"Now... Take off your pants."

Chapter Seven

The scowl Liza shot Matt amused him.

"Excuse me?" she asked haughtily.

Matt ignored her shocked outrage as he crossed to the bathroom, where he wet a washcloth with warm water before reaching beneath the sink to grab the first aid kit.

Liza was still standing next to the bed—in her jeans—when he returned, her hands on her hips. "Listen, Matt—" she started, but he cut her off.

"Your jeans are still on, Liza," he said impatiently. From her flushed cheeks, he knew exactly how she was interpreting his request. Clearly, she hadn't seen the kit in his hands, or if she had, she hadn't managed to register his intent.

"And they're staying that way. While I appreciate you offering to help me get to Hawaii, there's no way—"

Matt held up the first aid kit. "Your knee is dirty. I can see bits of gravel in it from here. We need to clean it before it gets infected."

"Oh." She quickly shut her mouth, flushing slightly now that she realized he wasn't propositioning her.

Or at least, he let her think he wasn't.

She held out her hands for the kit and washcloth. "I can clean it."

Matt held them away from her. "You had plenty of opportunities to do this yourself and you failed to take any of them. So now, I'm doing it."

He'd been annoyed at the Initiative offices when she'd explained her injury. He'd nearly lost his shit at the thought of her changing a tire on the side of the highway. She could have been struck by a car, could have been killed. Then she'd ignored her injured knee, bypassing God only knew how many restrooms at the airport. And while he understood she'd been trying to catch a flight initially, that didn't account for the ones she'd passed on the way out of the airport after she'd missed it.

Liza hadn't done a very good job taking care of herself today, so he was taking over.

"Matt," she said again, this time quieter, perhaps a bit uncertain.

"There's no need to be shy. There's nothing under those jeans I haven't seen before. Up close and personal."

His words struck the way he expected, Liza's temper flaring. He didn't have a clue what it said about him but seeing her outraged like this had his dick growing hard. Those brown eyes of hers—flashing fire—were a serious turn-on.

"And there's nothing under these jeans you'll ever see again," she insisted, her voice loud. "We're going for professionalism, remember?"

He fought not to grin as she threw that back in his face. She obviously didn't like the way they'd ended things last time. Good. That would only make it easier for him when he told her that ship had sailed.

Matt placed the washcloth and first aid kit on the dresser, stepping in front of her. "You can take them off yourself, or I can do it for you. Choose. Now."

Her anger wavered in the face of his threat...just as he expected. Because he had come to learn there was a hierarchy when it came to Liza's emotions. Anger fell just a little lower on the list...right under her desire to submit.

Matt spent the past three weeks considering this trip to Hawaii and how he planned to change the rules. He'd allowed himself to get mired in dark thoughts in the month following the Snowflake Gala, and it had left him acting out of character, forgetting who he was at heart. He'd let his grip slip, convincing himself that the best way forward was to keep Liza out of the picture.

That had been a fool's errand because his attraction to her had burrowed deep under his skin.

So it was time to revert back to the man he was deep down inside. In all things, business and personal, Matt was always in control.

He was a Russo, for God's sake. He'd been raised to take what he wanted and offer no apologies for it.

He wasn't the type of man who denied himself pleasure. Why would he? He could afford the best—private jets, luxurious suites, expensive wine and food—so denying himself Liza had gone against every single instinct he possessed.

The second he'd realized that, his eyes had been opened, and he'd decided that he didn't have to push Liza away. He just had to control the situation. Set parameters. Find a way to make sure they kept emotions out of it.

"Liza." He reached out, intent on ripping the dirty denim off her with his bare hands.

"Fine," Liza replied hastily, through gritted teeth, as she put a few feet between them. She backed up toward the bed and unfastened her jeans. The confidence she'd revealed the night of the gala returned full force as she kept her chin up, toeing off her flats, then taking off her jeans.

Matt didn't bother to pretend he wasn't looking.

She smirked.

"Take a good long look because this is the last time you're going to see this particular view."

He was tempted to fuck that snarky tone right out of her—with his dick in her mouth.

She wore a T-shirt with a thick cardigan on top. The cardigan did a good job. Too good. Covering her from mid-thigh and up. He considered telling her to lose the sweater too, but they weren't there yet. He needed to lay his cards on the table. If he was lucky, she'd go along with his ground rules. If he wasn't, he'd seduce the hell out of her until she agreed.

Matt gestured toward the mattress, inviting her to sit down. He didn't miss the slight wince when she bent her injured knee, and his temper piqued again.

"You were reckless today."

She rolled her eyes. "I changed a tire and scraped my knee. I'm really living life on the edge."

Matt held his tongue. If she were his, he'd have a hell of a lot more to say about her changing a tire on the side of a busy highway. And he wouldn't just say it. He'd back his opinion up with a spanking that would remind her to take care with what belonged to him.

Fuck. Matt pushed that thought away because she wasn't his. Couldn't be his. Not truly.

Grabbing the first aid kit and washcloth, he knelt on the floor in front of her. Her soft intake of breath told him she was recalling the same thing he was. How he'd knelt in front of her the night of the gala, lifted one knee—the now-injured one—over his shoulder and driven her to her first orgasm with his tongue.

Neither of them spoke as he gently cleaned the cut, blowing on it to alleviate any sting. Then he put antibiotic cream on a large Band-Aid and covered the scrape. Leaning back on his haunches, he looked up, wondering at the amusement tugging at the tips of her lips.

"No kiss to make it better?" she teased.

She was good at issuing dares he couldn't resist. Matt leaned forward to give her knee a soft kiss.

Liza jerked in surprise, not expecting him to take her up on her offer. He'd seen that same shock in her eyes when he'd responded to her comment about him overcompensating in the SUV.

"Thanks," she said, her brows lowered in confusion. She was struggling to keep up, which made sense. After all, the last time they talked, he'd made that dumbass comment about keeping their relationship professional. He'd also allowed her to continue to believe he was dating Patricia. His actions today were in direct opposition to all of that.

"You're welcome."

Time to pull back on the flirting until they had time to discuss where the two of them were going from here.

Liza reached down to retrieve her jeans from the floor, but he picked them up before she could, tossing them onto a chair in the corner of the room.

"Stay there," he said, rising and walking over to the dresser. "I keep sleepwear on the plane." Opening the drawer, he pulled out a pair of lounge pants. "These might be a bit big, but they have a drawstring, so you should be able to keep them up with no problem."

He handed the pants to Liza, who thanked him. While she put the lounge pants on, Matt opened his suitcase, pulling out a pair of jeans and a T-shirt. "Give me a moment to change into something more comfortable and then we can go back to the main cabin. We should be taking off very soon."

He changed in the bathroom, and when he stepped back into the bedroom, he discovered Liza already gone, so he returned to the main cabin, claiming the seat opposite her once more. She'd managed to snag her glass of wine. Matt requested the same, each of them sipping their merlot.

The flight attendant informed them they were about to take off. Buckling their seat belts, they gazed out the window as the jet taxied to the runway. Silence had fallen between them, but it wasn't awkward. He'd spent too many evenings with women who felt as if they had to fill every moment with conversation, Patricia the worst offender of them all. Liza was the first woman he'd ever spent time with who appreciated the value of quiet companionship.

Once they reached their cruising altitude, the flight attendant refilled their wine glasses, then prepared the cabin for dinner. Liza watched the setup with interest—and a bit of awe—grinning at the ostentatiousness of it all.

"A tablecloth and real crystal goblets?" she murmured softly when the attendant returned to the kitchen area.

Matt smirked but said nothing in reply.

Once the table was set, they moved across the aisle to claim their seats, carrying their wine glasses with them. Placing napkins on their laps, they both thanked the flight attendant as she served the salad course.

"Can I ask you something?" Liza started.

"Of course."

"Why isn't Patricia your date for the wedding?"

That hadn't taken long. He'd intended to bring up the subject himself because he couldn't move forward with his plans for Liza as long as she believed he was dating the other woman.

"Contrary to what the tabloids say, Patricia and I are no longer dating. You know that, because you saw me break things off in the lobby of the Ritz."

"Yet you were out with her the next night. You gave her the diamond tennis bracelet."

"A parting gift. Nothing more. I do a lot of business with her father. I thought it best to clear the air between us so that my association with Richard Eddington wasn't awkward."

Liza wasn't convinced. "Why was she in your office if you were still broken up?"

"Patricia is of the opinion that the two of us should get married." Matt decided full disclosure was in his best interest when it came to Liza.

"She's in love with you?"

Of course that was where Liza's thoughts would go. In the

world the Morettis inhabited, two things were certain—and it wasn't Benjamin Franklin's death and taxes. It was love and marriage.

"Not at all," he said.

Liza frowned. "I don't understand. Why marry someone you don't love?"

"I should think that would be obvious. Money."

Liza snorted—until she realized he was serious. "Because the two of you don't have enough already?"

"People like Patricia will never have enough."

"What about you?" Liza asked.

"I have plenty."

"So you're not going to marry her?"

Matt shook his head, grateful for this opening. If they were going to continue forward in the manner Matt hoped, Liza needed to understand one very vital thing about him. "No. I'm not marrying her. I'm not marrying anyone. *Ever*," he stressed.

Liza paused, and he sensed she was trying to let that sink in. "Gage told us that already. When Penny mentioned she was worried about you marrying Patricia."

"Penny was worried?" Matt hadn't realized that stupid online article had made the rounds as far as it had.

"She wasn't looking forward to spending holidays and family outings with Queen of the Mean Girls."

"I didn't know she'd seen the article. I would have put her fears to rest immediately."

"Gage handled that for you. Said you were married to your work."

Matt lifted one shoulder casually. "I'm not sure I would say it exactly that way. Work is work. Marriage is...something for other people. Something I have no interest in."

"Why not?"

He knew Liza, knew she'd keep pushing until she got the answers to all her questions. She was destined for disappointment because there were parts of himself he'd vowed never to share.

And while he could make up some lie about enjoying his bachelorhood, or employ the billionaire concerns about gold diggers and huge divorce settlements, he preferred to give her the same honesty she kept offering to him.

"I have reasons, Liza, but they're personal." It was as much as he could give her.

Liza leaned back and took another sip of her wine. The flight attendant served the rest of their dinner and refilled their glasses.

Rather than let Liza push for more once they were alone again, he cut her off at the pass because he needed to be certain of her single state as well. "Who was the man you were dancing with on New Year's Eve?"

Her confusion appeased that unwanted jealous side of him because it was obvious she didn't have a clue who he was talking about. Then the light went on. "Oh! You mean Miles? He's Joey's cohost on *ManPower*."

"Is that a thing?"

"No. He's a nice guy, but we were just dancing. I'm not dating anyone at the moment. You saw my last attempt crash and burn."

She was referring to Davis Taylor, her date for the Snowflake Gala. The man had overplayed his hand that night, revealing not only his chauvinistic side but his overly ambitious one as well.

They ate quietly for a little while, and when Liza began speaking again, he realized she was still thinking about their conversation. "While you're clinging to your swinging-single card, I'm trading mine in someday because I definitely want to get married."

"Why?" he asked, lobbing her question back at her.

"Personal reasons," she said with a shit-eating grin.

Matt lifted his wine glass, a silent touché to her smart-assery.

Then she answered anyway. "I've spent the last ten years as a single woman, living and eating alone, and I hate it. I want what my parents and grandparents have—companionship, love, and a big family."

"A big family," he said, not bothering to hide his disdain. "Why is it you Morettis feel compelled to pack every house with a hundred bodies?"

Liza laughed. "Gage filled you in on Christmas Eve, I see."

"He did."

"Did he tell you how much he loved it?"

Matt lifted one shoulder noncommittally, though the truth was Gage had spent the better part of an hour describing the Moretti holiday as if it was Mardi Gras, Rio Carnival, and Times Square on New Year's Eve all rolled into one.

"You know what your problem is, Mr. Russo?" she asked in a teasing tone. "You wouldn't know a good time if it bit you on the ass."

Matt reached across the table, grasping Liza's hand, pulling it until she was bent over the table. Kissing the back of her hand, he stroked the soft skin with his tongue, giving her one brief lick that had her expression morphing from playful to outright lust. "That's not true. I had a good time the night of the gala."

Liza's eyes widened for a split second before she offered him another taste of that open honesty. "I did too," she murmured. "It was one of the best nights of my life."

Her words warmed him in ways he couldn't begin to understand. "You said you discovered something about yourself."

She nodded. "You know I did. You were there."

"You're right. I *was* there," he admitted. "And I could be there again." This was how Matt intended to entice her back into his bed. While he couldn't give her marriage or kids or forever, there was something else she wanted...perhaps just as much.

"But—"

"I was wrong to dismiss what we shared out of hand. While I'm not interested in an emotional relationship, I am *very* attracted to you, Liza. I can't offer you love and marriage, but exploring our sexual desires, expanding on our similar needs, is no longer off the table."

She closed her mouth, rather than reply, but he could see his words sinking in.

Before they could continue the conversation, the flight attendant approached, offering coffee and dessert. Liza accepted both, though he wasn't sure if she really wanted them or just needed more time to wrap her head around what he'd proposed.

Once they were alone again, she took a deep breath, and he could read the rejection in her eyes. He had a pretty good idea about why she was hesitant. After all, she'd just told him point-blank she wanted a relationship, but he hoped to convince her to set that aside for a little while. He wasn't taking no for an answer.

"Matt—" she started.

He shook his head. "No, Liza. Don't answer me tonight. Take some time to think about it."

"Okay."

"Would you like to watch a movie?" he asked, letting her off the hook.

For now.

"A movie would be great."

They stood from the table, Matt leading her to the couch. Lowering the blinds, the two of them chose a movie, some action-adventure film he'd already seen. Liza attempted to maintain a polite distance from him, but the time for that had passed.

He reached out, tugging her against him, his arm draped over her shoulders. He was pleased when she sank into the embrace rather than seek to move away. Neither of them spoke during the movie, though Matt was certain she wasn't paying any more attention to it than he was. They'd paused it briefly to return to their seats when they landed in Denver. Once on the ground, they pushed play again, and it ended just as they were about to take off, the plane now refueled and ready for the longer leg of the journey.

Once they were back in the air, Matt unfastened his seat belt. "You can take the bed," he said, reaching down to help Liza stand. "I'll sleep out here. These seats recline."

Liza shook her head. "No. I'm not stealing your bed. I was

planning to sleep sitting up in the economy section anyway. The lovely recliner is already a huge step up."

Matt placed his hand on her lower back, propelling her toward the bedroom. "I'm not going to argue about it. You're taking the bed."

He purposely lowered his voice, aware of the way she responded whenever he used *that* tone.

Liza sighed, allowing him to push her forward. She opened the door, and he followed her in.

"Let me just change out of these jeans and into a pair of lounge pants." He walked over to his suitcase, rummaging around as Liza sank down on the edge of the mattress.

"If you want," she started, glancing back at the large bed. "We could share the bed. Platonically," she hastened to add.

Matt turned to face her, thrilled by the invite. She might not be ready to accept his offer yet, but she was definitely weakening.

"Okay."

He walked to the opposite side of the bed, not bothering with loungewear at all. Instead, he stripped off his jeans, left his T-shirt and boxers on, then crawled beneath the duvet.

Liza remained where she was, staring at him until he rolled over to face her.

"Get in bed, Liza. I don't intend to say this to you very often, but for tonight, I will be a perfect gentleman."

She huffed out a breathy laugh, then climbed into the bed next to him.

For the first time in over a month, the world felt right.

Matt didn't know what to do with that feeling, so instead he shut it down, ignored it, and turned off the light.

Chapter Eight

"What the—" Liza jerked awake, sitting up in the unfamiliar bed. It took her a moment to remember where she was, and when the plane shook again, she understood what had woken her up.

"Liza," a gruff voice said in the darkness. "You okay?"

Matt. She was in bed with Matt.

Again.

It spoke to just how screwed up her day was that she'd climbed into bed with the man who had essentially trashed her sleep for the past two months and *fell asleep*. Granted, she'd slept like extra shit the night before because she'd been too damn excited about the wedding and the trip, her mind whirling as she mentally checked off her "do I have everything?" list, making sure she'd packed what she needed.

When she combined those three hours of restless sleep with the nonstop highs and lows that followed, she could almost understand how she'd closed her eyes and fallen asleep within minutes.

Almost.

"I didn't mean to wake you up. It was the—" The plane shook again. "Shit."

Matt sat up and turned on the bedside lamp. "It's just turbulence."

"Should we go back to the main cabin and buckle up?"

"Let me call the pilot, see if that's necessary." Matt picked up the receiver on an intercom-style phone next to the bed that Liza hadn't noticed before. "Jack," he said, pausing to listen. "I see," he said in response to something Liza couldn't hear. "Sounds good."

Matt hung up the phone. "We've hit a pocket of weather," he explained to her. "So we're probably looking at a half an hour of turbulence. Jack, the pilot, doesn't think it'll get rough enough that we need to return to our seats, but he'll call if that changes."

"Oh. Okay." She picked up her smart watch and glanced at the time. She'd managed to grab a two-hour catnap. Just enough to help her find her second wind.

Which meant the fog had lifted from her brain enough that everything Matt had said over dinner was finally sinking in. A few weeks ago, he'd been preaching professionalism, telling her they couldn't expand on that one-night stand.

Tonight, he made it very clear he'd changed his mind.

"Damn," she muttered as the plane shook again, flattening her hands against the mattress to steady herself. Liza fought to school her expression because, while she hated turbulence, she hated appearing weak more. She pasted on a fake smile. "Bit like a ride at an amusement park."

Matt reached out, brushing her hair over one shoulder before gripping the back of her neck, giving her a too-brief kiss on the forehead. It was a simple enough touch, but the way Matt did it, it screamed of possession. Instead of pissing her off, which felt like the normal response, it turned her on.

"Lay down," he said, releasing her.

She did as he asked, settling on her back until he shook his head.

"Turn away from me," he commanded.

"Why?"

Matt lifted one brow. "Because I told you to."

Normal, everyday Liza would cut someone down to size for that comment, but instead she had to squeeze her legs together, trying to ignore the way her panties were suddenly damp.

She turned her back to him, facing the side wall, startling when Matt's arm snuck around her waist so that he could spoon her.

"Are you doing an impersonation of a seat belt?" she teased, loving the pure strength in his arm. Matt was well-built, muscular, powerful. And that power didn't just end in the physical realm. It was as if it was woven into every fiber of his being.

"Yes. Unless you prefer I tie your hands to the headboard."

Dammit, Matt had countered every single one of her jokes today with those steamy innuendoes that sent her mind straight to the gutter.

She was just about to take him up on his offer of bondage, but he spoke first.

"Go to sleep, Liza."

She sighed, grateful he couldn't see her face. It would give her time to wipe the pout off it without him noticing.

Matt's grip tightened around her; their bodies connected from shoulders to feet as he molded his position to match hers, right down to her bent knees. It was hard to ignore the fact her ass was perfectly cupped by his crotch and upper thighs. It was equally hard to ignore his very erect cock nestled beneath his boxer briefs.

Sleep was not going to come easily again.

She didn't want it to.

Matt was interested in expanding on their sexual experiences. Practicality suggested that she take the time he was offering and think about what she wanted from an affair with Matt.

Marriage and love were off the table, and in a lot of ways, that made Liza's decision much simpler. The two of them shared a physical chemistry, one so strong she thought she'd go mad from it. If they limited this thing between them to just sex...it would make things easier.

No messy emotions. No feuding relatives. No past to hash out.

Liza had pretty much dated every single man between the ages of twenty and forty over the past decade, so she had enough data to know that if she wanted to explore this newly discovered submissive side, Matt was her best option. Maybe her only option because no other lover had made her feel this way before.

She was terrified that if she didn't take this chance, she wouldn't get another.

Matt's arm was slack around her, and she wondered if he'd already fallen back to sleep. She hoped not because…well, she'd already made up her mind.

She wiggled her ass against his crotch, rubbing against the obvious bulge.

"Hold still," his deep voice murmured in her ear.

She didn't reply. Just wiggled again.

"Liza," Matt warned.

She glanced over her shoulder, feigning innocence. "What?"

"You're playing with fire."

She didn't reply. Instead, she grinned as she pushed her ass harder against his erection before doing another little shimmy.

Matt lifted the hand wrapped around her waist to her throat, loosely cupping the front of it, shifting until his lips were right next to her ear. "Bad girls get punished."

She laughed softly. "What do good girls get?"

"Doesn't matter. Because you're not a good girl."

They'd discussed her name being on the naughty list before the holidays. She gave him a wink, her smile pure wickedness when she said, "Good girls are boring." She backed that pronouncement up with one more bold shake of her ass.

Matt reacted quickly, pushing her to her stomach, his lips still by her ear. "Your safe word is red."

With that, his body left hers, his hands gripping her waist, tugging her to her hands and knees.

She sucked in a harsh breath at the sting of the sudden weight on her cut knee.

"Shit," Matt said, releasing her. "Your knee."

"It's fine." She'd been touched by his concern earlier, more than she cared to admit. While she was an independent woman, perfectly capable of changing a tire and cleaning up a cut, it had been a long time since someone had taken care of her. It felt good, even if it did drive home just how lonely she was.

Regardless of her reassurance, she could tell he intended to pull back, so she took the decision away from him. Taunting him with a seductive smile, she shook her ass one last time. "Punish me. Now," she whispered.

Matt's eyes narrowed briefly, and she immediately recognized her mistake. She'd spent her entire adult life having to ask for what she wanted in the bedroom.

Well, not exactly *asking*.

Liza made demands, like the one she'd just issued to him. Her past lovers had always followed her lead, most of them needing her guidance. Dominance and self-assurance in the bedroom were seriously lacking in her generation of the male species. Gen X parents had a lot to answer for.

Matt possessed an abundance of both, so he made her pay for her demand...by making her wait.

He slowly slid her pants and panties halfway down her thighs, not taking them completely off. The elastic of the panties as well as the drawstring made it difficult for her to part her legs. Not that she was trying. Just the opposite. She needed friction, so she squeezed her legs together, squirming to appease the pulsing need.

Matt placed his hand on her ass firmly. "Hold still."

She started to shake her head, but some instinct she'd never acknowledged stopped her, telling her this would all go easier if she just obeyed. She hated that word in ninety-nine out of a hundred scenarios. This was the one exception.

"Please," she begged.

Matt stroked her ass, his touch so light it almost tickled. "I like it when you beg."

"Matt." Mercifully, his name came out on a huff of breath that masked the whine inside it. "Please."

He didn't reply, just kept caressing her ass, his fingers dipping lower, to the backs of her thighs. The one place he didn't touch her was where she needed it most. She tried to part her legs on the downswing of his fingers, but all that got her was his palm cupping one ass cheek, squeezing it in warning.

Liza lowered her head, her forehead resting on the fluffy pillow beneath her. She tried to hold steady, but all the party places below her waist were throbbing.

"Ple—"

Her plea was cut off when Matt lifted his hand and brought it down on her ass.

Hard.

She gasped, her hands clenching into fists as she tried to adjust to the pain.

Not that Matt was giving her much time. Or any.

He lifted his hand again. And again. And—*God*, ten more times. His hand smacked every inch of her ass and upper thighs. The initial stings hurt enough that she almost said the safe word, but just when she thought she couldn't take another slap, her arousal kicked in.

Electricity shimmered and pulsed through every nerve ending, and her pussy clenched with a painful need.

Matt stroked the skin he'd just spanked, then cupped her ass again, squeezing harder, igniting a different kind of burn. This one sunk deep, struck gold.

Liza's back arched, silently begging for mercy, for more.

She blew out a long breath when his fingers slid along her slit. She fought against the pants and panties that prevented her from spreading her thighs wide. She wanted to be open to him completely, wanted him to find all those places now screaming for his touch.

Matt slid two fingers through her wet heat, starting at her clit —which needed so much more attention than the brief stroke— before sliding over her opening and back to her ass.

"Are you going to be good?" he asked.

Liza was still pressed down on the pillow, but she didn't need to lift her head to respond. She shook it. "No."

He chuckled darkly. "Correct answer." He drove two fingers inside her pussy.

Liza gasped, especially when she realized she was already on the verge of coming. There was no way. This was too fast.

Her back arched, her entire body caving in on itself as the orgasm struck with the force of a two-ton truck.

"God! Matt!"

He finger fucked her all the way through the orgasm, not letting up until the last vestiges of it faded away.

Then he pulled them out, gripped her waist, and flipped her to her back.

"I'm going to fuck you hard," he growled. "But I don't want to hurt your knee." As he spoke, he dragged her pants and panties off, tossing them to the floor before tugging his T-shirt over his head.

"Take that shirt off," he demanded, looking at her top like it was an affront to mankind.

She sat up to strip it and her bra off before flopping back down as he stood briefly, adding his boxers to the pile of clothes on the floor by the bed.

Crawling back onto the mattress, he shoved her legs apart, his gaze taking in her naked body. He stroked a single fingertip down the center of her chest, starting at the base of her throat, stopping just below her navel.

Liza shivered at the soft stroke, her eyes locked on his thick, hard cock. She'd been lying to herself a lot since the gala, trying to convince herself his dick hadn't been that fucking spectacular, that his body didn't look like it was chiseled from stone.

All those lies were blown out of the water now because the truth was, he was better than she remembered.

Matt bent forward, reaching for the nightstand drawer to pull out a condom. She watched as he slid it on, her body growing tight with anticipation.

Once covered, Matt wasted no time caging her beneath him. The almost savage look in his eyes told her that she hadn't been the only one slowly going insane without this.

He placed the head of his dick at her opening and then, he did exactly as he'd promised—or maybe threatened. He took her hard, fast, with that thick cock stretching her to the limits of comfort and a little beyond.

Liza's finger dug into his shoulders as he rocked her body roughly with each pounding thrust.

Within a dozen relentless strokes, he had her there again, right on the precipice of coming. She dragged one hand down her stomach, intent on firing the kill shot. Her fingers never reached her clit as Matt grasped her wrist, pulling it to the pillow beneath her head. Then he grabbed the other, placing it in the same position, one that felt a hell of a lot like surrender.

His movements—dammit—slowed as well.

"What do you think you're doing?"

Her initial thought was "oh shit" because there was no denying he was pissed.

"I was right there," she explained lamely.

"So?"

"So I always...I need to...usually with other lovers—"

"Don't *ever* talk about other men when you're in bed with me." His tone was harsh, loud, laced with...jealousy? "I'm in charge of your orgasms. Only me. Do you understand?"

She nodded, then, strangely, felt compelled to say, "I'm sorry."

Her apology appeased him, his features smoothing out. "I know you're used to taking care of yourself...in bed."

Had he paused after "yourself"?

"But I take care of what's mine, and in this bedroom, *you are mine*. Understand?"

She nodded again because, quite frankly, speech was beyond her at this point. Christ, the entire conversation had taken place with Matt still buried to the hilt inside her.

Matt held her gaze for a moment longer, and though she didn't have a clue what the hell he saw on her face, apparently it convinced him that she got it.

Withdrawing several inches, Matt shoved back in, resuming the relentless, glorious pace he'd set before. Liza never moved her hands from where he'd placed them on the pillow, even though he wasn't holding them there.

She didn't need her hands anyway.

Her orgasm fluttered back to life and Matt, the clever bastard, put his money where his mouth was. His fingers stroked her clit with the perfect amount of pressure and speed, and all Liza could do was hold on for the ride as she splintered into a million sparkling pieces.

Her vision went white, which felt wrong because she wasn't entirely sure she hadn't blacked out for a few seconds.

When she recovered enough to notice her surroundings, she discovered Matt was still fucking her, still taking her like a man possessed.

"Fuck!" she cried as a harder, more piercing climax struck, this one taking Matt down with it.

He fell to his elbows, his labored breathing hot on her face. He remained inside her, neither of them in a hurry to part. His dick, even soft, made her feel full.

After what felt like ages, he lifted his head, his face inches from hers. He hadn't kissed her through the entire thing, and suddenly it occurred to her that she wanted that, she missed it.

Matt's eyes were locked with hers. "Stay with me in Hawaii."

His invitation took her by surprise, though perhaps it shouldn't have. He'd expressed an interest in a sexual relationship with her, and she'd obviously given him the all systems go when she wiggled her ass.

"Is that a request or a command?" she asked with a grin.

"Yes."

She laughed at his succinct reply. "Okay. But just so you know, it's not very professional."

Matt smiled widely, the happy expression rare enough that it took Liza's breath away. Because Matt's hotness factor increased a thousand percent when he smiled.

Her agreement acquired, Matt pulled away, climbing out of bed and walking to the bathroom to dispose of the condom.

Liza considered washing up, but her bones had been liquified, and she wasn't sure she could walk if she tried.

She lay there in the quiet of the room, the hum of the plane engines' white noise in the background. She had no idea if they'd had any more turbulence, the two of them shaking the bed enough to overshadow everything happening around them.

Liza stared at the ceiling, letting what she'd just done sink in.

She'd slept with Matt again. More than that, she'd agreed to an affair with him. An affair neither of them had put any timeline on. She supposed that took them out of the enemies category and put them in the—hmm—fuck buddies one?

She waited for the regret to show up, but so far, nothing.

Given her expansive backlog of disappointing, lukewarm sexual encounters, she suspected it would take some time before regret reared its head because she wasn't a bit sorry about anything that happened in this bed, too overwhelmed by the desire to do it all again.

Of course, Matt had fucked her to within an inch of her life, so she should probably give herself a bye on thinking too deeply about anything tonight.

The bathroom door opened and Matt returned, naked as the day he was born.

God, he was gorgeous. His smirk proved he knew she was appreciating the view, but she didn't bother playing innocent.

Just gave him a smirk of her own, shamelessly winking as he climbed back into bed with her.

Matt drew the duvet they'd kicked off over them, twisting her away from him and spooning her the way he had earlier.

"Good night, Matt," she whispered, her eyelids suddenly very heavy.

"Good night, Ms. Moretti."

Liza fell asleep quickly, and with a smile on her face.

Chapter Nine

Matt glanced over at the sound of Liza's happy sigh and cursed himself for being a fool. She'd had his dick twisted in a knot since the night of the gala, which was a huge problem since that was the body part he was thinking with these days.

He'd had his head turned by Liza from the first moment he'd seen her, and if he'd been able to keep it in his pants, remembering she was the forbidden fruit, he would have been fine. But he'd taken that taste after the gala, then another on New Year's, and he'd foolishly convinced himself he could go back for more without any serious repercussions.

Now, as he looked at her profile, her lips slightly upturned as she soaked up the sun, there was no pretending this wasn't going to end badly. For both of them.

Liza was someone he could easily fall in love with if he allowed it to happen.

In the past, he always drew a line in the sand when it came to lovers, and he'd never stepped a toe over it. Sex was sex and emotion played no part in it.

Last night, he'd attempted to draw that line with Liza,

offering her sex without strings. And then...he'd immediately crossed it by inviting her to share his hotel suite with him.

Even now, he couldn't figure what the hell had provoked him to do such an utterly stupid thing. He'd been laying on top of her, his cock still tucked inside her body, and all he could think was that he needed to grab as much of her as he could, as quickly as he could, because this was going to implode too soon.

"I swear it's going to take an entire week of this gorgeous sunshine to thaw me out from everything Philadelphia has thrown at us the last few months," she said, her eyes closed beneath her sunglasses. She was laying on the lounger next to him, the ocean waves rolling along the white sand beach about twenty feet away. A light breeze blew in from the sea, so even though the sun was bright, it wasn't hot or humid. It was perfect weather.

"It *has* been a brutal winter." He reached for the drink the cabana boy had delivered earlier. They'd both ordered mai tais. He typically didn't go for fruity drinks, but when in Rome...

It had been nearly four a.m. Hawaii time before they'd checked into their suite, and while they'd caught several hours of sleep on the plane, they agreed it would be smart to get a few hours more in order to avoid jet lag.

They woke up around eight, neither of them in a hurry to get out of bed.

Now that they'd opened the floodgates on sex without strings, Matt hadn't been able to resist caging her beneath him and fucking her like his life depended on it. It had been shortly before ten when they'd managed to drag themselves away from each other. Showering separately—because they agreed a joint shower would ensure they missed lunch as well as breakfast—they'd gone in search of brunch after working up one hell of a hunger.

While eating, they discussed the day's plan like they were travel companions. That was when Matt should have said "catch you later in bed" and spent the day fortifying his walls. Instead, his dick made the call, so here he was, lying next to her on a lounge chair so they could—as Liza suggested—recuperate from their day of travel by taking it easy.

In addition to attending the wedding, which was taking place in three days, Liza shared the list of touristy things she planned to do over the course of the week, since she'd never been to Hawaii. Matt had traveled to the islands a few times, and he'd even done several of the things on her list. Regardless of that, he'd agreed to accompany her to *all of it*. He was a sucker, drunk on sex. It was the only explanation he could come up with.

For the first hour on the beach, they both read as they sunbathed, but then Liza had put her book down and started a conversation. For the past three hours, the two of them had talked about every subject under the sun, including politics, movies, music tastes, and favorite Philly haunts. Liza was interesting and a witty storyteller, who spoke not just in words but with her expressions and Italian hand gestures. His father had broken Matt's habit of speaking with his hands long ago, calling the gestures common, but as he watched Liza animatedly waving her hands around, she was nothing short of adorable.

Matt preferred to play his cards close to his chest, but Liza had a way of asking him simple questions, then drawing out more and more, until he found himself telling her things he'd never told anyone. Not that he'd revealed any big secrets.

Instead, he'd talked about his childhood with Gage and Conor, the games they'd played, how he'd had a stellar tenth birthday party complete with pony rides, and how he'd apparently been quite the little liar in kindergarten, telling his teacher that his grandfather had been run over by a fire truck—he hadn't—and how his dad had broken both legs after falling off a ladder—also untrue. Matt's mother used to bring the story up quite often to him, laughing about her confusion when his teacher had called to offer her sympathy over their family's tragedies.

Liza had roared with laughter, teasing him that she wasn't surprised in the slightest he'd been a "little shit" when he was young.

That was when it occurred to Matt that he'd done such a good job repressing past memories, that he'd lost the happy ones along with the bad.

Then Liza regaled him for the better part of an hour about her girlfriends' "bad habit" of falling for her cousins and brothers. Matt always tried to give her family a wide berth, thanks to bad blood and past sins, so most of what she shared was news to him. Gage probably knew all these stories, but by tacit agreement, his brother didn't share a lot of details about his newfound Moretti friends, and Matt didn't ask.

While Liza joked about her friends' new romances, it was clear she was enthralled by the love matches and thrilled that her best friends were either now family or on their way there.

Her brother Elio had married Gianna Duncan, the two becoming parents last September. That was the relationship that felt normal to him.

Because her brother Aldo and cousin Tony were both currently in committed threesomes, something Matt struggled to wrap his head around. Of course, that was probably because he'd spent the better part of his life resisting the idea of shacking up with *one* person. Spending the rest of his life with two partners? No thanks.

Liza pulled off her sunglasses and rolled to her stomach.

"Did you put sunscreen on your back?"

She lifted her head, shaking it slightly and squinting at him. "Can't reach."

Matt pushed up from his chair, grabbing the bottle of sunscreen from her bag. Perching on the edge of her lounge chair, he poured some onto his palm and began rubbing it onto her upper back.

"Mmm," she hummed. "That feels good. You're spoiling me."

Matt opened his mouth to say he liked taking care of her, but he shut up quick. Admissions like that would continue to muddy waters that were already thick with sludge. Rather than speak, he stroked her back and shoulders, letting his hands do the talking as he rubbed the sunscreen in.

She was wearing a red string bikini, and it had driven him to distraction all afternoon.

Untying the string at the back, he kept touching her, massaging her skin under the guise of lathering her with sunscreen, when really, he had just reached the point where he couldn't keep his hands off her for a second longer.

Liza looked up at him over her shoulder, desire smoldering in her gaze.

"Better not miss this spot." Matt squirted more sunscreen on his palms, cupping her ass cheeks and squeezing them hard enough that she gasped, then he started his rubbing motions. "The only thing that's going to make this gorgeous ass red is my hand...or my belt."

Liza squirmed on the chair, his touches having the desired effect. He'd been riding half-mast ever since she walked out of the bathroom in this bikini. It was time she did a bit of suffering too.

"Matt," she whispered, as his fingertips drifted between her upper thighs. One tiny stroke and then he drew his hands lower, spreading the sunscreen on the backs of her legs.

"Hmm?" He pretended not to understand her distress as he snapped the cap closed on the bottle, tossed it back into her bag, retied her bikini top, and returned to his chair.

Liza's eyes narrowed. "You're a terrible tease."

He chuckled. "I'll make it up to you later."

"You better," she muttered, dropping her head back down, her eyes closing once more, though her cheeks were now flushed... and not from the heat.

"Maybe we should put some of this downtime to good use," he said before taking another sip of his drink.

"How?" she asked lazily.

"I think we determined last night that you're okay with being spanked."

She was clearly all in on this topic, as she sat up, facing him. "More than okay with it."

"Where do you stand on bondage?"

Liza tilted her head, considering the question for a moment. "It's definitely a turn-on for me, but only in an academic, masturbation-fantasy way. I've never dated a guy I trusted enough to try it with."

It was a good answer, but one that might bite him in the ass because his and Liza's past association had been rocky at best. "Trust is important."

She studied his face hard, then bit her lower lip, almost nervously. "Would it freak you out to know that I trust you?"

It freaked him out more than he could admit. But it also made him feel like he was ten feet tall and bulletproof.

He wanted Liza's trust, even though he knew he was going to betray it.

Rather than admit that, he simply shook his head. "No, it doesn't," he lied. "So bondage is on the table. How about anal?"

This time, her response was instantaneous. "No."

"Why not?" He tried not to chuckle at the outright panic on her face.

"Not to inflate that already overinflated ego of yours, but that beast between your legs just about fits in my..." Rather than say the word vagina, she gestured to it with her hands.

Matt shook his head as if disappointed. "No guts, no glory."

"I can live with that."

He didn't push her on that decision, though he made a mental note to revisit the topic when they were in bed and he could give her a tease of what he was offering—because he was definitely putting a butt plug in that gorgeous ass of hers.

Matt moved on to the next item on his mental list. He intended to put this time in Hawaii to good use because—while they hadn't put a time limit on this affair—he suspected things would become more difficult once they returned to Philadelphia and real life. "I know you enjoyed the spanking, but I'll confess

I'm not into serious pain—yours or mine. If that's something you want—"

She shook her head. "It isn't. That's not one of my kinks. Truthfully, I'm probably pretty vanilla. For me, it's the..." She paused.

"It's the submission you want to explore."

Liza nodded. "I'm struggling to understand where this desire is coming from because I've never felt this burning need with past lovers. Never felt compelled to obey—God, I really hate that word—someone else's demands."

"There's nothing wrong with wanting someone else to take control in the bedroom. It's a common turn-on for a lot of people —male and female."

"And you don't mind? I mean...being the one to..." She waved her hands around rather than speak the words.

"I'm a control freak, Liza. Perhaps you've noticed."

She snickered.

"That character trait doesn't turn off when I step into a bedroom. If anything, it's stronger there."

"So, I guess this," she gestured between them, "makes sense. We're sexually compatible and we're both single. Feels like a win-win."

"It does."

"Even if you are a Russo," she tacked on with a wicked grin.

"No one is more surprised by this than me, Ms. Moretti." He enjoyed the way she laughed at his joke, and he recalled Christmas Eve dinner with his brothers. The way Conor and Gage had cracked up at each other's jokes. Yet with him, they became more serious, less fun.

Liza's lighthearted behavior sharply contrasted how other people acted around him. Perhaps that was part of her appeal. She didn't act like he was the world's most miserable bastard; rather, she seemed to enjoy his company. Then he realized the same held true of Arnold and Johnnie.

"Taking out the relationship factor makes this a lot easier for me too," Liza continued.

Matt knew why, though it chafed.

If the two of them maintained a casual affair—without commitment or emotion—she could keep her association with him a secret from her family and friends, most of whom would not approve of her sleeping with him.

Those sins of the past reared their ugly head again. Memories of the things he'd done to her family—and to his—had ensured he'd spent years wallowing in self-loathing and regret.

The constant drip-drip-drip of water.

Dark red blood congealed on the snowy-white tiles.

The blue-tinged skin of a lifeless arm.

Look deeper.

Matt restrained a shudder. There'd been a time when he thought he had managed to put those horrors behind him. Then Gage shared the guilt he'd felt in regard to their mother's suicide and sent Matt back to those days just following her death.

Liza picked up her mai tai and took a long drink, finishing it. "Should we head inside? Shower and relax for a little while, then figure out dinner?"

Matt rose, grateful for the reprieve she'd just offered. He'd excuse himself once they returned to the room, hide out on the porch until he could shut down these unwanted thoughts.

"That's a good idea. I need to check my messages. Make sure Gage and Conor haven't driven Russo Enterprises into the ground in the past twenty-four hours."

"I don't think you have to worry about Conor. I get the feeling he's as big a workaholic as you are."

"He is," Matt confirmed.

"Gage, on the hand, is another story entirely," Liza added, as they gathered up their things and started walking back to the hotel. "The cat's away, so I suspect your IT mice are spending a lot of time playing in that game room you foolishly let your brother build at work."

Matt sighed. "He insisted it was to test the games produced by the tech company he bought, but I'm afraid you're probably right. I spend a lot of time debating whether Penny has been a good or bad influence on my brother. In the past, Gage at least attempted to hide his nerdy side. Now it's hanging out there all the time for the whole world to see."

"Which probably means Russo Enterprises is safe," Liza said, grinning widely. "Because those two won't put the video game controllers down long enough for him to do any lasting damage."

"Another excellent point." Matt gestured for Liza to proceed him through the revolving doorway entrance to the hotel.

They were halfway across the lobby when they heard their names being called.

"Matt! Liza!"

Matt smiled as Johnnie and Arnold approached them with a man who appeared to be about Liza's age.

"Hey, guys." Liza hugged the grooms. Arnold had texted them both this morning to see if they'd made it to Hawaii safely. They had each replied yes without informing their friend that they'd traveled together.

Arnold gave Matt a curious grin, obviously amused to find him with Liza. The subject of Ms. Moretti had somehow managed to come up each time he'd gone out with Arnold and Johnnie, both men big Liza fans. Matt had tried to assume a nonchalant attitude about her, feigning boredom whenever the subject rose, claiming countless times that she was nothing more than a colleague, and a pesky one at that. He suspected they'd seen through that act right from the start.

"I was just about to text you to make sure you were settling in okay. Looks like you got some sun," Arnold observed.

"It's a gorgeous day and this resort is incredible. I can't quite believe I'm here," Liza gushed. "I keep thinking I'll wake up in dreary, freezing Philly."

"There's no way we were getting married without you here,"

Johnnie insisted. "Oh, I'm being rude." He turned to the man next to him. "Liza, Matt, this is my nephew, Alani."

Alani stepped toward Liza, who raised her hand for a handshake. The nephew, however, lifted her fingers to his lips, kissing her knuckles. "I'm so happy to finally meet you. My uncle talks about you all the time, but he failed to mention how beautiful you are."

Liza grinned at his obvious flirting. "It's nice to meet you too."

"I'm looking forward to getting to know my uncle's friends better," Alani added, though it was clear there was only one friend he was interested in getting to know. Especially when he added, "I hope you'll save a dance for me at the reception, Liza."

Liza looked from Alani to Johnnie. "Obviously charm runs in the family."

Johnnie slapped his nephew on the shoulder. "He's a chip off the old uncle block."

Before he could think better of it—or before Liza could respond to Alani's request—Matt gripped the back of Liza's neck familiarly. The move was possessive as hell, but he couldn't help himself.

Then he stuck his other hand out, forcing Alani to let go of Liza's.

"Matt Russo," he said, practically growling.

Alani took note of Matt's hands—both of them—and offered him a forced smile. "It's a pleasure to meet you," he said, returning the handshake before wisely backing away from Liza.

Matt's gaze drifted over to Arnold and Johnnie, and he knew in an instant he'd overplayed his hand in front of his new friends, given their intrigued looks. The only person who didn't seem to notice was Liza, who relaxed the moment he'd touched her, even shifting closer to him. She may just be realizing her submissive side, but her responses came instinctually, without thought, and they called to the raging alpha inside him like a siren's song.

"Matt and I are looking for dinner recs. Anywhere we should try?" Liza asked.

Johnnie and Alani offered them several suggestions of restaurants within walking distance of the resort, then all three men excused themselves to continue preparations for the big day.

Matt lowered his hand, placing it on Liza's back as they returned to their suite. She headed to the couch, intent on sitting down, but he stopped her, grasping her hand and tugging her toward the bedroom.

"How's your knee?" he asked, glancing down.

"Fine. Scabbed over. Doesn't hurt at all," she replied.

"Good." Matt grabbed a pillow from the bed, tossing it to the floor between them. He had intended to take a time-out, but that went out the window the second Alani kissed Liza's hand.

Liza's eyes darkened with desire. Before he could give the command, she dropped to her knees in front of him, her fingers slipping beneath the elastic of his swim trunks, pulling them down.

He hadn't bothered with a shirt when they'd headed to the beach, so all he needed to do was toe off his sandals and shorts and he was completely naked.

Liza started to reach for his erect dick, but he caught her wrist before she could touch him.

"Don't move," he commanded, stepping around her. Untying her bikini top, he slipped it off and bent over, using the strings to bind her hands behind her back.

Liza gave him a heated yet curious look. "No hands?"

Matt moved back in front of her, cupping her jaw, tilting her face up. "This isn't a blow job, Liza. I'm going to fuck your mouth."

A soft "oh" fell from her lips as she licked them.

Matt grabbed the base of his cock, rubbing it over her lush lips, back and forth, painting them with the pre-come beaded at the tip.

"Stick your tongue out. Taste me."

Liza responded instantly, running her tongue around the head of his dick. Her gaze lowered, but that wasn't right.

He tapped his knuckles under her chin twice. "Eyes up here. Don't look away from me."

Her dark chocolate-brown eyes found his beneath her thick lashes, their gazes locked as Matt guided the head of his cock back to her mouth.

"Open for me."

Her lips parted and he pushed the mushroom-shaped head inside. Liza had commented on his "beast," her description amusing him at the time, but now the monster was out of its lair and ready to roar.

Matt cupped the sides of her head, pushing deeper. His dick was wide—something his past lovers either raved or complained about—so he was stretching her mouth enough that it was probably uncomfortable.

Or so he thought. Until her eyelids grew heavy, and she moaned with desire as he pushed in another inch. The tip brushed the back of her throat, and Matt paused, took a deep breath, then three more, trying to calm himself down. It was that, or this would be over before it began.

He pushed in a tiny bit more, aware he was deep enough that he was limiting the amount of air she could draw into her lungs.

Her face flushed, and he withdrew until just the head was still buried inside her mouth. Liza sucked in a deep breath through her nose.

"Take another," he urged, and she did so.

Then he shoved back inside, deeper, stretching her mouth, encouraging her to open her throat. Liza's eyes glistened, tearing up, even as she tried to take more of him.

Matt tightened his grip on her head, his fists clenching around her thick hair, attempting to maintain control. She fought him until he tugged on her hair, pulling it hard enough to capture her attention.

"You're fighting me for control. Take what I give you, Liza. *Only* what I give you."

She blinked a few times, then stopped struggling against him. Her expression softened and he noted the exact second she put all the power in his hands. She'd dropped just enough comments about past lovers that he knew she'd most likely been the top in most of her sexual encounters. Or at the least, an equal partner.

Matt wondered how any man could take a woman like Liza to bed and not see this side of her. How they could not see this incredible, sensual, giving woman.

Liza remained still, letting Matt set the pace as he thrust in and out of her warm mouth. Every now and then, he felt the stroke of her tongue, but he could see in her eyes, her actions weren't driven by a need to reclaim control but rather by outright arousal.

His thrusts grew shallower but faster, as Matt's balls began to constrict. He was right there. On the edge.

"Liza!" he barked when her eyes drifted shut. They flew open, finding his again.

Jesus Christ. She was beautiful and—God help him—close to coming herself.

Matt was sorry he'd bound her hands because he suspected if he'd ordered her to touch herself, they would have reached their climaxes together.

Next time.

He held her gaze, let her see what was coming. He wouldn't order her to swallow—this time—mainly because he wanted to see what she would do on her own. Where her preferences lie.

He groaned as the first spurt of come splashed against her throat. His fingers were still gripping her hair—too tightly—but he couldn't make himself loosen that hold. The way Liza moaned told him she liked the sting.

Of course, that moan reverberating against his dick added the perfect sensation, and Matt called out her name, cursed, as he shot the rest of his come into her mouth.

"Liza. *Fuck*."

She held true to his command, her eyes never leaving his, even as his own vision turned fuzzy. He grunted, his pleasure almost an agony when she swallowed every drop.

Matt held her there until the last vestiges of his climax faded and his cock softened. Then he pulled out, Liza seemingly reluctant to let him go. The image of her trying to keep him inside her mouth was too much for him. Reaching down, he dragged her from the floor, pushing her backward until her knees hit the edge of the mattress. Quickly, he untied her hands, tossing her bikini top to the floor.

With a strong hand on her shoulder, he urged her back and lifted her legs, placing her feet flat on the edge of the mattress before shoving her knees apart.

Matt dropped between her legs, taking Liza like a man possessed, fucking her with his tongue, his teeth, his lips. Stroking her clit rapidly with his thumb, he drove his tongue inside her, Liza squirming beneath him. He wasn't the only one out of his mind with need.

He hadn't misread her desire during the blow job. Her orgasm struck quickly, her back arching as she cried out loudly. Matt drew the climax out, keeping pressure on her clit, tasting her arousal, feeling her pussy clench against his tongue.

It was Liza's hands on his head, weakly trying to push him away, that finally had him retreating.

"Too much," she gasped. "Too good!"

Matt helped her into the middle of the bed, claiming the spot next to her. Wrapping his arm around her waist, he murmured, "Nap, shower, dinner."

Liza mumbled something he couldn't make out in reply, and he realized she'd beat him to the first item on his list. Her eyes closed, her breathing slow and steady.

It didn't take Matt more than a minute to join her there, his last contradictory thoughts wavering between an awestruck "holy fuck" and then just plain "fuck."

* * *

The constant drip-drip-drip of water.
   Dark red blood congealed on the snowy-white tiles.
   The blue-tinged skin of a lifeless arm.
   "No! No! No!"
   Look deeper.

Matt bolted straight up in bed, beads of sweat running down the side of his face, his heart racing, his lungs tight with anguish. It took him a full minute before he recalled where he was. Then he hastily glanced down, relieved he hadn't woken Liza, her bare back turned toward him, the sheet pooling around her waist.

They'd accomplished the nap earlier and the second thing on his list—a shower—but because it had been a joint one, during which he'd pushed her face-first against the wall, fucking her from behind as the steamy water streamed over them, they'd opted for room service rather than trying one of the restaurants Johnnie had suggested for dinner.

They'd fed each other in bed, then fucked twice more before falling asleep together.

The nightmares he'd suffered after his mother's suicide had subsided after his father passed away, and Matt had foolishly believed that Dante Russo's unmourned departure from this world had freed him from them.

For ten years, he'd cockily believed his past sins had been laid to rest with Dad.

Then Gage fell in love with Penny, and Matt learned that his brother blamed himself for Mom's suicide.

That realization had ripped a hole in the space-time continuum, Matt's guilt returning full force, eating him alive.

So...for the past year, the nightmares had begun again. Not as frequently as all those years ago, but they still packed a punch whenever they struck, taking Matt down hard.

Asking Liza to stay with him in his suite had been a mistake, not just because it was blurring the lines between what this thing between them was and what it had to be. But because he'd left himself vulnerable.

Carefully rising so as not to wake her, he walked to the bathroom to splash cold water on his face. Returning, he walked past the bed, moving into the living room. Grabbing a blanket, he lay down on the couch.

He should never have started this. He knew better than to play with a fire he couldn't contain, but she'd been too fucking tempting, and he'd truly believed he could take her without paying a price.

All he'd proven was that he was powerless when it came to Liza Moretti.

Time to put on the brakes, to put this Matt Russo—the one wearing a false face—away and introduce Liza to the man he truly was.

He was going to put their fate in her hands, because before this week was over, she'd do what he couldn't.

Walk away forever.

Chapter Ten

"So...you're going to have to explain to me how Matt Russo came to be invited to your wedding," Liza said, two seconds after joining Arnold at the table.

He'd texted this morning to invite her and Matt to join him for lunch. She'd accepted instantly, but Matt had turned Arnold down, claiming he had a Zoom meeting that would take up most of his afternoon.

The meeting was news to her because Matt had agreed to accompany Liza on all her Hawaii excursions. This afternoon, she'd planned for the two of them to take a glass-bottom boat tour, but Matt had canceled, claiming he couldn't miss the meeting he'd failed to mention before. He insisted she go without him, and while she'd originally intended to do this tour and all the others alone, since she'd thought she would be here stag, now she wasn't as excited about seeing the island as she had been.

Matt had been awake before her this morning, already dressed and working on the deck when she woke up. She'd expected/hoped for more sex this morning, so she'd been disappointed to discover him not just up and about but distractedly texting away on his phone.

"I told you Matt's been hanging out at the Promise House

quite a bit since the holidays," Arnold said. "He's also gone out for dinner and drinks with me and Johnnie a few times."

"Mmm-hmm," Liza hummed, not buying that answer. "So obviously, based on that one month of budding friendship, you thought you'd invite him to your destination wedding in Hawaii."

Arnold chuckled. "What are you accusing me of, dear Liza?"

"Matchmaking," she replied instantly.

Arnold's only response was a wink.

"I knew it. Arnold, this is *your* wedding!"

"So what? I've been with Johnnie for twenty-five years. The only reason we're getting married is to make his mama happy. The poor woman's been beside herself over the fact we've been 'living in sin,'" he finger-quoted, "all these years."

Liza had heard countless stories about Johnnie's mother, Judy. So many that she wasn't sure if she was looking forward to or dreading meeting the woman. "Even so, this is your special day. Inviting someone you barely know because of the things I shared with you is...well, it's either the sweetest thing anyone's ever done for me or totally insane."

"I want you to be as happy as I am with Johnnie." Arnold reached out, patting her hand.

"And you think you're accomplishing that by pushing me and Matt together?" she asked. "How did you know he wouldn't bring Patricia as his date?"

"I told you Matt wouldn't date that woman, and I was right, wasn't I?"

She nodded. "Yes, but you were taking a hell of a risk."

Arnold took a sip of water. "I saw the sparks flying between you two yesterday, saw the way he went all caveman when Alani flirted with you."

Liza wasn't sure how to reply to that because, at the time, she'd wondered about Matt's very possessive grip on her neck. It had felt like a jealous move but given what the two of them were embarking on, she'd chalked her feeling up to wishful thinking. Matt had insisted there was no future for the two of them beyond what they shared in the bedroom. She'd agreed to the fuck-buddies offer because it was the perfect way to explore her sexual proclivities in what she'd thought was a safe manner.

He *didn't* want more, and she *shouldn't* want more.

Her family had opened their arms to Gage, but Matt would always be a different story. Hadn't her cousins confirmed that on Christmas Eve?

"Is it too soon to start gloating about my brilliance in bringing the two of you together?" Arnold asked.

"Maybe. I think I've made a mistake, Arnold. Another mistake."

He frowned. "Oh no. It's not going well?"

She sighed. "It's going too well. The sex..." She stopped herself, though her flushed cheeks were a dead giveaway.

Arnold lifted his iced tea glass, tapping it against hers. "Hot damn. That's what I was hoping to hear. So it's everything you hoped it would be?"

She nodded. "And more. And it's not just the sex. It's him. He's so much more than I expected. Easy to talk to, to be with. I'll admit, I haven't gotten a laugh out of him yet, but his smiles are coming a lot easier. He jokes and teases and..." Liza stopped, aware she was gushing, saying too much.

"You're smitten."

Leave it to Arnold to hit the nail on the head. "Yes. But I can't be."

"Why not?" he asked.

"Because Matt has made it very clear he's not interested in a commitment. No marriage. No kids. This is sex without strings."

Arnold leaned back, giving her a stern look that instantly had her feeling guilty. "Why on earth would you agree to that?"

"Because I thought it was the best way to—"

"Easiest, Liza," Arnold interjected. "Not best."

"I wanted to explore these newfound submissive tendencies—tendencies Matt awakened, by the way," she reminded him.

Arnold sighed. "I know he did."

"I'm not a stranger to casual sex, Arnold. I'm a thirty-year-old woman who's dated a handful of men I actually refer to as ex-boyfriends and only a couple of those relationships lasted longer than six months. My longest relationship ended just shy of a year, and the reason it lasted that long was because the guy was a pilot and out of town more than he was in. We broke up when we decided to take a weeklong trip to the beach together. By day four, we could both read the writing on the wall. To be perfectly honest, casual sex is all I've ever had."

"Fair enough. I'll give you that. And if it were any other man in the world, I suspect you would have had no problem with this affair either. But I've seen the two of you together. You aren't as indifferent to the man as you might hope."

She wasn't. The words "she doth protest too much" were starting to ring a little too true as she considered all the bitching she'd done about Matt over the past year and a half. Part of her wondered now if she'd placed him in that role of arch-nemesis as an attempt to keep herself safe.

From him.

From the things he made her feel.

"And the same holds true for Matt," Arnold added.

Liza hated how much she hoped her friend was seeing some-thing she wasn't.

"You're right. I'm not indifferent. The past couple of days have been really amazing."

She didn't mention that things with Matt had felt a bit off this morning. He was perfectly nice, not rude, but the closeness they'd shared the previous day was gone. When he mentioned the meeting, she'd dismissed her concerns. The man was a self-confessed workaholic, so maybe he couldn't turn that off for more than twenty-four hours at a time. She could relate—to a point—because she was also unable to disconnect from work whenever she was in the middle of a big project.

Arnold pointed a finger at her. "Then I think you owe it to

yourself to stop thinking of this thing between you and Matt as just sex. Look at the man—with his clothes on."

Liza laughed loudly.

"See if there's something worth building on. Because to be honest, as I've gotten to know Matt better, I believe he may be your perfect match."

Liza rolled her eyes. "This wedding has you looking at everything through the romance lens."

"Don't knock it until you've tried it."

The waitress returned to take their orders, and the rest of the lunch passed in pleasant conversation as Arnold filled her in on all the typical pre-wedding drama, like a company delivering the wrong topper for the cake—two brides rather than two grooms—concern about a groomsman not making it at all due to illness, and some nasty argument between two of Johnnie's female cousins leading to a last-minute redo of the seating chart at the reception. Despite all of it, Arnold's smile never faded, and Liza couldn't help but feel the tiniest twinge of jealousy toward her friend because his love and happiness were almost tangible things.

"Okay, you're both coming to the rehearsal dinner tomorrow," Arnold reminded her as the meal ended and they stood to leave. Neither she nor Matt had a role in the wedding, but as out-of-town guests, they'd been invited to the dinner.

"Wouldn't miss it."

"I'll see you later." Arnold excused himself, heading off with a list of chores Johnnie had handed him before he came to meet her for lunch.

Liza glanced at her phone. She needed to leave right now in order to make it to the dock in time for her tour. She was tempted to return to the suite to see if she could persuade Matt to change his mind, to blow off his meeting and come with her, but she refused to look clingy or needy.

Damn Arnold had planted a dangerous seed and it was already starting to take root.

"No," she muttered to herself. An afternoon to herself was

just what she needed. To think about where she wanted to go from here.

* * *

"We saw sooooo many sea turtles," Liza said, taking a sip of wine. "I swear some of them were bigger than my car. I had no idea they got that huge. They were nothing like the box turtle my brother Aldo kept as a pet for a few weeks before the creature finally managed to escape him and our backyard."

"Sounds like quite the excursion." Matt had joined her for dinner, though she couldn't help but feel he'd been reluctant to do so.

Officially out of sightseeing stories, Liza took another sip of wine and silence fell between them. Matt picked up the menu, reading it with a fervent interest rivaling that of a rabid fan grabbing the newest release from their favorite author.

The distance she'd noticed this morning was still there, though it wasn't something she could call him on, given he was being polite, if somewhat quieter than yesterday.

She couldn't help but wonder if he regretted inviting her to stay in his suite with him.

What if his interest in her was waning? What if he felt as if she was overstaying her welcome?

"How was your meeting?" she asked at last, drawing Matt's attention away from the damn menu.

He gave her a puzzled look for just long enough that she suddenly questioned if there'd even been a meeting at all. A few seconds too late, he cleared his throat and said, "It was fine," before turning his attention back to the menu.

"Anything look good?" Liza tried. "I've got my eye on the lomi lomi salmon or maybe the poke. How about you?"

"I haven't decided yet."

Wow. This was going to be a long night if she couldn't pull him out of whatever mood he was in.

Then she recalled her luncheon with Arnold. If she couldn't draw him into conversation, maybe she could entertain him with something scandalous and slightly funny, so she recounted the story of the two cousins, Maggie and Maya, who were fighting over the same man. "Arnold is concerned they'll make a scene at the reception, especially since Maggie's plus-one was Maya's boyfriend before she found out the two of them were cheating on her. They thought Maggie would be smart enough to leave the guy at home considering her cousin was going to be there. Of course, Johnnie is hoping for some juicy drama to liven things up."

"Sleeping with a person who's dating someone else is guaranteed to produce bad feelings." Matt's comment, spoken in such a monotone voice, suddenly struck a little too close to home, and she realized her story had hit a nerve without her intending it to.

"I guess so," she hedged.

"You and I both know I speak from experience."

Now that Matt had opened the door, Liza decided to walk through. She'd heard the story of Matt sleeping with her cousin Tony's girlfriend countless times in the past—always from Tony's perspective. She was curious to hear Matt's side of the story.

"I guess it's a tricky thing...two guys falling for the same girl."

Matt chuckled, but it wasn't an amused sound. Rather, it was cold and slightly sinister. "Tony and I didn't fall for the same girl, Liza. Is that what you've thought all these years?"

It wasn't. Because that wasn't how Tony told the tale. "Tony said you slept with his girlfriend to get even with him for winning class president."

"He also stole the position of quarterback when his family moved back to Philly from Baltimore. Your cousin was a pain in my ass senior year."

Liza hated the vehemence in Matt's tone. It had her back going up because defending her family was second nature to her. However, she was trying to give Matt the benefit of the doubt, for some reason.

"It was high school." Time to find a way out of this minefield she'd stepped onto. "Things always seem to matter a hell of a lot at eighteen."

Matt fell silent, and she thought perhaps he would let the conversation end there. Unfortunately, he didn't. "Not exactly. If there was one thing my father pounded into my brain growing up, it was that Russos always come out on top."

"Well, that's hardly true, is it?" she couldn't help but counter.

"Isn't it? Tony may have won the positions, but I got revenge."

Liza had grown up listening to countless stories about the Russos striking back hard against her family whenever they didn't get what they wanted. After all, Matt's grandfather had destroyed Nonno's business by any and every means necessary, just because Nonna had chosen Nonno over him.

"So Tony's version of the story...that you seduced his girlfriend in a place where you knew he'd catch the two of you..."

"Was the truth," Matt finished.

Liza shook her head, though she wasn't sure why. Maybe it was because she'd been seeing a different side of Matt since the gala. Actually, her impression of him had been slowly evolving over the past year or so.

When Penny mentioned some generous thing Matt had done for the Russo Enterprises employees or for his brothers.

When Arnold and Devonte sang his praises after the pickup basketball games.

When he gave Jess a job to help keep her and Jasper off the streets.

When he'd sent her obnoxious date, Davis Taylor, packing at the gala.

When he'd offered to share his flight to Hawaii after she missed hers.

Matt didn't match the stories she'd been told about him when he was in high school, so she'd thought they were exaggerated or maybe even wrong.

"I always thoufght..." she began. "There are two sides to every story."

Matt shook his head. "No. There's only ever one story, with the storytellers trying to sell their version of it to others."

"It doesn't feel like you're pleading your own case here," she pointed out.

"Because people's perceptions of me don't matter. I found a way for revenge and I took it. If that makes me what others believe to be 'the bad guy,'" he finger-quoted, "then so be it."

Liza wasn't buying a damn thing he was selling, but she had to hand it to him. Matt was one hell of a snake oil salesman. He was obviously trying to get a rise out of her, piss her off, and convince her that he was an asshole.

What she couldn't understand was why? What had changed between last night and this morning?

Regardless of what he said, there was a disconnect between the old Matt and the one she'd spent the last few days with, but he seemed determined to make sure all she saw was this "bad" side.

"So you didn't care about Adriana at all?" Liza kept searching for something that made sense here. She'd genuinely liked Tony's first girlfriend. Six years younger, Liza had idolized Adriana, who was pretty and popular and all those things awkward middle school girls aspire to become.

Matt frowned. "Who's Adriana?"

Liza's temper spiked, despite her efforts to remain calm. "Guess that answers my question. That was Tony's girlfriend, the one you seduced."

He shrugged. "I didn't remember that was her name. Didn't really matter. After all, she'd served her purpose, and I didn't need her anymore."

"Served her purpose," Liza muttered.

"Her only usefulness to me was that she was dating Tony Moretti."

"Usefulness?" she snapped loudly, hating that she was starting to sound like a damn parrot.

"If there's one thing I've learned in life, it's how to use people to get what I want. Adriana was a means to an end, nothing more."

Liza beat back her anger, taking a couple of deep breaths, trying to figure out what the hell was going on. Because she didn't have a doubt now that Matt was purposely trying to push her away.

"You seem to like portraying the villain in that story."

"You don't think I was?" he drawled.

She didn't reply, her silence revealing more than she probably should. Because she still didn't want to think that.

Which confirmed she was officially an idiot.

Matt scoffed. "Only stupid people try to justify bad actions in others. You aren't stupid, Liza, so stop looking at me like you're going to see something different than what's right in front of you."

Arnold was right. Liza wasn't approaching this thing between her and Matt as casual. If what she felt for him was just sexual attraction, this conversation would have had her waving the Moretti flag in his face, calling him a heartless bastard, and telling him to take his sex without strings and shove it up his ass.

But physical desire wasn't the stronger emotion here. She was certain there was a good man inside him, one stubbornly determined to hold people at arm's reach. The same question—why?—rattled around in her brain. What the hell was holding him back? It almost felt like he was a man paying penance, but for what?

Or was he right? Was she looking for justifications that didn't exist, simply so she could excuse the fact that he made her heart race and her palms sweaty even though she knew he'd intentionally hurt someone she cared about?

Liza put her menu down. She didn't want to be with him right now. Not when he was acting like this. Not when her thoughts were scattered and flipped right-side up and upside down like a thousand-piece jigsaw puzzle.

"I'm not hungry," she lied.

Matt looked at her. "Should we go?"

She shook her head. "You don't have to leave on my account. You stay and eat. We're only a few blocks from the hotel. I can walk on my own. I might..." It was on the tip of her tongue to tell him she was going to see if she could get her own room, but she couldn't force herself to say the words. If he said that was a good idea, she'd be... Fuck. *Hurt*. And if he asked her to reconsider and stay with him then...*fuck*...she would.

Matt rose, dropping enough money on the table to cover the wine they'd drunk, plus a good tip. "Come on." He placed his hand on her lower back, guiding her out of the restaurant. When they reached the curb, she twisted, forcing him to stop touching her.

"Are you using me?" she asked, hating the way he'd referred to Adriana as a means to an end. Given their families' history of animosity, she couldn't help but wonder if she was serving some nefarious purpose as well. If so, she didn't have a clue what it could be.

"To what end?" He turned to walk back to the hotel, giving her no choice but to follow.

"You tell me," she replied.

"Is this some sort of Moretti paranoia?" he asked with that smug smirk she hadn't seen since the night of the gala.

"Don't do that. Don't make me feel like an idiot for asking a perfectly legitimate question. You went out of your way at that table to let me know that people are pawns you use for your own benefit. So, are you using me?"

"Yes," Matt said, barely glancing her direction, walking faster.

She wasn't sure if she was imagining it or if he really had picked up the pace, but she was struggling to keep up.

"I *am* using you, Liza. For sex. Nothing more. Nothing less."

"Sex," the parrot repeated. This conversation had gone completely off the rails. The whole day had. She'd woken up in one frame of mind, and he'd woken up in another—unfortunately, his was the one they'd agreed on.

Just sex.

When they reached the hotel, Matt's hand found its way to her back again, guiding her across the lobby. She slowed down as they passed the reception desk, but Matt urged her forward.

"I'm going to—" she started.

"We're not finished," he said in a harsh tone, laced with an underlying warning that told her he'd die on that hill before he'd let her get her own room.

Liza stared him down, refusing to move. "I think I need to explain a few things to you, Mr. Russo."

His eyes narrowed, but he gave her a brief nod in agreement. "You can explain in the room," he said shortly.

She looked around them, taking note the number of happy tourists milling around the lobby, perfectly aware that if she started this here, they would make one hell of a scene.

Liza would be smart to refuse him, to get her own room and table this whole discussion until she got her temper under control.

But she needed to show him she wasn't someone he could push around. Backing down in a fight wasn't something that came natural to her, so she brushed by him and the reception desk, walking to their room, forcing him to follow in her wake.

Storming toward their suite, she fumed, hating how he'd gone out of his way to ruin things between them. The bastard had sensed her feelings were changing and he'd found a way to put her back on his track.

The "just sex" track. The track she'd agreed to two days earlier.

Fuck that, she thought, recalling all the bullshit he'd just spewed at her.

Entering the suite together, Liza spun around as Matt closed the door behind them. "You want this fight?"

He nodded.

She stepped closer to him, driving her finger into his shoulder. "You're an asshole. That's the lesson I was supposed to take away from all of this shit today, right?"

Matt stared at her for two heartbeats too long before he gave her a single bob of the head.

She slow clapped. "Well done."

"I've never lied to you about what this would be," he said, as if that made his actions excusable.

"You haven't. Apparently, I've given you the wrong impression of me."

"What impression is that?" he growled.

"Clearly you consider me a pushover."

"I don't think—"

"Of course you do. But let me make one thing very, very clear. My submissiveness begins and ends at the door to the bedroom. Got it?"

He scowled, responding through gritted teeth. "Got it."

"So if this is just sex, then I'm going to get my money's worth, going to use you every bit as much as you use me. And then I'm getting my own room."

Matt looked ready to argue that last point, but she didn't give him the chance.

Once again, she walked away from him, crossing the suite to the bedroom. As soon as she crossed the threshold, she pulled her T-shirt over her head, tossing it to the floor. Matt's lack of patience rivaled hers, three buttons to his shirt already unfastened.

"Take off those shorts," he demanded irritably, even though her fingers were already working the button free.

She narrowed her eyes, even as she did as he said. Guess she didn't have to like Matt Russo to follow his commands and let him fuck her brains out.

Liza stripped off the rest of her clothes, her bra—the last article to come off—falling to the floor. Matt was completely naked a split second later.

"Come here." He crooked a finger at her.

She didn't move. Kept her feet planted right where they were. This might just be sex, but that didn't mean she was going to make it easy for him.

"Liza," Matt growled. "I don't repeat myself."

Every instinct inside responded to that tone, told her to do as he said, and that was when she realized exactly how deeply ingrained her submissive tendencies were.

However, Liza was thirty years old with a list of lackluster lovers as long as her arm. She was no stranger to ignoring her desires.

She was also still pissed as fuck. So she remained where she was.

"Make me," she taunted.

A smile—a wholly unpleasant smile—crossed Matt's face. "Is this your attempt at payback? You're pissed off that I'm not pretending to be Prince fucking Charming?"

Liza crossed her arms, aware the position pushed her breasts up, something Matt took more than a few moments to enjoy.

Tit. For. Tat.

"Answer me," he barked.

She gave him the brattiest grin she could produce and then shook her head, her lips closed tightly.

"You want to play, kitten?"

Oh God, where did that nickname come from, and why was it so deadly to her restraint?

Matt stalked toward her. "Then let's play. Just remember what I said in the restaurant. Russos always come out on top."

Matt's expression told her there could only be one alpha in this room, and he knew it would be him.

Sadly, she did too.

Gripping her upper arm, he dragged her to the bed, unceremoniously shoving her face down on the mattress. "Safe word?"

"Red," she replied, though hell would freeze over before she used it.

Matt held her down with one hand on her upper back, the

other spanking every inch of her ass and thighs until she was gasping for breath.

"Open your legs." Matt used his foot, nudging her ankles apart impatiently.

Liza from ten minutes ago would have goaded him longer, but the spanking had jarred something loose, something feral, something wild. Her anger fled, drowned by the arousal roaring through her body.

Parting her thighs, she hissed when Matt spanked her pussy—three hard smacks that had her shifting up on her toes, pain and pleasure mingling until she was mindless.

"Please!" she gasped.

She expected Matt to crow over her plea or demand she beg him for more, but she wasn't the only one operating on anger and arousal and sheer carnal need.

The head of his cock bumped against her clit, then he guided it to her opening, slamming in with one hard, teeth-chattering thrust.

She lifted her head as much as his strong grip would allow, looking at him over her shoulder. "Fuck me hard. Make it hurt."

Liza put just enough strength behind her demand to let Matt know he hadn't completely conquered her.

Pride was going to give submission a run for its money, and the tune to "The Race is On" played in her mind. Then the music was drowned out by a cacophony of drumbeats—the pounding of her heart thudding in her ears, the headboard of the bed banging against the wall, as he gave her exactly what she'd asked for.

Matt's thrusts were brutal, rough, and nowhere near as controlled as she'd come to expect from him.

"God, Liza," he cried out when she felt the first twinges of her orgasm. Her pussy throbbed around his dick, her vision blurred, unfocused. Her climax struck hard, and she screamed as she splintered apart.

"Can't. Stop," Matt grunted, his own climax coming on the

heels of hers. "Can't stop," he repeated, though his words rang different the second time.

By the time he said them once more, his tone pure anguish, Liza realized he wasn't talking about sex or coming.

"I can't stop!"

He was talking about them.

Chapter Eleven

Matt leaned back in his chair, watching as Liza stopped by Arnold and Johnnie's table on her way back from the bar, chatting with the grooms. She was clearly stalling, doing whatever she could to avoid coming back to the table. She'd been giving him the cold shoulder ever since she returned from her tour of Pearl Harbor earlier this afternoon. There had been no more discussion about her getting her own room, though he suspected she still planned to. She probably would have gotten one this morning if they hadn't overslept, making her late to leave for her tour.

He tried to remind himself her feelings were none of his concern. After all, he'd made no bones about the fact that this affair was sex only.

So if that was the case, why did he wish she was sitting here, smiling at him, talking to him about her day? He'd enjoyed that first afternoon he'd spent by the ocean with her more than any day in years. God, he'd even raptly listened to her family stories, and he couldn't stand the damn Morettis.

He lifted his glass of whiskey, taking a large sip. He should probably slow down. This was his third drink and the bartender's pours were very, *very* generous. He was hoping the alcohol would fog his brain enough that he wouldn't have to think about how badly he'd fucked things up with Liza yesterday...and today.

After the nightmare, he'd decided his best course of action would be to put some distance between the two of them. Liza had begun to look at him in ways that made him...uncomfortable. She was starting to see things in him that simply weren't there.

While she gave off an air of being tough as nails, now that he'd gotten to know her better, Liza had become more transparent to him. As such, he could see that she wore her heart on her sleeve.

So yesterday morning, he'd lied about having a big meeting, hoping the physical distance would help break whatever spell had fallen over them. He'd spent all afternoon hunkered down in the room, pretending to work on his laptop.

What he'd really done was far more concerning. Because the second she'd left the room, he had pulled out a piece of paper and a pen and drawn a sketch of her.

He hadn't indulged his interest in art since he was fourteen, and his father caught him sketching his brothers when they were outside playing one afternoon. As always, he'd been in his father's office, doing homework, listening to Dad read one of his employees the riot act, when laughter from the window captured his attention. His brothers were tossing a football back and forth, talking and laughing.

Matt remembered how much he'd longed to go out and join them. Aware that wasn't possible, he'd started drawing them. He had almost finished the picture when his father saw it. Dad had torn it to pieces, yelling at him for wasting his time on stupid "girlie shit."

Dad wasn't averse to corporal punishment, so Matt had gotten the belt more than a few times when he was a kid. His father had also been known to backhand him whenever Matt got smart-mouthed. But Dante's preferred method of punishment was discovering what someone loved, then destroying it.

Up until that point, Matt's art had been keeping him sane,

but the idea of his father destroying all his work put an end to that.

Liza had become an unwelcome distraction and a huge disruption to his well-ordered routine, so he'd sought out the long-forgotten go-to, turning to art for peace. And it had worked...right up until he put the pen down and spent the remainder of the afternoon gazing at what he'd created.

He'd drawn her in her elegant red ball gown, the one she'd worn to the Snowflake Gala. In the picture, she was standing in profile next to the large picture windows, staring out at the cold night, lost in thought, and his own thoughts had drifted back to their first dance...and what came after.

Reliving every minute of that night had set him back in terms of the strides he'd made in setting safe boundaries with her. Rather than reinforce the fact this couldn't be more than sex, remembering her in that dress had him longing to find her, to drag her back here so he could spend the rest of this trip with her tied to his bed as he lost himself inside her.

After returning from the tour yesterday, Liza had cheerfully invited him to join her for dinner because he'd allowed her to believe that they were on holiday together by inviting her to stay in his suite.

So he'd had to change up his game plan, increase the emotional distance as well as the physical. It had been easier than he cared to admit, pulling out the old Matt. The one his father had raised him to be—cold, arrogant, unapologetic. While that version of himself still existed and had made more than a few appearances over the years—usually whenever dealing with someone who was a threat to his family or his business—typically he was able to keep his mask of indifference in place, tucking the darker, less savory parts of himself away.

When the conversation about Johnnie's cousins came up, Matt had spied a way to open her eyes to who he really was. He didn't like rehashing the past because he never came out of the stories looking good, but he could tell Liza was trying to rewrite an old story, to create a better version of the night he'd seduced Tony's girlfriend.

No such version existed because he'd done everything her cousin had accused him of, and he'd done it all with malicious intent.

Matt had been relieved when Liza's temper sparked because it felt familiar and safe, like they were on solid ground again. In his mind, he'd already gone back to the hotel, moved her into her own room, and was prepared to ignore her for the rest of the trip. He'd even considered offering his apologies to the grooms, hopping on his jet, and getting the hell out of dodge. Coming here had been a huge mistake.

The best way forward was for them to go backward, to continue being workplace nemeses, old family enemies, and somewhere down the road—in a decade or eight—he'd find a way to break free of his obsession with Liza Moretti.

Of course, that plan went to hell when she paused by the reception desk, and he'd snapped at the idea of letting her walk away from him. As was becoming his habit where she was concerned, he instantly lost the ground he'd made by dragging her back to his suite and fucking her like a meteor was about to strike the planet.

Mercifully, Matt had made it through the night without another bad dream, but that was only because he'd tossed and turned, too anxious to ever reach REM sleep. This morning when Liza had asked him if he wanted to join her on her tour of Pearl Harbor, he'd bailed, claiming he needed to work again. Matt had hated the hurt look on her face. So much so, he'd almost caved and accompanied her, but fortunately, he'd managed to refrain. Instead, he'd drawn another sketch of her. This time, it was of Liza standing under that streetlamp on New Year's Eve, snow flurries falling as she looked up into the night sky.

Once that was done, he'd done the unthinkable and ordered a bunch of art supplies online. They would all be delivered to his home by the time he returned from Hawaii.

Liza smiled at him as she returned to the table, but it wasn't the easygoing one she'd graced him with a couple of days ago. This smile was less sunny, uncertain, maybe even a bit annoyed. Not that he could blame her. He'd acted like a bear with a thorn in his paw ever since they sat down for the rehearsal dinner. The meal had ended, their tablemates circulating the room, socializing with other guests.

"Johnnie said they're about to start hula lessons. I think I'm going to give it a whirl. Wanna try it?" It was the most she had said to him since she'd returned from Pearl Harbor.

"Pass," he said.

Liza sighed. "It's Hawaii, Matt. The perfect place to forget about work and cut loose. Besides, I'm pretty sure hula lessons are a required part of the touristy fun. Think it was in the fine print when we booked our flights." He appreciated her efforts to make peace. He didn't enjoy the two of them being at odds, even if he'd been the one to put them there.

"I didn't book a flight," he reminded her. "Besides, wiggling my ass in front of a bunch of strangers isn't what I call fun."

"What is it with you and wiggling asses?" The unexpected tease was sultry as hell, reminding him of the night they spent together on his jet. Liza's wiggling ass had been far too tempting for him to resist that night, so he'd given in, taken her.

With one question, she'd thrust them right back to that place he was trying to escape. Now, rather than walk away, he found himself not only closing the door to the exit but locking it as well.

Leaning forward, he lowered his voice. "Behave."

The word and the gruff tone had the desired effect as her eyelids grew heavy, her cheeks flushed, and for a moment, he hoped she'd issue that same dare she tossed at him last night.

When she'd told him to "make her," the alpha inside had crashed out of him like the goddamn Kool-Aid Man. Spanking Liza ranked in his top five favorite things ever and he couldn't wait to do it again. If he had his way, he'd fill all five of his top spots with it.

This time, Liza's smile was bratty as hell. And, for a moment, he thought he was going to get his wish.

Unfortunately, someone gave Johnnie a microphone and he invited guests to the floor for the hula lesson.

Tease forgotten, Liza rose from the table and walked to the floor. She glanced back over her shoulder at him a couple of times, obviously hoping he'd join her. The second time she looked, he shook his head.

He'd rather remain here with an unobstructed view of his naughty girl.

The instructor demonstrated several moves that everyone copied, while explaining the proper technique for hip swaying and the use of hands. There was a lot of laughing, everyone enjoying the lesson, taking it with varying degrees of seriousness.

Arnold's hula was so wooden, Matt wasn't sure he was moving his hips at all. Probably because all his concentration was on the arm movements, which were flailing so wildly, he was concerned the man might take flight. After a few minutes, Arnold threw in the towel, loudly proclaiming that there was a problem at the bar. As far as Matt could tell, the only problem was Arnold's drink was ready and waiting for him.

Johnnie was, of course, an amazing hula dancer. As was Liza. God, she was a natural, and if Matt didn't look away soon, he was going to have to excuse himself to take care of some business. His dick had been rock-hard since the first sway of her hips.

The instructor started playing a hula song, guiding everyone through the simple routine she'd just taught them. Liza's happy expression told Matt how much she was enjoying herself, and he couldn't help but smile as well.

Until an attractive man stepped up behind her.

Matt didn't know who the man was, but it was clear he was a native of the island, as he'd been chipping in to help the instructor, the two of them moving among the guests, giving personal help where needed.

Matt saw red when the man placed his hands on Liza's hips, as if to correct the way they were swaying. She'd been nailing the routine, so the move was a ploy, a weak attempt at getting closer to an attractive woman.

Liza looked over her shoulder at the man, laughing at something he said, and Matt's eyes narrowed.

"Clench that jaw much harder and you'll break your teeth."

Matt glanced up at Arnold, who'd made his way from the bar to Matt's table. If Matt had been in the proper frame of mind, he would have turned his attention away from the dance floor and made pleasant small talk.

He *wasn't* in the proper frame.

"Who's the wannabe hula instructor?" Matt asked.

"One of Johnnie's countless nephews," Arnold replied. "Did I ever mention that Johnnie has five sisters? All married with at least twelve kids apiece."

Arnold was going for levity, trying to calm him down. Matt might have appreciated the effort if the nephew's hands hadn't just slipped upward from Liza's hips, gripping her waist in a way that was way too fucking familiar.

"Is the nephew a nice guy?" Matt growled. He'd told Liza this thing between them was just sex, so he could hardly get in the way of her flirting with someone else. They'd made no commitment to each other, and he had gone out of his way to make sure she knew it.

Because he was a goddamn idiot.

Arnold shook his head, studying the couple. "No. That particular nephew is a huge prick."

Matt took his eyes off Liza to see if Arnold was being serious or pulling his leg. "He is?"

"His wife is at home in San Francisco. She just had their second baby two weeks ago."

"You're kidding?" Matt said hotly.

Arnold raised a hand and pointed to his soon-to-be husband. "Johnnie's clenching his teeth harder than you. He noticed earlier that the asshole wasn't wearing his ring."

The nephew brushed Liza's hair over her shoulder, whispering something in her ear that had her blushing.

"Excuse me," Matt said, storming onto the dance floor.

Liza jerked with surprise when Matt grabbed her hand and tugged her against his chest.

"Matt? What are you doing?" She tried to pull her hand from his. Wisely, the married nephew took one look at the murderous expression on his face and moved away—fast.

Matt used his free hand to cup the back of Liza's neck, pulling her closer until his lips were next to her ear. "What's the rule about wiggling those hips, bad girl?"

Liza stopped trying to pull away, her body going soft as she leaned closer to him. "There's a rule?" she whispered, her breath hot against his cheek.

He shifted back just far enough that he could look her in the eye. "You only wiggle them for *me*."

Liza's eyes narrowed, half desire, half anger. Only she could pull off a look like that.

"Careful, Matt," she warned. "You're treading very close to a line you don't want to cross. *Only* is a dangerous word."

His jealousy replied before he could talk it down. "Only," he repeated darkly.

Matt tightened his grip on the back of her neck. It was a possessive hold, one he'd never used in his life before her, but the stake he needed to claim on Liza was too big for anything as subtle as holding her hand or placing his own on her lower back. If he'd gotten any sense it made her uncomfortable, he would have released her, but every time he touched her this way, he felt her shoulders relax, and his inner caveman beat his chest as she gave herself over to him.

He tried to use the grip to guide her off the floor, but Liza resisted. Not that he could blame her.

He'd been a regular Dr. Jekyll and Mr. Hyde since they'd landed on the island. Too much more of this bullshit, and they'd both wind up with a wicked case of whiplash.

Regardless, Liza had unwittingly lit a fire fueled by jealousy when she responded to the nephew's flirting.

"Walk out on your own steam, Ms. Moretti, or I'll throw you over my shoulder."

She glared at him. "Are you serious right now?"

"Test me. I dare you."

Angry sparks flared between them. He'd thought she was pissed off last night, but that anger didn't hold a candle to this rage.

Good. There was no reason he should be the only one on the cusp of outright fury.

Perhaps if that was all he felt, he'd back off, but mingled with all that fury was so much arousal, he was surprised the two of them weren't drowning in it.

Liza stopped resisting, following him off the floor and to their table.

"Get your purse," he barked.

She grabbed it as Matt looked over at Arnold, who was still standing in the same spot, watching them with a great deal of interest.

"Thanks for dinner," Matt said, working hard to sound polite and failing. "We're looking forward to the wedding tomorrow."

Why did he use the pronoun "we?" He should have said "I."

"You two have a good night," Arnold replied with a knowing, too-pleased grin. Matt was pretty sure he'd been invited to this wedding as part of the older man's matchmaking scheme. Matt should be pissed about that. Instead, he felt like taking Arnold out for a big-ass steak dinner as thanks.

Liza opened her mouth to speak, but Matt didn't trust what she planned to say, so he quickly guided her toward the exit of the restaurant. Johnnie and Arnold had booked the entire thing for their rehearsal dinner, the sign on the door they walked through proclaiming the place was closed for a private party.

Fortunately, it was less than a block away from the hotel. Once outside, Matt released her neck, lowering his hand to her back. He expected her to twist away from his grip and give him holy hell, so he was pleasantly surprised when she let it remain there.

Neither of them spoke as they walked. Matt tried to get his jealousy under control, but it was an emotion he had no experience with. None at all.

Entering the hotel and crossing the foyer, he fought to take several deep breaths, but they didn't help. Especially when the two of them entered the suite and Liza slammed the door closed.

"What the hell is your prob—"

That was as much as she managed to say before he shoved her against the closed door, crushing her with a bruising kiss.

It was their first kiss since New Year's.

That wasn't a fluke. It was by design.

Matt had specifically avoided her lips, treating them like his own personal Bermuda Triangle. Sex with Liza posed enough of a risk, but adding the intimacy of kissing?

Now that the gate had been opened, Matt was screwed six ways to Sunday, but he didn't give a shit. She tasted like wine and dessert, like home and happiness, like sunshine and...

Her tongue stroked his as he reached beneath her knee, lifting one of her legs, driving his crotch against her panties-clad pussy. She'd worn a sundress to the rehearsal dinner, one with spaghetti straps, which meant he'd spent too much of the night thinking about the fact she wasn't wearing a bra.

Her hands looped around his neck as she tilted her hips toward him.

She turned her head away, breaking the kiss. Matt growled because he was nowhere near finished with her lips. He grasped her jaw, turning her face back to his.

"Stop manhandling me," she said, though there was no force behind the words. She didn't help her case when her gaze dropped to his mouth as she licked her lips. Then she completely lost the argument when she initiated the next kiss. It was all tongue, teeth, and hot breaths.

Matt pulled away next. "You were flirting with another man."

They were the worst words he could possibly say because they made what was happening here a hell of a lot less fuzzy. Shit, with one sentence, he'd granted her twenty-twenty vision. He tried to erase his faux pas with another kiss, one that started at her lips and continued along her cheek to her ear, down the side of her neck.

"It's a free world," she responded. "And I'm a free woman."

Oh yeah. Fuck that.

He released her, dropping her leg, but only so that he could grab the hem of her sundress, ripping it over her head in one rough pull. Liza's response was to grip his neck once more, pulling him back for another explosive kiss.

Matt unfastened his pants as they devoured each other with the kiss. Shoving them and his boxer briefs to mid-thigh, he pulled her panties to the side, lifted her leg again, and thrust inside.

He closed his eyes, groaning with pleasure as he pounded inside her. Her pussy muscles quivered against him, her back sliding up the door with each thrust.

This wasn't sex. It was punishment.

His and hers.

When Liza's fingers closed around his hair, pulling it roughly...when she bit his lower lip, he knew they were both seeking retribution.

She deserved to punish him after the roller-coaster ride he'd put her on the past few days.

"Matt!" she cried out, already there, her inner muscles clamping down so hard, he saw stars. He fucked her through her first orgasm *and* the second because he couldn't stop.

Those were the same words he'd said to her last night. He knew what he should do, but for the first time in his life, he couldn't regain control and he didn't want to.

Liza made him want things he shouldn't want. But more than that, she made him believe that maybe...just maybe...he could have them.

"God!" she yelled, her head falling back against the door with a bang. She'd lost her grip on his hair, her hands hanging over his shoulders, her strength deserting her as she trembled. Two orgasms did that to a person. "It's too much."

"No," he barked. "It's not enough."

"I can't..." Liza's words fell away the second he reached between them, his finger stroking her clit.

"No more flirting with other men," he said through gritted teeth, punctuating each of his next words with a hard thrust. "You're. Here. With. Me."

"With you," she whispered, though he couldn't tell if her words were an agreement or a question.

"Mine."

The power of that one word—the sheer force of that single syllable—pulled the trigger, taking them both down hard. Liza's body shook as her third orgasm struck. Matt's eyes rolled back in his head as he came with her. He had to lock his knees to keep them both from collapsing to the floor.

When he managed to open his eyes, his surroundings coming back to him slowly, he felt Liza's cheek pressed against his chest, heard her rapid panting.

He cupped her head, holding her there as he shifted, pulling out.

Matt hadn't used a condom last night, or this time either. Now that he'd experienced the ecstasy of being bare inside her, he didn't think he could ever go back. She'd told him the night of the gala, after they'd fucked, that she had an IUD. He assumed she'd shared the information that they'd been doubly protected to comfort him. At the time, neither of them had anticipated going back for a repeat performance, so he understood her desire to assure him nothing would come from that one-night stand except for the earth-shattering orgasms.

"Liza," he started. "Do you still have the IUD?"

She lifted her head slowly. "Of course I do. Do you think I would have let you inside me without a condom if I didn't?"

He grinned, even as he shook his head. "Glad one of us has a level head," he said, placing a kiss on her forehead before reaching down to pull his pants back up.

Liza smirked at him, pushing him back a few inches so she could walk into the hotel room. They hadn't made it a foot from the door before they'd attacked each other like wild beasts.

"So what was that, back at the restaurant?" she asked. "Jealousy?"

It was, but Matt had already used too many of the wrong words tonight. "That guy you were flirting with, Johnnie's nephew, is married."

Liza frowned. "He wasn't wearing a ring."

The fact she'd checked it out had Matt seeing red, because his jealous mind was telling him that was a sign of her interest. "He has two kids. His wife is back home in San Francisco with their two-week-old newborn."

Liza's eyes widened with rage. "That cheating bastard." She bent over, picking up her dress, shaking it out as if she planned to put it back on.

Matt gripped her wrist. "What are you doing?"

"Going back to the restaurant to knee that son of a bitch in the nuts."

Matt took in the fury in her eyes, amused when he realized she meant what she said. God, he loved her fire, her spirit.

"Tomorrow," he said, pulling the dress out of her hands. "You can do it at the reception. A wedding gift for Johnnie. Didn't you say he was hoping for some drama?"

Liza grinned. "He is." Her amusement faded too quickly, and he understood why.

"Liza..." he started.

She must have assumed he was going to put this conversation off or maybe even push her away again, because she cut him off. "You're going to have to give me something here, Matt. You're worse than that Katy Perry song. Hot, cold, up, down, in, out. It's exhausting."

"You're right. It is."

"So do you want to talk about some of those words you just threw my way. Because they don't fit the 'just sex' mold."

Matt considered his dwindling options, measured all the things he'd tried and failed.

Which meant there was only one thing left to do.

He did as she asked. He gave her something, repeating all the words, putting them together in a way that would leave no doubt in her mind. Cupping her cheek affectionately, he looked deep into her eyes and let her see exactly what she'd done to him. "You're with *me*, Liza. Only me. Mine."

He wasn't sure how he expected her to respond to that. After the way he'd behaved the past two days, she would be perfectly justified in telling him to go take a flying leap, but she didn't.

Instead, she gave him a smile so genuine, so happy, it took his breath away. No one had ever looked at him like that. Like he was...good.

It made Matt want to give her the world. Made him want to be a man worthy of someone as special as her.

He wasn't sure he could do it, but for her...

He would try.

Chapter Twelve

Liza stood on the edge of the floor, watching the grooms dance their first dance. The wedding took place on the beach a few hours earlier, and it had been perfect.

And Matt had been perfect.

Last night, things had shifted between them, and Liza had felt the urge to pinch herself all day, just to make sure she was awake and not dreaming. After dumping that stupid "just sex" descriptor, Matt led her to the bed, pushed her to her back, went down on her, and kept her on edge for nearly an hour, withholding her orgasm until she was a live wire, sparking like mad.

Matt had refused to let her come until she gave him back every single one of his words—with interest—demanding she declare over and over that she was his. *Only* his.

Then he'd used his fingers and tongue to drive her to the most explosive orgasm of her life, before crawling over her body and fucking her into oblivion.

And even as incredible as the night had been, she'd still woken up this morning wondering which Matt would be there. The cold, distant man, intent on pushing her away, or...

Or the Matt she knew without a shadow of a doubt was the man of her dreams.

The man she was falling in love with.

She'd opened her eyes, prepared to find herself alone in bed, just as she had the previous two mornings. Instead, he'd been laying there next to her, wide awake, propped up on his elbow and watching her sleep. She'd made a joke about him being a creeper, but rather than laugh, he'd kissed her slowly but oh so completely, then told her she was the most beautiful woman he'd ever seen.

Shit. She could pinch herself a thousand times and still never believe this was real because she'd spent too many years longing for something she feared she would never find.

"You're one of those people, aren't you?" Matt stepped behind her, wrapping his arm around her waist. He placed a sweet kiss on the top of her head. He was a tall guy, a couple inches over six feet, his large, muscular frame making her feel tiny in comparison. The difference in their sizes added another element to her attraction toward him, fed into her desire to be with someone dominant, someone powerful. Matt fit the bill physically and personality-wise.

She looked over her shoulder. "What do you mean?"

"You're one of those people who cry during the wedding ceremony." He knew she was because she *had*. He'd been the one to offer her a tissue.

"You're one of those people who stand at the edge of the dance floor, snapping a million pictures of the first dance."

Not a million, but she'd snapped a few...or maybe like twenty.

"You're one of those people who're first in line for the cake and front row when the bouquet is tossed," Matt continued.

Her grin had grown throughout the list, letting him know without words that he was spot-on.

"You say all that like it's a bad thing."

Matt tightened his grip around her waist. "Not a bad thing. In truth, I suspect it's hereditary, passed down through those Moretti genes of yours because it's true of everyone in your family, isn't it?"

"You were at Gage and Penny's wedding, so you got to witness it firsthand."

"I did," he said, though she noticed he wasn't using the same slightly annoyed tone that seemed reserved for conversations about her family.

Mention of her family sent her thoughts down paths she'd been trying to avoid since hopping on the plane with Matt. Her family was wonderful, so if this thing between her and Matt went the distance, she was confident they'd support her decision.

Regardless, she was going to have to be a lot more certain of the relationship before she opened that can of worms. It felt as if they'd turned a corner after the rehearsal dinner, but Liza was too much of a realist to bet the whole farm on one incredible, amazing, perfect night.

And because of that damn pragmatist personality, she couldn't let go of her concerns regarding what might happen when they returned to Philadelphia. Spending time together on holiday was easy, carefree, and fun. How would this thing between her and Matt translate when they were dumped down in the middle of their real lives?

Matt turned her with a hand on her waist until she faced him, then he gave her a kiss. Last night was the first time he'd kissed her since New Year's Eve, and now that they'd added it to the mix, it felt as if they couldn't stop. They'd shared at least a hundred kisses today.

Not that she was complaining. Matt's kisses made her feel warm and fuzzy.

The deejay invited other couples to join the grooms on the dance floor. Matt took her hand and led her just a few feet away from where they'd been standing. He wrapped his arms around her as she placed her cheek on his chest, and she was reminded of their first dance, the night of the gala. Even that night, when she'd still considered him her arch enemy, she'd felt safe, cared for, comfortable—words she never used in regard to her relationship with Matt.

Arnold and Johnnie had opted for a casual dress code for the wedding, most of the men in lightweight pants and Hawaiian shirts, the women in sundresses. She'd opted for a pale pink twist dress, the skirt cut high in the front, low in the back, with flowy cap sleeves. It was much simpler than the elegant gown she'd worn to the Snowflake Gala.

Just before leaving for the wedding, Matt had given her a gift. She reached up to touch the necklace briefly, wanting to make sure it was still there. The ruby teardrop pendant was topped with a diamond and hanging from an 18K rose gold chain. She'd tried to give it back, exclaiming it cost too much.

Matt refused, demanding that she turn around—in that tone —so that he could put it on her. She'd never owned anything so beautiful or expensive, so she was scared to death of losing it.

"It's still there," Matt murmured against her hair.

"You shouldn't have spent so much." This wasn't the first time she'd made that comment.

"I'm going to spoil you, Liza. You might want to get used to that."

She lifted her face to his. "Thank you," she whispered.

"You already thanked me," he reminded her. "Three times in the room, in the elevator, on the walk to the beach before the wedding, during dinner."

She laughed. "I'm just trying to show my appreciation."

Matt's hand slid from her waist to the small of her back as he pulled her more snugly against him. "Mmm. Later, when we get back to the room, I'll let you *show* me all night."

Oh God. There were so many ways she wanted to show him. "What did you have in mind?" she whispered, lifting on tiptoe so that her lips were next to his jaw, his well-trimmed beard tickling her. Unable to resist, she gave him a quick kiss.

"I'm going to tie you to the bed, kitten. Going to use that vibrator you packed on you."

"That sounds backward. I thought I was showing you my appreciation. That sounds like me receiving, you giving."

Matt's brows furrowed. "You think there's something I want more than you tied up and at my mercy while I give you your other gift?"

She stopped swaying. "There's another one?"

"You're not dripping in rubies yet," he said, his tone pure seduction.

She knew exactly what he was hinting at. The night of the gala, he'd told her all the places he'd put rubies on her. Her neck was the most innocent, and while she loved this necklace more than she could say, she was more excited about the idea he might have ruby nipple clamps or—sweet Jesus—he mentioned a clamp for her clit and a butt plug. Her curiosity sparked over what it might be.

"You didn't leave my side all day. How did you get these gifts?" They'd spent the morning by the pool, soaking up the sun. Since the wedding was scheduled for midafternoon, they didn't have time to do any sightseeing on the island.

"I have a phone, an amazing personal assistant, and unlimited funds. There's very little I want that I can't acquire."

Liza had grown up in a middle-class family and while she made a good salary, she lived within a budget and was an accomplished bargain hunter. "Must be nice."

He winked at her. "It's very nice, kitten."

"Why kitten?"

Matt never missed a beat, his expression pure amusement. "Because you're soft and sweet and adorable, but you also have very sharp claws."

She narrowed her eyes, feigning a warning tone when she said, "And don't you forget it."

"Never," Matt murmured.

They continued swaying in time to the music, Liza too distracted by thoughts of what Matt had planned for the rest of their evening. She loved Johnnie and Arnold dearly, but she couldn't help but wonder how early was too early to bail on someone's reception.

Matt, ever astute, chuckled. "We've got all night, Liza. Let's enjoy the rest of the party."

She grimaced but nodded. She'd spent a lot of time offering input while Johnnie planned the wedding. He'd be hurt if she missed a huge part of the reception because of her raging hormones.

The slow song ended, a fast one starting. Matt, no fan of dancing, grasped her hand and led her off the floor.

"Wine?" he asked.

She nodded and the two of them made their way to the bar.

The rest of the evening passed more quickly than Liza anticipated, as Matt stole every single one of her slow dances. They spent more than a few minutes chatting with the grooms, who were absolutely aglow with happiness. There hadn't been a bit of drama regarding the warring cousins, Maya and Maggie, and Johnnie had jokingly bitched about how they'd appeared to make amends.

As the evening wound down, she and Matt said their good-byes, walking hand in hand back to their room. Closing the door behind them, Matt gestured toward the bar in the suite. Because, of course, Matt had a suite with a substantial bar. "Want a nightcap?"

She shook her head. "Nope. I want to show my appreciation." As she spoke, she began to unbutton his Hawaiian shirt, aware there was nothing this man wore that didn't look incredible on him. He was the sexiest man she'd ever seen, whether he was wearing a bespoke suit, jeans and a tee, or even khaki linen pants and a Hawaiian shirt.

Matt tsked, gripping her wrists tightly. "Did I give you permission to do that?"

Her breath caught in her chest, her heart racing. "Do I need permission?" She'd intended to put some pretend heat behind the question, but it was too airy, too needy.

Matt pulled her wrists behind her back, gripping them together with one hand as the other cupped her jaw. His lips brushed her cheek. "You're going to do everything I say tonight."

"Everything?" she repeated.

"You're going to be a good girl."

Those words rubbed up against her feminist side, and she was tempted to push back despite the fact those last two words also ensured her panties were drenched. Her gaze lifted to his and she saw something shift behind them, something dark and dangerous. The dominant man was emerging, and he was testing her.

For a second, she tried to decide if it would be better to pass or to fail.

"I've never punished you, Liza."

God, how was he so good at reading her thoughts? Then she scoffed. "I beg to differ."

"Those spankings were foreplay, not correction. You don't want to discover what the difference is. So tonight, you are going to be *my* good girl."

Liza stood there, letting the words sink in—really sink in—and then she just let it all go. There was no one in this bedroom except the two of them. They weren't subject to societal norms, didn't have to answer to judgmental pricks, didn't have to hide their kinks, their darkest desires, their wildest fantasies. She didn't have to use her public face, the one that revealed her as a strong, capable woman who took no shit. The idea of not having to try so hard, to analyze every action, every word, felt like a gift.

Right here, right now, with him, she could just be. Thinking wasn't necessary. All she had to do was trust him and feel.

Matt must have noticed the change in her because he smiled, placing a soft kiss on her cheek. "There you are," he whispered.

He released her wrists, and she whimpered, instantly missing the restriction.

Matt brushed the back of his knuckles along the side of her face. "You're perfect," he murmured. "Go to the bedroom, kitten. Take off all your clothes and lay down in the middle of the bed."

Liza moved without hesitance, wanting nothing more than to

please him. She worked quickly, efficiently, stripping off the dress, her bra, her panties, and sandals, then assuming the position he'd demanded. The only thing she didn't remove was the necklace.

Dripping in rubies, he'd said.

Matt hadn't followed her into the bedroom. Instead, she heard ice tinkling in a glass. Her curiosity was piqued, but not enough to disobey him. He'd told her where he wanted her, so that was where she was going to stay.

A minute or two later, Matt walked into the room carrying a highball glass. There was only about an inch of brown liquid in it. She'd discovered this week that he was a big fan of Scotch, ordering Glengoyne the one night they'd actually made it out of the room for dinner. From the way the waiter's eyebrows arched, she could tell Matt had asked for an extremely expensive brand.

His gaze drifted over her naked form, taking in the necklace and her hands. She'd placed them on the pillow next to her head, palms up, the ultimate pose of surrender.

Stepping next to the bed, he placed the drink on the nightstand, staring down at her. He was still dressed—dammit—and he appeared to be in no hurry to change that state.

Once he'd looked his fill, he walked over to his suitcase, returning with several neckties. Liza squeezed her legs together, her arousal off the charts. She'd always—ALWAYS—wanted to be tied up in bed, and that tiny taste he'd given her the day he'd used her bikini to bind her hands behind her back hadn't been enough. It had only whetted her desire for more. She didn't doubt for a moment that Matt would make the experience amazing.

He placed one knee on the bed next to her hip, reaching for her hands. Using one of the ties, he bound her wrists together with one end, then wrapped the rest around a slat in the center of the headboard.

He moved to the bottom of the bed, securing her right ankle to one footpost, her left to the other. She tested the knots, amazed by how well the silky material held. She'd assumed the ties would be more suggestive than effective, simply there to give the illusion of being defenseless, but damn if Matt hadn't managed to render her truly helpless.

Her heart began to race, though not in a bad way.

"Safe word," he murmured.

"Red," she whispered. This. This was why she trusted him. Because even as he made every single one of her darker fantasies come true, he still ensured her safety—even from him. With that one word, he was taking care of her mentally as well as physically.

She expected Matt to touch her, so she was surprised when he picked up the glass, tossing back the Scotch. It hadn't been more than a shot. A shot and two ice cubes.

Rather than put the glass down, he lifted it again, sucking one of the chunks of ice into his mouth. Liza never took her eyes off him, fascinated and turned on by every damn thing he did.

Putting the glass on the nightstand, he sat down on the edge of the bed, his torso turned toward her. Lowering his head, his cold lips landed just under her jaw. She shivered when, rather than kiss her, he held the ice cube between his teeth and ran it down the side of her neck, then along her collarbone.

Matt left a trail of icy water as he progressed farther down her body. She gasped when he ran the ice over her nipple, and for the first time, she fought against the ties around her hands, trying to lower them so she could escape the cold.

"Matt," she whispered.

He took the ice from his mouth as he shook his head, giving her a stern look. "I didn't give you permission to speak."

"But—" she started.

Matt scowled and leaned over her, his face a mere inch from hers, the smell of the Scotch on his breath impacting her in strange ways. Since when did whiskey become an aphrodisiac?

"Speak again and I'll gag you."

At some point—not now—Liza was going to let him know just how far his sensual threats missed the mark. She licked her lips, hoping he'd take her up on the invitation to kiss her.

He didn't. Rising until he was sitting next to her once more, he drew the slowly melting ice in a circle around one budded nipple, the intense cold on the cusp of painful.

When he finally moved the cube away, she held her breath, expecting him to treat the other nipple to the same. Instead, he put the cube back in the glass.

Liza closed her eyes and relaxed, but it was a brief respite.

"Open your eyes, kitten. I have another gift for you."

Liza's eyelids lifted as Matt grabbed a square box from the nightstand drawer. Removing the lid, he withdrew another ruby, this one smaller than the pendant on her necklace, though it also dangled.

She'd never experimented with nipple clamps, not with other lovers or even alone. To be honest, before Matt, she hadn't considered her breasts one of her key erogenous zones. Apparently, that was because past lovers hadn't known how to play with them the way Matt did.

He drew the clamp toward her tight, cold nipple. No pause. No questioning look. He'd given her the safe word, so he clearly didn't feel the need to double-check for her willingness. If she didn't want it, all she had to say was red.

Hell would freeze over first.

Or that was what she thought. Until he snapped the clamp onto her nipple, and she gasped in pain. She panicked for a moment, afraid she'd broken the no-talking rule because she'd screamed out a few curse words. Mercifully, she realized they'd all been in her head.

Matt admired his work for a moment, then lifted his gaze. "Take a deep breath. In through your nose, out through your mouth. Give your body a chance to adjust."

She didn't see that happening, even as she followed his instructions. Three breaths later, she was still tempted to say the word. Until Matt jiggled the ruby with his finger, toying with it. "Beautiful."

His word was the salve, the stinging pain fading away until it almost felt as if her nipple had its own heartbeat. It pulsed in time with the quivering of her pussy, and she knew there was no way she was going to make it through this without breaking his rule, without begging him to take her.

Matt, adept at reading her, must have sensed the tide had turned because he grabbed what remained of the first piece of ice and repeated the same torturous process on the other nipple. This time, when he snapped the second clamp on, she was better prepared, already utilizing his deep breathing techniques. It still stung, but it was tolerable because she knew what was on the other side.

Once both nipples were clamped, Matt rose from the bed, crossing to her suitcase.

He'd discovered her vibrator by accident earlier today. She'd just gotten out of the shower when she realized she had forgotten clean panties. She'd called out to Matt, who was dressing in the bedroom, asking if he would grab a pair from her suitcase. When he'd entered the bathroom with an amused smirk, she'd known he was up to something before he said a word.

Leaning in the doorway between the bathroom and bedroom, he'd watched as she slipped on her panties and bra.

"Do you always travel with your vibrator?" he'd asked with a shit-eating grin.

Liza had groaned, then started to confess the truth. "Not usually, but my sex drive has been in full swing since the night of the..." She'd paused, mentally kicking herself for not playing it cool. After all, Matt was a huge flight risk.

He'd filled in the blanks for himself, then admitted, "I've had the same problem since the gala."

They'd grinned at each other like a couple of lovestruck fools, then he'd continued getting dressed for the wedding, and he hadn't mentioned it again until their first dance at the reception.

Returning to the bed, he stopped at the foot of the mattress, crawling onto it between her outstretched legs.

Matt ran his fingers along her slit, lifting the shiny tips up for her to see. "Nice and wet," he reported, before turning on the toy.

It was a standard vibrator—no bells or whistles. It had three speeds and was a decent enough size that—when paired with her recent fantasies of Matt—it managed to do the trick quite efficiently.

She expected Matt to push it inside her, so she jerked—startled—when he pressed the vibrating tip against her clit.

A rush of air and a loud moan escaped. "Oh God," she gasped, her eyes closed, her hips shifting as much as the ties on her legs would allow.

Her eyes flew open when the toy was silenced instantly.

Shit.

She wasn't supposed to speak. It was on the tip of her tongue to apologize, but that was more talking, and she didn't know what was better. Saying sorry or following his order.

In the end, she opted for silence.

Matt studied her, let her squirm—both with need and discomfort—then he nodded just once. "Good girl."

This time, the only thing those words provoked in her was happiness, and she smiled.

Matt turned the toy back on, pressing it to her clit, circling the sensitive nub until Liza was out of her mind, biting her lip so hard to hold back the pleas, she was shocked she wasn't bleeding.

While the stimulation was amazing, it wasn't enough. She needed more. Preferably him. Inside her.

Her breathing was labored, her body covered with a sheen of sweat. When did the room get so damn hot?

"Don't come, Liza."

The second he forbade it, her body responded, and suddenly she was aware she could come exactly like this, without anything inside her.

That wasn't good.

She shook her head, fighting with everything she had not to come, not to scream obscenities at him.

Matt recognized her struggle, but the bastard didn't ease up. Not a bit.

When he moved the vibrator away from her clit, she moaned —in relief, in disappointment. She missed the touch instantly.

Then he pushed the vibrator inside her, just an inch or so. Holding it there.

She frowned, wondering what new fresh hell this was. She thought she'd cleared the hurdle, thought he was ready to give her what she so desperately needed.

"You can speak now, kitten," he said. "I miss your voice. Beg. Beg me for what you want."

"Please," she said, clearing her throat. "Please let me come."

Matt thrust the toy in and out a half dozen times before turning the speed on high. Liza's entire body trembled, but he hadn't given her permission. Hadn't told her she could come.

Circling his thumb around her clit, he slammed the toy in harder, faster.

Bright stars flew behind her eyes and then...

"Come, Liza."

And then she was one of them. A brilliant white ball of light floating in space.

Her orgasm lingered, even after Matt turned the vibrator off and took it out. It had just about faded when he fanned it back to life, removing both nipple clamps at the same time.

She cried out, in pain, in bliss. Especially when he lowered his head and gently stroked her tender nipples with his tongue, whispering soothing words, sweet nothings.

Liza wasn't sure how much time had passed when she managed to land, to focus. The first thing she realized was she wasn't tied up anymore. The second was that Matt was naked and lying next to her in bed.

"You're back," he whispered.

Now that Liza could speak, she couldn't find the words, so she turned, reaching out to pull his body over hers, her legs parting in invitation.

Matt held his weight on his elbows, kissing her. His thick erection slid in slowly, but Liza still shuddered as he stroked the oversensitized muscles. Once he was seated to the hilt, he held in place, breaking the kiss so that he could look at her, his expression one she'd spent her entire life waiting for.

She cupped his cheeks affectionately, letting her face reflect those same amazing emotions, though neither of them spoke the words. They didn't need to.

Because she could read what he couldn't say in those deep brown eyes of his, and they were the most beautiful words she'd ever heard.

Chapter Thirteen

Matt finished his wine, wiped his mouth, leaned back, and sighed, wondering if he'd ever felt this genuinely relaxed.

Liza had assumed a similar pose across the table from him. "That was delicious. I'm pretty sure you've ruined me for commercial air travel for the rest of my life."

He was glad. Because if he had his way, the two of them would always be on this jet together. Then Matt found himself making a mental list of all the places he'd love to travel to with her. "I still can't believe you've never flown outside of the country."

"We weren't all born with private planes and silver spoons," she joked. "But I do have a bucket list of places I want to see."

"Given your heritage, Ms. Moretti, I hope Italy is on your list. You would love Lake Como and Positano."

"Oh. I'll add those to my list, right next to Amsterdam, Nice, and Rome."

"All very good places to travel."

Her eyes widened. "You've been to all of them?"

Matt nodded. "When I was younger, my father took us on a couple big trips each year, insisting that my brothers and I needed culture. Italy was our annual overseas trip, while the second trip abroad was always somewhere different."

"Hmpf," Liza huffed. "The most culture I ever got was on a high school trip to New York City with the drama club. We saw Les Mis and Phantom."

"Ah...that explains why you're so dramatic," he teased.

She stuck her tongue out at him, and he chuckled. "It must have been wonderful to see so much of the world."

"It was. Though, when I look back on those vacations now, I can't help but wonder if they were just another way for Dad to flaunt his wealth to his peers, considering he typically spent most of the holiday working in the hotel, while Mom was the one who took us sightseeing."

He smiled as he recalled Mom traipsing all over Pompeii with three preteen boys who never tired of pointing out every stone phallus they saw, and damn if there weren't *a lot*. Mom laughed every single time they spotted another dick, endlessly patient with their constant tittering over the "everything penis" city. Gage had even started calling it Pompenis.

Matt paused, considering what he'd just said. What he'd just remembered. He didn't have a clue where his comment had come from. Talking about his parents was difficult, so he didn't do it. Then he realized it was the first time he'd thought of his mother and not felt that unbearable crushing weight on his chest.

And because Liza was Liza, she latched onto the nugget like it was gold and immediately started digging for more.

"Your dad was a workaholic, huh? Sounds like someone I know," she said, one eyebrow raised, reminding him of the two days he'd wasted hiding in the hotel under the guise of work. The problem was Liza was comparing him to Dad, something that— unbeknownst to her—cut like glass.

"Do you think you take after your dad?" she asked, pouring more salt on the unseen wound. "Or are you more like your mom? My dad swears I'm my mother's twin, the two of us cut from the same cloth—looks-wise and personality-wise, and at least half the time, I think he means that as a compliment," she said, laughing.

"And now, I'm interested in meeting your mom to see if that's true. I took after my dad," Matt admitted, though it brought him no joy to say so. "He made sure of it."

"What do you mean?"

Matt wasn't sure why he was opening this vein, but after keeping his own counsel for so many years, it felt...good to be able to talk to someone else. "When I was thirteen, Dad decided it was time I stopped fucking around doing kid stuff and started learning the business."

Liza's eyes widened. "Thirteen?"

"From the moment we were born, Dad had assigned my brothers and me our roles. I was the heir, Gage the spare, and Conor was extra insurance, though if you ask my youngest brother, I suspect he'd use the word unnecessary." He tried to temper the bitterness in his tone, but he was certain he was failing.

"Sounds...terrible. What business could you have done at thirteen?" Liza asked. "You were still in school."

"I was, but when I got home every afternoon, I reported to his office. I did my homework there, a silent observer to my father's meetings and business dealings. I believe his intention was that I would learn how to emulate him. And it worked."

"How so?"

"In business, he was cold, calculating, and ruthless. Dad was the one who taught me to how to discover someone's worth, then exploit it for gain. Dante Russo was a wealth of old-school wisdom. In addition to the *Russos always come out on top* gem, he had strong opinions about politics, marriage, and children."

"Do I want to know what those opinions were?"

Now that Matt had started, he found he didn't want to stop. "Probably not. But, since you asked... His opinions were pretty simple. His only use for politics was for financial gain. Grease the right palm with enough cash and you can have anything you wanted. As for marriage, the only purpose of a wife was as arm candy and to provide heirs. And an oldie but a goodie, as far as child-rearing—"

"Let me guess. Children should be seen, not heard."

Matt nodded, tapping his nose once. "You got it in one."

"Wow. That's some pretty shitty advice. My dad just taught me how to ride a bike and fish," Liza said with a kind smile, trying to lighten the mood.

Matt returned it, appreciating her efforts.

"And you really think you're like him?" Liza probably hoped she was leading him to some great reveal, that this would be the point where he would admit he wasn't anything like his old man.

"I was."

She noticed the past tense, waited for him to expound on it.

"I idolized my dad, Liza. From the time I was fifteen until I was twenty-three, I didn't just think the sun rose and set on my father's shoulders, I believed he paid someone to do it—that God himself answered to Dante Russo. I strove to be exactly like him, and in truth, I succeeded."

"So you're nothing like your mom?"

Matt started to shake his head, then stopped. "Mom was a talented artist. When she wasn't playing video games with Gage or trading books with Conor, she drew. Primarily comic books."

"That's cool," Liza gushed. "I can't draw a stick figure."

"I shared her interest in art for a while. She and I had a sketch-book that we shared. We passed it back and forth. She'd start a drawing, then I would finish it. Then I'd start one and give it back to her to finish."

"Wow. I love that."

Matt nodded, his throat constricting. He hadn't thought about that sketchbook in years. The last time he'd seen it was right after Dad had destroyed his drawing of his brothers playing foot-ball. He'd taken the sketchbook back to Mom without finishing her drawing. He told her he was done with art, that it was a stupid thing to do, a waste of time. Every word he'd spoken was chan-neled straight from Dad, and he'd seen how much they hurt her.

He couldn't tell her that he was trying to save their art, certain that if his father ever found the sketchbook, he'd burn it. When he looked back now, he wondered if his cruel comments that day weren't just his attempt to preserve the art but to keep Mom safe as well. Dad had already curtailed the amount of time Matt spent with her, claiming he couldn't "suck at that tit forever."

Had Matt pulled away so that Dad wouldn't find another, more permanent way to separate him from Mom?

Mom had accepted the sketchbook, telling him, "You know who you are, Matt."

Unfortunately, asshole Matt had been in full force that day, so he'd turned around, sneered, and tossed back a pitch perfect Dante Russo reply.

"I know *exactly* who I am, Mother. I'm a Russo."

Mom shook her head, holding his gaze for a moment or two. "Look deeper," she'd whispered.

He'd had to turn away quickly because the disappointment in Mom's eyes had cut deep. After that, he'd avoided his mom as much as possible, and the rift he'd torn grew until it was as wide as the Grand Canyon.

"Where's the sketchbook now?" Liza asked.

Matt shrugged. "I haven't seen it in years."

Liza, an astute listener, then recalled something he really shouldn't have said. She tilted her head. "What happened when you were twenty-three?"

Shit. Matt hadn't meant to share all of that. He'd decided in Hawaii that he didn't want to keep fighting this thing between him and Liza, but old habits died hard. Because here he was, still trying to warn her, still trying to save her...from him.

Her question reminded him why he never cracked the door on the past. Because he'd just given Liza the opportunity to fling it wide open.

Matt refused to step through. He couldn't. Not if he hoped to hold on to this thing between them. Losing her would snuff out the tiny bit of humanity he still possessed.

"Life happened," he said dismissively, making it clear he'd said as much as he was going to. "So your dad taught you to fish?"

Liza hesitated. He could see she wanted to push the subject, but—on this—he wouldn't budge. He recognized the moment she realized.

"My family vacations were a lot simpler than yours. Mom and Dad own a cabin in the Poconos, so when we traveled, we went there. Fishing and swimming in the pond in the summer, ice skating in the winter. Lots of hiking and campfires with s'mores. That cabin is still one of my happy places."

The way Liza described her family was so different from the memories he had of his. His happy times and places had been erased by all the pain and remorse that came after.

"One of your happy places, huh?"

She nodded. "Yep. Where's yours?"

Matt didn't have a response for that because he didn't have a happy place. Then he realized, he did. His happy place was with her...but that wasn't a confession he was ready to make, so he lied. "My penthouse, I suppose. The perfect bachelor pad."

"Let me guess...black silk sheets, mirrored ceiling above the bed, mood lighting, and soft jazz playing at all times. Maybe Kenny G?"

"Clearly, I've decorated all wrong. I have white Egyptian cotton sheets, no mirror on the ceiling, a bedside lamp, and my white noise is the TV—finance shows mostly, so I can keep up-to-date with the stock market."

Liza rolled her eyes. "God. That's even worse than what I described. What are you? Ninety?"

"Not quite, but at least I can make a definite decision and narrow my happy place down to just one. You need two?" Matt was amused by their back-and-forth. He spent too much of his time around sycophants. It was nice to have someone unafraid to give him shit.

She leaned forward. "Absolutely. Because the second is my nonna and nonno's house. They throw the greatest celebrations ever—holidays, birthdays, special life-changing events. You name it."

"You Morettis seem to find a lot of reasons to overindulge in food and drink."

Liza didn't take offense, quite the opposite. "You say that like it's a bad thing."

"Give me an example of a life-changing event."

"Those are some of the best parties because they're unexpected and special. We had a party when Joey announced that he'd landed the hosting gig on *ManPower*. Then we had one where Elio and Gianna told us they were expecting. We had a huge bash when Uncle Frank and Uncle Renzo started Moretti Brothers Restorations. That party was epic. I was only ten, but Uncle Renzo poured me the tiniest bit of champagne in a real champagne glass, and I remember feeling so grown up. He probably hadn't given me more than a single sip, but I loved how fizzy it was and how the bubbles went up my nose."

Matt enjoyed listening to her stories, though it was difficult to hear them without viewing her relatives through the Russo lens. He'd spent most of his childhood listening to his own nonno and father talk trash about Liza's uncles and grandfathers. Whether the stories he'd been told were true or the exaggerated bitterness of two angry, lonely men, it was still hard to not think of the Morettis as blue-collar buffoons—his father's favorite description for them.

Liza continued. "I know I shouldn't say this, but Uncle Renzo was my favorite uncle. He had this larger-than-life personality and booming laugh. He had a way of making me feel like I was the most special person in the world."

Matt had known her uncle, and therefore knew he had passed away of a heart attack, though he didn't admit that.

"He's been gone nearly five years and I miss him every day," she admitted. "And while it might sound silly, I still pour myself a tiny glass of champagne at every family gathering in his memory."

"That's not silly. It's nice."

"Yeah, I guess. He died too young. We all miss him. Especially Aunt Berta."

"She was his wife?"

Liza nodded. "The two of them never had any kids. Around the same time Uncle Renzo passed away, Tony and Rhys bought the building where they currently live and work. So, as part of the renovations, they included an apartment for Aunt Berta on the same floor as the Moretti Brothers Restorations offices. That way she wouldn't be lonely, and Tony could keep an eye on her. Not that she's in bad health or anything. It was just...Uncle Renzo's death hit her hard, and it took her a long time to find her way out of her sadness."

"That was a thoughtful thing for Tony to do."

"Careful, Mr. Russo," Liza teased. "Because I'm not sure if you know it or not, but you just paid Tony a compliment."

Matt narrowed his eyes, pretending to be annoyed. "My mistake."

She reached out and smacked his hand playfully.

"Did your aunt keep her half in the company or did Tony and his brothers buy her out?" Matt asked.

"Aunt Berta still owns half. Calls it her nest egg."

"Pretty nice nest egg," he mused.

"You're not kidding," Liza agreed. "The company is doing amazing. Tony said last year was their best ever financially, and they already have enough projects lined up this year to beat that. Over Christmas, he, Gio, and Luca were talking about plans for expansion. They're looking to buy another local company, bring it under the Moretti Brothers umbrella. They're all so talented and smart," Liza gushed.

Matt wondered what it would feel like to be on the receiving end of such praise. Liza adored her family, proud of them and their accomplishments. Despite Matt working his ass off, doing everything in his power to prove himself to Dad, he couldn't recall a single time his father had ever given him a simple "good job."

Mom might have felt pride for him at some point, but Matt

couldn't confirm that. When Dad stepped in to take over the primary parenting role to train his heir, Matt had all but cut her out of his life. By the last few years of her life, they rarely spoke, his father's demeaning comments about Mom sinking in as deeply as his hatred for the Morettis.

There'd been a time when he'd believed his dad's lies...believed his mom was stupid and weak, believed the Morettis were white trash.

Matt swallowed hard, refusing to go there. It was hard to remember how susceptible he'd been, how brainwashed. It was why he fought so hard to remain in control now. He would never allow anyone the same power over him that he'd bestowed upon his father.

Time to end this conversation.

Glancing across the table at Liza, he knew the best way to shut down all the shit. "We have several hours before we land in Denver to refuel. Do you want to watch a movie or..."

When Liza's eyes grew dark, her lids heavy, he knew she'd chosen correctly. Rising from the table, he offered his hand.

Yesterday—their last day in Hawaii—had been one of the best days of Matt's life. The two of them had slept—he used that word loosely—so late they'd missed breakfast and lunch.

After pulling themselves out of bed, they'd frolicked in the ocean, sunbathed, then done scandalous things in the hot tub on the deck of their suite.

Walking down the aisle of the plane, they entered the bedroom together. Matt closed the door behind him and leaned on it, as Liza sank down on the bed, looking at him.

The past week had been nothing but passionate, frantic, frenetic sex, the two of them all but ripping each other's clothes off and fucking like it was the last thing they'd ever do.

Tonight felt different. Probably because they were headed home after their too-brief break from reality.

"Matt," Liza started. "We haven't talked about what comes next."

They hadn't. Matt had considered starting the conversation last night at dinner, but he wasn't ready to leave the bubble of bliss they'd been bouncing merrily along in. Talking about what came next meant adding in a lot of variables, like work, family, friends, his place or her place, conflicting schedules, and God only knew what else. In Hawaii, it was just them in a shared bed with nothing but time to spend wrapped around each other.

"We haven't." Matt noticed Liza's stiff posture, the unease in her eyes. She'd been comfortable with him since the night of the rehearsal dinner, so he hated seeing doubt creep back in. However, she didn't let her nervousness stop her from putting herself out there, from asking the hard questions.

"I'd like to keep seeing you. Dating you. Just you," she clarified. The wariness in her tone proved she knew just how big a risk she was taking. Because before this, Matt hadn't done committed relationships. Hell, he hadn't done relationships at all.

This was the fork in the road Matt had been avoiding last night. Not because he didn't know which direction he wanted to go, but because—no matter how hard he pretended otherwise— he was making a bad decision. One that would most likely lead to heartbreak for both of them.

Regardless, he dove into the mistake headfirst. "I'd like that too, Liza."

Liza blinked several times, and he got the sense she was wondering if she'd misheard him. "You would?"

Matt pushed away from the door, brushing her chestnut-brown hair over her shoulder, cupping her cheek affectionately. "I would. Stand up."

Liza rose. Matt didn't shift back, not even an inch, so their chests were pressed together, her face still lifted to his.

Cupping her face in his hands, he kissed her forehead, her closed eyes, the tip of her upturned nose, before claiming her lush lips.

Liza's lips parted, their tongues entering the dance. They'd kissed countless times over the course of the past couple of days, but every single one had felt different, unique. He could spend a lifetime studying her lips and still find something new.

For several minutes, they simply stood there, locked together, as they let the weight, the importance, the specialness of the commitment they'd just made to each other sink in.

Liza was the first to break away, to suck in a deep breath. The stunning smile she gave him had his heart skipping a few beats.

After that, they moved together, slowly undressing each other as they continued stealing kiss after glorious kiss.

Once naked, Matt drew back the duvet and they climbed into bed together. So far, their sexual encounters had been explorations, a give-and-take as they learned each other's turn-ons.

There was none of that now.

This wasn't about fantasies or kinks. It wasn't about dominating or submitting. It was about Matt and Liza, on the verge of something big. He should be afraid. God, he should be terrified, but as he climbed over her body, the two of them connected from chest to feet, Matt was overwhelmed by a sense of rightness.

He hadn't fit in his own skin since he was thirteen years old and his father had ripped him from his happy childhood, from his brothers—who'd been his best friends—and from his mother.

"Matt," Liza whispered, drawing the back of her fingers over his cheek, his bearded jaw.

"Hmm?" Matt hummed, giving her a quick kiss.

"Make love to me."

Four small words, but when put together like that...oh so powerful. Matt had never made love to a woman in his life, never wanted to.

But now that she'd made the request, he couldn't imagine doing anything else with her...for the rest of his life.

If only.

Liza's legs parted in invitation and Matt slid inside. She was wet and warm, and he sank in deep, his lips still locked to hers. He set an easy motion, his thrusts gentle but steady as Liza wrapped her legs around his waist, tilting her hips in that way that allowed him to sink in even farther.

The only sounds in the room—besides the white noise of the jet's engines—was their heavy breathing, the slight smacking of their kisses, and their matching groans of pure delight.

Matt felt the telltale fluttering of her pussy walls that told him she was close. Ordinarily, he would wring a couple orgasms out of her before coming, but tonight, he wanted to be right there with her.

"Come with me, Liza," he said, though the words were unnecessary. He'd become attuned to her tells, her soft panting breaths, the cute little moans, the flush of her cheeks, her tightly closed eyes.

Reaching between them, he stroked her clit—her self-destruct button, as she referred to it—then he increased his speed, his force.

Liza fell over first, her back arching, the tight constriction of her pussy his undoing.

He pushed inside her once, twice, three times more, and then he threw himself over the cliff with her, their bodies still connected, though now slick with sweat.

Matt drew in several deep breaths, then placed a million little kisses all over her face and neck before twisting to the side, pulling her with him until her head was cushioned on his chest.

The two of them lay in silence for a long time, though he could tell she wasn't asleep. Like him, it seemed as if she was lost in her thoughts.

After twenty minutes or so, Liza lifted her head to look at him. "That was incredible."

Matt smiled. "Every time with you is..." He paused, trying to find a big enough word, then decided hers worked just fine. "Incredible."

"I have to admit, sleeping with you is a far cry from my humble sexual beginnings."

Matt chuckled. "Rough start?"

"I lost my virginity in the backseat of Rory Jensen's ancient Honda Civic."

"Romantic," Matt teased.

Liza giggled. "Not in the slightest. Rory had zero game when it came to sex, which was a shame because he was hot as hell."

"Nice to know you're not one of those shallow women who places value on appearances."

Liza ran her fingertip from his sternum to his belly button. "At seventeen, looks were a very important factor, and Rory had that California surfer look complete with blond hair, blue eyes, and dimples going for him."

"You lost your virginity to Ken. Got it." Matt followed his joke up with a wink.

"Tease all you want, but I bet your first time was in the back of a limo with some bleach-blonde, big-boobed Barbie wannabe."

Once again, Liza had unwittingly found a way to lead their conversation down an unsavory path. "Not exactly."

When he didn't offer more, Liza took a subtler, more patient approach. "How old were you when you lost your virginity?"

"Fifteen."

"Seems pretty young. High school girlfriend?"

Matt shook his head. "No. She was actually older than me."

He could see he'd piqued Liza's curiosity. "How much older?"

"Twenty-four."

Liza's eyes widened. "Um. I'm pretty sure that's illegal."

"Only if someone reports it as a crime. Considering my dad set it up, it wasn't likely anyone was going to jail."

Liza remained quiet, her gaze locked on his face, letting the dust settle on his confession. "Maybe you could fill in some blanks on that story."

"Which blanks?" he asked.

"All of them."

"I told you that my after-school hours were spent with my dad, except for football practices and games in the fall, so I didn't have a lot of time for dating. My father had very definite ideas about when certain things should happen in my life. I think he just basically looked at the ages when he started doing shit and decided I should follow suit. So, at thirteen, I was forced out of my 'child' stage. At fifteen, Dad thought I should learn about sex, so he set me up with his mistress at the time."

Liza's mouth fell open, and Matt couldn't resist pushing his finger beneath her chin to close it. "Don't look so scandalized, Ms. Moretti."

"Your dad had a mistress, and he got her to tutor you in sex?"

"Yes."

"I think that's child abuse."

Matt chuckled. "I was a horny fifteen-year-old boy, and she was gorgeous, submissive, and very good at feeding my ego. It didn't feel like abuse. It just felt fucking good."

"Matt—" she started.

Matt placed his fingers over her lips. "I know it was wrong, Liza, but hindsight is twenty-twenty. I told you how I felt about my father. At the time, it felt like just one more step in becoming the man I wanted to be. *Him.*"

"I know you think you're like your father, but you're nothing like him," she insisted.

"I'm exactly like him. Cold, calculating, ruthless, remember?"

"In business," she added, as if separating certain parts out would make it easier for her to accept.

"Trust me, those attributes carry over from my professional life to my personal. You've seen my relationship with my brothers. Strained doesn't even begin to describe it."

"I *have* seen your brothers with you, so I know you could erase the strain in five minutes if you wanted to. Gage talks about you all the time, and whenever I'm at Enigma—which isn't much, granted—you've been there with Conor. Why?"

"He likes to get my advice on business things."

She raised her hand as if he'd just proven her point. "Because he respects your opinion."

Matt considered her arguments. He'd built a wall around

himself a long time ago, not to hide but to protect others he cared about.

What if he tore it down? Reached out to his brothers, tried to get back to what they had as kids?

No. That was something he could never do without coming clean about their past, and once that particular Pandora's box was opened, he'd lose his brothers forever. Even if he didn't have a close relationship with them, they were a part of his life. He couldn't give that up, couldn't give *them* up.

He sighed. "You're going to have to understand that we're not all Morettis. Most families share blood and very little else."

Liza pursed her lips, obviously annoyed that she hadn't swayed him. Mercifully, she let it go, placing her head back on his chest.

Silence prevailed for a few minutes, and he thought she'd fallen asleep until she spoke.

"You wanna know something, Matt?"

"What?"

"Your pillow talk sucks."

He laughed loudly as Liza lifted her head once more.

"I think that's the first time I've ever heard you laugh."

Matt knew that was the truth because it felt rusty as hell. Rusty, but good.

"You should laugh more often," she said.

"Maybe you could help me with that...and my pillow talk." He pushed her to her back once more, positioning his cock at her entrance, before placing a soft kiss on her cheek and whispering in her ear, "Let's practice now."

Chapter Fourteen

L iza and Devonte laughed as they did an over-the-top victory dance they were making up on the spot. Matt rolled his eyes at their antics, his arms crossed, drawing her attention to the way his sweat-drenched T-shirt clung to his muscular shoulders. That Superman "man of steel" descriptor seriously applied to Matt, or it would if the superhero had also sported a sexy, close-trimmed beard.

Matt was bulky and built, his abs, biceps, and all the other sexy muscles chiseled by hours spent in the gym lifting weights. Yesterday, she discovered he was a member of a boxing club and currently enjoying an impressive winning streak, undefeated in his last twelve matches.

However, Matt could not boast the same champion status at the Promise House. That title rested with Devonte, whose team was celebrating—according to Arnold—their eighth win in a row against Matt's team.

Tonight was the first time she and Matt had visited the Promise House since returning from Hawaii a week earlier. It was also the first time they'd been here together. Liza hadn't meant to stay away so long, but she found it difficult to split her free time.

Every second she and Matt weren't at work, they were at her place. Or more specifically, in her bed.

Control wasn't something either of them seemed to possess anymore. Liza, queen of lackluster dating, had never approached a relationship with an all-in attitude before. But there was no denying she was one gazillion percent dedicated to taking this thing between her and Matt all the way to the finish line.

And while he hadn't said anything beyond his desire to date her and only her, she couldn't help but feel like Matt was as fully committed as she was. Her evidence was the fact he had toiletries in her bathroom, his own side of the bed, his favorite beer in her fridge, and not one, not two, but three suits hanging in her closet. For God's sake, he walked around her place barefoot these days, which she realized shouldn't be such a turn-on, but it totally was.

"Celebrate now," Matt taunted, "but just remember, I get first pick next time for teams." He waved his thumb over his shoulder at his team behind him. "And we're taking Liza."

Matt's current team—who were, for the most part, his permanent team, all cheered, while Devonte groaned.

Liza had come to know Devonte well enough to understand that the hustler was already trying to work an angle, to come up with a way to make sure she remained on his team. "I was thinking since our teams don't change that much, we should just stick with who we got. Maybe come up with team names, make T-shirts and shit like that."

Matt shook his head. "Nope. Variety is the spice of life."

Devonte frowned, probably trying to figure out what the hell Matt was talking about. "Come on, man. You can't steal my best player."

This was her first time participating in Devonte and Matt's pickup game. Typically, her time spent shooting hoops here was during her occasional one-on-one games with Devonte after she finished tutoring Ashley.

Liza grinned. "Yeah, Matt. You can't steal his best player."

While the games were all in good fun, she could see losing

tweaked her competitive boyfriend—she was calling Matt her boyfriend in her head—and right before her very eyes, she watched as the cutthroat businessman emerged. "I can and I will steal you. We're not changing the rules just because you joined the game, Moretti."

She laughed, then rolled her eyes. "Russo is a sore loser, Devonte. Looks like we're going to have to soothe his wounded pride next time."

Devonte didn't seem as willing to concede, but when Arnold placed a hand on the young boy's shoulder, reminding him about some conversation the two of them apparently had about good sportsmanship, he begrudgingly backed down.

Arnold and Johnnie had returned home from Hawaii a couple of days ago. They'd remained on the islands for a few days following their wedding—a short honeymoon—then returned to Philadelphia as they'd both needed to get back to work. Liza had been somewhat surprised when Arnold told her he was taking a full two-week vacation for the wedding ceremony and honey-moon because the man practically lived at Promise House, working way more hours than he should.

She and Matt had gone out to dinner with the newlyweds last night because, as Johnnie said, the cupboards were bare and neither of them had the energy to shop and cook after their long flight home. After a lovely meal at the restaurant, she and Matt had returned to her apartment where Matt had bent her over the side of her bed and fucked her to within an inch of her life. She'd loved every second of it. Then they'd crawled under the covers, talking for nearly an hour. That was when she had learned about his amateur boxing and when she shared that she had played forward on the girls' basketball team in high school. Matt had immediately suggested she join him at Promise House for his rematch with Devonte.

She suspected he was regretting that invite now.

"You ready to head out?" Matt asked, slipping his sweaty arm over her shoulder playfully. She tried to escape, proclaiming he stunk, but he just tightened his grip, to the amusement of the kids in the gym.

"I guess we better before Arnold has to pay someone to come in here and fumigate," she teased, holding her nose.

Matt ruffled her hair and the two of them said their goodbyes, promising to return early next week for another game.

Once they were on the sidewalk, Matt took her hand and led her to his car. He'd picked her up at her place after work so that they could both change out of their professional attire and into their shorts and T-shirts. Neither of them bothered putting their sweatshirts on for the quick walk from the building to the car, letting the brisk winter air cool them off.

"That was fun," Liza said, once they were on the road.

"I think Devonte has a crush on you."

Liza shook her head, giggling. "That's funny because I think he has one on you."

Matt rolled his eyes. "Devonte likes my money. He's asked me on more than one occasion how he can score a lot of guap so he can be drippin' like me. I swear talking to Devonte is like talking to Gage and his friends, except instead of nerd-speak, it's Gen-Z slang. It sounds like English, but it might as well be spoken in pig Latin for all I understand."

"I feel your pain with Devonte. I've gotten really good at using context clues to piece together the shit he says. It's sort of depressing because I keep wondering when in the hell I got old," she admitted.

Matt laughed, something she'd noticed he was doing more and more often. "I've got nearly a decade on you. Trust me, you're not old."

"Seven years is not a decade," she pointed out, though it wasn't even that much. Matt had just turned thirty-seven in late November, while she was only a month away from thirty-one.

She looked around and realized Matt had missed his turn. "Wait. My apartment is that way." She pointed behind her.

"I'm aware. We're going to spend tonight at my place."

Liza's brows rose. "What? You're letting me into the inner sanctum?" While she was attempting to make light of it, she knew without Matt saying so that him inviting her back to his penthouse was a big deal.

"Yeah, I am." He glanced over at her, and she got the sense he was as surprised as she was. "To be honest, I've never taken a woman to my place."

"So why me?"

Matt huffed out a breath, then gave her a pretty simple answer that she sensed possessed more layers than were immediately apparent. "Because I want you to see where I live."

"Why haven't you taken anyone else to see it?"

Matt gave her a crooked grin. He'd told her on more than one occasion that she asked too many questions, and while that might have been a complaint at the beginning, she could tell he was more amused than annoyed nowadays.

"I'm a private man, Liza, and I've never trusted any of the women I dated enough to take them into my home."

His admission warmed her because the idea that he trusted her meant the world to her. Every second she was with him, she fell deeper and deeper in love. Not that she'd told him that yet. After all, they were only a couple weeks into this thing and given both of their lack of long-term relationships, she'd be smart to let a little more time pass before making such a huge declaration.

"Thank you," she said softly, reaching across the console to place her hand on his thigh. Matt grasped it, placing a kiss on her palm then lacing their fingers together, squeezing her hand affectionately.

They'd had a few discussions about their past relationships— or lack thereof in Matt's case. He'd made it clear that he took lovers to his bed for sex and sex only, so it stood to reason, he wouldn't have taken them to his home. In addition to being private, Matt was also extremely wealthy and, according to him, gold-diggers were a very real threat. He'd spent the better part of an hour telling her about some of the extremes women had gone to in order to land him or his brothers. Billionaire hunters, he'd called them, and his stories had made Liza ashamed of her gender.

"I would have packed an overnight bag—some pajamas, toiletries, or even just thrown my toothbrush in my purse if I'd known," she said, when she realized all she had with her were the sweaty clothes she was wearing.

"I made a note of the brands and scents in your bathroom and had them stocked in mine. And you don't sleep in pajamas when you're in bed with me," he added in a deliciously dark voice.

He'd made that rule the first night they were back from Hawaii, informing her that wearing pajamas to bed was a punishable offense. She hadn't had the chance to test that theory because clothes were the first thing to go when they got home from work, and by the time they were ready to fall asleep, she was too physically wrung out from orgasms—multiple—to even think about getting out of bed in search of pj's.

She was touched Matt had taken the time to buy her what she needed, but even so, she didn't look forward to having to put these smelly clothes back on in the morning. He could have given her a heads-up. "Do you own a washer and dryer?" she asked. "Or do you rich guys just send all your clothes to the dry cleaners? Or maybe you buy everything new because doing laundry is so middle class," she teased.

"Smart-ass." Matt tugged on her ponytail, grinning at her joke. "I have lounge pants and a sweatshirt you can use in the morning. I'll drive you home early enough that you can change for work. Unless you prefer I call my PA and have him purchase and deliver a new wardrobe to my place tonight."

She rolled her eyes, even though she didn't doubt he could do as he offered. "Lounge pants work."

Tomorrow was Friday—TGIF. Working a full week following that trip to paradise would have been hard enough, but she also had to add in her unquenchable desire to spend every waking hour wrapped up in Matt's arms. Consequently, the days had crept at a snail's pace, while the evenings passed in the blink of an eye.

The rest of the ride was made in companionable silence. Liza perked up when Matt pulled into a parking garage beneath a large building.

"Russo Enterprises owns quite a few apartment buildings in the city," Matt explained. "My brothers and I each claimed the top two floors of three of them, creating the penthouses that we call our homes."

Matt pulled into his reserved spot and the two got out of the car, walking hand-in-hand to the elevator.

"Mine's the biggest," he said with a grin when they got into the elevator.

"Of course it is," she teased. "It's that overcompensation thing all over again."

"You know what they say...big jet, big penthouse, big..." Matt wiggled his eyebrows and she laughed. He used a key card to push the button to the top floor, then wrapped his arm around Liza's waist, tucking her close.

Liza wasn't sure what she expected when the elevator doors slid open, but she *didn't* expect to step directly into Matt's home. The elevator literally opened *into* his living room.

"Holy shit," she breathed as she took in the floor-to-ceiling windows that offered the best view of Philadelphia she'd ever seen.

Matt stood next to her but didn't say anything as she stepped farther inside, slowly making her way around the room. It was clear to Liza that the place had been decorated by a professional rather than Matt himself, because—while it was tasteful and elegant and magazine-worthy—it didn't feel like Matt's style.

"How about a shower first, then we can figure out dinner," Matt suggested. "I'll give you the grand tour of the place once we're out of these sticky clothes."

Liza's workout clothes were clinging to her, so she was all for getting out of them. "That sounds great."

As they traversed the hall, Matt quickly pointed out the

kitchen and dining room, his home office, and the theater room on the first floor, before they climbed the circular staircase to the second story, which consisted of two guest rooms and a huge master suite complete with a bathroom that was bigger than her entire home.

"It occurs to me you've been slumming it this past week at my apartment," she said, only half joking.

Matt laughed. "I love your place. It's warm and comfortable and every inch of it is you."

He glanced around as if he just realized the same couldn't be said for his own place. Not that the penthouse wasn't comfortable. It simply didn't have any personal touches that told her who lived here. Now that she considered it, she wasn't sure she'd seen a single family photo, all the walls covered with what she was sure was very expensive artwork.

Not that she dwelled on that thought for long. Matt tugged her farther into his bathroom, pulling off her T-shirt, bra, shorts, and panties with an efficiency that proved just how many times he'd undressed her the past couple of weeks.

Liza gazed longingly at the huge jacuzzi tub in one corner of the bathroom. She wasn't sure what to make of the candles that lined two edges of it, creating what looked like quite the romantic space to her. He said he'd never brought a woman back here, but...

"I never use the candles," Matt pointed out, aware of her focus. "I paid an interior designer to decorate the place for me and she put a few candles there. I have a maid who comes in daily, and she asked several years ago if she could decorate the house according to the seasons. I said it would be fine, and since then, she changes the candles, throw pillows, bathroom towels, and a bunch of other stuff to represent whatever the time of year is. This year, she went a little overboard, putting a bunch of small pumpkins all over the place in October."

He wasn't lying. The candles—cinnamon-scented—hadn't been burned, then she recalled the almost-whimsical snowflake throw pillows on the couch in his living room that didn't seem like something a guy would pick out.

"How long have you lived here?"

"Twelve years." Matt crossed the room to turn on the water in his large shower. He had five—FIVE—showerheads, one coming from each of the opposite walls, a rain-shower-style one in the center, and two handhelds.

"Twelve years," she repeated as she looked around the bathroom, searching for something—anything—personal that might offer some insight into Matt's life. Apart from his toiletries—all high end—there was nothing, especially now that she knew the maid had chosen the scented candles, plush navy-blue towels, and snowflake vase with a realistic-looking fake plant in the corner of the vanity.

Matt undressed, stepping under the steamy jets before reaching out for her to join him. She followed him in, groaning in relief as the hot water beat down on her sore muscles. It had been a long time since she'd played basketball at such an extreme pace. Her one-on-one games against Devonte were more trash talk than actual exertion. Tonight, she'd been in it to win it, and her thirty-year-old body was reminding her that she wasn't in high school anymore. It was also reminding her that jogging a couple days a week wasn't enough exercise and she should probably try to be more consistent.

Then she grinned, deciding her nightly workouts with Matt surely must count as cardio.

"What's that smile about?" Matt asked, twisting her until their bare chests were touching, both of them standing beneath the rain showerhead.

"I'm happy." Everything about him made her smile, made her hopeful...made her, yeah, happy.

Matt gave her a quick kiss. "I'm glad. I only ever want you to be happy."

He started to pull away, but she grasped his waist, pulling him tighter against her, reaching on tiptoe to initiate another, better, longer kiss. His beard tickled her lips and the skin around her mouth, but that wasn't a complaint. Some nights, as they lay together in the wee hours, she couldn't resist running her fingers over the scratchy hair. Matt had offered to shave if it bothered her, but she'd put the kibosh on that idea instantly.

Because his beard?

So fucking hot.

Their kiss lingered, slowly becoming hungrier, more passionate. Liza knew the second the tide had turned, and this shower wasn't about getting clean. Nope. It was going to be a very, very dirty one.

Matt broke the kiss, his eyes dark with a need she recognized and responded to.

This wasn't Matt, the lover. This was Matt, the conqueror.

Pushing Liza backward, he moved her until she was pressed against the wall, water from the showerhead above spraying over her, making her feel like she was standing behind a waterfall.

Matt reached for the handheld, pointing the stream at her as he changed the setting from the normal spray to a powerful pulsating one. He directed the bursts of water at her left nipple, the steady thrum drawing it taut. Then he repeated the action on her right nipple.

Liza placed her hands on his shoulders, but Matt shook his head, his expression suddenly strict.

"No touching, kitten. Only surrendering. Put your hands next to your head against that wall."

Liza's hands were halfway to the position he demanded before she could consider her actions. There was something about that tone of his that made her want to please him. During the day, when they were apart, she'd sometimes imagine disobeying him, just to see how he would respond.

Those thoughts were easy to entertain when they weren't together. Now, with all six feet two muscular inches of him standing just a few inches away from her, she was helpless to deny him anything. She didn't know what this power he possessed was, but she didn't mind being in his thrall.

Not. At. All.

With her hands pressed against the tile by her head, Liza's eyes closed as Matt continued to torment her breasts with pulsating water. They flew open when the jet traveled lower. God help her.

Matt wasn't looking at her. Instead, all his attention was focused on the jet. Using his free hand, Matt parted the lips of her labia and directed the pulse on her clit.

Liza cried out and started to twist her hips away from the overstimulating sensation.

"Don't move!" Matt said sharply. Liza stopped in an instant. So quickly, in fact, Matt didn't even have time to threaten her with punishment if she failed to comply.

Dammit. While he hadn't had to follow through, every time he talked about spanking her ass or withholding her orgasms or tying her hands, arousal soaked her panties.

He held the jet steady, pummeling her clit until Liza's body began to tremble, the telltale sign that her first orgasm was imminent.

She'd started numbering her orgasms in her head with Matt. With past lovers, that wasn't necessary because she rarely passed the number one. Hell, sometimes she didn't even make it that far.

With Matt, she counted them, coveted each and every one. Maybe she'd remind him that his personal best was six orgasms in one night—just to see if he'd rise to the challenge and try to break the record.

The current orgasm record had been set their last night in Hawaii, when everything between them was brand spanking new, and shit like having to get up early for work hadn't been a concern.

"Matt," she gasped, her head falling back, her eyes shutting when he moved the showerhead closer, the water hitting harder.

"You know better than that," he chastised. "Eyes open."

His demand was a common one. Matt always wanted her looking at him when she came. She didn't ask why because she didn't need to. She felt the power of that connection as keenly as he did.

She looked into his deep brown eyes and saw his intense determination that in any other situation would actually be frightening.

"Come for me." As he spoke, he pressed two fingers inside her pussy, the jets of water still pounding hard against her clit.

His words freed her, sent her to that magical place where everything was perfect, where stress, fear, and self-doubt didn't exist. Where it was only her and him and that happiness seeping out of every pore.

The second Liza's climax subsided, Matt returned the showerhead to its cradle, gripping her hips to turn her away from him. His chest pressed firmly against her back, pushing until her entire front was flush against the warm tiles.

"I'm going to fuck you," he murmured, his lips next to her ear. "Keep your hands flat against the wall and hold on."

Her hands were already there, and she had no intention of lowering them. She was going to need them to protect herself from being crushed against the wall.

Matt nipped at her earlobe, his lips traveling along the side of her neck. He lifted one hand, wrapping it around her throat—not tightly but in a way that teased of danger. She'd discovered that along with her desire to submit, Liza liked her sex with a darker edge, turned on by Matt's touches that felt as threatening as they did arousing. He'd never physically hurt her, but he had pushed her limits, drawing out more and more of her kinks with each encounter. One night, she'd confessed that the way he—for lack of a better term—manhandled her in bed was a huge turn-on.

That confession appeared to be the green light Matt had been looking for because since then, he'd taken off the kid gloves, making sure she felt his strength, his control as he put her where he wanted and kept her there.

Like now, as he placed his hand around her throat, his thumb lightly stroking her pulse point reminding her that right here, right now, he held all the power.

"You're mine."

Every time he said those words, she melted inside.

"I own every inch of you, Liza Moretti." His deep tone was menacing, the words sounding almost like a threat, even though they were the truth.

She was his. Completely.

"Your body," Matt continued. "Your kisses. Your orgasms. Even the air you breathe." Matt applied a bit more pressure to her throat. Not enough to cut off her air. Just enough to flip the switch on the part of her brain that said this was the hottest moment of her life.

"Please," she whispered.

Matt tightened his grip the tiniest bit more. "Beg me."

"Please, Matt. Please fuck me!"

Too many nights, Matt had drawn the foreplay out for so long Liza thought she'd lose her mind. This wasn't going to be one of those nights. Thank God.

Matt gripped her hips, pulling her away from the wall until she was bent at the waist. He lost no time lining up his cock with her opening and slamming in. Liza's second orgasm struck three thrusts later, but Matt fucked his way through that one, pounding harder with each re-entry—and her third.

Liza's legs turned to jelly, Matt supporting more of her weight than she was. His grip on her hips was unyielding, firm, as he beat a brutally beautiful rhythm inside her oversensitive pussy.

"God," she called out hoarsely. Her voice was all but gone after the pleading and screaming. "I can't—"

"You can!" Matt barked, cutting her off. He grabbed a fistful of her hair, using it to pull her body upright. He never stopped fucking her as he pushed her forward until her chest was once again flat against the tiles. Matt's fingers tightened around her hair, her scalp stinging, setting off a nuclear reaction in every single one of her nerve endings.

"*Mine*, Liza."

What the hell was it with that word? One second, Liza was sure she'd never find the strength to come again; the next, she was diving over that goddamn cliff with Matt. Orgasm number four hurt, it felt so fucking good.

He gripped her hip tight enough to bruise, but that pain, just like the stinging of her scalp, only served to make her hotter, hornier.

Matt called out her name as he came inside her. He was the first man she'd ever let take her without a condom, and her ticking clock was waking up and taking notice. Liza had always wanted kids—plural—hoping for a big family like the one she'd grown up in. So while thirty-one might seem too early to start hearing that tick-tick-tick, she decided that wasn't true for a woman longing for three or four babies.

Matt would probably have a coronary if he knew where her thoughts had traveled. Gently, he released her hair while keeping a supportive hand on her hip as he kissed the side of her head.

"Okay?"

"So okay," she breathed.

Silence fell as they reveled in the afterglow, each taking turns washing the other. Shutting off the water, they dried themselves with his oversized, super-soft towels, then Matt reached out for her, hugging her in a way that told her this thing between them wasn't just sex.

Matt's embrace was one of genuine fondness, not foreplay.

"Dinner?" he asked. "We can order in or rummage around in my kitchen for something to fix."

She and Matt had eaten far too much takeout this week, sex edging out cooking every time. "Rummage," she said, warming up to the idea of doing something domestic like making a meal with him. Besides, she was curious to see if his kitchen was just as Matt-less as his bedroom and bathroom.

Matt loaned her a T-shirt, the soft cotton falling to mid-thigh, but he'd refused her request for a pair of boxers, telling her she was lucky he was letting her wear the shirt. She didn't kick up much of a fuss because he'd donned the boxers—and nothing else. His bare chest was drool-worthy.

In the kitchen, they found the makings for BLTs and Matt pulled out a can of tomato soup to add to the meal. The kitchen —devoid of any personal effects—appeared to be yet another place where she and Matt worked well together, each dividing the duties, creating the simple fare that they ate side by side sitting at the bar that separated his kitchen and dining room.

After dinner, Matt gave her a proper tour, which left her equal parts impressed and sad. His penthouse was absolutely gorgeous. However, the only room that gave the barest hint that Matt owned the penthouse was his home office, which made sense. The man was a true workaholic, so Liza suspected with the exception of him sleeping in his bedroom, this was the room he spent the most time in when he was home.

In his office, she discovered several framed pictures of Gage and Penny on their wedding day, and another of Conor standing in front of his restaurant, Chives, at its Grand Opening, and another of his youngest brother holding a trophy after winning what looked like a golf tournament. There were no photos of his parents, and Matt wasn't in any of the photographs either. It was like he purposely kept himself apart from his family. There, but only on the outer fringes.

Whenever Matt talked about his brothers, his fondness shone through, though he didn't seem to spend much time with either of them outside of work. Meanwhile, Liza wasn't sure she'd ever gone a full week without seeing her parents and brothers, or at the very least, talking to them on the phone. Her family had a big text thread that saw action pretty much every day, someone sharing a funny meme, sending a "current situation" picture if they were somewhere great, or even just to brag about getting the Wordle in two guesses.

Once the tour was over, Liza couldn't manage to stifle a yawn. She was still a bit jet-lagged, due to having to return to work the day after getting back from Hawaii. Between fighting to return to East Coast time and staying up too late, thanks to sexy nights with Matt, it was a wonder she could keep her eyes open at all.

"Come on. Time to tuck you in, kitten." Matt led her up the stairs to his bedroom.

"Just me?"

Matt pulled back the duvet and pushed his boxers off. "Nope. I think we both need a good night's sleep. We've been burning the candle at both ends this past week."

Liza crawled onto the bed, moaning in delight over his soft mattress. "I love this bed," she said, as she sank into it, every muscle in her body relaxing.

"Good," Matt whispered, as he slid in next to her. "Because you're going to spend a lot of time in it."

She smiled, then the two of them kissed. Unlike their previous kisses, this one was short and sweet.

"Good night, Ms. Moretti," Matt said as he wrapped her up in his arms, his chest her pillow.

"Good night, Mr. Russo," she said, making a silent wish to spend every night for the rest of her life sleeping next to him.

Chapter Fifteen

Matt leaned back in his chair as he looked out of the window of his office. It was a sunny day, the sky blue without a single cloud, the temperature unseasonably warm for early March. It was the kind of end-of-winter day that had some people longing for snow and others ready for spring.

Matt had never been the type to give a shit what the weather was because the temperature was always the same in his office. Hot or cold, all the days drifted along in the same relentless, monotonous way.

Today, however, he was straddling the line between the seasons, imagining he and Liza taking walks in the snow, getting into snowball fights, curling up in front of a roaring fire. And as much as he wanted to do all of that, he wouldn't mind seeing her in less clothing, sitting next to him on a blanket while they had a picnic in the park or standing on the deck of his yacht, sipping cocktails and breathing in the salty sea air.

After a lifetime of nondescript seasons—most spent right here at this damn desk—he was suddenly envisioning countless days filled with new adventures and Liza.

She found a way to make everything fun, something he hadn't realized he missed until she helped him find his laugh again.

Even better, the nightmares had stopped.

Matt hoped forever.

He wasn't sure what had possessed him to take Liza back to his penthouse last night, but—as he told her—he'd been overwhelmed by the desire to share a part of himself he didn't show to others. Of course, as he took her around his home, he became painfully aware of how sterile the place was. Liza's apartment was a cacophony of colors and her. Pictures of her family and friends adorned nearly every wall, and she seemed to have a story behind every piece of furniture—be it a treasured family heirloom, something her cousin, Gio, had built, or some amazing deal she'd found at a yard sale.

He'd teased her, pretending not to have a clue what a yard sale was, and she'd believed him, describing it while he reacted in fake horror to her buying other people's crap. She'd punched him on the arm when she realized he was pulling her leg.

"Hey, Matt." Gage walked in without knocking. Matt didn't take his brother to task because he never knocked either. Gage stopped halfway across the office, frowning.

"What's wrong?" Matt asked.

"Are you smiling?"

Shit. Matt couldn't think about Liza without smiling.

He schooled his features, quickly resuming his usual dour expression. "What do you want, Gage?" he asked, ignoring his brother's question.

For a moment, he thought Gage might push the subject but he let it go. "Wanted to talk to you about that new tech upstart I'm looking at buying."

Gage's interests in videogames had made its way into Russo Enterprises, his brother investing in a couple of tech upstarts over the past year. Matt had been skeptical when Gage first talked about expanding into gaming, but there was no denying his brother, Penny, Toby, and the rest of the self-proclaimed nerd circle had a Midas touch when it came to recognizing quality games. The venture had become quite profitable for the company.

"What about it?"

For the next twenty minutes or so, they discussed figures and prospective plans. For the first few years following their parents' deaths, Gage had been lost, drinking and fucking his way through his grief, work concerns much lower on his list. Hell, it was probably accurate to say work hadn't been a concern for Gage during that time at all. Eventually he found his way back, and since then, he'd proven himself to be as savvy a businessman as Conor and Matt.

"Haven't had a chance to talk to you much since you got back from Hawaii. How was the wedding?" Gage was clearly surprised Matt had taken an entire week off to fly to the islands for the nuptials of two men he didn't know particularly well.

Liza had revealed on the flight back to Philadelphia that Matt's invitation had been a matchmaking move on Arnold's part. Matt had thanked the man two nights ago when he and Liza joined the newlyweds for dinner, much to Johnnie and Liza's amusement.

"It was a good trip." Matt was aware his descriptor was completely wrong. It had been the greatest vacation of his life.

Gage rolled his eyes. "Only you could travel to paradise in the dead of winter and refer to it in the most boring way possible. No hula girl hookups? No blackout drunk on Mai Tai antics?"

"What do you think?" Matt asked sardonically.

Gage shook his head, disappointed. "You need to live a little, bro. Put yourself out there, have some fun."

Matt didn't respond. With the exception of Arnold and Johnnie, no one else in his or Liza's life was privy to their changed relationship status. And while Matt was tempted to confide in his brother, there was that nagging voice in the back of his head that kept telling him this couldn't last.

He'd gotten adept at shutting it down, but right now it was there again, reminding him he was overreaching, taking something that wasn't his to keep. Especially as he sat here, looking at his brother and recalling how tenuous all his relationships were. Too many secrets could bring his entire life crashing down on his head.

So, he kept his mouth shut.

Matt asked about Penny as a distraction because Gage was always happy to talk about his beloved wife. The conversation was just winding down when Matt's cellphone rang.

He sighed when he read the name on the screen. "Sorry, Gage. I need to take this."

Matt hadn't spoken to Richard Eddington since the Patricia breakup, even though the man had called his cell several times over the past couple of weeks. Matt had sent them all to voicemail, then hadn't bothered to call him back because he hadn't wanted to deal with the bullshit again. However, it was becoming clear the fruit didn't fall far from the tree. The father was as tenacious as the daughter. Time to see where he stood with the man.

Gage nodded, then saw himself out.

"Richard," he said, answering the phone.

"You're a hard man to track down." Richard was undoubtedly annoyed at being ignored so long.

"I was out of town for a short vacation. Spent most of this week playing catch-up. You know how it is."

Richard didn't respond to his excuse because they both knew it was a lie. "You and I have a bit of a problem."

"How so?"

"You know my baby girl, Matt. When she has her heart set on something, she doesn't let it go."

Matt rubbed his temple wearily. It was on the tip of his tongue to suggest that Richard's life might be easier now if he'd done a better job of child-rearing, but he managed to refrain, not willing to burn his bridge with the man quite that completely.

Regardless, Matt suspected irrevocable harm to their business association was inevitable if Patricia didn't back down.

"I'm not sure what that has to do with me," Matt said.

"Matt," Richard said in a *don't bullshit a bullshitter* tone. "Patricia has expressed her interest in marrying you, and to be honest, I think she's made some very good points about why this would be an advantageous match. In the past, I've given my daughter a lot of leeway when it comes to her romantic attachments, taking a backseat as she searched for a life partner, but if I'm being honest, I never cared for any of her fiancés. None of them were good enough for her, not enough drive or ambition. None of them were on the same level you and I are. I'm certain those other men looked at my daughter and saw the fortune rather than the woman. I know you don't have children, but trust me when I say, no man wants that for his little girl."

The more Richard talked, the more obvious it became that Patricia hadn't spelled out everything she'd offered Matt along with the marriage.

Like the infidelity hall pass.

Patricia wanted his name and his money, not his love. Matt wondered if filling in that blank for Richard would make a difference, then he realized...it wouldn't. Patricia pointed at something, said "I want it now" in her best Veruca Salt voice, and Richard pulled out his Amex.

"I'm sure you don't want that for your daughter. But as I've already expressed to Patricia—several times—I have no interest in getting married...to anyone," he forced himself to add, though it suddenly dawned on him that statement was no longer accurate. Because he could very much see himself married to Liza, a realization that wasn't as terrifying as he would have expected.

Richard dismissed that assertion by ignoring it. "You and I are businessmen, first and foremost, which means you'll understand when I say there is always a bottom line. So let's get down to it. I recall you mentioning once that you were interested in Russo Enterprises branching out into the casino/resort line of business."

Matt had made that comment when he was younger, just starting out at Russo Enterprises. Richard had discouraged the idea, claiming a good future CEO should know not to spread the company business too thin. He'd then offered unsolicited advice, telling Matt it was better to stick to the Russo brands, the companies they were already invested in, and grow them.

Matt had seen through the so-called words of wisdom, understanding that Richard felt threatened by potential competition. He'd let the idea go, however, because Dad hadn't been interested in stepping on his country club buddy's toes. Dad told Matt the best way to remain on top was to stay in his lane and keep his enemies close.

"That was a long time ago," Matt reminded Richard.

"You assumed leadership of Russo Enterprises at a young age, but you've stepped in and filled the large shoes left behind by your father. You should be proud of that."

Matt swallowed the bile clogging his throat as Eddington compared him to his dad.

"I've been very impressed with your tenacity and work ethic. The truth is, I'm not getting any younger, Matt. Patricia is my only child, and sadly, she's never expressed any interest in taking over the family business."

Matt wasn't stupid enough to fall for that crap. He'd sipped one too many bourbons in the company of Richard Eddington not to know the man was the world's biggest misogynist. He'd never encouraged his daughter to do anything more than smile, look pretty in her designer clothing, and follow in her mother's socialite footsteps, which essentially meant she should be the perfect Stepford Wife.

However, Richard's comments were enlightening, and now Matt couldn't help but wonder if Patricia had thrown back the first four fiancés...or if it had been Richard who'd suggested she look higher up on the food chain.

"Russo Enterprises keeps me very busy," Matt started.

"I'm sure it does, but you also have two brothers to help you, both of whom are capable of taking on additional responsibilities should you acquire more."

Again with that fucking word. The Eddingtons loved the word *more* as much as they detested the word *no*.

"I'm not sure either of them is interested in expanding upon their roles here. They're busy with their own interests."

"Not even if it meant acquiring Edgewood Resorts and Casinos?"

Matt fell silent. Not because he was considering the offer but because he was so shocked by it. Edgewood was the flagship brand of the Eddington Group, which was the second-largest hotel chain after Hilton. Under that same umbrella, the Edgewood brand included a large string of casinos up and down the East Coast.

"I can tell I've piqued your interest," Richard said smugly.

Matt had let the silence drift too long. "I think it's safer to say you caught me by surprise."

"If you consent to marry Patricia, Edgewood is yours. Then, after the birth of each of your children, I'll gift you another chain. With your marriage, the Eddington Group would belong to you and Patricia, as well as your heirs, and this gives me a way to slowly retire, confident that the company I've dedicated my life to building is in good hands."

Matt rolled his eyes, grateful this wasn't a video call. Richard Eddington had inherited everything he owned. The company had continued to grow thanks to a competent board, who operated without the man's guidance. Richard preferred to spend most of his days on the golf course in warm weather and skiing in Aspen and Switzerland during the winter months.

"It's a very generous offer," Matt began.

"It is indeed. So should I have my lawyers call yours? Get the ball rolling? Patricia has her heart set on a June wedding."

"You didn't let me finish," Matt said. "It's a generous offer, but I'm going to have to refuse."

This time, the silence came from the other end of the line, but it didn't last for long. "You can't refuse!" Richard roared. "I'm offering you the chance to inherit *billions*. How dare you—"

"Richard," Matt interjected, aware this phone conversation was only going to go downhill from here. "I know you and Patricia like the idea of expanding your empire and your fortune, but I have more money than I can spend in a hundred lifetimes. I don't need or want any more."

A billion dollars was nowhere near enough to shackle himself to Patricia for the rest of his life, but Matt left that part unsaid.

"Are you refusing because of your affair with the Moretti woman?"

Once again, Richard had taken him by surprise, something Matt hated. He wasn't sure how Richard knew about Liza, but obviously someone, somewhere, had talked.

"I have no idea what you're talking about." Hell would freeze over before Matt exposed Liza to the likes of the Eddingtons.

"You know exactly what I'm talking about. Don't let your dick do your thinking for you. That woman is a gold-digger and nothing more."

"This conversation is over," Matt said, ready to disconnect the call. He'd had enough of the Eddingtons to last him a lifetime.

"You're making a big mistake," Richard growled.

"Perhaps, but my answer remains the same. Good day, Richard."

He hung up before Richard could continue to berate him.

Matt sighed, aware he should probably fire off an email to his brothers to warn them he'd just made an enemy of the Eddingtons. Gage did the tech for a lot of the Eddington Group properties, and Conor had been in negotiations to open a restaurant in a new casino Richard was building in Atlantic City. Matt wasn't sure how much pull Richard had within the company, but the man was certainly vindictive enough to kill those contracts and deals if he could.

Leaning his head back, he pushed all thoughts of the Eddingtons from his mind.

Instead, he let himself think back to this morning, to waking up with Liza in his bed. She was as warm and soft as a kitten, curled up in his arms.

Then he recalled his earlier desire to celebrate every single season with her.

Picking up his office phone, he hit the button for his PA.

"Yes, sir," Henri said, answering promptly.

"I'm thinking of taking a weekend ski trip to Vermont. I need you to arrange for the jet to be fueled up and ready to leave this evening, returning Sunday. Then see if you can find a nice cabin to rent, one bedroom is fine so long as it has a big bed. You know what I like. Oh, and make sure it has a fireplace."

"Of course. Will you be traveling alone?" Henri asked.

"No. I'm taking a date. Speaking of which, I'm going to send you some women's clothing sizes as well as a shopping list for toiletries—the brand names and scents are noted. I need you to buy a complete ski ensemble for her, as well as jeans, sweaters, and boots." He intended to pick up Liza straight from work and whisk her to the jet, keeping their destination a secret until they arrived.

"Very well. Should I also purchase a gift for your companion?" Henri was very accomplished when it came to buying baubles for his "dates." Matt never thought of them as gifts as much as insurance policies, an easy way to extract himself after sex. Diamonds went a long way toward buying him an easy exit.

"No, thank you." Matt intended to be the only man who bought Liza gifts from now on.

"I'll make the preparations now."

Matt hung up, then spun his chair back to the large windows, grinning to himself as he planned out the rest of the day. He and Liza were going to make the most of what was left of winter. Then when spring hit, they were going to do the same. Maybe he'd fly her to Paris in April, to Bora Bora in the summer, to the Scottish Highlands in the fall.

Matt glanced at the clock. Only six more hours to kill until their spontaneous weekend trip began. He couldn't wait to see Liza's face.

* * *

Matt signed the paperwork in front of him as Henri listed off what each page consisted of. He listened with half an ear, too busy basking in the afterglow of his incredible weekend. Liza had been thrilled by his surprise, so thrilled, the two of them had added quite a few scandalous acts to their mile-high club list while flying to and from Vermont.

After a great day of skiing on Saturday—Liza was a natural and she enjoyed the activity as much as he did—they made his dream of making love on a bearskin rug before a fire come true in spectacular fashion.

Closing his eyes, he could recall the way Liza's skin had shimmered in the firelight. How she'd gone down on him, taking him deep into her mouth as he tugged on the chain he'd attached to her nipple and clit clamps. He hadn't touched her in any other way, so he'd been shocked when they had both come at exactly the same time. Liza's sexual appetite matched his right down the line.

Once he signed everything, Henri gave him a quick rundown of his day, then excused himself to return to his own desk outside Matt's office. Alone, Matt forced himself to concentrate on his work. He managed with varying degrees of success.

He groaned when he glanced at his watch and realized he'd only been here an hour. He used to be able to immerse himself so deeply in work that day would turn to night without him even realizing it. Now, the days passed way too slowly as he counted every minute until he could be with Liza again.

Matt was starting to feel like a teenage boy with his first crush. Then, he realized that he'd skipped that falling-in-love stuff in high school, which meant he really was experiencing those emotions now for the first time.

Opening his email, he worked his way through the inbox, putting out the most immediate fires.

Another peek at the clock.

"Shit," he muttered. It was only ten-fifteen, exactly fifteen minutes later than the last time he checked.

Before he could return to his email, the door to his office opened.

"Yes," he said to Henri, as he walked in.

"Ms. Edd—"

That was as much as his PA got out before Patricia sashayed around Henri and into the office. Henri looked ready to blow a gasket, but Matt lifted his hand, gesturing that it was okay.

It wasn't, but he was the one who'd made the monumental mistake of asking Patricia out that first time—and too many times after. She was his cross to bear, not Henri's.

Henri sniffed in annoyance, then left, closing the door behind him.

"Patricia," Matt said, remaining seated. "I thought we agreed the last time you were here that you would make an appointment."

He'd grown accustomed to Patricia's fake smiles and laughs, so he wasn't quite sure what to do with the menacing grin she shot in his direction. Patricia was well-known for her temper tantrums, something he was in no mood for today. If it came to that, he'd call security and have them toss her out on her ass.

"How was Hawaii?" Patricia asked, dropping down in the chair opposite him. She crossed her legs, looking far too comfortable.

Matt schooled his features, though he was curious how she'd known he was out of town, let alone where he was. Then he recalled Richard's question about Liza. Were the Eddingtons so far gone on this stupid marriage idea that they were stalking him?

"Hawaii was nice."

"I stopped by to see you a couple weeks ago. Your PA said you were out of town."

Matt frowned. Henri was the last person on Matt's list of people who would feed the Eddingtons information. Matt prized Henri as an assistant because the man was very good at protecting his privacy, so he struggled to believe Henri was the one to tell Patricia where he was.

Rather than respond, Matt remained quiet. He wasn't interested in whatever game Patricia was playing. He hoped by refusing to participate, she'd get to the point, then get out.

"He was ridiculously closemouthed about where," she bitched.

Matt fought to hide his smile. So, Henri *hadn't* been the one telling tales. Good to know his trust hadn't been misplaced.

"Daddy keeps his private plane in the same hangar as you at Northeast, so it wasn't difficult for him to make a few calls and find out you'd flown to Hawaii. And that you had a female passenger with you."

And there it was. The leak.

No doubt Richard had greased a few palms, but Matt didn't give a shit. He would place a call to the airport once Patricia was gone to ensure whoever the hell was sharing his flight details was fired.

"One call to the Philadelphia Initiative later, and I found out Liza was out of town too, for a wedding in Hawaii." Patricia's skin glowed green, jealousy dripping from every word.

Matt had dropped the niceties at the end of their last conversation, and he felt no need to pick them back up again. So instead, he gave her a slow clap. "Remarkable detective skills," he replied drolly. "Any point to them?"

"Daddy said he called and offered you Edgewood Resorts."

"He did."

"And you refused."

"I did."

"Why?" she countered.

Matt wasn't doing this again. As soon as Patricia left, he was calling security, informing them she was no longer allowed in the building. Then he would make sure Henri knew that he wasn't accepting calls from either Eddington in the future. As for his cell, he'd just block their numbers. "Patricia, if there's a reason for this conversation, make it and leave."

Patricia scowled, and he almost imagined the smoke coming from her ears. "You took Liza to a wedding as your date?"

Matt rolled his eyes. "Is that what this is about? You're jealous?"

Patricia snarled. "I will never be jealous of that white-trash bitch!"

Matt's temper rose, and he reached for the phone. Fuck it. He was calling security now.

Before he picked up the receiver, Patricia rose and slammed a piece of paper down on his desk.

Matt recognized it instantly, even though it was a copy. The original was tucked in Matt's office safe. "Where did you get this?" It was a stupid question. Obviously, Richard was determined to make good on his threat to make Matt sorry. However, Matt had anticipated the attacks to involve his business. Not his personal life.

"Does Liza know you can break her family financially?"

Matt remained stone-faced, aware of Patricia's laser-like focus on him. She was searching for weakness, or perhaps confirmation that he and Liza were in a relationship.

When he refused to answer her question, she picked up the paper again, dangling it between two fingers, waving it back and forth. "I wonder what Tony Moretti will say when he sees this. If rumors are to be believed, there's bad blood between the two of you. How will he feel when he learns you hold him and that ridiculous construction company of his in the palm of your hand?"

Matt stared her down, refusing to rise to her bait.

"All it would take is one little call and Moretti Brothers Restorations could be yours. Liza is close to her neanderthal blue-collar cousins, is she not? I can't imagine she would be happy to learn what you did all those years ago. It's an unforgiveable offense."

"So this is your plan?" Matt gestured at the paper in her hands. "Your father couldn't *pay* me to marry you, so you're trying to blackmail me into it? Pretty pathetic when you think about it."

"You messed with the wrong family." Patricia's face twisted in anger. Matt couldn't believe he'd ever thought the woman was pretty. Now, with her true nature on display, she was as hideous as an old crone. "We were offering you the world, and you stupidly rejected it for that gold-digging whore!"

Matt rose, pressing his fists against the top of his desk to stop himself from reaching out and throttling the woman. "Say another disparaging word about Liza," he said darkly, "and it'll be the last words you ever speak."

It was an empty threat—maybe—but it was delivered with enough malice that Patricia took a half step away from his desk.

"I have the power to make this go away," she said, forging on. "Make certain the Morettis never learn what you did all those years ago, what you can do to them now."

Matt couldn't understand this maliciousness, this tenacity. It was too over-the-top, too fucking much. "You don't give a shit about me, Patricia, so you're going to have to explain why you won't let this go." The second Matt asked, the light went on. "It's because I said no, isn't it? No one's ever said that to you."

Patricia sneered. "I always get what I want."

"But you don't want me," he said.

"Of course I do," Patricia said, smiling evilly. "Because *she* does."

That was when Matt grasped he'd hit the trifecta when it came to setting off the selfish, spoiled woman. He'd refused to give her "more," he'd said the word "no" repeatedly, and he'd had the audacity to choose another woman over her.

"So, what do you say, Matt?"

"I don't negotiate with terrorists."

It wasn't the response she'd expected. Her frown was rife with confusion, but that emotion only lingered a moment before the anger returned. "You want to dig your own grave? So be it."

And with that, Patricia spun on her heel and stormed out of his office.

Matt dropped back down into his chair, aware of what he'd unleashed. Patricia would follow through on her threat, and when she did, this house of cards he'd built was going to fall down. He'd been a fool to believe he could hide the sins of his past.

This time, that niggling little voice was no longer quiet. It was loud and condescending and...right.

Closing his eyes, the images flashed, each one reigniting the pain he thought he'd overcome.

The constant drip-drip-drip of water.

Dark red blood congealed on the snowy-white tiles.

The blue-tinged skin of a lifeless arm.

"No! No! No!"

"How could she do this to me?!"

Look deeper.

Matt bowed his head, not even bothering to fight the heavy feelings, the anguish, the desolation. He'd learned the hard way there was no way to rewrite the past, no matter how much he wanted to. As such, he couldn't change what he'd done all those years ago.

He was as sure of that as he was of...

Liza's response.

She'd never forgive him.

Chapter Sixteen

"Are you sure I can't help you do something?" Liza asked her aunt Berta for the third time.

Aunt Berta, now as always, was immovable. "No, no, no. I'm just putting the finishing touches on the sandwiches. You sit there and relax."

Liza grinned as her aunt fluttered around the kitchen, slicing a tomato, washing the leaves of lettuce, digging through the dill pickle jar. Aunt Berta had been inviting her over for lunch ever since Liza returned from Hawaii, but she'd been so slammed after missing a week of work that she'd eaten lunch at her desk every day last week, plowing through all the crap that had piled up during her absence.

Today, Liza decided enough was enough. She hadn't seen anyone in her family since she'd returned. Simply because she'd earmarked every free second of her day as Matt's.

"Now then," Aunt Berta said, carrying two plates to the table. "Tell me all about your trip to Hawaii."

Liza went into great detail about the wedding ceremony, the reception, the resort where she stayed, and all the food she'd eaten. The only thing she made no mention of was Matt.

Not because she didn't want to tell Aunt Berta but because

she and Matt hadn't discussed "coming out" to their families and friends yet. She'd bring the subject up tonight after work. Now that she was here, chatting with her beloved aunt, she realized she was dying to tell everyone.

The problem was that, while that realist side of hers was telling her to err on the side of caution, the too-inexperienced-with-romance woman inside was flittering around like a girl who'd just gotten her first kiss.

The second she thought about kissing, she recalled the X-rated kiss Matt had given her girlie parts this weekend in Vermont. They'd been making out like teenagers on the bearskin rug, laughing, tickling, talking. Then, alpha Matt had emerged, stripped her out of her clothes, and French-kissed her pussy until she thought the top of her head would fly off.

Mercifully, Aunt Berta chose that moment to grab the iced tea pitcher from the refrigerator to refill their glasses. Otherwise, Liza would have to come up with an excuse for her suddenly flushed cheeks.

Liza still couldn't believe Matt had whisked her off for a ski weekend. It was hands down the most romantic thing any man had ever done for her. Her feet hadn't touched the ground since they returned last night, Matt driving them directly back to his penthouse, the two of them soaking in—and initiating—the gigantic Jacuzzi tub in his bathroom. Afterward, they'd laughed as they made a list of all the rooms and pieces of furniture they planned to "initiate" in his penthouse, his office at Russo, and her apartment.

And as perfect as everything had been—seriously, she'd been in a sex haze for two weeks, completely enthralled by the countless orgasms—she knew they were rapidly approaching the time when they should begin to broach some real-world topics. Things like the future, their families, and whether or not his view on marriage and kids had changed. Because—fuck her—that was going to be a deal breaker.

If Liza wasn't so well-sexed, she'd probably take a minute to admit the thought of bringing those subjects up tied her insides in nervous knots. But for now, she preferred to remain safely ensconced in this "ignorance is bliss" state a while longer.

"Well, it sounds like you had a wonderful time." Aunt Berta topped up their glasses and sat back down. Ever since she began working at the Initiative, Liza had enjoyed a standing weekly lunch date with Aunt Berta in her small apartment on the same floor as Moretti Brothers Restorations. Liza had always loved her aunt's kitchen because it was clearly Berta's favorite room. There were all sorts of cool cooking knickknacks, countless spices lining a shelf above the stove, colorful pictures of Italy and Philadelphia and family adorning the walls. There was a much-cherished recipe card framed and hanging above the table, the instructions and ingredients handwritten by Aunt Berta's grandmother.

But it wasn't the décor that left Liza with a warm feeling every time she visited. It was the smells. If Heaven had a scent, it would be called Aunt Berta's Kitchen. Tomatoes and garlic and basil and cheese and, God, Liza's mouth always started watering the second she stepped inside the apartment.

She and her aunt chatted for a few minutes more before they both rose and Liza helped her load their dishes into the dishwasher.

Liza was just about to head back to work when the door to Aunt Berta's apartment flew open.

"Heavens, Tony!" Aunt Berta exclaimed, her hand on her chest. "You startled me."

Liza watched as Tony and Luca entered with matching expressions, though she couldn't tell if they were angry or upset.

Tony, in a normal state of mind, would have apologized for scaring Aunt Berta. Actually, normal Tony would have knocked rather than barging in.

"What's wrong?" Liza asked.

Tony sighed rather than respond, and she knew exactly what he was thinking. Her brothers and cousins had spent their entire lives trying to protect the females in the family—with varying degrees of success. "Liza, if you could just give us a minute alone with—"

"I'm not leaving." Liza crossed her arms. "So you might as well spit it out."

"Tony? What is it?" Aunt Berta asked, clearly alarmed.

Tony gestured toward the living room. "Maybe we should all sit down."

Liza and Aunt Berta sank down side by side on the couch, while Tony claimed the overstuffed chair to Aunt Berta's left. Luca didn't bother sitting down. Instead, he paced the length of the room, back and forth, like a caged lion.

Tony placed a piece of paper on the coffee table. Liza was only able to scan it for a second before her attention was distracted by Aunt Berta's gasp.

Liza turned, panicking when she realized her aunt had turned white as a ghost. "Aunt Berta," she said, wrapping her arm around Berta's shoulders. "Are you okay?"

Tony shifted closer as well, and Luca stopped walking, standing on the opposite side of the coffee table, concern now mingled with anger.

"You know what that is," Tony said softly.

Aunt Berta nodded, her hands shaking slightly. "We thought...I thought...I..." Aunt Berta lowered her head to her hands, and Liza's panic increased tenfold. The only time Liza had ever seen her aunt this visibly shaken was when she'd learned Uncle Renzo had died.

"So it's real?" Luca asked.

Despite the powerful emotions coursing through her cousins, Liza could tell they were trying to gentle their tones to keep Aunt Berta calm.

"It's real," Berta whispered brokenly.

Liza turned her attention back to the paper, trying to determine what the hell could be so bad.

Scanning the document, she saw it appeared to be...a gambling marker?

"I don't understand what this is." Liza could see Renzo's name, an ungodly amount of debt, an interest rate so high that it had to be a typo, and then...

Liza's heart stopped when her eyes landed on the name at the bottom.

Matt Russo.

"You've seen this before?" Tony asked Aunt Berta.

"No. But Renzo told me about it. I thought—I hoped—that maybe it had been forgiven."

Tony rubbed his eyes wearily. "I don't understand, Aunt Berta. Why would Uncle Renzo go to Matt Russo for a loan? Why would he agree to those ridiculous rates?"

Aunt Berta wrung her hands before lifting one to wipe away a tear. "I never wanted you kids to find out. You loved your uncle Renzo, and you should have. He was an amazing man. It's just..."

"Did Uncle Renzo have a gambling problem?" Liza asked.

Aunt Berta sucked in a shaky breath. "He...yes, he did. But he got it under control long before he died."

"Maybe you should start at the beginning, Aunt Berta. Talk us through this. Because if this debt is real..." Tony didn't finish his thought. Probably because they could all do the math and figure out Uncle Renzo's debt—given the weekly interest and the length of time since the loan was issued—was in the seven-figure range.

"He liked to gamble," Aunt Berta started. "He always did. Shortly after he and Frank opened the restoration business, he started hitting the tables at one of the local casinos after work to blow off steam. I didn't know at first. I thought he'd just been working long hours, but then one day, the bank called to tell me I'd bounced a check at the grocery store. I couldn't understand how. When I confronted Renzo, he told me about the casino, about the string of bad luck."

"I never knew," Tony said. "I'm sure Dad didn't either."

"He was so ashamed of himself, and he promised he would stop. He did...for a while."

"Obviously, he started back up," Luca said, prompting Aunt Berta to continue.

"By the time I realized he was gambling again, he'd racked up a substantial debt with the casino."

"The Russos don't own casinos," Liza pointed out, trying to figure out how Matt's name ended up on this marker.

"But the Eddingtons do," Tony said. "Isn't Russo dating Patricia Eddington? Obviously, the Russos pulled in a favor with their country club buddies."

Liza swallowed deeply, trying to dislodge the lump there. None of this made sense. But...maybe it did. Had Matt discovered the debt and bought it as a way to help her family?

She glanced at the document again, that too-wonderful-to-be-true dream dashed when she saw that Matt had purchased this marker fifteen years ago. He would have been twenty-two at the time.

Why would he buy something like this?

Liza scoffed at herself. She might be an idiot in love, but she wasn't stupid.

Matt had seen the debt as a way to hurt her family.

What didn't make sense was why he'd decided to cash it in *now*. The man she'd spent the last two weeks falling head over heels for wouldn't do something like this. He just wouldn't.

"Why didn't you tell us we were in debt to Matt Russo after Uncle Renzo died?" Luca asked.

"I didn't know who the debt was to. Renzo never told me. I knew he owed the casino quite a lot of money. We took out a second mortgage on the house, but—"

"When you sold the house, you told me you didn't know why Uncle Renzo took out that second mortgage." Tony looked as confused as Liza felt.

"I shouldn't have lied to you, but..." Aunt Berta wiped away another tear. Liza reached over to the end table closest to her and grabbed a box of tissues. Her aunt gave her a grateful smile as she took one. "You loved your uncle, looked up to him, and I didn't want you to think less of him. He was a good man, but he wasn't perfect."

"So some of the debt has been paid?" Liza wondered if perhaps this was a moot point. If the second mortgage had covered it.

"Renzo went to the casino to give them the money. It wasn't enough to pay off the loan, but he hoped it would buy him time to figure out how to come up with the rest. He even considered selling his half of the business, but it still wouldn't have been enough."

"But he paid some of it off?" Luca asked, seeking clarification of exactly what they were up against.

"Renzo was gone a long time that day, and I worried he'd bypassed the cashier window and hit the tables again. When he returned, he still had the money. Said that the marker had been bought by a powerful man."

"Matt Russo," Tony spat the name in a way that made Liza's chest hurt.

"Renzo refused to tell me who, but I could tell that whoever it was...it was bad."

"Did he give Matt the money?"

Aunt Berta shrugged. "I don't know. Renzo never talked to me about what happened that day, and while I knew that marker existed, this is the first time I've ever seen it. But not a day went by that Renzo didn't think of and worry about the debt. Whenever I asked him about it, all he would say was the loan hadn't come due yet. I didn't understand what that meant. All I know is he lived every single day of his life waiting for that knock on the door."

"That must have been unbearable," Liza murmured.

"His blood pressure had always been high, and he'd taken medicine to keep it under control from the time he was in his twenties. But with the added anxiety of knowing we could lose everything in the blink of an eye, well, the doctor increased his dose shortly after."

Liza felt sick to think her uncle had spent so many years—*an entire decade and a half*—waiting for a phone call that could destroy him, Aunt Berta, their family, the business. Sure, he'd dug the hole, but this debt was clearly exploited—it was obvious from the high interest rate.

When she attached Matt's name as the person who tormented Renzo, a wave of nausea left her light-headed.

"When he died, I waited, certain I wouldn't be able to settle his estate until the debt was cleared. But it didn't show up anywhere in the bank records and no one came looking for the money. So I hoped that maybe it was forgiven," Aunt Berta said, though it was apparent she didn't believe what she was saying.

"Loans aren't forgiven, Aunt Berta," Tony said. "Obviously, Matt sat on this until the interest on the principal was high enough he knew we couldn't afford to pay it."

Aunt Berta sniffled, a soft cry escaping. "I'm so sorry!"

Liza tightened her grip around her aunt's shoulders, tugging her closer. "It's okay, Aunt Berta. It's all going to be okay." She locked gazes with Tony, whose jaw was clenched tight in anger and despair.

She suspected he had a lot more he wanted to say, but he didn't want to upset their aunt any more than they already had.

Liza glanced at the marker again, still struggling to understand. "Where did you get that, Tony?" she asked, nodded at the paper.

"Someone delivered it to the Moretti Brothers offices about a half hour ago," Tony replied.

"Who delivered it?" Liza asked.

"Isn't it obvious? Russo had one of his lackeys bring it to us."

Liza slowly shook her head, refusing to believe that. She and Matt had made love no more than seven hours earlier. It had been slow and passionate and perfect. He hadn't been a man set on revenge. He'd been gentle and warm and...goddammit...*perfect*.

Luca ran his hand through his hair, anger winning as the dominant emotion. "Looks like the fruit didn't fall far from the tree. Matt's decided to continue the path of destruction put in place by his grandfather and father with this fucking sucker punch."

"Come on, Luca," Tony said, rising.

"Where are you going?" Liza asked.

"To see Russo," Tony replied. "I'm not waiting around for the asshole's next move."

"No." Liza stood as well, picking up the piece of paper. "I'll go."

Luca and Tony scoffed in unison. "No way."

Liza raised her hand before they could continue. "I know Matt. We have a...working relationship." She hoped no one noticed her pause before *working*. She'd almost skipped that word entirely. Now probably wasn't the best time to mention she'd been shacking up with Matt for the past couple of weeks. She hadn't slept alone in a bed since Hawaii.

"Liza, there's no way—"

"I can talk to him," she interjected. "Reason with him. Try to figure out what his end game is. If you go, it'll be less talk, more fists. That won't help anyone."

"I'm not going to hit him," Tony insisted. "At least not immediately."

She rolled her eyes. "Please let me handle this."

Tony sighed, then exchanged a glance with Luca, who shrugged.

"You can come with us," Tony conceded.

"I'm doing all the talking," she added, though she knew Tony wouldn't be able to stop himself from stepping into the fray. Tony Moretti was an intimidating force, and when something arose that threatened his loved ones...God help them.

That marker had made Aunt Berta cry, it had caused Uncle Renzo years of stress, and it had the potential to bankrupt Moretti Brothers. At the end of the day, all of that was ultimately Uncle Renzo's fault, but Liza wasn't certain Tony was seeing it that way at the moment.

There was no way she'd be able to hold Tony back if it turned out Matt was indeed calling in the debt.

Blood would be shed.

"Please, Tony," she persisted, desperate to find some way out of this mess, some way back to the pure happiness she'd felt not thirty minutes ago.

"We'll go together." Tony hadn't agreed to let her do the talking, but it was as good a deal as she was going to get.

As they left Aunt Berta's, Liza prayed the entire way to the Russo Enterprises building that this had been some big misunderstanding. That Matt, the man she'd fallen hopelessly in love with, wasn't trying to destroy her family.

Chapter Seventeen

"You can't go in there!"

Matt looked up as the door to his office slammed open, Henri hot on the heels of Tony and Luca Moretti.

"Sir," Henri exclaimed, rushing into the room. "I tried to stop them. Should I call security?"

Henri's question was justified. Tony and Luca looked ready to commit murder.

A wise man would request backup, but instead, Matt shook his head. "No. I've been expecting them."

"You have?"

At the sound of her voice, Matt's stomach clenched painfully, because that was when he realized Liza was standing in the threshold of the door, hidden behind her cousins' large frames.

Matt stood, swallowing hard. When Patricia had issued her threat, he'd known this showdown was imminent. He'd expected her to go to Tony. After all, he was the one she'd specifically mentioned, and he'd taken a small amount of comfort in that. Tony's anger, he could deal with. But Liza's?

This conversation was going to be difficult enough as it was, and given his and Tony's contentious past, Matt would be lucky if it didn't come to blows. Tony certainly looked furious enough to throw a few punches.

If it had just been Tony and Luca, Matt could have powered through. But doing this, becoming the man he used to be, in front of Liza...

Matt took a deep breath and steeled himself for what came next. Glancing at his assistant, he said, "You can go back to your desk, Henri. There's no need to call security. I can handle this."

Henri's gaze traveled from Tony to Luca, then back to Matt, and while his slight PA wasn't more than five feet six and a hundred and fifty pounds soaking wet, he shot Matt a determined, fearless "got your back" look.

Matt was going to give the man one hell of a bonus come evaluation time.

"It's okay," Matt reassured him again, giving Henri an appreciative nod.

Henri walked out of the room, closing the door behind him, and Tony wasted no time, storming over to his desk and slamming the marker down on the surface. "You want to explain to me what this is?"

Matt didn't give the marker more than a cursory glance. He knew what the paper said. Matt lifted one eyebrow and kept his eyes locked on Tony's face. As long as he didn't look at Liza, he could handle this. A lifetime of animosity toward Tony bubbled to the surface, allowing Matt to slide back into his role as the villain in this fucking Greek tragedy more easily than he expected. He'd tried to show this man to Liza in Hawaii, tried to make her see he wasn't the man she thought he was. "You need me to explain the loan to you?"

Tony gritted his teeth. "No, I don't."

"Perhaps you need me to do the math for you. Interest can be tricky." His words and tone hit their marks. Luca, who'd been standing slightly behind Tony, deferring the lead to his older brother, moved closer until the two were standing side by side in front of his desk. He should probably dial back the snark because there was no way this would be a fair fight. Not that that was his goal.

Whatever he got…he had coming.

"Knew the Russos' hands were fucking dirty, but I didn't realize just how low you sank. You sit here in your fancy office and act like a big shot, but you're nothing more than a goddamned loan shark," Luca snarled.

In this particular instance, that's absolutely what Matt was. He'd chosen his victim, preyed on his weakness, then struck fast and hard, a black mamba lying in wait. The insanely high interest, charged weekly, had been put in place on purpose, since Matt's original goal had been to inflict as much pain as possible.

Then, his mom committed suicide and life changed those goals. He'd put the marker aside, all but forgotten, until Patricia shoved it in his face this morning. The truth was he had never intended to collect on it, but now…

Now he saw a different use for it.

"This debt is fifteen years old," Tony said. "That's a long time to sit on a loan without collecting payment."

"Maybe so, but if I'd called in the debt fifteen years ago, this piece of paper," Matt tapped his finger on the marker, "would be worth a lot less."

He heard Liza gasp at the cruel callousness in his voice, but he didn't spare her a glance. He couldn't.

"How did you come into possession of this?" Luca asked. "The Eddingtons own the casino that issued this marker, not Russo Enterprises."

This…

This was the part he didn't want to say in front of Liza. This was why he'd tried to stay away from her initially. He'd been a fool to think the past would stay dead and buried. He had too many skeletons in his closet…done too many truly terrible things.

Horrible things that wouldn't just ensure he lost Liza's trust and affection, but his brothers' as well.

For fourteen years, he'd been living with an ax over his head.

Maybe it was time to just let it fall, let it chop the head off this shell of a man he'd become and live the rest of his miserable life alone.

"My father and Richard Eddington were good friends. As such, he was aware of the animosity between our families. One night at the club, Richard mentioned that your uncle Renzo had built up a bit of gambling debt. Twenty thousand dollars, to be exact."

Tony's gaze fell to the paper. Matt knew why. The numbers didn't add up. "I convinced Richard to extend your uncle more credit. Told him I would cover the loan, buy the marker. We agreed on a number and then Renzo dug the hole. That's the one reliable thing about gamblers. They're always certain they can solve their problems with just one more deal of the cards."

Richard was as big an asshole as Matt's dad, and he'd been all too happy to agree to Matt's scheme, pleased to be a part of the twisted game his family liked to play with the Morettis. He could recall the way he, Dad, and Richard had all clinked their glasses of Scotch together, amused by the thought of playing God, destroying a man simply because they could.

"You made sure he got in too deep, over his head with a debt he couldn't hope to pay." Tony's voice was quiet but lethal as he started connecting the dots.

Matt crossed his arms. "No one held a gun to your uncle's head at those tables. He lost the money all on his own."

"He shouldn't have been able to gamble so much," Luca said, slamming his fist on the top of the desk. "If he'd been cut off before—"

Matt interrupted the man mid-rant. "He would have gone to another casino and racked up more debt with someone else. I ensured that didn't happen. Because this way, it all comes to me."

Tony's fists clenched, fury carved in every groove on his face, and Matt braced himself for the punch.

"He had a gambling problem," Liza said softly. "We didn't know about it until that marker showed up today."

Apparently, her uncle Renzo had taken his secret to the grave, though Matt didn't believe he could have hidden it from everyone. "Surely his wife knew."

Matt had felt Liza's eyes on him throughout the conversation, but he hadn't glanced her direction once. He couldn't. Not if he hoped to do what needed to be done. He ignored her comment, his attention locked on Tony and Luca.

"Aunt Berta knew," Liza admitted.

Tony huffed out a disgusted laugh, shaking his head. "You really know how to play the long game, don't you, Russo? Obviously, the original debt is a drop in the bucket to you. It's why you waited. You don't need that fucking money, so you waited until you could do the most damage."

"My patience is endless," Matt replied, the cold, cutting words coming easily...too easily. This was the role he was raised to play.

"All this just because you lost a stupid election in high school?" Tony asked. "Are you really *that* petty? Is your ego that fucking fragile?"

Matt had been twenty-two when he'd bought the marker, a cocky, selfish son of a bitch with too much money and even more pride. Hell yeah, his ego had been fragile.

He began to wonder if the reason he'd tolerated Patricia as long as he had was because he understood her. Children raised with silver spoons, never wanting for a single thing, saw the world much differently than most.

"What's the end game?" Luca asked, calmer after his outburst. "Why send the marker now?"

Matt could come clean here, tell them he hadn't sent the marker, but he doubted Tony and Luca would believe him... though he knew Liza would.

"Your aunt Berta owes me a great deal of money," Matt forced himself to say.

"It was me," Liza whispered with so much anguish, Matt turned to her before he could stop himself. Her pain always called to him, always made him seek to end it, which was ridiculous because in this instance, he was the one hurting her.

Jesus. The look in her eyes. He'd put that there. *He'd* done that.

"What was you?" he forced himself to ask, uncertain if he wanted to hear her answer.

"I told you Aunt Berta owned half of Moretti Brothers. I told you how well the company was doing."

She had. And at the time, Matt had lain there next to her, wondering what it would be like to be a part of such a huge, loving family. The pride and love in her voice as she talked about how amazing her aunt and cousins were had glowed so brightly, he'd longed to have someone shine that kind of light on him...just once.

Now she was interpreting that conversation differently, viewing him as the panther lying in wait.

He'd told her he was a user, that he took what he needed from people then discarded them, but he refused to let her assume the blame for any of this. She didn't do a damn thing wrong. "I didn't need to be told that, Liza. A simple Google search would have revealed the same."

Matt started to turn back to Tony and Luca, but Liza stepped next to him, took his hand in hers. Her hand was ice cold, her expression steeped in grief and fear. He'd always hated seeing resignation in her eyes, but this...this was a thousand times worse.

"Did your dad do this?" she asked.

Matt shook his head in disbelief. Even after everything she just heard him say, she was still looking for another explanation. One that would cast him in a better light. He pointed to the marker, tapped his finger on his name. "I bought the marker with my own money. My dad had nothing to do with this, nor did Russo Enterprises. I found a useful Moretti, one whose weakness offered me a way to take your family down. I exploited it."

Liza stared at him, searching hard for something he couldn't show her. If this was where his list of sins ended...maybe. Maybe he could apologize for his actions, find a way to earn her forgiveness. But this was just the tip of the iceberg.

Finally, something in her expression broke. There wasn't a sign of the happiness and joy he'd witnessed in Hawaii, or even last night when she'd lain next to him in his bed. Now, there was nothing but a deep sadness he was helpless to take away.

"We can't pay that debt," she said softly.

"It's not *your* debt."

His words struck a chord, and he saw a flash of that fire he admired so.

"We're a family," she asserted. "It is *our* debt." Unfortunately, the spark of temper sputtered out too quickly, replaced by confusion. "I just...you have to help me, Matt. Have to explain this to me. Why? Why are you doing this? After everything..." Her voice faltered, clueing him in that she still hadn't revealed their affair to her family.

"I told you who I was, Liza. I never lied about it."

"This isn't who you are," she insisted.

Matt's ability to hold it together crumbled as she stood there, determined to see the best in him. "This is exactly who I am! Open your eyes and *look* at me." He reached for her upper arms, gripping them. From the corner of his eye, he saw Tony and Luca both take a step toward him, but Liza shook her head, waved them off. "Really look at me!"

Liza's gaze never wavered. "I am."

He released her instantly, her words a punch to the gut, as she looked at him with that fucking misplaced hope in her eyes.

How? How could she still look at him like...like he was worthy of anything more than disdain?

Turning to his desk, he opened the top desk drawer. After Patricia's visit, he'd retrieved the original marker from the safe in his office. He flipped open the file, aware that all three Morettis were watching, that they saw what he had in his hands.

"This is the original marker. What you have is just a copy."

Matt stared at Tony, pushing down the rush of emotions rising to the surface, each one capable of shredding him to pieces.

He took a steadying breath, then turned to Liza. "You want to settle the debt?" he asked woodenly.

She didn't respond immediately. His clever girl was too astute not to understand that what he was offering would come with a catch.

Finally, she nodded, just once.

He handed her the marker. "Accept that this is me, agree to walk away, and you can tear that up."

"Walk away?" she whispered, her hands trembling slightly as she held the paper.

"From me. From us."

He didn't bother to look at Tony and Luca. He could feel their shock without having to see it.

"No."

He'd expected that response, had been prepared for it. "Then pay me the money."

Matt forced himself to look at her, to see the tears glistening in her eyes. They were his punishment, his to bear.

"Matt."

"Decide quickly, Liza, because this offer isn't going to last much longer." He was going for cold, but he feared his words sounded too desperate to pull it off.

"Tell me why," she demanded.

Matt wanted to refuse, but even now he could tell she was trying to give him the benefit of the doubt, searching for something that might excuse all of this.

"I...can't. We should never have started this, should never have let things go so far. I'm not the man you think I am. This marker is just the beginning of my sins."

Liza frowned. "You have more ways to hurt my family?"

He shook his head. "No. This is the only threat to the Morettis."

"Then tell me the rest and let me decide."

She was fierce and beautiful and so goddamned courageous. But what she didn't understand was that not all sins could be forgiven.

Besides, how could he ask her to forgive something for which he couldn't forgive himself?

Matt clenched his teeth and did what needed to be done. "No. Make your decision. Tear it up and walk away. Or…"

"Or?" she prodded.

"I'll take your family for everything. Destroy them."

"You wouldn't." She was right. He wouldn't, but he hated that for the first time, she didn't look or sound very sure of that.

Which meant it was time to finish this once and for all. He raised one cruel eyebrow, his expression the very definition of a *dare*. "Are you willing to risk your family's livelihood on that assumption?"

She reached up to wipe away a tear and before he could think better of it, he took a small step closer, lowered his voice. "It's better for everyone if we make a clean break."

"Everyone," she repeated angrily. "The *everyone* in this scenario is just you and me, and this isn't better for me." She sniffled, blinking back her tears. He knew she despised crying in front of people, and he hated that he'd provoked her to it.

Until that moment, he'd thought he was going to make it through to the other side. He could see the finish line. It was just there…only a few steps away.

But then Liza closed the distance between them, tilted her face up to his, and swung the death blow. "Please don't do this. I love you, Matt."

Matt felt all the blood drain from his face.

Love.

She loved him.

He knew that, felt it every time he held her. Because he felt it too.

Love.

He was in love with her…which was why he had to let her go.

Liza stared at him for several long minutes, waiting for his reply. Waiting for something he wanted to give her but couldn't. Because his love would destroy her, just as surely as hers was killing him.

His continued silence worked more effectively than any harsh words.

Liza took a step away from him. "So you're the everyone in the scenario," she said at last, her voice devoid of emotion. "Got it."

She lifted the paper, tearing it in half. It might as well have been Matt's heart in her hands. The tears she'd been valiantly fighting finally defeated her, flowing down her cheeks.

"Goodbye, Matt," she whispered, turning and walking out of the office. Matt could only assume it was shock and concern that had Tony and Luca following her without saying another word.

The second the door closed behind them, Matt sank down onto his desk chair, numbness and exhaustion claiming him quickly.

She loved him.

He'd lost her. Lost them both.

The constant drip-drip-drip of water.

Dark red blood congealed on the snowy-white tiles.

The blue-tinged skin of a lifeless arm.

"No! No! No!"

"How could she do this to me?!"

Look deeper.

Matt bowed his head in his hands and did something he hadn't done since he was a young boy.

He cried.

Chapter Eighteen

"**W**hat the fuck was that?" Tony said the second the elevator doors closed behind them.

"Tony," Luca said warningly.

Numbness sank in so deep, Liza felt as if she was suffocating, even though she felt the same way Tony did.

Because what the fuck *was* that?

"Liza," Tony pressed.

"Please, Tony." She was barely keeping it together. If she could just make it back to her apartment, she could fall apart completely, but she refused to do that here in front of them.

Luca placed a hand on his brother's shoulder, giving it a squeeze. She and Luca had grown closer this past year—two of the last men standing in what had been their gang of single friends/family. With the exception of Luca and Joey, everyone else was shacked up and working on their happily ever afters. This morning, Liza had woken up thinking she might be switching to that club from the lonely hearts one.

She should have known better.

Regardless, it felt like she owed her cousins an explanation. After all, she hadn't given them any warning that the status quo between her and Matt had changed from enemies to lovers. "I...

We..." she started. She couldn't speak the words, her tremulous control hanging on by a thread. "Matt..." Her voice broke the second she said his name.

"Shit," Tony murmured, his voice calmer. "I didn't know. I'm so sorry." He reached out and gave her a hug. Liza tried to let that compassion bolster her. And it sort of worked until he released her, his gaze zeroed in on her own. "Can you explain to us what just happened in there?"

Liza took a deep breath, then gave them as much as she could say, aware her voice was small, tight. "I've been seeing Matt off and on for two months...actually a little more." That wasn't exactly true, but in her mind, the one-night stand after the gala and the New Year's Eve kiss had started to count, the moment they'd become a monogamous couple.

"Jesus Christ, Liza," Tony breathed, shaking his head as if she'd admitted to committing some heinous crime.

His reaction, though muted for him—considering how deep his disdain ran for Matt—helped, because if there was one thing Liza could do in her sleep, it was go toe-to-toe with her overprotective, opinionated relatives.

Bruno, Elio, and Aldo—the world's greatest brothers—put her through her paces when they were younger, and she'd put a lot of time and effort into breaking their bad habits of intimidating her dates or expressing very strong views whenever she went out with someone they didn't approve of.

Obviously, she'd done a better job breaking her brothers' spirits than Layla had done with *her* big brothers, Tony, Luca, Gio, and Joey. Liza was beginning to understand why her cousin had moved to Baltimore.

"Don't start with me, Tony Moretti," she said hotly, trying to pick a fight, anger a preferable emotion to the excruciating anguish currently short-circuiting every internal system she had. The idea of curling into a fetal position in the corner of this elevator held a definite appeal.

Unfortunately, Tony wasn't picking up what she was

throwing down, his response too calm, too conciliatory. "I won't start because that was..."

He didn't finish that thought, so she did it for him.

"Horrible."

Tony didn't nod, though she could tell he agreed. "You're gonna have to give me a minute to let this soak in, let me get used to it, sweetheart. You kind of sprung that on us out of nowhere. You and Matt." The last sentence was muttered more to himself than to her.

His comment killed her weak-willed attempt at anger, and she sniffled, fighting hard not to cry again. "There's nothing to get used to," she said thickly.

"I don't know about that," Luca disagreed.

"You were in there," she said, blinking when her vision blurred with tears. "It's pretty fucking awful when you tell someone you love them for the first time, only to realize they don't feel the same."

Luca and Tony exchanged a look, then glanced back at her with matching bewildered expressions.

"You're kidding, right?" Luca asked incredulously.

Tony rubbed the back of his neck, and she could tell he took no pleasure in what he said next. "Liza. That man is so fucking in love with you, he can't see straight."

Liza shook her head. "He..." She replayed the scene in the office, trying to see what her cousins apparently had. She'd been so blinded by her anger, her confusion, her sadness, it was a wonder she'd managed to speak at all.

"He broke things off," she finally said.

"He canceled the debt," Luca pointed out. "That was a fuck-ton of money, and he just let you tear up the marker."

"If that's true, then why..." Her voice broke and she hated it. "Why did he break up with me? I thought... We were..." She struggled to catch her breath, but her throat completely closed up until talking simply wasn't possible. In the end, she just shook her head, turning away from them as much as she could so she could bat away a few stray tears.

"He's fighting it hard, and men like Matt Russo always go down swinging," Tony said, placing a comforting hand on her shoulder. "Take it from me. I was one of those guys. Took me way too long to admit Jess and Rhys were my future."

"That guy's obviously got some bad shit rattling around in his head," Luca added. "I don't think what happened in there has *anything* to do with you. It felt less like he didn't want you and more like he was trying to save you."

"From what?" she asked.

Luca lifted one shoulder casually. "From him."

"What if I don't want to be saved?" she asked, wiping the tears sliding down her cheeks with the back of her hand.

Luca leaned closer. "Are you questioning that?"

"Do you think the stress of this marker caused Uncle Renzo's heart attack?"

Tony and Luca exchanged a glance. She expected Luca to respond, so she was surprised when Tony did. "Honestly, I don't. I mean...it might have been a contributing factor, but Uncle Renzo's diet consisted of red meat, homemade pasta, wine, and whiskey. Add in the pack a day of cigarettes and lack of exercise..."

"He didn't exactly live a healthy lifestyle, Liza," Luca agreed.

Liza knew all of that, but hearing Tony say it, even after everything that had happened upstairs, helped. "What the hell am I supposed to do now?"

The doors to the elevator slid open when they reached the lobby, but Luca held his arm out, keeping her and Tony inside.

"We're gonna ask for help." When the doors closed once more, Luca hit the button to another floor.

While Matt's office was on one of the top floors, Russo Enterprises' IT department was on the third floor, so it only took them a second to backtrack.

Twenty minutes later, Gage walked into the IT department,

glancing around the room in surprise when he saw her, Tony, and Luca standing with Penny, Toby, and Rich.

Penny had called her husband, asking him to come to IT, though she hadn't told him why. Mainly because she didn't *know* why. Liza had asked if she could wait to explain their presence at Russo Enterprises until Gage got there. She wasn't sure she had it in her to recount what had just happened, twice.

Gage frowned. "Shit. Did I forget someone's birthday?"

Penny shook her head.

"Is it *my* birthday?" he asked with a grin.

Liza used to wonder if Gage had been dropped at the wrong house by the stork because his easygoing nature and great sense of humor were so different from that of his brothers.

Then she'd gotten to know Matt better, and she realized he shared the same quick wit, the same amazing laugh.

"Not your birthday," Penny said with a laugh.

Gage looked around the room. "Anyone want to give me a hint?"

Liza stepped forward. "How do I get your brother to admit he's in love with me?"

Gage frowned. "I didn't think you and Conor knew each other that well."

"Oh," Penny breathed, her eyes wide. Clearly, she understood what her husband did not.

"Not Conor," Liza clarified. "Matt."

Gage burst out with a loud laugh—one that died quickly when no one else joined in. Gage looked over at his wife.

"Is it April Fools?" he asked, though his previous joking attitude was gone. He looked confused, while Penny just looked concerned.

Penny shook her head, and Gage turned his attention back to Liza. "Matt's in love with you?"

Liza wanted to nod, wanted to believe that was true. Luca and Tony were convinced, but her heart—still shattered from what just went down—couldn't give him a definitive answer.

Luca, bless him, answered for her. "He is."

"Damn," Gage whispered. "That's…" He studied Liza's face, and she knew she was doing a shit job hiding her outright devastation. "Maybe you should start at the beginning."

Liza repeated what she'd told Tony and Luca in the elevator. How she and Matt had engaged in an affair before the holidays and that it had picked up steam when they were in Hawaii together. She tried to tell him about the debt, but there was no way she could speak the words without falling apart.

Mercifully, Luca and Tony covered that part, explaining about the debt and Matt's condition for forgiving it.

Gage rubbed his forehead wearily. "My brother is such an idiot."

"Why is he so against relationships? Against marriage?" she asked.

Gage shrugged. "I'm afraid I don't know why. Matt and I were close as kids, but once Dad got his claws into him…"

Liza knew about that. "He told me about your father, how he raised Matt in his image, to be his heir."

Gage's eyebrows lifted. "He told you?" It was clear he hadn't expected Matt to have confided something so personal.

She nodded.

"To be honest, I pulled away from Matt back then. Because he'd taken Dad's lessons to heart. For quite a few years, he and our old man were carbon copies of each other, which wasn't a good thing because Dad was…well, not to speak ill of the dead…but he was a grade-A asshole. And by the time Matt graduated from college and joined Russo Enterprises, he was the same. Cold, callous, distant. Not to mention misogynistic, arrogant, and cruel."

Matt had used a few of those same words to describe himself back when he was trying to warn Liza away. It didn't matter how many times they were bandied about because Liza still couldn't see any of that in the man she'd fallen in love with.

"Misogynistic?" That one was new, though, and it sparked Liza's curiosity.

"Matt was sort of a womanizer."

"He's not like that now," Liza insisted.

"I know he's not," Gage agreed. "He changed after our mom died. Went from being Dad's mini-me to the angriest man I've ever met. He cut everyone out of his life—including Dad—who, up until then, he'd been working overtime to impress. He did *everything* with our dad—work, golf on weekends, drinks at the club."

"It makes sense he would be angry over losing his mom." Liza was trying to pick up a couple of these scattered pieces Gage was tossing her way in hopes of putting them together, but she wasn't having any luck.

Gage didn't seem convinced that was the reason for Matt's change. "I've never seen anger run that deep, burn that hot. It was scary. And then Dad died, and it was like...all Matt's rage evaporated. Just disappeared like it had never been there. After that, he became the guy he is today. Workaholic with those impenetrable walls around him."

Liza sighed, and Gage gave her a sad smile.

"I don't know why Matt is fighting this thing between you, Liza. And even if I did, I couldn't tell you. There are some stories a guy's just gotta tell himself."

Gage and Penny exchanged a look, one filled with sadness and understanding. Liza didn't know what it meant, but it told her that Matt didn't appear to be the only Russo who'd struggled with love.

Penny reached out and grasped Gage's hand, giving it a squeeze.

"Liza," he began. "I want you with my brother. You're perfect for him, and there would be zero Mean Girl vibes at the Christmas Eve dinner."

Penny grinned. "We could be sisters," she whispered.

Liza tried to smile back, but that dream felt unachievable at the moment.

"You're strong, beautiful, and you won't let him believe his own press. He needs someone to keep that cockiness of his in check. But..." Gage paused.

"But?" Liza prodded.

"Matt's kept his own council for a very long time. Habits like that are going to be hard to break. The guy's been a shell of a man since he was twenty-three years old."

"Are you telling me to walk away?"

Gage shook his head. "No. I mean, walking away is one option if you can't forgive him for that crap he just pulled up in his office, because that was a big old pile of steaming bullshit."

"Seriously," Luca muttered.

"What's my other option?" she asked.

"Right now? Give him some time. Let the dust settle on this. Because I don't think it's going to take my brother long to figure out he made one hell of a mistake."

"Patience isn't a Moretti trait. We lean toward impulsive," Luca said.

Liza could have kissed her cousin because he said exactly what she was thinking. She didn't want to wait Matt out. That wasn't her speed. It was taking everything she had not to go back up to his office right now and demand answers.

"I'm not saying wait forever. But I know him well enough to know that the more you push, the more he'll resist."

Liza considered Patricia's pursuit of Matt, and she realized Gage was right.

"It took me a week to come to my senses when I was a jackass and stupidly tried to break things off with Penny," Gage said. "Matt's a stubborn son of a bitch, so it might take him longer."

Liza rubbed the back of her neck wearily, then remembered all the times Matt would grip her there, pull her toward him for a kiss. Her heart panged and she sniffled. Somehow she was going to have to hold these tears in until she got home.

Penny reached out, grasping her hand. "Want me to call the girls? Set up a happy hour for later in the week?"

Liza couldn't think beyond the rest of today. "Let me see how I feel. I'll text everyone if I'm up for it."

Penny gave her a gentle smile, then pulled her close. "For what it's worth, I think everything is going to work out."

"You do?" Liza felt like a fool for latching onto those words like they were some sort of lifeline.

"I do."

Gage offered her a hug. "If Matt is truly in love with you, being without you is going to fucking hurt. I'm just not sure he'll..."

"You think he'll dig his heels in?" she asked.

Gage shrugged, his expression proving he knew as well as she did that was a definite possibility. His silence told her what she didn't want to hear—that she shouldn't wait *too* long. But it didn't matter what Gage thought.

Because, while she'd never admit it, Liza would wait for Matt until the end of time.

$$Chapter\ Nineteen$$

"**O**kay. Time's up."

Matt looked up from his computer, blinking wearily after so many screen hours without a break, frowning as Gage and Conor walked in. He hadn't had a good night's sleep in over a week, the nightmares returning with a vengeance, attacking nightly.

Arnold, worried about him, had been blowing up his phone, texting and calling, inviting Matt to return to the Promise House or to join him and Johnnie for dinner. Every text and voicemail the man left had gone unanswered as Matt attempted to revert back to character, to become the man who lived in solitude. Opening himself up to others had only led to this unending ache in his chest.

"Did we have a meeting scheduled?" He looked behind them for Henri. For once, his guard dog PA was surprisingly absent.

"Nope." Gage closed the door behind them. He and Conor claimed the two chairs opposite his desk, settling in like they intended to be there for a while.

Matt didn't have the energy for whatever this was. "I'm busy," he barked. "Call Henri and schedule a meeting."

Gage and Conor both chuckled, unfazed by his grumpiness.

"Yeah," Conor said. "That's not going to happen."

"Is there a reason for this visit?" Matt had barricaded himself in this office and the one in his penthouse for the past ten days, working from dawn until midnight.

The only truly productive thing he'd accomplished was seeking retribution against the Eddingtons. By awakening the monster within, Matt had found it far too simple to reach into Dante Russo's bag of tricks. Hiring a private investigator immediately following Patricia's visit with the marker had yielded some interested information. Information Matt had shared with the right people.

As such, Richard Eddington was currently under investigation for sexual harassment. Matt had encouraged a former personal assistant to come forward to tell her story. That initial report had opened the door, and three other women had since filed their own grievances. The evidence—and Eddington's attempts to buy the women off—had been irrefutable, and last Matt had heard, the board of directors was calling for Richard's resignation.

Meanwhile, the tabloids were having a field day with the news that the self-proclaimed "all-natural beauty" Patricia had, in fact, undergone several plastic surgery operations, something she'd always vehemently denied, declaring she didn't need it.

Sadly, revenge wasn't the balm it had been in his younger days.

He'd thrown himself into his work with a vengeance, ensuring he was so fucking exhausted by the time he fell into bed that sleep took him immediately. Though it never lasted for long, the bad dreams waking him up in a cold sweat.

When he was awake, work kept him distracted enough that he didn't have time to think about—

He shut that down, refusing to say her name even in his thoughts.

"Of course there's a reason for our visit," Gage said. "This is your intervention."

Matt sighed. "Is this some sort of payback?"

Back when Gage had first started seeing Penny, Matt and Conor had shanghaied Gage in his office when it became apparent their brother was falling apart.

Which meant Matt hadn't been doing a very good job hiding his own mental breakdown.

"It's not payback," Conor hastened to say. "We just thought it might be time to step in before you drive every employee we have out of the building. I give Henri another week before he starts keeping a flask in his desk drawer."

Matt rubbed his eyes. He'd been a fucking bear, barking at anyone unfortunate enough to catch his attention. It was no wonder Henri hadn't announced his brothers' arrival. His poor PA had taken the brunt of Matt's very bad mood. He'd no doubt hit his limit on ass-chewings.

"Fine," Matt said. "I'll stop being an asshole. So if that's all—"

Gage laughed as he looked at Conor. "Aw. Isn't that cute? He thinks we're going to let him off easy."

Matt scowled. "You do remember that technically I'm the boss, right? I could fire both your asses."

Gage rolled his eyes in response to that empty threat, while Conor just stared him down, one eyebrow raised.

"Fine. Obviously you have something on your mind. Stop beating around the fucking bush and say it. I've got work to do."

"What's the deal with you and Liza Moretti?" Gage went right for the jugular, and given Conor's lack of shock, he'd clearly filled their kid brother in on what had gone down.

While he didn't know exactly how much Gage knew, Matt wasn't surprised he'd heard at least some of it. Penny and Liza were friends, after all.

"There *is* no deal."

Saying those words hurt. Matt kept waiting for the pain to subside, but every single day he woke up struggling to breathe, his chest tight. He was starting to think this was his new normal.

"Because you decided to play loan shark with her uncle?" Conor asked.

Matt started to nod, but he stopped. "No."

He truly believed that if he'd simply torn the marker up the second Liza, Tony, and Luca had stormed into his office and begged for her forgiveness, she would have given it to him. Liza wasn't like Patricia. She didn't hold grudges. He'd tested her forgiving nature countless times in Hawaii with his hands-off, hands-on bullshit enough to know for sure that was true.

Gage leaned forward. "Then why? You clearly have feelings for her, apparent by this wounded beast routine you've got going on."

Matt stared at his brothers and felt all the carefully constructed walls he'd erected over the years begin to shake.

He was tired. *So fucking tired.* Of pain, regrets, anger...

Secrets.

He couldn't do this anymore. But more than that...he didn't want to.

"I know why Mom killed herself."

His words were the equivalent of a bomb going off. Gage and Conor both jerked as if he'd struck them.

Silence fell for an uncomfortable amount of time before Gage hoarsely said, "What?"

Matt closed his eyes. "I was with her the night..." He swallowed thickly. "The night she committed suicide."

"You never told us that," Conor said, speaking up when it was apparent Gage couldn't. Gage was always the closest to Mom, and Matt knew his brother had been seeking answers, trying to figure out why she took her own life.

Matt could never bring himself to tell Gage why. Because he was a selfish son of a bitch who was too fucking afraid of losing the only family he had left. Not that it mattered. The secret had taken its toll and created a distance between him and his brothers anyway.

"Tell us now," Gage demanded.

Matt took a long look at his brothers, certain that what he said next would destroy what was left of him, of them.

Fatigue took over as he opened the door on the memory, his words wooden as he let his mind drift back to that night. "It was a few days after New Year's. You'd spent the holidays skiing with a friend, Conor, and..." He turned to look at Gage. "You'd gone back to college early for a frat party or something." Gage nodded just once, confirming the truth. "Mom had been pestering me to go out to dinner with her to celebrate my birthday."

"Your birthday is the end of November," Conor pointed out.

"I know. I'd canceled on her...a lot, always claiming I had too much work to do. Finally, I ran out of excuses and just decided to get it over with." Bile rose because that was truly how he'd viewed that night. As an unwanted chore, something to grin and bear.

God. What would he give to spend one more birthday with Mom?

"Start at the beginning," Conor said, when Matt stopped talking. His brother was right. This story was long overdue. He'd tell it from beginning to end and then...

He couldn't think about what came after.

"I picked Mom up and drove us to the restaurant," he started, the story coming out in starts and stops as he forced himself to say every painful word.

Matt guided Mom inside, the restaurant crowded as most people were still hesitant to give up holiday mode. He'd called ahead and made reservations, so he wasn't worried about having to wait for a table.

Mom held a wrapped birthday package in her hands. He'd offered to open it in the car, so she didn't have to carry it into the restaurant, but she insisted that they do it at the table, that she wanted to see his face clearly when he opened it.

"Mr. Russo, if you'll follow me," the hostess said, leading

them through the crowded dining room. Matt was almost to the table when he realized Mom had stopped walking.

Turning back, he noticed she was looking at something across the restaurant. Matt followed her gaze, cursing under his breath. "Fuck."

There, in a corner booth, was Dad and his latest mistress. Given the close, somewhat awkward way they were sitting—Dad's arms spread out along the back of the seat, the woman's hands under the table—as well as her flushed face, Matt was willing to bet she was giving his father a hand job.

If Mom hadn't been there, Matt would have smirked and admired his dad's brazenness.

One of the first lessons Matt had learned from his father was that marriage didn't equate to fidelity. It had been a rude awakening at fourteen to learn that Dad was cheating on Mom, but as always, Dante Russo found a way to explain it as if it was the most normal thing in the world.

He'd told Matt that Mom was perfectly aware of his cheating. Then he'd explained that, out of respect to the mother of his children, a real man never flaunted his mistresses or mentioned them. Made Matt swear to never speak to his mother or brothers about it, told him it was their "little secret" with a wink and a leer, like they were part of some bad boys club.

After that, Dad had launched into an even bigger lecture on the levels of mistresses, beginning with one-night stands all the way through the "kept" woman, who was monogamous to him in exchange for an apartment, clothing, an allowance. Matt wasn't sure where this latest woman ranked on the list.

Stepping back next to her, Matt said, "Shit. I'm sorry, Mom. I didn't know they'd be here. We can go somewhere else if you want."

Mom's gaze jerked from Dad to him, her eyes wide with surprise—and hurt. Dad said he didn't flaunt his other women. Was this the first time she'd ever seen it up close and personal?

Guilt wasn't something Matt suffered from much, but he definitely felt it now when his mother looked so wounded.

"I guess you've never seen him out with one of his..." Matt stopped. He hated saying the word "mistress" to his mom.

"One of them?" Mom asked. "There have been others?"

Matt didn't know how to reply to that. Because her question didn't fit what Dad had told him.

"I..." he started, still stumbling over how to answer. In the end, he just said, "Yes."

"And you knew," she whispered.

Her words struck hard and deep—and he was left to wonder what was hurting her worse. Finding out that Dad was cheating on her or learning that Matt had been a silent witness to it all these years.

"Do you want to eat somewhere else?" he asked again, hoping to distract her.

Mom shook her head, taking one last look at Dad. "Actually, I have a bit of a headache. I think I'd like to go home."

He nodded, guiding her back out of the restaurant, relieved at getting off so easy. For a second, he'd been concerned she would made a scene. They drove home in silence, his mother looking resolutely out the passenger-side window.

When Matt pulled up to the house, he put the car in park but didn't turn off the engine. "You need me to come inside with you?"

Mom shook her head. "No." She glanced down as if just now realizing she was still holding his birthday gift. "Here," she said, handing him the package. "I want you to have this."

"Thanks," he said, taking it, though he made no move to open it. "You sure you're okay?"

Mom nodded.

"Sorry tonight didn't work out."

Mom looked at him for a long time. Too long. Matt waited for her pain to morph into something scarier, darker. He was no stranger to her depression, to those times when she seemed to go blank. It always felt like she was going away somewhere in her head, but tonight, none of that was there.

In truth, she almost looked at peace. It should have set his mind at ease, but instead...it terrified him.

"Mom..."

"You know who you are, Matt," she whispered.

Her words took Matt back to the day he'd given her the sketchbook and said he didn't want to draw with her anymore.

"I'm a..." He didn't finish, couldn't.

She gave him a sad smile, then cupped his cheek. "Look deeper."

Before he could offer any reply, she closed the car door and walked inside.

Matt drove home, inundated with too many conflicting thoughts and feelings. Dad had sworn Mom knew about his cheating and turned a blind eye because, as his father like to say, women were simple creatures. Buy them a piece of jewelry and they forget everything.

But...now...

She hadn't known about the infidelity, and it had hurt her. Badly. Just as Matt's knowledge about it had.

When he got home, he went to his office, determined to turn off the heavy thoughts and get some work done, but he couldn't ignore the little voice in the back of his head that said something was very, very wrong.

So, after an hour, he climbed back into his car and drove back to his parents' house. His dad was in his office, smoking a cigar and drinking bourbon. He looked up in surprise when Matt walked in.

"Late for a visit," Dad said.

"Have you been home long?" he asked.

Dad shook his head. "Just got back a few minutes ago." Then, Dad had the audacity to wiggle his eyebrows. "Had a date with Genevieve. That woman has talented fingers."

"Where's Mom?"

Dad scowled. "I'm assuming bed."

"She saw you tonight."

"What?" Dad asked.

"At the restaurant. I'd made reservations for the two of us to dine there."

"Why the fuck would you take her there?" Dad barked, as if Matt should know his cheating schedule.

Matt wasn't going to stand there and take another of his father's many dressing-downs. His gut was telling him something was wrong, so he left Dad's office, heading to the stairs. He heard Dad calling his name, pissed at being ignored, but Matt disregarded him, climbing the steps to Mom's room.

"Mom," he said softly, knocking on the door.

There was no answer, so Matt opened it, praying she was asleep.

The moon cast enough light from the window that he could see the bed was empty.

Glancing over toward the bathroom, he saw light peeking from beneath the closed door. He forced himself across the room even though...

He knocked, but all he could hear was the constant drip-drip-drip of water.

He cracked the door a little, not looking in. "Mom?"

She didn't reply, so he pushed it open completely.

Dark red blood congealed on the snowy-white tiles.

Matt's eyes locked onto the puddle, refusing to move, to see anything else. He didn't want to look into the bathtub. He didn't need to because he could see enough to know...

The blue-tinged skin of a lifeless arm hung over the edge of the tub.

Her arm.

"Mom," he whispered. While inside he was screaming, *No! No! No!*

He didn't hear Dad walk in, but he smelled the cigar smoke as his father stepped into the room, roaring with rage. "What the fuck? How could she do this to me?!"

To *him*?

Matt turned to his father, fury erupting like lava from a volcano. He led with his right, punching his father square in the face, then shoving him back against the wall hard.

"What the fuck is wrong with you?" Dad barked.

Dad didn't get it. He'd *never* get it. And the rose-colored glasses Matt had donned in regards to his old man shattered instantly, opening his eyes to all the things he should have seen.

The selfishness, the lack of compassion, the arrogance, the *evil*.

You know who you are, Matt. Look deeper.

His mother's last words to him.

Matt hadn't bothered to look the first time she'd said that to him all those years earlier. He'd been so busy emulating an asshole, turning himself into one in the process, just so he could earn his father's favor.

Now...now he didn't have a fucking clue who he was.

Unable to deal with his grief, Matt latched onto anger. It was the only emotion he could control, so he wrapped it around himself like a blanket, letting it warm him from the inside out.

Anger at his father—and at himself—allowed him to do what came next.

Call his brothers and tell them Mom was dead.

Once that was done, the fury kept him moving through the next few days—the funeral, the burial—then it just kept burning over the weeks...months...years.

Until he got a midnight call from his father's latest mistress, telling him Dad had died of a heart attack.

And that was when the anger faded, replaced by regret and sorrow and guilt so thick, he could hardly breathe.

. . .

"I left her alone," Matt said brokenly, as he reached the end of his story. "I should never have left her alone." He bowed his head because he didn't have the strength to face his brothers' wrath. "I'm sorry," he whispered, his gaze averted. "I'm so sorry."

Neither Gage nor Conor spoke, the silence in the room drifting for several long minutes as Matt stared resolutely at his lap, drowning in a sea of anguish, the deafening beat of his heart thudding in his ears.

For all he knew, his brothers had stood up and walked out. He wouldn't blame them. Matt had left their mother alone at her most vulnerable moment. She had a long history of depression, something she'd been taking medication for. It wasn't until last year, during Gage's intervention, that Matt learned from Conor that Mom had stopped taking the meds, which made his actions even worse. She'd had no life preserver that night. None at all.

"Matt."

He jerked when he felt a hand on his shoulder. He hadn't heard Gage move.

"Matt, look at us."

Matt shook his head. Shame suffusing him. "I'm sorry," he said again, though those words would never be enough, never erase what he'd done.

Gage's grip on his shoulder tightened. "Look at us."

Matt lifted his head. Conor was still sitting across from him, his brother's pale, grief-stricken face the first thing he focused on.

None of the anger he'd expected to see was there. Instead, Conor's face was lined with the same pain Matt was drowning in.

"You've held that in for a long time," Conor said quietly.

Now that it was out, Matt felt drained, empty. He was out of words, out of emotions, out of everything, so he just nodded.

"You should have told us all of that when it happened," Gage said.

Matt looked up at him. "I didn't know how. I left her alone. I... It was my fault."

Gage sighed. "No, Matt. It wasn't. You spent years under

Dad's thumb, listening to all those bullshit lessons of his. You were just a kid when he started indoctrinating you. It's easy to look back now and see just how big a narcissist he truly was, but at the time, when we were there, all we saw was our dad. The man who took us on family vacations, sat down to dinner with us every night, who gave us money when we got good grades in school, who went to our football games and school plays—occasionally," Gage filled in, because Dad was out of town for work as much as he was in. "Sure, he was a cold, arrogant, selfish bastard, but he was still there, still our dad, and besides, we didn't know anything different. Looking back at it now, we see it through the eyes of our family's history, our experiences. Maybe you think all this shit should have been obvious, but Matt...*nothing* was obvious back then."

"What's that saying?" Conor asked. "Hindsight is twenty-twenty. We grew up in a tough house. Dad's coldness, his high expectations, Mom's depression. We were forced to find ways to adapt, to hold on. You threw yourself into your art, and then when Dad dragged you away from that, you used work as a way to deal. Gage escaped through video games, me into books. It's a wonder we're not all locked up in padded rooms right now," he added with a thin smile.

"Why aren't you angry at me?" Matt asked. "Didn't you hear what I said?"

"We heard you," Conor said in that gentle tone of his. Matt could count on one hand the number of times he'd seen his steady-as-a-rock brother break, and he'd still have fingers left over. "We also heard you say you went back. Mom's death wasn't your fault."

"It was," Matt insisted.

Conor shook his head. "She made that choice, and even if you'd walked into the house with her that night, I think..." His brother swallowed deeply, his voice thick. "She'd made her decision. If not that night, another."

Gage knelt next to Matt's chair. "You told me once that the

only person standing in my way with Penny was me. You were right. So I'm going to offer you some similar advice. We don't blame you, so there's nothing we can offer to make this right for you. There's only one person's forgiveness you need right now, and that's your own. Find a way to forgive yourself, Matt, and the rest will take care of itself."

"I..." Matt started.

Can't.

Gage stood, then reached down. Matt took his brother's hand, allowing Gage to pull him up from the chair.

Matt froze, shocked when Gage wrapped his arms around him, hugging him tightly. "I'm sorry you felt like you couldn't tell us. Sorry we let this stupid distance between us go on for so long. We should never have forgotten that first and foremost, we're family. We're brothers."

Matt lifted his arms, returning the embrace, so stunned by their understanding he didn't know what else to say or do.

He'd expected contempt. He'd received compassion.

"I love you," Gage said.

Matt wanted to say the words. Wanted to give them back to his brothers.

But now, just like when Liza had said them, he couldn't get the words out. He'd lived a lifetime without love, pretending it was a silly, useless emotion.

He'd been lying to himself because the truth was, love had always felt like something he didn't deserve.

When they separated, Gage gripped his neck, pressed their foreheads together. Just for a second. Then he walked back around the desk as Conor rose.

"You going to be okay?" Conor asked.

Matt felt as if his insides had been ripped out and tossed through the shredder. Regardless, he nodded. "Yeah."

Because, while the pain was still there, it was mingled now with the tiniest bit of hope. He'd told his brothers the truth and they hadn't walked away.

Matt had let his fear of losing them rule him for far too long.

"Eventually," he added. "I just need to figure some things out."

"Is Liza one of those things?" Gage asked.

"I hurt her."

"She's tough," Gage said. "Don't write off what the two of you shared. If you reach out to her, she'll help you through this."

Matt had fought like the devil to keep this away from her, certain her disgust over his callous actions would drive her away. The second she tore up that marker and walked out of his office, he crumbled, because without her...

Conor gave him an encouraging smile. "Call us if you need us. We can hold as many interventions as it takes. And you know, therapy isn't a bad thing. Pretty sure our health plan covers it," he added with a wink.

Matt chuckled. "Yeah. I probably need a few...thousand sessions. Thank you."

His brothers left as Matt sat back down, swiveling his chair toward the windows, staring outside without seeing anything.

Gage told him he needed to forgive himself. Matt wasn't sure how the hell to do that, but he needed to find a way.

For himself.

For Liza.

Chapter Twenty

An hour later, Matt let himself into his penthouse. He'd had Henri cancel the rest of his meetings for the day and called for his driver to take him home. He hadn't been in the right state of mind to get behind the steering wheel of a car.

He considered climbing the stairs to his room, burrowing himself under his thick duvet, and sleeping for the next twenty years or so.

Instead, he turned toward his office. He knew what was pulling him there, though he wasn't sure if he could follow through with what came next.

Sitting at his desk, he took a deep, calming breath, then reached down to open the bottom drawer. He never opened this drawer because it only contained one thing. One thing he'd attempted to keep hidden away along with his guilt, his regret, his grief.

Matt pulled out the birthday package, the wrapping still as pristine as the night Mom had given it to him. He'd found the forgotten gift on his desk after Mom's funeral. He hadn't been able to open it then, his fury burning too hot, so he'd shoved it in the drawer and put it out of his mind for fourteen years.

He carefully unwrapped the paper, then lifted the lid on the box, gasping when he discovered the sketchbook he and his mother had shared.

Matt's hands shook as he pulled it from the box. When he hadn't found it as they'd packed up his mother's belongings following her death, Matt had assumed she'd destroyed it. That idea, combined with the night she'd died, convinced him that he'd broken Mom's heart irrevocably, that he'd lost her due to his callousness.

Matt ran his finger over the cover, the sketchbook tatty from so many years of being passed back and forth between them. There were smudges of ink and pencil and deep creases that spoke of frequent use. In calligraphy, his mother had written, "The Artwork of Bianca and Matt Russo."

Opening the book, Matt spent hours slowly leafing through the pages, studying the drawings, recalling what had inspired each of them, what had been happening in his life at the time. He'd been eight years old when his mother gave him the sketchbook with the first incomplete drawing—a funny picture of a dog on water-skis that Matt had finished by adding a crazy-looking cat driving the boat. His mom had titled it "Rex and Boots, Unlikely Summer Buddies."

He laughed, admiring his mother's talent, and his definite lack of skill in that first sketch.

He watched his skill improve with each drawing, as he and Mom tackled everything from silly caricatures to nature to still life to portraits. Every single sketch evoked a memory, some happy, some sad, all of them forgotten until right now, as his past came back in a display of pencil, ink, watercolors, charcoal, and even pastels. Mom was clearly a huge fan of color and shading, while Matt's additions were always heavy on delicate strokes of the pencil, with an eye for fine detail.

Once a drawing was complete, Mom would choose the title, adding it to the page, then they'd both signed it with a flourish, as if they believed their silly sketches would someday be displayed in a museum or sold to art collectors for millions of dollars.

When Matt flipped to the last page, he stilled, staring at a drawing he'd never seen before. His mother had started one last "incomplete" sketch.

It was of him. An unfinished portrait.

Matt stared at the younger version of himself, studying that twenty-something man and trying to assimilate that face with the one that greeted him in the mirror nowadays. She'd drawn him with a smile on his face, sitting at a desk, concentrating on something on the surface. At first glance, he assumed he was working, but when he peered closer, he realized he was drawing in this very sketchbook. The page was blank.

Mom was the most talented artist he'd ever known, but this drawing...it was next level. There were so many layers, Matt could hardly take it all in, from the details in his eyes, his lips, the curve of his jaw, to the bright rays of sun streaking along the floor. The handsome man in the drawing sat up straight and tall, he looked confident, strong, ready to take on the world. What he *didn't* look like was Dad—no frown, no harsh lines, no furrowed eyebrows, no anger in his eyes.

The Matt she'd drawn looked peaceful, happy.

Then his eyes landed on the bottom of the page, on the title of the piece.

"Look Deeper."

Matt's vision clouded with unshed tears as he saw his mother as she'd been that last night. She'd said the same thing to him, even as she'd sat there, ready to end her own life.

Were those words a reference to this drawing? Her way of telling him she loved him?

How could she have seen those positive things in him when he couldn't even see them in himself?

Matt wasn't sure how long he sat there, bombarded by memories and feelings he'd buried years ago. When it all became too much, he reached into the top desk drawer for the new art pencils he'd ordered when he was in Hawaii. He hadn't touched them because, at first, he'd been too wrapped up in Liza, and for the last week and a half, too wrapped up in himself.

Bending toward Mom's unfinished portrait, he did what he always did.

He finished it.

He decided to fill in that blank page in the drawing of the sketchbook. Mom—aware of his ability to create a lot of detail in a small space—had scaled it so that he would have plenty of room to add his part.

Working from memory, he drew a much smaller portrait of his mom. He only had enough room for her face, but that was all he needed. He didn't want anything extra to pull his focus away from her. He sketched her as he wanted to remember her, smiling widely, looking at him with love and affection. Just as she had that day in Pompenis, as she'd traipsed around behind three unruly, silly boys, laughing at their antics.

Once the drawing was done, he leaned back to study it...and the calm he sensed in that younger version of himself washed through him. And for the first time since Mom had uttered those words, he looked deeper, trying to discover who he was, who he wanted to be.

Then he realized he'd already found shades of that man, thanks to Liza. She'd brought back his laughter, taught him how to trust again, forced him to stop focusing inward and to see the world and the people around him.

Without realizing it, she'd given him the strength to talk to his brothers. At the time, he'd thought he was giving up, but now, he could see she'd opened his eyes to the importance of family, of how much he longed to not just be present in Gage and Conor's life but to be a part of it.

Turning the page in the sketchbook, Matt picked up his pencil and began a new drawing.

This one was of Liza, playing basketball with the kids in Promise House, her hair pulled back in a ponytail, knees bent as she prepared to shoot the ball. In the background, he sketched Devonte cheering her on as Matt stood in front of her, prepared to block.

Matt worked on the drawing until he couldn't keep his eyes open. Crawling into bed, he had his first sound sleep since the day he'd pushed Liza away.

When he woke up, he was not only refreshed, he was optimistic. He returned to his desk, to the sketchbook, his fingers flying over the pages as too many years of images fought to find their way out. Every emotion bled out of him onto the page. Therapy through art.

He recreated the drawing his dad had destroyed of Gage and Conor tossing the football; he added one of Arnold and Johnnie sharing their first dance after their wedding; another one of Mom, playing video games in the living room with Gage as Conor sat nearby, his nose buried in a book.

However, most of his drawings were of Liza—her basking in the sun in Hawaii, dancing the hula, sprawled out in his bed as his boring Egyptian cotton sheets just barely covered her naked body. He tucked the two sketches of her that he'd drawn in Hawaii—of her at the gala and on New Year's Eve—into the sketchbook as well.

Then he spent hours working on a portrait of her, struggling to capture those expressive brown eyes of hers. Probably because they were a kaleidoscope of the emotions he'd put there—resignation, happiness, mischief, sadness, confusion, hope...love. That was the one he was trying to recreate, but seeing it in his mind's eye hurt too much, so he kept losing sight of it.

Three days later, Henri was probably crying at work after another request from Matt that he clear his schedule, while he remained at his desk at home, drawing as if his life depended on it.

Staring at his portrait of Liza, he knew it was time.

Time to find her, to try to make things right.

Rising, he left his office and was about to head upstairs to take a shower.

Matt turned at the sound of the elevator doors opening. Only his brothers had access to these floors, so he wasn't surprised when he turned to find Gage standing there, giving him an annoyed look.

"Okay. Time's up, Matt."

Matt grinned. "You're too late. I've already figured that out."

Gage must have anticipated a fight because it took a few seconds before his scowl faded replaced with a smile. "Perfect. And because I'm such a good brother, I'm going to help you."

* * *

Matt stepped out of his car, thanking his driver, who would return upon request. Taking a deep breath, he prepared himself for the coming evening.

Gage had stopped by his apartment a few hours earlier, issuing an invitation to some "surprise" celebration dinner. Matt, anxious to find Liza, had started to refuse until Gage told him she would be there.

Matt had lived most of his adult life with regrets, the biggest being his decision to leave his mother alone the night she died.

He didn't want to do that anymore.

Couldn't do that.

Forcing Liza to leave had been another colossal mistake. One he had to try to make right. For his sanity, for his broken heart.

Somehow, someway, he'd find a way to earn her forgiveness for the things he'd done to her family, for the times he'd pushed her away, for...God...for all of it.

He was a Russo.

Which meant he was strong, strong enough to admit when he was wrong.

He was ruthless, ruthless enough to fight tooth and nail to deserve the love of the woman he couldn't live without.

He was smart, smart enough to turn the tide, to point his ship in the right direction by apologizing for past sins and hurts.

He was determined, determined enough to put in the work, to put in however much time it took to win her back, to show her how fucking much he loved her.

Matt had looked deeper, and now, he was going to show the world who he really was.

Walking toward the entrance of Chives, he smiled when he saw Conor leaning against the front door.

"What are you doing outside?" Matt asked.

"Waiting for reinforcements," Conor said, only half-jokingly. "Gage's guest list, for whatever this is, is very Moretti-heavy."

Matt glanced through the restaurant window, sighing when he spotted Tony and Luca. Tonight was going to be harder than he'd thought, but now that he was here, and Liza was so near, he refused to walk away.

He slapped Conor on the shoulder, a show of camaraderie. "You'd probably be smarter to go in before me. Get clear of the door. I'm going to be public enemy number one in there."

Conor shook his head. "Gage assured me there would be no bloodshed. It was the only way I would agree to let him hold this weird shindig in my restaurant."

That was when Matt realized there was a sign on the door that said, "Closed for private function."

"You closed the whole restaurant?" Matt asked.

"Gage insisted this was one of those go big or go home occasions."

"Okay." Matt had no clue what to make of that. "Well, ready or not?" He'd intended for his words to bolster them, not come out as a question.

Conor gave him a "why not" shrug, and the two of them walked inside, stopping just over the threshold.

"See why I needed you?" Conor said. "I swear to God every single Moretti is here. Even the two female cousins who moved to Baltimore."

Matt's gaze traveled from one corner of the restaurant to the next, not that he was taking note of exactly who was there like his brother. He was searching for one person, and one only.

He wasn't sure whether to feel relieved or disappointed when he didn't spy Liza anywhere in the crowd.

"You made it!"

Matt grinned as Gage approached, two beers in his hands. He offered one to Matt and one to Conor. Conor accepted it gratefully, chugging half down in one gulp. Matt took it but didn't risk a drink. He'd need his wits about him if he was going to make his way through this land mine of—no doubt—angry relatives to find Liza.

"You weren't exactly forthcoming about your guest list," Matt said. Gage had used the words "small celebration with a few friends," then he'd mentioned Liza was attending, dangling that carrot effectively. Matt had envisioned Liza and Gage's much *smaller* group of friends, not the entire damn family. It had been his hope to pull her away for a moment to talk in private. There wasn't a private corner in this entire restaurant. He recalled joking once with Liza about her family's fondness of packing every house full of relatives. Tonight definitely fit that bill.

Gage laughed. "If I'd told you it was a big party, one with a bunch of Morettis on the guest list, would you have come?"

"This isn't a bunch," Matt grumbled. "This is all of them."

Gage, the shameless bastard, just grinned. Matt wanted to be annoyed with his brother, but he couldn't. For the first time since they were kids, Matt felt genuinely close to Gage and Conor. Both of them had called him daily since their intervention to check on him, and he got a feeling nothing was going to dim his happiness over that for a long time. Not even a Moretti party.

"I'm happy you're both here," Gage said.

"Are you going to tell us what this is all about?" Conor asked.

Gage shook his head. "Not yet. Soon. Promise. Come in, join the party. Stop blocking the entrance. It's a fire hazard." And with that, he walked away, joining a huge group of Morettis who immediately laughed loudly at something his brother said.

"Charming fucking bastard," Conor muttered.

Matt chuckled. "Should we..." He gestured toward the dining area. Some of the tables had been shifted out of the center and lined up against the wall, where huge steaming trays of food were set up buffet-style. "Different menu tonight?"

Conor shook his head. "Catered by the Moretti women. Every style of pasta known to man is over there. And it smells fucking incredible."

The area cleared of tables was now being used as a makeshift dance floor, though there were only a few people on it—Jess and Rhys spinning their son, Jasper, around to "Old Time Rock & Roll," while the boy laughed; Liza's brother Elio and his wife, Gianna, swaying slower, their baby daughter between them, her arms and legs flailing wildly as if she was trying to dance as well.

Matt felt—Jesus—a pang of envy as he watched the parents with their children. What would he give to be out there on that dance floor with Liza, the two of them spinning their own kids around, laughing and acting silly.

A family of his own. Matt wanted it so bad he could taste it.

"Regardless of the delicious food, I'm happy staying right here," Conor said. "Close to the exit."

Matt laughed, but the sound faded quickly when Tony approached.

"Matt," Tony said, nodding his head once in greeting. "Conor."

"Hello." Matt braced himself. His last meeting with Moretti had been worse than the high school scene, but he'd vowed to start righting the wrongs of the past. Tony was a good place to start because he'd sure as hell wronged the man. "Listen, Tony—" he began.

Tony cut him off. "I didn't have a chance to thank you the last time we were together."

Matt wasn't expecting it when Tony stuck his hand out. He accepted the handshake, moving by rote, confused. "Thank me?"

He wondered why in the hell Tony thought he owed him anything more than a punch in the face.

"For forgiving my uncle's debt."

Matt was speechless for a moment, then he said, "No, Tony. I'm sorry. For your uncle, for all that shit I pulled back in high school. I don't have any excuse other than I...well...I was a grade-A douche and this apology is long overdue."

Tony smiled. "Apology accepted."

"Just like that?"

Tony laughed. "We're almost forty, man. A lot of that shit happened nearly twenty years ago. Besides, according to Rhys, grudges give you wrinkles, though I doubt he has any medical research to back that up. He just says it to shut me up when I bitch nonstop about losing a bet over a hockey game to my brother, Joey."

Matt hadn't expected this to be so easy. "Brothers," he joked, aware Conor was standing there listening. "Always bring out our competitive worst."

"Hey," Conor interjected.

The three of them laughed.

"Thank you," Matt said sincerely to Tony.

"There you are!"

Matt turned, confused when an older woman barreled directly toward him.

"I've been waiting for you," the woman said.

"For me?" Matt asked, wondering who she was.

Tony offered the introduction. "Matt, this is my aunt Berta. Renzo's wife."

Shit.

"Mrs. Moretti," Matt began, anxious to offer this apology as well. He hated knowing he'd caused Liza's beloved aunt and uncle so many years of stress and worry.

"No, no, no." The woman waved his words away. "Everyone calls me Aunt Berta."

Matt didn't have a clue if that was information or an invitation. He exchanged a glance with Conor, who shrugged, clearly as baffled as he was.

Before he could say more, the woman—Aunt Berta—was thrusting a covered tray into his hands. "These are for you. A batch of my homemade biscotti, fresh from the oven today."

Matt stared down at the tray, wondering if he'd somehow slipped into an alternate universe. Or maybe he'd suffered a total mental break and none of this was real at all. "I don't...understand."

Aunt Berta linked her arm through Tony's. "My nephews told me what you did."

Matt glanced at Tony. If that was true, shouldn't she be reading him the riot act rather than baking him cookies?

"Ms. Mor—" he started again, stopping when the woman raised one eyebrow. "I wanted to offer you an apology for...for my behavior. For causing your husband so much stress, for threatening his livelihood, his business."

"You tore up that marker. You forgave the debt," she said as if that was enough. Matt wasn't sure it was. "My Renzo was a good man. I know he..." Aunt Berta batted away a tear. "I know he wasn't perfect, but he was *good*. I wanted to thank you for not holding his weakness against our family."

"Please don't thank me," Matt said. "I don't deserve your thanks."

"Nonsense. Now, I plan to stop by your office one afternoon this week with a pan of my lasagna. A good Italian boy like you? I bet you love pasta." She didn't give him a chance to answer, just kept plowing forward. "Does Tuesday work for you?"

"Yes, but you don't have to—"

"Perfect. I'll bring some garlic bread as well. You can't have lasagna without garlic bread," she said, smiling widely. Then she stunned him even more by reaching out and hugging him tightly, whispering "thank you" once more before releasing him. "Tony told me where you work, so I'll see you Tuesday," she said, before returning to the party.

Tony snickered at Matt's outright shock. "You might want to get used to that. Aunt Berta's gratitude comes in the form of casseroles. Speaking of, I'm about to hit the buffet. Nonna made her eggplant parmesan. You might want to get over there and make a plate before my family devours it all." And with that, Tony walked away.

Matt turned to Conor. "We're in the twilight zone."

Conor clearly agreed. "Yeah. FYI—I'm coming to your place Tuesday night for dinner."

Matt laughed loudly, ready to tell Conor if the lasagna smelled as good as this restaurant did, he wasn't inclined to share.

Spoons chiming against wine glasses drew their attention as Gage and Penny stood up.

"We want to thank you for coming tonight." Gage's arm was wrapped around Penny's shoulders, looking down at her with a love that was almost tangible. "Penny and I wanted to do something special for our family and friends, for everyone who has supported us through our first year of marriage. We also wanted you to be the first to know…we're having a baby!"

A loud cheer rang throughout the restaurant as Penny and Gage kissed.

"Baby Russo will be arriving in August," Gage added, he and Penny taking off the sweaters they'd been wearing to reveal coordinating T-shirts. Gage's said "Daddy to Be," with a computer-loading image that said, "please wait" across his chest. Penny's was the same, only the words were over her stomach and said "Baby." Matt had to admit they were perfect for his tech-mad brother and his IT wife.

Conor slapped Matt on the back. "How about that? We're going to be uncles!"

Matt's smile mirrored his brother's. For so many years, their family had felt so small, so fractured, but now, piece by piece, it was growing, mending.

They waited patiently as countless family members hugged the couple, congratulating them before making their way over.

Matt gave Penny a kiss on the cheek, then hugged his brother. "I'm happy for you both."

"This is great news," Conor added before tacking on a tease. "But I thought most couples had the big-ass party for the gender reveal."

Gage smirked at Matt. "That was the original plan, but this guy needed a kick in the pants now. Not a couple months from now."

Matt frowned. "What does that mean?"

Gage leaned closer, lowering his voice. "Have you pulled your head out of your ass about Liza yet?"

Matt narrowed his eyes. "Are you telling me you had this party just to throw me and Liza together?"

Gage lifted one shoulder casually. "It only took me a week to figure out letting Penny go was the biggest mistake of my life. Crashed her birthday party to tell her so. You're way more stubborn than me, so I thought I'd better give you two weeks. Plus, if you're going to be with Liza, you need to get used to being surrounded by Morettis. This way, you can clear the slate in one fell swoop and then the two of you can get on with it."

Matt shook his head, chuckling. "I swear to God, you must have been dropped on your head as a baby."

Gage laughed. "Tell me I'm wrong."

His brother not only wasn't wrong, he was fucking brilliant. But Matt knew better than to feed that ego, so he crossed his arms. "I'm pleading the Fifth."

Conor sighed. "Shit. There'll be no living with the guy now." Conor raised a finger and pointed it at Gage. "And before you get any wild ideas in your head, I do not want or need you playing matchmaker in my life."

Gage shrugged. "I make no promises because if you're fucking up, I *will* step in. I think interventions and impromptu parties might be my new thing."

Matt was afraid his brothers were putting the cart before the horse when it came to him and Liza. He started to tell them so, but he didn't get the chance because Conor, Gage, and Penny were all distracted by something behind Matt.

"I think I'll go make a plate," Conor said, walking away without waiting for a response. Then Penny and Gage stepped away, pretending they'd just spotted someone they wanted to talk to.

Matt knew who was behind him. He could smell her perfume.

Taking a deep breath, he turned around.

Liza stood there, looking—fuck him—so gorgeous. She wore skin-tight blue jeans and a dark green sweater that hung off one shoulder. Her hair was down, curling slightly at the ends. He'd been dreaming of her eyes since the last time he saw her, trying to capture them in his sketch of her. Now he knew without a doubt, there was no way he'd ever manage to capture the depth, the emotion, the sheer beauty of them. Liza's eyes were truly the mirror to her soul.

As always, her gaze held his, his indomitable woman holding her own. The last time he'd seen her, he'd hurt her badly. Yet, here she stood, looking him straight in the eye. And for the first time in days, he managed to take a deep breath. Because she wasn't looking at him with anger or sadness or that fucking resignation he hated.

Instead, he saw hope. Hope, he could work with.

"I wasn't sure you'd come," she said.

"Liza," he said, reaching for her hand, grateful when she placed hers in his. He lifted it to his lips, kissing her palm. It was a bold move, but the fact she hadn't ripped it away from him sparked confidence, as did her flushing cheeks and heavy eyelids. "You look beautiful tonight."

Someone started playing a slow song, so Matt kept hold of her hand. "Dance with me."

She nodded, and he walked her to the dance floor, pulling her closer as he bent his head until their faces were mere inches apart. They began to sway slowly to Forest Blakk's "I Choose You."

"I'm sorry," he breathed. "So fucking sorry. I was wrong."

"Matt—" she began.

"No, please. Let me say this. I've done nothing but hurt you since this whole thing started, pushing you away, giving you mixed signals."

"Why did you do that?" she asked, without an ounce of hostility or anger in her tone. Instead, she sounded genuinely curious. God bless her, she was giving him a chance to explain his actions.

"I've done too many things in my past that I'm not proud of, things that proved to me that you deserved better."

She opened her mouth to speak again, but he shook his head, cut her off.

"No, wait. Liza, for so long, I've held myself apart, letting my regrets, my mistakes, and my fears rule me, convinced monsters were meant to live in the dark, away from people. Then you came along and suddenly, I hated the cave. I wanted to bask in your sunshine, your warmth, and I knew—all the way to the depths of my soul—that I wanted to be a man worthy of you and your love."

"You *are* worthy," she insisted.

He smiled, pressing his forehead against hers. "Even after all the crap I put you through...you really believe that, don't you?"

"Of course I do."

"If you'll let me, I want to show you who I am—all the parts of me—the good, the bad, the ugly. I thought I could hide the horrible stuff, bury it so deep it wouldn't hurt us, but I know now that's not how love works."

"Love?"

He took her face in his hands, tilting it up so that she could see his eyes, could read the truth in them. "I've never been in love before, so I screwed up, offered you only bits and pieces of me, thinking that would be enough to keep you. I was wrong."

"Can you trust me enough to show me who you are? Because I'm not afraid, Matt. I'm not worried."

"I don't have any choice *but* to show you. I can't live without you. You're as essential to my life as the air I breathe. I love you, Liza. So damn much."

Tears wet her lashes. "My heart recognized yours almost from the start. Every time I looked at you, it felt as if you were the only person in the world who understood me, who truly saw me. Somehow I knew you were meant just for me."

"I felt the same," he confessed.

Then because she was Liza, she added, "Even though I didn't want you to be the one."

"A Russo and a Moretti," he said with a grin. "Quite the scandal."

She drew one hand down the center of his chest suggestively. "I like being scandalous with you."

Matt growled, her words hitting him below the belt in a way that wasn't appropriate, considering they were standing in the middle of a room, surrounded by her grandparents, parents, and approximately four hundred other relatives.

"Behave," he murmured, loving the way her body softened, shifted even closer.

"I missed you," she whispered.

"I'm so sorry, Liza," he said again.

"I know. It's okay."

"Will you come home with me tonight? Give me a chance to explain, to show you who I am? Deep inside." Now that Matt held her close, he wasn't sure he could let her go again. He needed this woman in his life, his home, his bed, but she deserved to know everything. So he was going to put his heart on the line and come clean, and then he was going to pray she stayed.

She nodded. "Of course I will."

He kissed her gently, a quick one to seal his vow.

"Liza," he said, releasing her hand, the sounds of talking and forks clattering against plates and laughter that he'd reduced to white noise coming back into focus. A quick glance around the room proved there were quite a few people casting curious glances their way as they danced.

Being here, surrounded by Morettis, felt almost surreal.

Surreal and yet, somehow right.

Then he realized...

"This song," he murmured.

She smiled. "I wondered if you would remember. It's the same one we danced to the night of the Snowflake Gala. Aldo's serving as deejay tonight, so I asked him to play it."

They listened to the words, locked in each other's arms.

"This is our song," he declared. "Because I'm always going to choose you."

She cupped his cheek, and he bent his head to hers, giving her a long, slow kiss.

"Kitten," he murmured.

"Hmm?"

"Introduce me to your family."

Chapter Twenty-One

Liza followed Matt into his penthouse, and she was amazed by the feeling of coming home. The two of them hadn't spent more than two nights here together, yet as she walked into the living room, she was aware that this place felt as much like home as her own apartment. Simply because they were together.

"Wine?" he asked.

She shook her head. "I had a couple of glasses at the party. I probably shouldn't have any more."

Matt had been all smiles at the party, working hard to win over her family. Her mom, Nonna, and aunts had been charmed by him, while the males—hardheaded to a fault—had been much tougher nuts to crack. Matt still had his work cut out for him with her dad, uncles, and Nonno, but Tony had already opened the door, accepting Matt's apology for past sins. She noticed her cousins and brothers had been less arms crossed and scowling than the older generation of men, making a genuine effort to get to know Matt better...for her.

Now that they were here, she sensed his good mood dimming, nervousness creeping in. He'd promised to tell her why he kept pushing her away, and whatever it was, it must be pretty fucking terrible in his mind if it was the reason he'd lived such a solitary life for so many years.

He led her to the couch, the two of them sitting down next to each other. She toed off her shoes, tucking one foot under her opposite leg as she turned to face him.

Matt assumed a similar position, reaching for her hands. His hands had been on her the entire night, his arm wrapped around her waist or shoulders, his fingers tangling in her hair or clasped with hers.

He released a long, slow breath, and then he gave her what he'd promised—the good, the bad, and the ugly.

Liza listened as Matt talked about his childhood, about his love of art. He took her through what he now considered the dark years, when he'd become the worst version of himself. She noticed Matt didn't blame his father for his actions, for his cruelty and coldness. Matt took ownership of all of it, claiming he'd been weak and easily led, and while she wanted to argue he'd been young, she also respected that it was those years that had molded him into this man. One who was strong with a powerful sense of responsibility and compassion.

She cried as he talked about the night his mother committed suicide. Cried hard enough that Matt had pulled her onto his lap as if she was the one who needed soothing, not the other way around. She hated that for so many years, he'd carried his guilt around, letting it eat away at him like cancer.

The two of them talked for nearly two hours as Matt opened up about everything, even showing her his sketchbook. She'd been blown away by his talent, and so incredibly moved by the drawings he'd done of her. The idea that when he looked at her, he saw someone so beautiful, had her crying again. Happy tears this time.

With every revelation, every secret, she fell even more in love with him.

"Can I ask you something?" There was something Liza had been struggling to understand for the past two weeks. "Why did you send that marker to Tony?"

That was the part that didn't add up. Because how could Matt know she'd confront him with Luca and Tony? How could he know they'd even tell her about it? If she hadn't been at Aunt Berta's, she wouldn't have known. Even now, most of the family didn't. Primarily because, like Aunt Berta, she, Tony, and Luca hadn't wanted to diminish anyone's memories of Uncle Renzo.

"I didn't send it. The copy Tony had was from Edgewood Casinos. Which is owned by—"

"The Eddingtons," Liza interjected. "Patricia?"

Matt nodded. "She stopped by my office shortly before having that marker delivered to Tony, to give me an ultimatum."

"Ultimatum? To what end?"

"She hoped to burn shit down."

Liza frowned. "Shit between you and Tony was burned down years ago."

Matt didn't respond, and she got the feeling he was waiting until...

The light went on.

"Because of me?"

"I told you she hoped to marry me. Originally, her intention was to increase her own wealth and fame. Patricia loves the limelight, and merging the Russo and Eddington names would certainly catapult her into a stratosphere very few ever reach in terms of wealth."

"You said originally. Her intentions changed?" Liza was still trying to make sense of it all.

"*You* changed them. Jealousy is a powerful motivator for a woman as vain as Patricia. I had the audacity to choose you over her. Combine that with the fact I kept saying no to an extremely spoiled woman, and it was a recipe for disaster."

"So she sent that marker hoping to drive us apart."

Matt sighed. "I almost let her plan work. I thought...I was certain once you learned what I'd done to your uncle, how I'd plotted to destroy your family, you'd walk away."

"I thought about it," she confessed. "Thought about what

you'd put Aunt Berta and Uncle Renzo through. I know he dug the hole…"

"But I handed him the shovel."

"You were young," she said.

"I was an asshole," he clarified.

Liza was still on Matt's lap, the two of them unable to be so close to each other and not touching. "You pushed me away."

"While I was waiting for Tony to show up and confront me over the marker, a shit ton of guilt crashed down on my head, and I decided you deserved better than me."

She hated that he believed that, that he couldn't see the compassionate, wonderful man he'd become. "I'm sorry you felt that way."

"Gage pointed out a few days ago that the only person's forgiveness I needed was my own."

"He's a smart man."

"Never tell him that," Matt joked. "But you're right. He is. I've spent the last three days alone in this penthouse trying to find a way to do just that."

"Have you succeeded?"

Matt shook his head. "Not completely, no. I don't think it's something I can do on my own. So I've called a therapist and I'm going to start counseling."

"That's a wonderful idea."

"Regardless of that, I was coming to see you to beg for your forgiveness. Gage forced my hand with tonight's party, but I had already decided I couldn't go another day without talking to you, without trying to make things right. If he hadn't thrown that party, you still would have found me on your doorstep."

"I'm glad." Liza placed a soft kiss on Matt's cheek. "So…is that all of it?"

He nodded.

"I'm still here," she whispered, her heart doing flip-flops when Matt gave her the biggest smile she'd ever seen, pressing his forehead to hers.

"I promise you right now, I'll never cause you another second of pain. I'll spend every minute of the rest of my life making you happy, giving you the world."

"You're my world," she replied. "All I want is you."

"I hope you really mean that because..." Matt eased Liza to the cushion next to him, rising from the couch. Walking over to where they'd shed their coats, he dug through his pocket, pulling out a small rectangular box before returning to her.

Liza struggled to draw air into her lungs when he dropped down to one knee in front of her.

"Matt," she said breathlessly.

"I'm thirty-seven years old, Liza. I've spent a lifetime trying to convince myself that I was content with the life I'd chosen. Then you showed up and tossed everything I'd always believed I wanted right out the window. I tried to stay away from you, but I couldn't. The pull was too strong. I'll be honest with you. I'm not a romantic. I don't believe in stuff like love at first sight or soul mates."

"What *do* you believe in?" she whispered.

"You. I believe in you."

He opened the box, and Liza gasped at the most beautiful engagement ring she'd ever seen. It was a large ruby surrounded by diamonds. "You couldn't find anything bigger?" she asked, her soft laugh laced with a happy sob.

Matt chuckled. "I know this is fast, and while I'd like to say we can have a long engagement, the truth is, I don't want to wait. I want you as my wife. I want that big family you described, three, four kids, maybe a dog or a cat. A house. A white picket fence. I want to spend the rest of my life with you. Will you marry me?"

She nodded, aware there were tears streaming down her face. "Yes. God, yes!"

Matt slid the ring on her finger and tugged her toward him, kissing her as if they'd been apart for years.

"I love you," he said, his lips still pressed against hers. "I've never said that to anyone before and now, I can't seem to stop."

She laughed softly. "If you're expecting me to complain about that, you're destined for disappointment." Then her gaze drifted down to the ring. "I can't believe this," she whispered.

Liza had never experienced such a dream-come-true moment, a small part of her losing hope this would ever happen. That she could find the man she wanted to spend the rest of her life with, that he would be so incredible, so...

"I love you," she said, giving him the words back.

Matt kissed her again, his tongue stroking inside her mouth. Lifting his hands to her hair, he gripped it as the kiss grew hotter, hungrier, more passionate.

Liza twisted her head, searching for air, but Matt growled, pulling her right back.

"I need you." Every night they'd been apart, she had lain in her bed, replaying every single thing they'd ever done together. A few nights ago, she'd broken down and pulled out her vibrator, but it had failed to get her there, something she'd never experienced before.

That "he ruined me for all men" comment had always felt like utter bullshit to her. Until Matt. Because he hadn't just ruined her for men, but for her damn toys as well.

Matt came up for air, his hands stroking her face, gripping her shoulders, sliding down her arms to her waist. Once there, he grasped the hem of her sweater, pulling it over her head.

His eyes heated when he saw the ruby necklace he'd given her was tucked beneath. She hadn't taken it off, couldn't. She needed some part of him touching her, and if the necklace was all she could have, she'd been prepared to wear it for the rest of her life.

Matt touched the ruby, his fingertip brushing it before running along the top of her bra. He studied her so long and intensely, she wondered if he was making a mental note so that he could draw this later.

Liza ran her hand along his jaw, loving the roughness of his beard, the way it tickled when he went down on her.

Matt's gaze lifted to hers. "I feel like a kid in a candy store, kitten. I want to do everything with you—*to* you. There are so many options, I can't decide. Should I strip you out of your clothes right here? Bend you over the couch and fuck you from behind? Or should I carry you upstairs to my bedroom? Tie you to my bed and drive you to orgasm after orgasm until you're begging me for mercy? Or should I fill the Jacuzzi in my bathroom where you can ride me until we've flooded the entire penthouse?"

"Yes," she whispered, aware that wasn't exactly an answer, but equally aware she couldn't choose.

Matt chuckled, the deep timbre of it sending a rush of arousal to her pussy. "Such a greedy kitten. Did you play with yourself when we were apart?"

Liza nodded.

"Vibrator or dildo?"

Her body began to tremble, her need so great. "Vibrator."

"Were you thinking of me?"

"Yes," she replied.

"Tell me how I was taking you. Tell me which fantasy made that tight pussy of yours clench around that vibrator."

"I... I couldn't."

Matt clearly hadn't expected that answer. "What?"

"It wasn't you. I couldn't get myself there because it wasn't you."

He froze for just a moment, his eyes wide, then he kissed her again, this one rough, his lips bruising hers. "That's so fucking hot, kitten. Jesus! You *are* mine. Just mine."

She whimpered when he reached behind her, unfastening her bra, his fingers quickly finding her nipples, pinching them the way she loved. Liza tried to squeeze her legs together, seeking some sort of relief, friction, but Matt was wedged between her thighs, holding her open.

Lowering his head, he sucked her tight nipple into his mouth, licking and biting it until her head flew back, her fists clenched in his hair too tightly.

He played with her nipples as her pleas grew louder, more desperate.

Finally, he released her and rose, rapidly stripping her out of her clothing before unzipping his own jeans. She only caught a glimpse of his thick cock, and then he did exactly as he'd suggested, twisting her away from him, bending her over the couch.

She felt his fingers slide along her slit—just once—testing her, making sure she was wet, and then he was there, driving inside her with a force that pushed her forward until her face was pressed against the back of the couch.

Matt took her like a man possessed, every thrust filling her, stretching her. She came fast, but Matt ignored it, pounding and pounding until her first orgasm became a second, and then, God help her, a third.

That was the climax that claimed him, and he grunted, calling out her name, reminding her over and over that she was his. "Mine" was quickly becoming one of her all-time favorite words. After so many lonely years, the idea of belonging to someone was potent, powerful, wonderful.

Liza had only just come back to earth when he wrapped his arms around her waist, juggling her until he could lift her in his arms.

"Matt," she said as he headed toward the stairs. She was completely naked, while he was still fully dressed, only his jeans hanging open. "I can walk."

"And I can carry you."

When they reached the top, he took her straight to his bedroom, placing her in the center of the mattress.

"Lay on your back," he demanded in that dominant tone she found completely irresistible. "Put your hands on the pillow by your head. Surrender position."

As she lay there, Matt gave her a show of her own, quickly and efficiently undressing at the foot of the bed. His dick was already growing hard again.

"That's some impressive recovery time," she joked.

Matt winked at her, the playfulness there then gone, when his expression morphed to one of his power looks.

She shivered as he walked to the side of the bed. Reaching for the post, he withdrew the strap he had tucked there. He'd left them attached to the bed during her second night at the penthouse, declaring it pointless to take them off and on, considering his intentions to tie her up frequently.

Liza had picked a half-hearted fight about it, the crux of her argument being "what would the housekeeper say?"

He hadn't been swayed, and she decided fairly quickly it was a stupid fight because she definitely wanted bondage to be a regular occurrence in their sexual play.

Matt secured one hand to the bedpost, then crossed to the other side, doing the same. Standing next to the bed, he took his time, perusing her naked body, letting his gaze glide over every inch until she began to squirm, not with embarrassment but with need.

He hadn't tied her legs, so Liza started to close her thighs, quickly realizing Matt had been waiting for just that thing. He'd set the trap and she fell right into it.

Climbing onto the bed, he knelt between her legs, his hand slapping her pussy three times as she gasped, then groaned.

"Behave," he said, that word a serious trigger for her hormones.

Every time he uttered it, every part of her body lit up like a Christmas tree. "Please," she whispered, aware it was wasted breath. This game had only just begun.

Liza soon lost track of time and orgasms as Matt drove her to the peak over and over again with his fingers, his tongue. She was going to have beard burns on her nipples and her inner thighs, but she was beyond caring at this point.

Lifting himself above her, he kissed her deeply, and she tasted their combined flavors on his tongue.

She closed her eyes in utter bliss as his cock—finally—slid back inside.

"Open your eyes, Liza. Look at me."

She did as he said, their gazes locked as he made slow, beautiful love to her.

Liza lost focus as tears filled her eyes, her happiness so huge it couldn't be contained.

This time, the two of them came together, Matt clasping her face in his hands, placing soft kisses on her lips, her chin, her nose. "You are so beautiful," he whispered.

As their orgasms began to fade, Matt reached above her head to untie her. Gently massaging her shoulders, he asked if she was okay.

"Better than okay," she whispered.

Matt dropped to her side, gripping her waist to turn her until they were facing each other. "Make a doctor's appointment. Take out that damn IUD."

Liza laughed. "Jesus, Matt. Don't you think we should wait a few minutes to let the dust settle on the marriage proposal?"

He shook his head. "No. I don't need anything to settle. I told you I couldn't wait and I meant it. I want my wedding ring on your finger and my baby inside you."

Liza recalled the argument about the straps on the bed and realized picking this fight would be just as pointless. She wanted the exact same thing. "I'll call in the morning."

Matt's eyes widened in surprise. Clearly, he'd been expecting her to put up more resistance.

She was rewarded when he kissed her again, this one so reverent, she felt as if she was made of precious glass. How could the same man evoke so many different emotions from something as simple as a kiss?

They lay there for nearly half an hour, neither of them talking. They just looked at each other, grinning like a couple of goofy, lovestruck kids.

Liza would have expected to be exhausted after so many

orgasms, but Matt had lit a bonfire inside her and the thing appeared to have enough fuel to rage until dawn.

When Matt got out of bed and reached out for her hand, she took it, following him as he led her to the bathroom. And that was when she realized the kid in the candy store was about to get every damn thing he wanted.

Matt perched on the edge of the tub, running the water, then he found a lighter and lit all of those unused candles. Once the huge tub was filled, he stepped in and sat down, crooking his finger for her to join him.

She recalled his plan, so she joined him eagerly. Too eagerly.

Jesus, it was like the last fifty-seven orgasms had never happened.

Liza straddled his hips, impressed once more by the fact his dick was just as thick and hard as it had been when he took her over the couch downstairs.

She positioned him at her opening, sliding down slowly, and not stopping until every inch of him was inside her.

Once there, Matt gripped her waist, holding her still while he gave her a slow, sensual kiss that had her inner muscles clenching with need.

When the kiss ended, Liza began to ride him. At first, their motions were gentle, easy, two people taking their time because suddenly they had it. A lifetime of it.

That rhythm changed when Matt reached between them, his fingers stroking her clit.

Applying the perfect amount of pressure, he teased and tempted her to move faster, harder, until she felt like a cowgirl riding on a runaway horse without any reins.

Matt was with her stroke for stroke, tilting and lifting his hips on each return, the head of his dick stroking her G-spot until she reached the edge of the cliff and leapt off.

He came with her, the two of them gasping for air as Liza slumped forward, her head resting in the crook of his shoulder, his softening dick still tucked inside her.

Neither of them spoke for a long time until Liza finally found the strength to lift her head. Glancing around, she realized there was as much water on the floor as in the tub, and she giggled.

"That was quite a list," she murmured.

He chuckled. "That was just the beginning, Ms. Moretti, my naughty, sexy kitten. Believe me when I say there's a lot more where that came from."

"I'd be down for more."

Matt cupped her cheek with one hand, his expression suddenly serious. "Since the day I first saw you, you've tempted me to the brink of insanity."

Liza leaned forward and kissed him. "Take me."

onor sat alone in the restaurant, marveling at the efficiency of the Moretti family. He had to hand it to them, when they made a mess, they cleaned it up. He'd watched them reorganizing the tables and chairs this evening, shifting and moving everything, and all he could envision was his restaurant manager showing up tomorrow morning and suffering a coronary over having to put it all back to rights.

Looking around, he couldn't tell they'd moved a single chair.

The last of the partiers—Gage, Penny, Toby, and Rich—had left a few minutes earlier. Conor wasn't sure why he hadn't followed them out and locked the door behind him. It made more sense to go home and kick back on his comfy recliner rather than sit at this table.

Regardless, he didn't move. Couldn't find the energy.

Tonight had been wonderful. Gage was going to be a father, and if that slow dance Matt and Liza shared was any indication, his big brother was on his way to his own happily ever after.

Which left him the last Russo standing.

Alone.

What else was new?

He'd always felt like the odd guy out in his family, and now, with his brothers both in love and moving on with their lives, he was once more relegated to that role.

Conor had spent his entire life as the invisible kid, and now… man. All of Dad's attention had been focused on Matt, the oldest, his heir. Not that Conor begrudged Matt for that. Shit. If anything, Matt had taken one for the team as far as Conor was concerned.

And while Conor had been close to their mom, there was no denying she'd preferred Gage. Why wouldn't she? They had a million things in common, and Gage had followed her around like she hung the moon. Gage had also been a lot better at dealing with Mom's dark days. Whenever she went into a depression, remaining in bed for days at a time, Gage was the one who would sit with her, talk to her, try to draw her back out of the darkness.

During those times, Conor withdrew to his room because seeing her like that scared him. He'd always been prone to panic attacks and seeing Mom so lost and sad was a trigger. So, most days, he avoided her and the rest of his family, losing himself in his books. Fiction had been his escape from reality ever since he'd graduated to chapter books in first grade. Books were his way of disappearing from his real life when things felt too hard or too frightening.

He startled briefly when he heard a knock at the door. Glancing up, he was surprised to find Luca Moretti waving from the front window.

Shit.

While he was happy for his brothers, their newfound happiness meant Conor was more frequently subjected to things he'd prefer to forget.

Or maybe just one thing.

Luca.

Conor forced himself to rise, crossing the restaurant to unlock the door. "Hey. Is everything alright?"

Luca nodded. "Yeah. I'm glad I caught you. I was hoping someone would still be around. I think I left my phone here."

"Oh." Conor gestured for Luca to come in.

"Thanks." Luca headed to the booth where he and his twin brother, Gio, along with Gio's partners, Keeley and Rafe, had been sitting earlier.

Luca and Gio were a year older than Conor, so they'd all attended the same elementary school when they were kids, before Frank Moretti had moved his family to Baltimore. Frank moved back to Philadelphia with his five kids after his wife died, when the twins were freshmen in high school. However, their paths and Conor's didn't cross again until a year later, when Conor moved from middle to high school.

Unlike their brothers, Matt and Tony, Conor and the twins hadn't picked up the stupid feud that had been raging between their families for years.

Quite the opposite.

Conor had been just fifteen years old when he'd gotten his first, honest-to-God crush. Falling head over ass.

For a guy.

Luca Moretti.

Jesus, what the hell would his father have said if he'd come out not only as gay but in love with a Moretti?

Mercifully, that was a conversation Conor never had to have. Dad had been dead for nearly a decade.

It wasn't until he was in college that Conor realized he was bisexual, not gay, when he'd fallen for a girl who lived in his dorm. He'd lost his virginity to her, and after they eventually broke up, he lost a different virginity to a guy in his business law class.

Conor's gaze drifted to Luca's ass as the man bent over, checking the bench seat for his missing cell.

"Found it," he said, standing up and turning.

Conor's eyes flew to Luca's face, hoping the other man hadn't caught him ogling his ass. It appeared luck wasn't on his side when Luca gave him a look that was too knowing for Conor's peace of mind.

Conor cleared his throat uncomfortably. "Good."

Many, many years ago, he and Luca had been—if not friends —friendly acquaintances. Until Conor fucked it up. After that, he'd stonewalled, avoided, and ignored Luca until he graduated, and their paths no longer crossed on a daily basis.

Prior to Gage's wedding, he hadn't been in the same room with Luca Moretti since high school, something Conor preferred.

"It was a great party," Luca said, attempting to make small talk.

"It was," Conor agreed.

Luca glanced around the restaurant. "You here alone?"

Conor nodded. "Yeah. I was just about to lock up."

Considering Luca had seen him sitting by himself through the window at the front of the restaurant, it was apparent he was lying.

"Everything look okay? Anything left to put back or clean up? I can help, if so."

Conor shook his head. "No. I was actually just sitting here wondering what the odds were that I could hire your aunts and mom as chefs in my restaurants."

The edges of Luca's lips curled up, giving him a half smile, and Conor felt his dick twitch.

There was no denying the Morettis had good genes, but as far as he was concerned, Luca was the best-looking of the bunch. Which was ridiculous, considering the guy had an identical twin.

"I'd say the odds are slim, but I'll pass on your compliment just the same. They'll be pleased to know you liked the food."

Silence fell and lingered a shade too long, but Conor didn't have a clue how to break it. Social skills were way down on this list of things he could do. Rock bottom actually.

Luca glanced at the time on his phone. "Well, I guess I should head out. It was good to see you, Conor. Maybe we'll run into each other again sometime, especially since..."

Luca had seen the same thing Conor had tonight.

"Since my brother and your cousin are dating now," Conor finished.

"Yeah." Luca shook his head in disbelief, as if a Moretti and a Russo relationship was completely out of the realm of possibility. "That's going to take some getting used to."

Luca's words hurt, but Conor knew that wasn't his intention, so he just nodded. Luca was as straight as they came, something Conor had resigned himself to long ago. Any lingering fantasies he harbored toward the man were destined to remain dreams and nothing more.

"Well, good night," he finally managed to say, following Luca to the door so he could lock it once more.

"I'll see you around," Luca said as he took his leave.

Conor stood at the front window, watching Luca walk away down the sidewalk, sighing heavily.

Rather than heading to his own car, Conor went back to the table he'd just been occupying, dropping down into the chair again, reliving mistakes he hadn't thought of in years.

When those thoughts got too heavy, he pushed them away, instead letting himself dream of things he was afraid he'd never find.

Love.

Marriage.

And a place where he wasn't lost in the shadows.

Are you ready for more Italian Stallions?
Down and Dirty
Hard and Fast
Rough and Ready
Wild and Wicked
Hot and Heavy
Naughty and Nice (a holiday novella)
Tempted and Taken
Steady and Strong
Kiss and Tell

About the Author

Virginia native Mari Carr is a New York Times and USA TODAY bestseller of contemporary romance novels. With over three million copies of her books sold, Mari was the winner of the Romance Writers of America's Passionate Plume award for her novella, Erotic Research. She has over a hundred published works, including her popular Wild Irish and Italian Stallions books, along with the Trinity Masters series she writes with Lila Dubois.

Follow Mari:
www.maricarr.com
mari@maricarr.com

Join her newsletter so you don't miss new releases and for exclusive subscriber-only content.

www.ingramcontent.com/pod-product-compliance
Lightning Source LLC
Chambersburg PA
CBHW032114310726

48972CB00001B/224